THE
COLOUR
OF
DARKNESS

The Colour of Darkness

A Sebastian Foxley Medieval Mystery
Book 13

Copyright © 2025 Toni Mount
ISBN-13: 978-84-129716-2-0

M
MadeGlobal Publishing

For more information on
MadeGlobal Publishing, visit our
website
www.madeglobal.com

To Tim and Claire for all your
support over the past ten years

Toni.

Visit Sebastian Foxley's web page to discover more about his life and times?
www.SebastianFoxley.com

Prologue

The maiden was beautiful. Where she had come from, few knew. What was her purpose here? She had not said. In truth, she spoke little and answered no questions but the men of London were bewitched by such loveliness; words were unnecessary.

However, the women were suspicious of her and jealous—those who did not trust their husbands. Some thought she must be an angel come among them to give them heart and solace in times of trouble. Others claimed she was the Devil's minion, a witch, forwhy, hot upon her arrival came the dreaded pestilence of plague into the city.

Jude Foxley of Amen Lane found his new printing enterprise to be more of a challenge than he expected. He had succeeded against the odds in assembling the mighty contraption of the press—with a deal of aid from his friends—and thought it would then be an easy matter to learn the rudiments of the craft.

Firstly, the tiny lead letters—each one back to front—had to be arranged contrary-wise, right to left, to form words and sentences in reverse in the little box. Apparently, the printer's term for the line of letters was a 'slug'. No need to ask why for the procedure was accomplished at a slug's pace. The type being so small, it was hard to make out any mistakes. How many times had he put in a 'b' instead of a 'd'? He'd lost count and the faults only made themselves known once the page was printed. But he discovered how much ink to use by trial and error and how to handle the pristine paper without smudging it with inky finger marks and the need to let each newly printed sheet dry.

1

Beyond that, it wasn't unlike the stationer's craft he knew so well: correlating pages, stitching and binding. Practice. That was all it would take to have his business venture thriving: London's first printing press. It could not fail. Jude Foxley would soon be rich on the profits.

Except for one thing.

The great, fat worm in the rosy apple of his ambitions—his far more experienced rival with a press set up and running these last five years at Westminster. The name of Master William Caxton was anathema to Jude: the wretch and his workshop at the Sign of the Red Pale. Patronised by royalty and nobility, the fellow received all the most valuable commissions. It was so unfair. Being the first-ever printer in England, Caxton had every advantage and, thereby, was the destroyer of Jude's dreams, ruining all his efforts to make himself a wealthy man.

Something must be done to remedy the matter.

Jude had had thoughts upon this since autumn last; he'd even discussed certain 'possibilities' with that ne'er-do-well apprentice, Jack Tabor. Long gone were the days when he used to have the frequent satisfaction of giving the young rascal a good beating or a clout around the head—not that it had improved the lad one peck. But now Jack was doing well enough, learning the craft of carpentry and, whatever his legion misdemeanours, was become a hard-muscled mountain of a man and beyond punishing, if you valued your own safety. At times, Jude still felt tempted to strike him for his inconsiderate and irritating ways but refrained. Instead, he was coming to some kind of an understanding with Jack, whose strength and size might yet be of use. A friendship it was not, but it could prove of benefit to both parties.

A plan had been under consideration before Christmas but then the young scallywag came to grief. The story ran that he—being a kindly Christian sort, ha!—was intending to aid an elderly neighbour by sawing off a branch from an ancient pear tree which grew in the garden plot behind the old man's house. The branch had grown close enough to bang against the window whenever it was windy, both a nuisance and possible danger to the roof and window glass.

On Twelfth Night it was that Jack climbed the tree at dusk to set about the task. Why then, in fading light and after a bellyful of cider and ale at dinner, was ne'er explained. And where, Jude asked afterwards, was the saw or the axe to cut the branch? Was it merely a coincidence that the neighbour's shapely daughter was within the chamber at the time, readying herself, changing her gown for the evening's festivities?

Whatever the case, Jack's great weight had proved too onerous for the aged wood. He duly removed the offending bough but not as intended: it creaked horribly and broke. Jack fell awkwardly, landing on the frost-hardened ground.

Afterwards, in the Sunne in Splendour tavern, he'd bemoaned the outcome of his virtuous act over another jug of ale or two, his broken arm splinted and his head wreathed in a blood-stained bandage. He insisted that his bleary sight and wavering step were due to the blow to his head, which had quite astounded him, and not to an excess of drink taken solely for medicinal purposes. Jude had heard the like before and felt no sympathy for Jack. In truth, he was much angered as the plan, so long in the devising, would now have to wait upon the wretch's recovery.

But that was months since. Summer was now come. Gone were Jack's splints and his spurious claim to continued befuddlement of his head due to the whack received. Jude didn't believe a word of it. More like an excuse for idleness, the lazy dog. Jack was never one to labour if he might avoid it. But now it was well past time to put their plan into action and save Jude's new-born business from ruination.

Chapter 1

THE WINTER was a hard one, as Old Symkyn, the beggar whose bunions foretold the weather with nigh infallibility, had predicted and spring was right tardy in arriving. However, as be so often the way, Nature was now putting matters to rights. Since May Day, the sun had shone gloriously, crops grew in haste, lapping up the light and warmth and now, with the approach of midsummer, fields of corn ripened, grass spread a green sward, trees bowed under the burden of new leaves and gardens were bedecked with flowers.

England was beautiful and bounteous once more.

Even London's crowded, narrow streets looked at their best in the sunshine. The top of St Paul's spire gleamed gold, freshly white-washed houses dazzled the eye and, most radiant of all, folk were smiling again, relieved of the weight of winter at last.

And I, Sebastian Foxley, Master Stationer and Artist of Paternoster Row, was one who smiled broadest. My business thrived in our newly-enlarged premises. Customers and commissions came in goodly numbers to purchase books or writing stuffs or to place orders for illuminated volumes, portraits, shop signs and coats of arms. It had been thus since November last, upon our return from pilgrimage, and the cold, dreary months between passed in a blur of industry and hard work, often done with benumbed fingers, waiting whilst ink thawed on the hearthstone.

I had no complaints. My family and household were in good health—praised be God—my debts paid on time and I loved my craft. And now the summer brought the vivid hues of Nature back to life, expelling the colour of darkness, what more could an artist—or any man—wish for?

Trinity Sunday, the seventeenth day of June in the year of Our Lord 1481 The Foxley Place in Paternoster Row in the City of London

As was our custom, family and friends came to join us for dinner, it being the Lord's Day, but 'twas an especially joyous celebration, and doubly so, it being the feast of the Holy Trinity combined with our little Dickon's third anniversary of his birth. In truth, he was born upon the sixteenth day of June, but yesterday, being an Ember Day, was spent in prayer and fasting and thus was no occasion for feasting and making merry, so we had delayed until this day.

Parents must give grateful thanks unto the merciful Christ Jesu when their child attains another year of life, knowing how fragile be the existence of the very young. Every extra year was a blessing and we were no different in praising God for it, as all loving parents do.

Our recently enlarged house was full of laughter; children's happy voices rang from one chamber to another and out into the garden plot beyond as they played, Dickon's new hobby-horse being the centre of attention in every game. The garden was full of scents from herbs and flowers and, at the far end where the sun shone brightest—the house casting a shadow at midday—butterflies danced.

Fortunately, though inordinately proud of his toy, Dickon was willing to share it, to a certain degree, with the others. However, it must be noted that he was wary of doing so with young Nicholas Hutchinson, his elder by a year and more. Mishaps tended to occur whenever Nick was at hand, whether by chance or intent could not always be discerned but Adam and I kept close watch.

Everyone was there to celebrate: my brother Jude and his cross-dressing friend, John Rykenor—I tried to remember that he-she preferred to be addressed as Eleanor but, on occasion, I forgot—Stephen Appleyard, father to my first wife—Emily, may God assoil her soul—and Jack, once my unruly 'prentice and now Stephen's. There was Thaddeus Turner and Old Symkyn, along with all of our own household and Adam's adopted family. 'Twas quite a merry gathering.

Bess Chambers' apothecary shop, Bishopsgate

Bess Chambers, wise woman and apothecary, was busy in the stillroom behind her shop in Bishopsgate Street. With the heat of summer, her customers required remedies for all manner of agues, fevers and fluxes of the belly. In winter, it was treatments for coughs, chills and rheumaticks, but the sunshine brought its own assortment of ills. Worst of all was the pestilence, and tidings had come of a few cases in Shoreditch, just to the east of the city, and a couple across London Bridge in Southwark. It was as well to have both preventives and treatments ready-made for fear they might be needed at short notice.

Every year, the pestilence came claiming lives: sometimes a handful, sometimes a thousand, and though Bess made a livelihood from tending the sick, she hoped each summer that the plague's visitation would be brief and concern a very few. She knew full well, whether physicians would admit it or not, that only God or Mother Nature at His behest could cure it, so preventives and prayer were the best resort. The prayer she would leave to the priests whilst she stirred her herbs and distilled the liquors to ward off the dread disease.

Powdered dragon's blood, purchased from a reputable Portuguese merchant of close acquaintance, by its very nature, cleansed the humours and granted protection. Meadowsweet and betony treated all manner of ailments including headaches and lethargy; feverfew reduced the sweats, and marigold petals were good for skin lesions—all symptoms of the pestilence—so likely to strengthen a patient's ability to fight the sickness. Roses, as was well known, rendered any medicament twice as effective as otherwise, so red rose petals went into the potion. The roses, marigolds, feverfew and betony were all lush and blooming in her garden and she'd gathered them at their best before dawn on Monday last, it being the day of the Moon Mother who oversaw the flourishing of herbs.

Steeped in spring water, simmered and stirred thrice times three in the sun-wise direction when the Angelus bell rang at the first hour, the sixth and the twelfth hour of the day for each of three days, then distilled and cooled, the potion was now ready. With the addition of her own-made lavender water, six drops of her precious thyme oil and a half pennyweight of a secret ingredient—mugwort, learned from her mother—this completed the receipt. It could now be decanted into vials for sale as a preventive or treatment, as required, although those with wit enough would use it beforehand, rather than delay until they fell sick. A few drops taken in ale and a handful applied on exposed skin every morn, as instructed, should ward off the pestilence.

Thus, with the finest ingredients, this ought to prove a most efficacious remedy and she had high hopes that her customers would remain in good health throughout the summer.

Monday, the eighteenth day of June in the year of Our Lord Jesu 1481 The Foxley Place, Paternoster Row

Upon Friday last, our serving wench, Nessie, had a rash, so my goodwife, Rose, took her to visit Bess Chambers. Apparently, whilst Nessie showed the itchy, red blotches on her forearm with a deal of moaning and complaint, Bess saw that it was no more than nettle stings that the foolish wench had scratched at, making it a deal worse than it would be otherwise. Dispensing a soothing ointment, Bess introduced her niece who had come to study the apothecary's art and learn herb lore from her aunt.

'Her niece is a pretty young woman: clear of skin, green-eyed and her hair a mass of red locks which she wears uncovered—being yet unwed—tied back with a green ribbon,' Rose told us over dinner. 'Her gown is of dull brown homespun, neatly patched, with an apron of unbleached linen and she goes barefoot, I noticed. Bess says the lass is already attracting the menfolk of London as wasps to ripe fruit. She'll have to keep a watch on her.'

'Mayhap, I'll keep a watch on her myself,' Adam said, a gleam in his eye.

'Then have a care, cousin,' I laughed. 'Fall foul of the formidable Bess Chambers and you will not escape lightly.'

Thus, upon this Monday morn, right early, afore the day's labours commenced, I had cause to visit Bess Chambers for my own purposes.

Behind the counter-board, a cascade of copper-coloured curls caught my attention upon an instant. When the lass turned about, a shaft of sunlight through the east-facing door reflected in her eyes. And what eyes they were! As an artist who knows colours and tints as well as others know their catechism yet was I hard-pressed to name their hue. She looked me straight—no false modesty here—and I gazed overlong at such flawless beauty and, after much consideration, deemed the closest description of those eyes to be the green of malachite, gold-flecked.

I was not Bess's sole customer e'en so early in the morn. Most often, there were one or two goodwives in need of remedies for the family but this day, there was a queue out the door—all of men. One, a carpenter, to judge by the sawdust-besprinkled apron, held out his thumb for Bess to appraise the blackened nail yet, all the while, he gazed upon the lass behind the counter. Even I could see the injury to the nail was an old one; the blackish part nigh grown out but the fellow insisted an ointment or salve was required most urgently.

Much time was spent as Bess named this and that remedy for bruises but 'twas plain he listened not as he watched the lass arranging pots and vials upon a shelf. Eventually, he took a small covered flask without so much as looking at it, paid over the halfpenny demanded and retreated from the shop, snail slow, casting many a backward glance.

The next was a man of slight acquaintance who I knew to be a pewterer by trade. We greeted each other courteously afore he turned and spoke to Bess:

'I'm needing somethin' to grow me 'air back,' he said. 'See? It fell out last eve… all of it.' He removed his coif to reveal a pate, round and bald as a coot's egg.

His words I knew for a lie. He had been hairless as long as I had known him.

'I have no certain remedy for that, good master,' Bess apologised but it mattered not for all his attention was upon the lass.

'No matter. D'you 'ave somethin' for bunions? My wife suffers terrible. 'Ow long she been working 'ere?' He waved his grubby hand, grey from his metal-working, towards the assistant.

Bess indicated to the lass to fetch down an earthenware pot from the shelf.

'My niece arrived last week, as I think every man in London

knows by now.' She spooned a dollop of some thick, herbal-smelling mixture from the large pot into a smaller one and covered it with a piece of linen which she tied in place. 'There. That'll be three farthings, if you please, master.'

'Wot's that?'

'For your wife's bunions. Tell her to smear it on night and morn.'

'Oh, aye. Three farthings, you say? For 'er bunions?'

'That's what you asked for.'

'Oh, I s'pose I did, aye,' he muttered absently as he paid over the coin and departed out into Bishopsgate where the queue now trailed like a serpent's tail.

'Next!' Bess called out.

I stepped forward to be served but was shoved aside by a young fellow in a red hat. Such a deplorable lack of courtesy.

'I came to get a cure for the droops, if you take my meaning, mistress.' He winked and grinned lasciviously, licking his lips. 'But I've found the cure for free.' He leaned upon the counter-board, blatantly ogling the niece. 'Come home with me, wench. Warm my bed and I'll pay you well.'

Bess slapped his face, hard, so he cried out and stepped back, rubbing his cheek.

'Get out of my shop, you disgusting sot. Dogs have better manners than you.' She manhandled him to the door with me and another customer assisting. We threw the wretch into the street, silent in our tacit agreement to make certain he landed in a pile of fresh dung. It was a job well done, I thought, as I brushed invisible dirt from my hands, feeling soiled by laying hold of one so ill-mannered.

'God give you good day, Mistress Chambers,' I said formally, smiling as I doffed my cap in an attempt to make amends for the discourtesy of the previous customer. And, if I be honest, hoping to impress the new assistant.

'And to you, Master Foxley. How can I help you?'

'I be in need of azurite pigment and red ink, if you will oblige me, Bess.' How righteous I felt to be a genuine customer and not just here to gawp.

'I fear I can't offer you refreshment as usual, Seb, but you can see how busy we are this morn. However, let me make proper introductions. This is my sister's daughter, Sarra Shardlowe, come to learn my craft as my apprentice. Sarra, this is Master Sebastian Foxley, a stationer and artist of Paternoster Row and one of our best customers, so treat him well.'

'At your service, Sarra,' I said, making a small bow in reply to her bob of courtesy. 'Welcome to London.'

'Good day to you, Master Foxley,' she said. Oh, and those rose-red lips curved upwards and I felt my heart lift in unison.

'Sarra be so lovely a name... that of the wife of Abraham, renowned for her beauty and piety... if I recall aright,' I stammered.

'And one who birthed babes in her nineties, if you can believe that, Master Seb.' She spoke my name and it sounded as honey upon her tongue.

'Indeed, Sarra.' I bowed once again.

'Azurite; red ink.' Bess put two pots on the board. She was steely-eyed now: a look of reproof. 'Anything else, master?'

'Er, aye, some yellow ochre, if you have it? And a flask of lavender water, please.'

'We always have ochre in a half dozen hues, as you well know. As for lavender water, your wife, Rose...' She emphasised the last three words. 'She bought a large flask of it only Friday. Do you really need more?'

'You cannot have too much lavender scent, to my way of thinking.' I sounded quite the fool, talking nonsense.

'Now choose your ochre. Sarra will serve you whilst I attend the next customer.' Bess leaned close as I moved to examine the range of ochre pigments set in oyster shells upon the counter. 'You're a happily married man, Seb,' she whispered.

'Of course.' Why should she remind me? I was quite affronted.

As I made my way home, my scrip bulging with purchases, I recalled to mind female beauty, remembering my first wife Emily: she with autumn-hued hair, eyes of heavenly blue and a striking, clear-boned jaw. My dearest Rose, softer-featured, hair the colour of ripe wheat, hazel eyes and skin like the petals of a wild rose. The most wonderful woman in London. How surprised I had been to learn she was not named for the loveliest of flowers but after the busy street wherein her parents dwelt in Canterbury at the time of her birth.

But Sarra was different—what a portrait such a face would make. And a chalks-and-charcoal sketch would not suffice. It would have to be a painted likeness in joyous colours and, even then, could my talents do justice to the beauty of an angel... a veritable goddess stepped down from Olympus to bide among mere mortals.

Cease this, I told myself. 'Tis but foolish fantasy and you a respected citizen with a loving wife, a fine family and responsibilities. You should know better. The lass be but a pretty 'prentice, as ordinary as any country maid come from the shires to seek a means of making her livelihood.

As for my own livelihood, I needs must hasten home where the book commissioned last leaf-fall by the Prioress at Dartford awaited my further attentions. 'Twas a Gospel Book of the Four Evangelists intended to be read aloud whilst the nuns ate in the refectory. My instructions stated that it must be of a goodly size with the letters large enough that a sister with eyesight dimmed by age might yet read the words—apparently, most of the nuns at Dartford be past their youthful years. The pages must be of parchment, gold-edged, with a full-page image to commence each Gospel and twelve half-page images spread throughout.

During the winter, I had completed the Gospels of St Matthew and St Mark, sharing the writing of the texts with Adam and our new young journeyman Hugh—the latter doing all the historiated initials assisted with the details of decoration by my talented apprentice Kate, his betrothed. The pair worked right well together in harmony. As usual, the illuminated images were my responsibility and now, looking to St Luke's Gospel, the first full page was to be of Our Lord's Holy Nativity. For so important an image, I must be clear of eye and clean in mind and spirit. Sarra must be banished from my thoughts.

Upon our side of Paternoster Row, beyond the shadow cast by the walls of St Paul's Cathedral Precinct, the sun blazed down on the dusty cobbles and our customers were right glad of the shade provided by our new jettied upper storey which gave shade to those who would examine our wares for sale at the shop front. Our enlarged bedchamber above provided this unforeseen benefit and our shop space was doubled now that it extended into what had once been our neighbour's workshop until it burned down a year since. Our neighbours moved away after that hateful occurrence and, as their landlord, I took the opportunity to have the premises rebuilt and combined with our own home.

'Twas quite the grand house now with much oaken timber used and, on the ground floor, in-filled with the latest fashionable Dutch red brick—much to the envy of our fellow citizens. My one-time father-by-marriage, Stephen Appleyard, had done us proud. We now had glass in all the upper windows which faced the street and two chimneys. As an Assistant Deputy to the Warden Master of the Honourable Company of Stationers, I had to be seen as a reputable and prosperous guildsman. Appearances matter greatly in London and I must play the part.

'Well? What was she like?' Adam asked me the instant I entered the workshop. I had no need to enquire as to whom he meant. 'You should have let me go to Bess's place instead. I could have done the errand and seen her for myself.'

'You have Luke's Gospel to copy. 'Tis of far greater importance than staring at a lass. You be of an age to know better.'

'As are you, Seb.'

'I went to purchase pigments...'

'At least I'm unwed,' Adam continued, ignoring my excuse. He took a freshly ruled sheet, turned the page of the exemplar from which he was working, dipped his pen and began a new verse. 'So? Was she worth the trouble of your visit? Is she as lovely as rumour tells?'

'I hardly noted.'

'Of course, you did. You notice every detail of every face you see, so don't lie to me, Seb. Tell us or, better yet, draw her likeness for us.'

'Oh, very well.' I sighed as one resigned to an unwelcome task but Adam knew me too well and was not deceived.

I could have drawn a sketch in but a few minutes yet, somehow, Sarra's likeness could not be done in haste. As I sat with my drawing board, charcoal and red and white chalks, her image took form upon the paper and a small crowd gathered behind me to watch—not only all those in my employ but customers from the shop. And few became many as neighbours and passers-by joined the throng. By dinnertime, I had drawn— and sold—three copies of the pretty 'prentice's portrait with orders for a half dozen more to be done after our meal.

'You should've charged more than a groat a picture,' Adam scolded me as we sat at dinner in the kitchen. 'Sixpence at least, if not eight. You can sell them by the hundred… such a fair lass as she could make our fortune.'

Rose banged her ladle upon the iron cook pot.

'Hush, Adam. You make her sound like a loose woman with Seb selling her favours to any rogue upon the street. It won't do!' Rose was right stern upon the matter and I saw she served my kinsman less than his usually-generous helping of chicken and chestnuts in a coffin with buttered worts.

But my wife was correct and I felt my face flush with shame at my actions. In truth, I had no right to make money from Sarra's beauty without her knowledge and permission and even then… she, but an innocent lass… I was much at fault. Yet I had struck contracts with other folk for more sketches of her. A

15

contract is binding—verbal though it may be—and I did not wish arguments to ensue if I failed to fulfil my obligations. My reputation was precious to me. Thus, despite Rose's obvious and deep disapproval, I made six further likenesses of Sarra but no more, refusing all offers of coin to do so. A merchant offered me a shilling but I would not draw another for him. Eventually, though, he had his desire, purchasing a sketch from a customer whom I had obliged earlier, giving him fourteen pence to part with his drawing for which the fellow had paid but sixpence an hour before. Even beauty loses out to profit, so it seems, and my conscience was troubled also at having made money in this immoral manner. Upon the morrow, I vowed, I would go to Bess Chambers, confess all, give over the illicit coin thus garnered and I should not sleep until it was done.

That eve, at our time of quiet conversation once the children were abed, Rose asked me straight:

'Is Sarra truly so beautiful, Seb?' Yet she did not look up from the darning she was doing, mending Adam's hose with tiny stitches, frowning in the fading daylight from the parlour window.

'You saw her yourself upon Friday last.'

'Aye, but through a woman's eyes. Men see women differently.'

'I suppose she be of such youthful age as gives any woman a beauteous countenance.' I chose my words with care.

'Seb Foxley, you're as poor a liar as ever. She's a veritable goddess, isn't she, as every man with eyes is saying?'

'Well, aye. 'Tis not to be denied but she cannot hold a candle to you, my dear one. Your loveliness of heart outshines all others.'

'False flatterer! Away with you.' Despite her words, my wife was smiling and set aside her mending. 'I've heard men say she is an angel come from heaven.'

'And what do the women say of her?'

'Beattie Thatcher reckons she's the Devil's own; the new Eve,

16

sent to tempt men to stray, especially since her Harry has visited the apothecary twice in three days for potions and salves to soothe his piles... spent a small fortune on them.'

'You cannot blame him for that. Such a painful affliction...'

'But Beattie says he doesn't suffer from piles and never has. It's an excuse, is all. And you're nigh as bad: buying yet more lavender water when I have a full flask of it on the shelf, as you well know.'

'It slipped my mind for the moment.'

'Because Sarra's beauty befuddled your brain, no doubt. They say she is bewitching men. Those candles she's selling...'

'Who says that? What candles?'

''Tis common gossip all along Cheapside, so beware of her, Seb. I would not have you fall prey to her womanly wiles. They say Bess Chambers is letting her niece make the beeswax candles and she's adding a secret ingredient which makes men over-lusty.'

I laughed at that and reached out to her, pulling her closer.

'Rose, Sarra be a pretty lass and no more than that to me, so speak not another word on this. *You* are my soul-mate, my beloved. And if you would have me prove it, then our bedchamber awaits... and I have no need of candles with secret ingredients.' I kissed her right heartily, tasting her honeyed lips as Sarra was dispelled from my thoughts, forgotten as last week's soured ale.

Chapter 2

Tuesday, the nineteenth day of June
The Foxley Place, Paternoster Row

WE WERE at the kitchen board, all of us, breaking our fast upon a mess of eggs with herbs and slices of boiled ham, when Stephen Appleyard arrived by way of our side gate off the alleyway.

'God give you good day, Stephen,' I greeted him. 'Join us, will you not? Nessie, set another place at table.'

'No, no, Seb,' Stephen gasped, out of breath. 'That's not why I came… unless Jack is here?'

'Jack? Why would he be here? He breaks his fast at your house these days.'

'Aye, but not this morn. And you know he never misses a meal. I thought he might have come to you for some reason.'

'Mayhap he downed a surfeit of ale at the Sunne in Splendour tavern last eve and slept neath a bench there. Has his bed been slept in?'

Stephen shrugged.

'Can't tell. The idle rascal never tidies his bed unless I order him to and I've given up of late. If he wants to sleep in a mare's nest, that's his affair, though I make sure he changes the sheets first of every month. You know, he had the cheek to complain on St David's feast day, the first day of March, telling me that, February being a short month, his bed linen didn't need laundering. I gave him short shrift, I can tell you, Seb. I'll not abide an unclean house, as God's my witness.

'Anyhow, I'm right worried, Seb. I haven't seen him since

18

dinner yesterday, so he missed supper also.'

'Was he not working for you yester afternoon?'

'I sent him upon an errand to order iron nails from the wire-drawers and smiths by Dowgate. That's the last I saw of him. You know Jack as well as I do and I fear he might have got into trouble. You know… with the law. I wondered if you might ask around, Bailiff Turner and his constables and anyone else, discreetly, if you will… for fear he could be held in a lock-up or the Sheriff's Compter or some such. I'll willingly pay his bail or fine or whatever's needful… being my 'prentice, the lad's my responsibility. I do hope…'

'Fear not, Stephen. I shall make due enquiry at Guildhall as soon as breakfast be done.

'Sit you down, Master Appleyard, and eat with us. You'll feel restored with a full belly,' Rose insisted, already beating more eggs and tipping them into the hot pan afore sprinkling chopped chives, thyme and marjoram into the mix. 'Help yourself to bread and ale while this cooks.'

'And if it should come to pass that Jack does have to pay a fine,' I went on, 'I shall pay half as you do. 'Tis not so long since I was responsible for his raising, so I be partly to blame for his wild ways.'

'Nay, Seb, Jack was born wild as any beast of the field and forest. His feral ways are in his blood and not of our doing. We've done our best to tame the young rascal.'

'Aye, but we may yet find him asleep in an outhouse or under a tree. Last night was warm enough that he will have come to no harm, if he did so. I shall also ask my brother if he saw him at the tavern yesterday, since both of them frequent the Sunne oftentimes.'

At this hour, 'twas too early to visit Jude who, these days, was ne'er one for rising with the sun, if he might avoid it. I suppose lying abed be most comfortable for his damaged knee, which all my fervent prayers at St Thomas Becket's shrine in Canterbury in October last had done naught to improve, sorrowfully. Thus,

I determined that I should first wait upon my good friend, Thaddeus Turner, the City Bailiff, at Guildhall.

London looked its best in the fresh light of a new day. However, the brassy sky promised much heat for later and already the stench from the Shambles was wafting along the streets on the soft but tainted westerly breeze. It could but get worse as the day progressed. Every pile of animal dung in the street had its own cloud of flies which rose briefly as I walked near only to settle back precisely as afore. The goodwives emptying the night's pisspots in the gutters by their doors added to the rank smells and foul odours made all the stronger by the warmth of the sun. The stink from one such over-burdened gully, blocked by refuse, caught in my throat as I turned into Catte Street and set me coughing even as I waved away the buzz of flies.

Guildhall

Thaddeus was outside in the porch of Guildhall, munching a great pie in the shade, juices dripping and running over his hands, greasing the sleeve ends of his leather jerkin.

'God give you good day, Thaddeus,' I began but he indicated as best he might to bid me wait whilst he slurped up gravy and saved a gobbet of meat from escaping his lips.

'And to you, Seb,' he said at last, throwing a pastry crust to a passing stray dog and wiping the back of his hand across his mouth afore pulling out the hem of his shirt to finish cleansing himself of the pie juices. 'I hoped to make more of savouring that coney and bacon pasty, Seb, and you've made me rush it. Still, there's never any peace for the wicked, is there?' He grinned at me. 'So, what brings you here, disturbing my breakfast, eh? Not more trouble, I hope.'

'Aye, there may be trouble, I fear, for young Jack Tabor.'

'What's that scallywag done now?'

'Mayhap naught at all,' I said, attempting to sound

confident, 'But Stephen Appleyard has not espied him since dinner yesterday. He missed supper and, unlike your good self, Thaddeus, he did not avail himself of breakfast either and we all know the lad for his keenness as a trencherman.'

'Probably wheedled his meals for free somewhere.'

''Tis possible but both Stephen and I fear he may have become entangled with the law. Have you heard aught concerning him?'

'No, but last night's watch reports aren't all collected yet. My constables will be here soon: they'll know if Jack's fallen foul of any beadle or watchman.' Angus the Scot, a long-serving, reliable man, despite his heritage, and the younger, enthusiastic Thomas Hardacre were the City Bailiff's constables and I knew them well.

I wriggled inside my shirt which clung to my back like a wet dish-clout e'en so soon when I donned it barely an hour since. Seeing my discomfort, Thaddeus suggested we wait inside for the constables in the relative coolness of his chamber. I felt tempted.

'This heat is too much, isn't it?' he continued. 'And there are already rumours of pestilence in St Olave's parish, may God have mercy.' His gloomy expression prevailed for an instant afore he cheered. 'I have a jug of fresh ale keeping cold in a bucket of well-water.'

I found the mention too enticing to resist.

'Oh, in which case...' I followed him within, across the chequered tiles, smooth under my shoes, to his place of work. 'Chamber' was too lofty a word for a space just large enough for a chair and two stools with a high, barred window, small as a table napkin, but the plastered and lime-washed walls were cool to the touch.

Thaddeus took the chair as of right, leaving me a choice of stool—one four-legged which ne'er stood even, the other three-legged, the seat worn thin by a thousand backsides, oftentimes those of a criminal kind. I chose this latter all the same. It was my usual perch when scribing for the bailiff with a board balanced across my knees and my inkwell on the floor beside. In the corner sat the blessed ale jug in a bucket and two treenware cups upon the window ledge.

My friend took a cup, blew the dust from it and wiped away a cobweb with his much-misused shirt-tail, then filled it with liquid gold from the moisture-coated jug. 'There you are, Seb: The Bull Inn's finest brew, fresh this morn. Oh, no, yesterday... Tom fetched it... but still the best in London.'

I agreed that it was refreshing, indeed.

'No doubt but you've heard we've got a new Deputy Coroner appointed last week?' Thaddeus eyed me over the rim of his cup.

'Nay. To whom has the king given this thankless task?'

'Andrew Dymmock. You know him?'

I shook my head.

'I cannot recall the name. At least, he will spare you the labour of performing two offices at once. It cannot have been easy acting as Deputy Coroner as well as City Bailiff this last year.'

'That remains to be seen. He's a lawyer, trained at Lincoln's Inn. Calls himself "gentleman".'

I pulled a face and, glancing at my friend, saw that his grimace mirrored my own. We neither of us had any reason to like lawyers—the Duke of Gloucester's man of law, old Miles Metcalfe, being the exception which proved the rule. In general, I felt their kind required coin to grease their palm afore they would trouble themselves to bid you 'good day'.

'Have you had any dealings with Dymmock as yet?' I asked.

Thaddeus grunted and curled his lip, tipping his chair back on two legs such that his shoulders were against the cool wall.

'Upon Thursday last... and it didn't bode well, Seb. He's an officious—is that the word?—little busy-body, requiring we adhere to the letter of the law down to the last dot of an "i". Did you hear of the slaying during a football game down Vintry Ward?'

'I heard there was trouble but naught of any perpetrator

taken into custody.'

'You won't and there will be no trial.'

'Oh? And is this Dymmock's doing?'

'No. It's just the way it happened. The victim, Michael Hedger—an apprentice wire-drawer—was playing football with many other 'prentices upon Thursday eve and matters got lively. They were racing along Thames Street when Hedger lunged for the pig's bladder, tripped, stumbled and fell with a cry, as the witnesses told of it. None paid any heed until they saw the blood. It seems Hedger somehow contrived to fall upon his own knife which he kept well-honed but wore in a thin leather sheath on his girdle. The leather was old and the blade sliced it through as he fell and pierced his thigh.

'His fellow gamesters fetched a surgeon and the priest from St Martin's Vintry. The blade had cut a major blood vessel, as the surgeon said to me after. The fellow was already senseless from loss of blood when he arrived at the place. There was naught to be done for him. By the time the priest came, Hedger was dead. So victim and perpetrator are one and the same: a simple case, as you might think.'

'But not as Dymmock saw it?' I hazarded a guess.

'Indeed not.' Thaddeus sighed heavily as he crashed his chair back onto all four feet, reached for the jug to replenish his cup and found but a dribble of ale remained. 'He insisted we rounded up and interviewed every witness, whether gamester or by-stander, passer-by or those who live in Thames Street. Can you imagine, Seb? There were nigh forty players in the game and twice as many watchers and Thames Street is a busy place. He chided me publicly because so many witnesses had gone home by the time we were summoned. "Question them all and record what they say", he demanded of me. What a fool!'

'Mayhap, since this be Dymmock's initiation as Deputy Coroner, he thinks to make an impression, being right thorough in the task. Mayhap, such diligence will diminish as time passes.'

'We can but hope. But Seb, you know my constables are not

lettered men. Angus can only make his mark and Tom takes an hour to pen his name and it's unreadable even so. And my scrawl… half the time I can't make out what I've written. They can't recall such an unnecessary excess of details. That's why I employ you, my friend.'

'But you have a secretary these days…'

Thaddeus made a derisive noise. I knew his secretary aided him little.

'That useless shat-monger. I sent Angus to seek him out and he was swiftly found in his usual place at the Green Dragon on Candlewick Street. He lay under a table board, drunk as a Bartholomew-Day bishop. What use is he to me like that? I tell you, Seb, if I have to work with the likes of him and Dymmock for another month, my hair will be whiter than Monday's linen.

'And it got worse when Dymmock instructed me to take the guilty knife—*me*, mark you, not a constable—to at least a dozen cutlers and blade-smiths to assess its worth for deodand, so the king can be recompensed for the murder. I told him it was worth a groat… four pence ha'penny at most but my years of experience count for naught, so it seems. The wretch insisted only the word of craftsmen in knives would serve and I had to do it because a constable was not to be trusted to complete the task in full.' Thaddeus grinned as he added: 'I thought Angus was about to knock him down when he said those words. The fool deserved it, insulting my good fellows.'

'And did you enquire the knife's value of so many cutlers?' I asked, certain I knew the answer in any case.

'What do you think?' my friend replied, laughing. 'But now I need you to write a list of cutlers and smiths and put a value for the blade beside each name.'

'I do not know so many of that craft,' I objected.

Thaddeus shrugged, rising from his seat.

'Paper and ink are on the window ledge. Invent the names, Seb. Dymmock won't know the difference. John Smith, Will Cutler, Jack Steel, Martin Blade… just be sure they agree with my valuation.'

'But that be a fraudulent act!'

'Meantime, I'll fetch more ale.'

'And what of Jack Tabor?' But my words fell upon empty air, forwhy the bailiff was gone to refill his jug.

Jude's house, Ave Maria Alley

'Bloody hell, Jack! You stink like a cesspit.' Such were Jude's words of welcome when the youngster stumbled through the door from the street. 'Did you get it?'

Jack was too exhausted to reply.

'Got any ale?' was all he could manage to say.

Jude called out from his seat:

'Ell! Is there any drink left from yesterday?'

John Rykenor, resplendent in patched blue silk this morn, came with a cup and a jug.

'Sorry, Jude, but the ale's on the turn in this hot weather. It'll have to serve 'til I buy fresh.'

'No matter. It'll do for him.' Jude cocked his chin in Jack's direction where the lad was sprawled on the lowest few stairs, eyes closed, face streaked with dirt, his breeches soaked in God knew what. 'Get the filthy devil cleaned up, will you, before the whole place reeks like the public shithouse?'

Eleanor roused Jack and gave him the cup which he drained in a single draught. He sighed with pleasure, wiped his mouth on his filthy sleeve and held out the cup for more. Sour or not, Jack was too thirsty to care.

Eleanor went off to fetch water, washcloths and a flask of rose water whilst Jack drank the ale jug dry.

'Got anyfing t'eat? I'm starved.'

'Later. When you don't stink,' Jude said. 'Did you get the ledger?'

'Wot ledger?'

'The order book… like I told you.'

25

'Don't know, do I? Can't read, can I, so 'ow do I know wot I got? I fetched a big book, like wot yer said.'

'Show it to me. If you took some useless antiphon or psalter, I'll wring your neck like a bloody chicken.' The threat was an empty one as both well knew. These days, Jack could overpower Jude as a bear could the aforementioned fowl. Gone was the time when the lad took regular beatings from the man.

'I ain't got it wiv me. That'd be stupid, wouldn't it? 'Ow could I 'ave crossed the city ditch an' climbed the wall wiv a great antifoner-salter fing under me arm, eh?'

'Where is it then?'

'Safe.'

'Where?'

'I ain't tellin' 'til yer pay me.'

'And I'm not paying you a bent farthing until I know you took the right bloody book.'

'Well, I ain't doin' nuffink unless I get breakfast. That mouldy cheese were 'orrible and that's all I've 'ad t'eat since yesserday morn.'

'Wash first, you great turd, then I might consider it. Ell! Where's that washing water?'

Jack stood bare-arsed naked in the midst of the floor whilst Eleanor washed him down.

'And his hair,' Jude insisted. 'He looks like he rolled in shit.'

Eleanor wet the lad's matted locks and tried to work up a lather with scented soap, rinsing it off with rosewater.

'Hey, leave off wiv that stuff else us'll smell like a buggerin' brothel.' Jack shoved the merry cross-dresser away. 'Where're me clouts?'

'Gone for laundering,' she said. 'You can't wear them so befouled.'

'Wot am I s'posed to wear then? Can't go out like this: the size o' me prick'll scare ev'rybody.'

Eleanor laughed but Jude sneered.

'That wouldn't frighten a virgin nun. Find him some of my

linen, Ell—not the decent ones, mind.'

'They won't fit us,' Jack muttered, pulling himself up to his considerable full height.

'They'll bloody serve to cover your toddling's pizzle.'

'Shut yer mouth or I won't tells yer where I hided the book. And give us some eats now I'm clean. Yer promised us.'

Over a platter of yesterday's bread, hard cheese and more half-sour ale, Jack told his tale betwixt mouthfuls:

'Well, yesserday aft'noon, I went to Wes'mister, like yer told us to, wiv me basket of stinky cheese fer me grandam—not that I've got 'un and why anybody'd b'lieve she'd eat that muck if I did 'ave 'un, I don't know...'

'Get on with it. I don't pay you to think.'

'You ain't paid us anyfink yet...'

'What did you do at Westminster?'

'So I put the cheese on top o' the little axe wot yer gived us an' them rags wot I'd soaked in tallow in a bowl, like yer said, wot smelled worser than the bloody cheese.'

'That was the point: the smell of the cheese disguised the stink of the tallow,' Jude explained with a sigh. 'How else would you be able to see what you were doing at Caxton's place in the bloody dark? Were you hoping he'd leave candles burning for you in a shop full of paper?'

'I knows it but the cheese woz 'orrible. Tasted 'orrible too, didn't it, when I tooked a bite cos I woz 'ungry?'

'You weren't supposed to eat it...'

'Worse than this wot yer call bloody breakfast. Master Seb eats bacon collops fer his breakfast. Now, where woz I?' Jack tore off a piece of dry bread crust with his teeth and chewed slowly.

'Westminster.'

'Oh, aye. But it weren't like wot yer said. The winder-shutter in the side alley weren't broke.'

'Well, I haven't been there for a six-and-twelve month, since my bloody accident. I suppose they mended it. So how did you get in?'

'I waited fer dark—which woz a long time comin'—and they wozn't in 'aste t'go t'bed neither, so I filched a couple o' pasties from a cook shop...'

'I told you to behave your bloody self until the job was done. If you'd been caught beforehand...'

'Well I wosn't. Too quick fer 'em, ain't I? Besides, yer can't do a job proper on an empty belly, can yer? So I uses me knife t' poke betwixt them shutters and lift the latch inside so they open. Then I climbs up wiv me basket and I'm in. Easy as pie!'

Jack was having trouble with a piece of tough crust and dipped it in his ale to soften it. Only once he had eaten it, despite Jude's huffing impatience, did he continue:

'I taked out them rags in their chafing dish and used me tinder to set 'em afire. It gived us a good light, like yer said it would. I could see right well t'search fer the book wot yer wanted.'

'Assuming you took the ledger and not some foolish moral tale or the History of bloody Troy, or some such damned nonsense. Where was it kept?'

'I'm comin' t' that bit, ain't I? Yer can't rush a good story. Master Seb told us that one time.' In truth, Jack was enjoying having an audience, even if they kept interrupting.

'Knowing my brother, he meant you can't rush the scribing of it, not the telling. And I haven't got all day to waste, listening to you. I want that bloody ledger. Now, where is it, you time-wasting knave?' Jude leapt up in agitation, forgetful of his knee, and almost fell.

'Be easy, Jude,' Eleanor calmed him and got him back to his bench, rearranging the dislodged cushion. 'Let Jack tell you in his own good time whilst I go buy us some fresh ale, eh?'

Jude muttered some curse or other, wincing as he tried to find a comfortable position for his leg, but he nodded.

'From the Sunne.' He referred to their favoured tavern at the sign of King Edward's device: the Sunne in Splendour. 'Not that cat's piss brew you bought last time.'

28

'I'll need coin, Jude.'

He fished in his purse for money and gave it to Eleanor who took it with a coy toss of her long, loose locks and a swish of silken skirts.

'And get pies,' Jack added, hopefully, receiving a playful clout across the ear from the erstwhile 'lady' before she swept out the door. 'Now she's gone, I can tell yer proper the rest of wot I done, can't I?'

Jude gave him a suspicious frown but said naught.

'See, I couldn't find no book wot looked like wot yer said: wiv lists an' monies writ down in column fings. It weren't layin' around so I reckoned it woz kept safe and there woz a iron-studded coffer wiv a stout lock. I took me axe to it, quiet like, usin' the blade t' prise off the 'asp o' the padlock. It took a while but I did it, didn't I? An' there woz this big, 'eavy levver-covered book wot I nearly dropped cos it were 'eavier than I 'spected. What a crash that would've made, eh? Would've woked up the whole 'ouse'old. And there woz bags o' silver... dozens of 'em...'

'You stole the money, you thieving little bastard!'

'Well, it seemed a sorry waste t' leave 'em there. Yer told us t' thieve the book... why not the coin? Anyway, I now 'ave t' get me boots mended, don't I? Look: strap's broked, so I need money fer that.'

'I told you to get the book and then ruin the printing press. Did you manage that?'

'O' course I did but not 'ow yer said. Choppin' up the platen fing an' wrecking the great lumps o' wood wiv the axe would make too much racket an' raise the 'ouse'old. So instead, I put piles o' paper on the platen an' all round the press. Then I tipped the flamin' tallow rags on top. Yer should've seen it. It went up like a St John's Eve bonfire! An' I left, swift as an arra from a bow...'

'Christ's bloody bollocks, Jack! What have you done? What of Will Caxton and his family? Did you rouse them in time?'

'Wot? Course not. They would've caught us, wouldn't they?

I ain't stupid.'

'So you left them to roast alive in their beds!'

'Nah. I 'spect they climbed out the winders.'

'Will Caxton is fat, gouty and has more trouble with his knees than I do and that was over a year ago. He's probably worse now. I can't imagine him making his escape through an upstairs window. Damn it, Jack, you would be better off being taken as a thief than a multiple murderer.'

Jack shrugged.

'Why? I'd get hanged jus' the same. This way, I've got money an' can run away, anywheres, start over in a new place. Las' night, I woz finking t' get on a ship, go t' Cally.'

'Where?'

'Cally… in France.'

'You mean Calais. Then maybe you should. But first, you'll bloody tell me where you've hidden the ledger. If Caxton's dead, his customers will be even more eager to use my services. I can see there may be more advantages for me in this…'

'See. It woz a good fing…'

'For me. Not for you, Jack. You're a bloody lost cause now. Always were. But there can be no way back from this for you. Where's the ledger?'

The harsh warnings bothered the lad not at all. His entire early life had been a dark garland of possible dire endings.

'Well, it's 'ard t' tell yer in words. I'll need t'show yer… after yer pay us.'

'Seems to me you've had coin enough out of this catastrophic bloody shambles.'

'But yer promised us two shillin's if I did this catterwotsit fing.'

'You didn't follow my instructions. Why should I pay a bloody murderer?'

'Then yer don't get the book.' Jack looked at him, bold as a Sunday strumpet, holding out his hand for wages due. 'Master Appleyard won't be payin' us this week so I needs every penny owed, don't I?'

Grudgingly, Jude opened his purse once more and counted out the pennies:

'...Twenty-two, twenty-three, twenty-four pence. There! Now take me to it.'

'Better wait 'til dark. I'm a wanted man now, ain't I?' Jack sounded pleased at his new status, his notoriety—not that he even knew such a word.

'Christ, give me bloody strength. I should have done the task myself.'

'Not wiv yer lame leg. Yer never could've got in that winder nor out agin after.'

'I would've found a way in and probably have left through the front door. And nobody would be dead.'

'They prob'ly ain't, anyways. Prob'ly got out in time.'

'You had better pray they did. Caxton serves King Randy Bollocks himself.' Jude had personal good reason for his calling King Edward thus. 'This is going to have serious consequences and it's all down to you.' Content to forget that he was the initial instigator of the crime, even if it hadn't been carried out as he intended, Jude decided he was blameless; his conscience—what little he possessed—clear. Almost.

'Wot's conserkwenters?'

'They're what you're going to suffer, you dim-witted gutter snipe. The forces of law and order...'

'If yer tells Bailiff Turner wot I done, I'll say it woz your idea cos it woz. Yer told me to thieve the damned stupid book an' wreck the press so it wouldn't work no more.'

'I never said you were to set the place ablaze...'

Jack shrugged.

'Worked tho', didn't it?'

How Jude kept his temper, God only knew.

'I don't care about waiting for dark,' he yelled, fists clenched. 'We're going to fetch this bloody book. Now! And then you'll stowaway on the first ship sailing from Queenhithe or Paul's Wharf, no matter where it's going: Cathay, the Indies or the

Garden of bloody Eden. If you don't, I will inform the City Bailiff—damn his eyes and bugger the consequences. You're going, Jack, and that's the end of the matter. You can keep all Caxton's coin. I don't care about that either but I want the ledger first.'

Chapter 3

Later that Tuesday
by the Fleet river

IT WAS hotter than Hell's mouth, Jude was convinced, a haze shimmering over the dusty way and he could've sworn the Fleet was steaming. Or, mayhap, that was the miasma rising from the fly-ridden muck and rubbish that tarnished its sluggish waters. Upstream, it was a pretty river, flower-strewn and clear, but here it was no better than the public jakes which emptied into it. He coughed on the stench and wiped the sweat from his brow with his cap—once of fine velvet but now crumpled and frayed, its trim of woven silver-thread braid dulled and coming unstitched in places. Like himself, it was past its best. The walk from home, through Newgate, then down Bailey, behind the Law Court, and along St George's Lane was farther than he had walked since the accident: in truth, not far at all but more than his knee could bear even with the use of a staff.

'Come on, make 'aste, can't yer?' Jack was yards ahead. 'I don't wanna be out too long. Don't want no bailiff, beadle nor constable seein' us, do we?'

Jude paused again, leaning against a crumbling wall of some long-abandoned building. Glancing down at his leg, it surprised him that its agonised throbbing wasn't visible through his hose, expanding and contracting in rhythm with his heart beat. Not for the first time, he wondered if Caxton's ledger—if Jack had even taken the correct book—was worth so much effort on his part. He pushed away from the moss-encrusted stone with

33

his staff and stumbled onwards. The lad was nigh out of sight, following the Fleet north toward Holbourne Hill. For Jude, the steep incline was adding to his torture and misery.

By a stand of willows which leaned out precariously across the murky water, Jack waded into the river to get around the trailing branches. That explained the state of him earlier, Jude realised as he caught up. If that ledger had got sodden, all would have been a waste of time.

'Give us the sack!' Jack called out.

Much against his better judgement, Jude pushed his way through the green willow curtain. He wasn't going to wade in the water and walk home in soaked boots, rousing suspicion with each squelching step. Mud oozed up around his feet, nigh pulling off his boots. Lacking the strength in that leg, he was unable to pull his left foot free of the sucking mud. He began to topple as his staff sank deep and lost his balance, falling awkwardly into the slime, arse first.

'Shit and fucking damnation!' He gagged on the stink which arose around him.

'Where's the sack?'

'Come and get it.'

Jack parted the leaves, sloshing water. One look at Jude and laughter rumbled up in his throat. He couldn't help it as mirth overflowed.

'I'm going to kill you when I get out of here.' Jude shook his fist.

'Catch us first.'

'You filthy whore's son.'

'Call *me* filfy?' the lad chuckled. 'Look at yerself. I never seen nobody wot's as filfy as you. An' pooh... yer stink worser 'n a dead dog. Give us that sack.' Jack snatched the now mud-plastered hessian bag, keeping his distance. Jude's idle threat didn't bother him but even a nose well used to vile stenches could only withstand so much.

Within less time than it took to recite an *Ave Maria*—but

time enough for Jude to realise he was incapable of getting himself upright—Jack returned with the sack over his shoulder, a large square shape bulging, corners poking through the loose weave. Clearly, it weighed heavy.

'Put that somewhere dry, then get me out of here.'

'I might jus' leave yer an' serve yer right, won't it, yer toofless ol' bear.'

Jude couldn't think of a suitable reply and refused to plead for aid. He held out a begrimed hand, hoping Jack would have pity upon him.

The wretch took his own good time—on purpose, no doubt—hiding the sack amongst some brambles higher up the bank. Then he stood, hands on hips, staring at the beleaguered man, drinking in his full fill of the spectacle: his childhood nemesis brought so low. At long last, he relented and took the outstretched hand.

Even with Jack's considerable strength, it was no easy task to pull Jude free. The mud was reluctant to give him up, much as it clung fast to the detritus of the city. With a great deal of sucking and oozing and Jack pulling him by the arms, Jude was able to turn onto his belly and crawl, one-kneed, dragging his bad leg, shoeless, up onto the grass. Whilst he lay, panting, sweating and exhausted from the struggle, the lad even took pity and trouble enough, going back to rescue the staff and the lost boot from the mire.

Christ be thanked that his ignominious plight had, for the most part, been hidden by the willow curtain yet naught could remedy the sight and stink of him but a good bath. The walk home was going to be an agony, both of body and spirit.

'Shall us go straight t' the Sunne an' 'ave some ale?' Jack suggested, shouldering the sack and grinning like a merry gargoyle.

Jude said naught, wishing for a cloak to hide him as they passed through Newgate and the gate-keeper shied away from them, holding his nose. A mangy cur came close to sniff at him and, this once, he had not the strength to shove it aside. Having to put his whole weight upon the staff and doing his utmost to force his good limb to support him and not buckle, Jude felt tired unto death. Home was a hundred yards hence but it seemed like a hundred miles. Crime, he realised, truly didn't pay. Not this time, leastwise.

Jack, too, was no longer grinning but scurried, head down, keeping to the shadowed side of the street forwhy they had heard a huckster speaking to the gate-keeper about 'that dreadful fire in Westminster last eve…' and making the sign of the Cross.

Jude's house, Ave Maria Alley

Arriving at my brother's abode, my fraudulent list of cutlers completed for Thaddeus—much against my inclinations—I was surprised to find Jude seated in a tub of grimy-looking water in the midst of the floor, his back to that great unwieldy printing press. His friend, Eleanor, was wiping him down with a sponge, sprinkling rosewater liberally. What e'er the reason for bathing at this hour, his countenance suggested 'twas not a pleasant one.

'What do you want? Can't you see I'm busy?'

'Indeed.' I omitted the usual courtesies of greeting. They seemed inappropriate, forwhy clearly God had not bestowed a 'good day' upon my brother. I detected a foul odour and espied a heap of soiled attire cast aside in the corner. It included Jude's velvet cap and I wondered what had befallen that even the cap was besmirched. But I thought it best not to ask; my brother's thunderous visage deterred comment. 'I came to enquire as to whether you may have seen young Jack. He has not been at Stephen's place since yesterday nor slept in his bed.'

'Why ask me?' he growled. 'Why should I know what that idle arse-wipe gets up to? Go ask the taverners and the brothel keepers. They're more likely to know. Or the beadles. Or your friend, Turner.'

'The authorities have heard naught of him and we are

becoming concerned. Jack having failed to appear at dinnertime, it could be a serious matter.'

'Forget the bugger. You have a business to run—as I do. There are more important things to deal with.'

'So you know not his whereabouts?'

'I bloody said so, didn't I? How much plainer can I say it? I haven't seen him for a week or more; I don't know where he is and don't care.'

'You saw him upon Sunday last at our place.'

'Did I? Well, that shows how little attention I give to the wretch. Go back to your desk, little brother, and forget about the verminous worm. He's not worth the trouble.' Jude was paying scrupulous attention to scraping dirt out from 'neath his fingernails with a paring knife. 'Cease your worrying. Jack's a crafty rogue and can take care of himself. He always does.' He dropped the knife on the floor. 'Where's that bloody soap, Ell? I can still smell the stink in my hair.'

'Here. I'm sure you're clean enough now, Jude.' Eleanor said, handing him the soap.

'Well, I don't feel clean. Probably never will again.'

'What came to pass?' I dared ask.

'Slipped. Bloody mud.'

I accepted his explanation without comment but where in this dusty city had my brother contrived to discover such an excess of mud? Since he could not venture far, it must be close at hand.

'Ell, get me out of this water before it goes cold. I'll take a chill, sitting here.'

Eleanor moved to assist but, even with her strong arms to aid him, Jude was struggling, unable to put any weight on his bad leg.

'Let me help you,' I offered.

'You think I can't bloody manage myself?'

In truth, I saw he could not. And no wonder for as his knee appeared above the cloudy, soap-scummed water, it was crimson, swollen like a pig's bladder. He likely injured it further when he fell. Whether he wished it or not, I had to assist Eleanor and, even so, 'twas difficult to lift him from the bath. His slick, wet skin and the stream of curses helped not at all.

Water splashed all about, including upon the platen of the press which, as even I knew, must remain ever spotless, else the paper will mark. I saw also that a mud-spattered sack sat atop the platen and once Jude was safe seated, I made to remove it.

'Leave that! Get away from my things, you nosey bugger,' he shouted, dropping the towel in order to push me aside.

I grabbed him in order that he should not fall.

'Fear not, Jude. I thought only to preserve the platen from soiling.'

'Well don't. It's naught to do with you.'

'Forgive me. I meant no offence.'

He growled some reply but I was unable to make out the words.

With Jude dried off, decently clad and seated in comfort upon the bench, Eleanor hastened to fetch ale for us all. We were in need of refreshment after our struggles: Jude be right heavy these days. I set a box of paper that might serve as a footstool so his leg was propped up. His hose were pulled so taut by his swollen knee, the cloth stretched, the seams about to split.

'I would advise one of Beth Chambers' poultices,' I said. 'Shall I call upon her and purchase what be needful?'

'No. Rest is all it needs; none of your quack's receipts and magick potions. It'll do well enough by tomorrow.'

'A cold compress or a salve may be helpful. Rose's meadowsweet remedy reduces inflammation. I could fetch it...'

'I said no! Stop bloody fussing me, Seb. You're worse than a mother hen. Go home and leave me in peace. Go write a bloody great bible or something. Just bugger off.'

'I trust I may finish my ale afore I leave?'

He did not deign to reply and we all sat in a discomforting silence for a while. In truth, I was enjoying the ale and also hoped for a word aside with Eleanor concerning Jude. He appeared so pale with shadows, dark as bruises, 'neath his eyes. Mayhap, 'twas the shock of the fall earlier but I feared him to be in far more pain than he would admit.

'Did you hear about the conflagration at Westminster last eve?' I said to break the silence.

'No,' Jude said. 'What's it to us, anyway, what happens there?'

'I heard tell that it was Master Caxton's place which caught afire.'

'So? What of it?'

'He being your fellow printer, I thought you might have an interest, is all.'

'Well, I don't.' Jude scowled at his ale cup. 'And I think it's time you left now.'

I stood up, draining my ale since my welcome was ended.

'What of Caxton and his family?' Eleanor asked the question which would concern most Christian souls. 'Are they safe?'

'Their lives were spared, God be praised. The household escaped the flames, barely. 'Twas too close for comfort, so they say, but the house and workshop are lost utterly. Poor Will Caxton… after years of hard work… to lose all.' I set down my cup. 'Take care of Jude, Eleanor, if you will.' Out of my brother's view, I took coin from my purse and gave it to her. 'That be for any medicaments you think he needs and send word, anytime, if you require assistance with him… for fear he should take another fall…'

She nodded.

'Fare you well, brother,' I called out as I departed but received no word in return.

The Foxley Place, Paternoster Row

'Any word of Jack?' Rose enquired the moment I entered the kitchen, turning from stirring the pot from which delicious aromas emanated, tickling my taste buds, causing my mouth to water.

'Nay, sweeting. Naught. Not a word. 'Tis as though he has taken flight and disappeared. I be right concerned for the lad.'

'Have you asked at the taverns?'

I laughed humourlessly.

'Jude suggested the same but it would take a month to visit every ale house and inn, as well as costing a fortune and making a drunkard of me. No tavern-keeper likes to part with an iota of information unless you buy his ale but I have asked at the Panyer Inn, the Sunne in Splendour and at the Barge, the Pope's Head and the Green Dragon.'

'And your wits aren't addled after all that ale?'

'I paid for it but drank no more than a mouthful. I tell you, lass, the stuff they call ale at that last establishment be unfit for human kind. A dog would not drink it if he was dying of thirst and I would not wash my feet in it. However, I have a Gospel Book requiring my attention. As you know, the Prioress at Dartford wrote a letter last week, enquiring as to its progress, so...'

'You must get on with it.'

'Aye.'

'Is there much more to do to finish it?'

'Adam, Hugh and Kate be well advanced with their contributions but as for the images, *mea culpa*, I be but at the beginning of St Luke's Gospel.'

'Then you must forget about Jack for the present. He can fend for himself well enough.'

'Aye. Jude said likewise and you both be correct: my work puts bread upon the board; scouring the taverns for the lad serves for naught.'

Rose kissed me, smiled, but then wagged a finger, mocking a scold.

'Then go to, husband, and no supper for you until you've done a day's labour... well, half an afternoon of it, at least. And tell Adam I've repaired young Nicholas's breeches—again.

They're more of patches than substance. The child needs new ones. I can sew them for him, if Adam wants me to, but I'll need to buy cloth and I know not what's best. Do I buy cheap cloth because the child will grow out of them soon enough but, since he's so hard on his clothes and careless of them, should I get better cloth to last longer? If they survive Nick's wearing, they can be passed on to little Mundy. What do you think, Seb?'

'Me? What do I know of such matters? Probably, cheap cloth will suffice… but then good cloth may be more economical in the way of lasting longer. Do not ask me, sweeting. 'Tis a woman's concern. But I shall mention it to Adam.'

'If you remember…'

I walked through to our workshop. It still brought a smile to my face whenever I saw our spacious new workplace: neat desks, two purpose-made for their occupants—one to allow for Ralf's bent back and Hugh's constructed to be convenient for his enforced left-handedness, lacking a right thumb as he did. Not that its lack encumbered him nor made his craftsmanship any less than exemplary. As my new journeyman, Hugh was proving a valuable addition to our workshop.

'Ah, you're back at last,' Adam greeted me, a note of exasperation in his voice. He put down his pen, being careful not to lay it too close by the page he was copying—St John's Gospel, the seventh chapter. 'We've had enquiries that only you can deal with. Sir Philip Allenby wants his coat-of-arms repainted as a matter of urgency… important guests visiting in a fortnight's time, apparently.'

'Re-painted? Is he the fellow who lives by the Crutched Friars in Hart Street? I do not recall that we ever made such a thing for him.'

'He is and we didn't. A limner did it but the paint is peeling though it's not yet a twelvemonth since it was made.'

'Improper preparation of the wood, no doubt. Sir Philip should complain to the Limners' Company and get them to repaint it at no cost.'

41

'That's what I told him but he said the less he has to do with "those corner-cutting charlatans", the better. He's determined you should do it and is willing to pay a goodly sum to have it done properly and within two weeks. But, in truth, I don't see how you'll have the time since these Dartford Gospels have to be finished by then...'

'Aye, but the daylight lasts long. Mayhap I could work on it in the evenings.'

'He's coming back after supper to ask you about it... And Master Rainer came by also, the pompous little ass. He wants to know the exact date when you will begin his portrait. He's getting tetchy about the delay and spoke right rudely, even in front of Kate, so I warned him to watch his words and he answered: "If that erstwhile artist of yours was ever here to work like a proper Christian, then I wouldn't have cause to enquire". I don't like the fellow, Seb, not one bit.'

'And I be no better than an erstwhile artist? If 'tis so—since no contract has yet been agreed nor a penny paid, I shall be less inclined than ever to paint his portrait. He hardly makes for a pleasing subject. I most assuredly would not want his likeness staring down at me from a place of honour upon the wall.'

'Aye. It would put me off my dinner,' Adam laughed, returning to a better humour.

'Did any other customers come by?'

'Lady Howard's servant brought in a Psalter book, asking that we might repair it for her ladyship. I told him we'd look at it and send word as to 'aye' or 'nay'. It's a family heirloom, so he said but, at a glance, I'm not certain it can be saved. See what you think of it: I've put it in the store room coffer for safe keeping as it's so fragile. Also, we sold two scholars' primers, four blank chap-books, a ream of best paper, a plain breviary and that little Book of Hours which you completed last month.'

'Well, that did not gather dust on the shelf for too long. Did you get the full price for it? I thought four marks might be somewhat too much to ask, although it be worth at least that, since I used lapis lazuli and saffron.'

'Aye, which is why I said it cost five marks.'

'You did?'

'And the fellow paid without demure. He could well afford it, being an Italian banker from Lombard Street.'

'Well done, Adam.'

'Indeed. Somebody has to keep our accounts in good stead.' He gave me a right steely look.

'And how is Simon's lettering progressing?'

'Very well. Simon is an excellent 'prentice, aren't you, lad?' Adam grinned, his ill humour with me deflected—as I knew it would be, forwhy his eldest step-son was proving a most able penman, and Adam was a proud stepfather. He went to the youngster's desk and ruffled his hair. 'He works hard and with his fine hand we'll soon have him scribing primers, won't we, my son?'

Simon had not yet been apprenticed here for six months but his previous schooling in St Paul's was proving a most sure grounding. His master there had taught him well. Once he knew all the proper scribal letter forms, such that he might do them in his sleep, his lessons would swiftly progress to preparing the pages: whiting parchment, pricking and ruling up—tedious stuff—but then would come the joys of decorated initials, at which young Kate excelled, and my favoured aspect: learning how to prepare and use pigments, the true secrets and mysteries of our craft.

'Thank you, Father.' Simon blushed at such praise and Adam's smile grew yet broader to be addressed as 'father'. In truth, their relationship was not yet confirmed under the law. The Lord Mayor had signed the indenture of apprenticeship as the lad's guardian at Christmastide last and we still awaited the completion of the legal convolutions that would recognise Adam as Simon's guardian. Despite this, the pair was as close as any parent and child: far closer than the lad had ever been to his murderous sire.

'Twas a sorrowful affair that Adam's marriage to the mother of the three lads, Mercy Hutchinson, proved to be bigamous when her hateful husband returned from the dead. Their happy union was void as the wretch reclaimed his wife… only to kill her, leaving their sons motherless and soon to be fatherless when he was hanged. With no other relatives to care for them, Adam continued in the role of stepfather and thus it remained for the present until the slow machinations of the law confirmed it. I knew Adam and Simon to be eager for that day, Nicholas and Edmund being too young to comprehend such matters.

I sat at my desk, uncovered the parchment upon which I had been working yesterday and considered the half-painted image of the Nativity that would open St Luke's Gospel. This day, I had not so much as lifted a brush. Stephen's anxious enquiries concerning Jack had precluded any work until now. How unfortunate that my efforts to learn of the lad had achieved naught but wasted the best part of the day. I must set that aside now.

Since Kate, Hugh and Ralf were fully immersed in their rightful tasks, I prepared my own pigment, breaking the egg and piercing the yolk sac that it should mix cleanly in the oyster shell with the crimson lake. This for the Virgin's kirtle and a faint blush upon her cheek. I needs must apply the colour swiftly, forwhy the June heat would dry the pigment in the shell all too soon, making it unworkable. Laying a small square of damp linen over the paint delayed but did not entirely prevent its drying out.

When Rose called us to supper, I near told her to put mine aside for later.

'This miniature requires my attention for the present, afore the pigment sets hard,' I said, not so much as glancing up from my work.

'You'll regret it, Seb. We have a most splendid dish, courtesy of Nessie.'

'What of Nessie? Are we celebrating some event or other?' I

continued to apply the crimson lake in sweeping brush strokes, each implying the fall of cloth in the Virgin's robe.

'Naught at all. In truth, I think the butcher must have made a mistake. I sent her with three farthings to buy scrag end of mutton for a pottage and she returns with stekys of best beef, thick and juicy, which must cost far more than that. So we have a right grand dish for this eve's supper. I've made an anise and cinnamon basting sauce to accompany the beef and I don't want it to spoil, waiting for you. The Virgin may keep until after we have supped.'

'But the pigment cannot. I will finish this and then...'

'Seb Foxley. If you do not come to the board within the time it takes me to recite five *Paternosters*, Gawain shall have your dish. At least he appreciates fine food and this windfall is unlikely to be repeated. Please don't let it spoil.'

'Oh, very well. But I dare not linger over it.' I washed out my brush and covered the pigment in a wet cloth, hoping it would remain usable. 'Best beef upon a Tuesday, Rose? Whatever next?' But my wife was away to the kitchen and I could hear her murmuring a *Paternoster* under her breath.

As it came to pass, I did indeed linger over our fine supper. Since the cut of meat was of such fine quality, Rose insisted the other dishes must do it justice. Thus, she had made an elderflower cheesecake, known as sambocade, decorated with bright blue alkanet blossoms from our garden. Meg served this with little griddled cakes made with buttermilk, flour, honey and raisins of Corinth. And spynoches, fresh and green, also from our garden plot, were briefly fried with grated nutmeg and pepper and garnished with saffron. This meal befitted a king's table—and all for no better reason than a butcher's error!

My good intentions regarding the Gospel of St Luke flew out of the window. All of us, replete after so much good food, sat over our last few morsels of cakes and ale.

'That beef was excellent, Rose,' Adam said, patting his belly and belching appreciatively. 'Which butcher did you go to?'

'Fattyng's, as always, in the Shambles by Newgate, but you can thank Nessie, not me.'

Adam gave a nod of acknowledgement towards our plump, buck-toothed maid servant who blushed as red as a cherry.

'It weren't no trouble, Master Adam, Warin gived us the beef for free on account of...'

'Is that Fattyng's ugly 'prentice: knock-kneed, chinless, weed-thin?' Adam continued.

Ralf chuckled:

'Spotty as a pard with a braying laugh like a donkey? I've seen him... and heard him.'

'He's not ugly!' Nessie screeched, leaping up and overturning her stool. 'Warin is kind and generous...'

'Ooh, Adam, it seems we Norfolk men have touched a tender place there.' Ralf went on laughing into his ale cup.

Nessie was sobbing loudly—as only she could.

'They meant no harm, lass.' Rose put a comforting arm around her and offered a table napkin to dry her tears.

'They but speak in jest,' I added, giving both men a sharp, reproving glance.

'Aye, that's so,' Adam muttered, smothering his mirth with his hand. 'I dare say this Warin fellow is a paragon... handsome, virile...'

Ralf laughed out loud and I could tell that Hugh, Kate and young Simon were hard put not to join in. The little ones burbled and chuckled without knowing the reason but because the adults did so. Only Meg did not seem inclined to merriment.

'Don't listen to them, Nessie,' she said, patting the maid's hand. 'They're men: ignorant and foolish. They don't understand. Come, let us walk in the garden and leave them to their ale-sodden jests.'

Ale-sodden jests? Hardly. We had consumed but a jug full betwixt us all.

With Meg and Nessie gone, the rest of us resumed our discourse, talking of naught of any consequence until there came a knock upon the street door.

'Who can that be?' Rose said, rising from her stool and hastening to attend the visitor.

'Probably Sir Philip Allenby, about his coat-of-arms,' Adam said. 'As I told you, Seb, he wants you to repaint it in haste before his important guests arrive.'

'Oh, aye. I recall you saying.' I sighed, having no desire to tangle with a difficult customer, if 'twas indeed Sir Philip, he who was so displeased with a limner's previous work on his heraldic piece. I silently prayed our visitor to be some other but Fortune was not of a mind to please me.

'Sir Philip Allenby awaits you in the parlour, Seb,' Rose said as she returned. 'I'll serve wine, shall I? And we have a few of Meg's griddle cakes left.'

'Aye, lass, that will be fitting for a knight but naught for me. I could not eat or drink another mouthful after so magnificent a repast.' I made for the parlour reluctantly.

Sir Philip was a man of middle years and well attired, as befitted a prosperous knight, though I suspected his miniver-lined velvet robe to be too weighty a garment for this warm summer's eve. He sat upon our cushioned settle, mopping his glistening brow with a kerchief, his greying hair clinging damply to his forehead.

'Master Foxley? Good even to you,' he wheezed, extending his hand which I held but briefly, finding it clammy.

'And also to you, Sir Philip. I apologise for being elsewhere when you came earlier. My good wife will bring wine for you shortly, then may we discuss business.'

'Indeed, Foxley. You must understand that my brother-by-marriage—my wife's brother—is a pompous ass, ever lauding his own importance. My own standing cannot be let down by a piece of shoddy workmanship, as you'll realise.' Sir Philip pulled at the neck of his close-fitting embroidered over-shirt. I saw he looked to be in some discomfort and pale.

'Be you quite well, sir?' I asked.

'The hot weather afflicts me somewhat... no use for this summer heat.'

I wondered if that was truly the cause, forwhy I should have expected one overcome by the heat to appear flushed of face, which he was not. I observed him as Rose served his wine. He drank it down greedily whilst his hands upon the cup shook. As she departed the parlour, leaving the wine jug for our visitor to help himself, she and I exchanged anxious glances concerning him.

'Will you oblige me, F-Foxley?' he continued. 'I haven't the time to waste u-upon those lick-spittle limners. Y-you come highly... recommended. I w-would p-pay you...' The knight's words faded into a groan as what little colour he had leeched away. The pewter cup fell from his grasp, clattered on the new tiles and rolled around, spilling the remainder of its ruby contents as he slumped sideways upon the cushions.

'Rose! Make haste,' I called out, much alarmed as I went to attend him. 'Our visitor be most unwell,' The smell of sour sweat was strong upon him and his skin felt clammy 'neath my touch. Moreover, he had brought fleas within our house for certain—I knew, forwhy I suffered bites upon my arm which much annoyed me.

We revived him with cold compresses and by burning a feather under his nose—a sharp stink which pervaded the parlour long after. Adam ran to Sir Philip Allenby's house by the Crutched Friars on Hart Street to fetch his servants to take him home.

Time passed all too tardily and it was some hours as St Paul's bell rang for Compline that the knight was taken home upon a litter by his household servants. I like to think myself a Christian soul but, in truth, I have ne'er been so eager to see a visitor depart.

Rose was wringing her hands, her eyes tear-filled. I put my arm around her as we watched Sir Philip's litter disappearing down Paternoster Row into Cheapside.

'Oh, Seb… may sweet Jesu Christ keep us all safe.'

'Amen to that, sweeting,' I replied as we both crossed ourselves. 'Twas a heartfelt prayer, forewhy, as we had bathed the knight's brow and loosened the ties of his shirt at the neck, we espied an ominous token there: a great ugly swelling.

Chapter 4

Wednesday, the twentieth day of June
The Foxley Place, Paternoster Row

I DID NOT sleep last night and Rose fared little better. All we could think about was that lump on Sir Philip Allenby's neck and what evil it might foretell for our household. I recalled that Thaddeus had mentioned cases of pestilence in St Olave's parish, where the knight dwelt, and now our happy home was at grave risk all because of one thoughtless customer. The man should never have been at large in the city, endangering the lives of everyone he touched or breathed upon. He ought to have shut himself away until the contagion passed and he recovered, or not, howsoever Almighty God willed it. But that was irrelevant now and, mayhap, the damage was already done to us.

Lying sleepless abed, Rose and I had discussed the matter at interminable length, wondering what we should do for the best whilst making provision, if the worst befell. Fortunately, I had drawn up my will last October, previous to embarking upon our pilgrimage to Canterbury, not knowing then what dangers we might encounter during the journey—and hazards there were indeed. The will could yet stand, meaning I need not trouble to write another. Also, we decided, there seemed no reason to tell the others what we had seen, not as yet, at least. Why give them needless nightmares if our concerns came to naught?

And what of the little ones: might we send them to safety elsewhere? If we did, the entire parish would realise something was amiss and likely guess the truth. We would be shunned, customers would not come and our livelihood would founder. Best to keep silent but take every precaution whilst continuing as usual. If we could… if Rose and I might maintain our merry countenances. 'Twould be no easy matter so to do.

Meanwhile, we fretted over possibilities: did other less deadly maladies also bear similar tokens? If we were unfortunate and succumbed, how long afore the first symptoms made themselves felt? What would be the chances of our survival? Folk did come through it, occasionally, I knew. Was there some preventive medicament we could take in the meantime to ward off the sickness before it began? These questions we could not answer but would consult Bess Chambers at the first opportunity upon the morrow.

'Oh, Seb, I'm so afeared,' Rose sobbed in my arms, her tears wet upon my breast. 'I love you so dearly… and the children and everyone… I couldn't bear to lose you.'

'Nor I you, my dearest one.' I kissed her smooth brow: warm and dry, God be thanked. 'But all may be well. Sir Philip was here for so short a space…'

'You forget that he visited earlier in your absence. He spoke at length with Adam and Meg served them refreshment. He seemed well enough this afternoon but Dickon, Nick and Mundy were by the shop door when he left, playing with knuckle bones. He could have breathed his deadly humours upon any of us. Seb, hold me close, closer… Tell me how much you love me.'

'You know I love you, Rose, queen of my heart, my eternal soul-mate. I shall love and cherish you until death and beyond, 'til the stars no longer shine, the salt seas taste sweet again and the sun and moon forget their differences, sharing the heavens together in everlasting unity. And you and I will be there, hand-in-hand, when the last grain of the sands of time trickles through God's hourglass and Judgement Day is come. Without you, I should be a lost soul, my life meaningless. You are everything to me, sweeting: the very reason I draw breath

and my heart beats...'

And thus, I believe she slept.

I rose at first light, there seeming no reason to delay the commencement of the day's tasks, for who could say how many days were yet left to us? But in so solemn a frame of mind with my thoughts in turmoil, I found it impossible to sit at my desk and take up the brush. As though to mock us, hours before Prime was rung, the sun shone down upon a beauteous morning. Not knowing how many more such mornings I might live to witness, I dared not miss the opportunity to enjoy this one to the full.

Calling to a sleepy Gawain, I took up my scrip and drawing stuff and slipped from the silent house by the back door. We went up to Newgate where the narrow wicket gave exit from the city afore the gates opened officially at Prime. The street lay empty, as yet untrodden, as I made my solitary way.

Along Bailey to Cock Lane, the hedgerows were bedecked with flowers of bramble and buttercups, moon daisies and mallow, foxgloves standing sentinel in royal purple array. In the orchid-strewn grass of Smithfield, beyond St Bartholomew's Hospital, I sketched the wild roses, each touched by dawn's first blush, petals like pale butterflies tumbling in the light. A golden circlet sat at the heart of every bloom: a reminder of Our Lord's ultimate crown of glory. I fixed the colours in my mind's eye and drew their forms: the five petals for the five wounds of Christ, the thorns for the crown He wore and, later, the red rosehips for the blood He shed. This, I imagined for the title page of St John's Gospel which I should begin painting as soon as the Nativity was completed.

Gawain chased an early-rising bumble bee, wetting his coat in the dew on the feathery cow parsley and long grasses by St Bartholomew's Precinct wall. A wren sang his sweet purring song from atop a hawthorn bush and skylarks carolled as they flew high above in the blue vault of Heaven. How could anything so amiss, so hideous as the pestilence, yet be abroad in God's own glorious Creation? Why was the Devil himself so intent on imposing ugliness and pain upon this lovely land? Was mankind's sinfulness so great that we all must suffer, even the youngest and most innocent among us?

As I sketched Gawain confronting a red-coated squirrel—I know not which of them was most put out by this whisker-twitching encounter—tears fell upon the paper, smudging the dark dust of charcoal.

It being Wednesday, we all went to St Michael le Quern for Low Mass, as usual, excepting Adam and his step-sons, who attended St Augustine's since the house Adam rented from me lay in that parish. But whilst Nessie, Kate, Hugh and Ralf—Meg preferring not to attend as was her way—prayed according to custom, for Rose and me, our prayers were of another kind. Never had we beseeched the Lord Jesu's mercy so fervently; never had we lighted so many candles afore each saint and at every chapel altar nor poured so many coins into the alms boxes.

'Is all well, Master Seb?' Ralf enquired with a quizzical expression as I emptied my purse into the collection box for monies towards repairing the nave roof. My old journeyman watched as Rose did likewise, tipping her coins into the alms box for the poor and destitute of the parish. Our generosity was raising eyebrows amongst our neighbours and I feared we should have used more discretion.

'Aye, Ralf. All be well. Why should it not?' I forced a smile, patting his misshapen shoulder.

'Just a-wondering, master,' he replied but I saw he was unconvinced by my assurance.

At home, Adam and his lads joined us in breaking our fast on fried whitebait—little Dickon's favoured fish—with new bread and fresh ale. Ale did not remain drinkable for long in this hot weather and Meg had fetched a jug-full from the Panyer Inn whilst we were at church. Her disillusionment with Almighty God resulted from a lifetime of misuse, first from her father and then from the Abbess of St Helen's in Bishopsgate. Our own priest, Father Thomas, and my one-time friend, Father Christian—may God assoil his soul—and I had attempted to persuade her otherwise and we each failed utterly. Now, though Meg knew it not, her reacceptance of Our Lord's mercy might become urgent. I must try anew to convince the lass.

Everyone at the board ate with good heart but for Rose and me. We neither of us had much appetite but then I watched as she sat, determined of countenance, and forced herself to take up a little silvery fish in her fingers, chew and swallow it. Our eyes met across the table and she mouthed the word 'eat' at me. She was correct, of course. If the contagion came upon us, we would require all our strength to fight it. Starving myself beforehand could do no good, so I did my best to clear the small helping of whitebait I had taken from the dish. Not a man's portion, I admit, but with a heel of bread and a half cup of ale, I could manage no more.

'I shall be away then, to Bess Chambers' shop,' I said, leaving the board. 'We have need of... er... white lead pigment.'

'There's a new box of it in the storeroom,' Adam said, helping himself to more fish. 'So you may spare yourself the walk, cousin.'

'I—I meant red lead... and yellow ochre.'

'But you bought ochre the other day and there's plenty of red lead. I checked our supplies last Saturday.'

'M-maybe so, Adam, but I think the pot of azurite be low...'

'It's not. I checked all the pigments.'

'Nonetheless, I be away to Bishopsgate for…'

'Fennel seed,' Rose said, coming to my rescue. 'We need fennel seed, Seb, if you will? Don't forget to put more coin in your purse. Father Thomas remarked upon your generosity this morn, saying another five marks or so should be sufficient to repair the nave roof. Won't that be splendid? We will no longer have to stand in puddles to hear mass when it's raining.'

'Aye, lass… a mercy to us all. I shall make haste now.'

Last night, we had discussed this morning's errand to the apothecary's shop: questions I must ask and purchases I should make. Our lives might depend upon this.

But as I departed the house with a refilled purse—who could say what the necessities might cost—and an empty scrip to contain them all, I saw Thaddeus striding towards me along Paternoster Row.

'God give you good day, my friend,' he called out. 'Am I too tardy for breakfast? I need you, Seb, to write up all the matters gleaned from witnesses regarding that football death.'

'Thaddeus, come no further. Breakfast be done and I have not time to scribe for you.'

'Oh, pity. I hoped…'

I saw his merry countenance fall but hardened my heart.

'Be gone. Take your meals elsewhere in future.'

'Am I not welcome any longer? What have I done amiss? How have I offended you?' His puzzlement was painful to see.

'You have not offended but stay away from our house… until I say otherwise.'

'What has happened, Seb? Is something wrong?' He stood before me, blocking my way.

'Naught of concern to you. Now, get you gone. Stand aside and do not speak to me or mine. Do you understand what I say?'

'Aye. Your words be clear enough but I don't know why you would say these things to me. We're friends… or, at least, I thought we were. If you need help, Seb…'

'I do not. I simply have matters to deal with that be not of your business. Go away, Thaddeus.' With which harsh words, I walked around him, careful not to brush against him nor breathe upon him. I hated having to treat him thus but I would not imperil the life of my good friend nor ask his aid. Besides, what could he do? Sharing the truth of our situation would but spread panic throughout the neighbourhood. There would be time enough for that if the worse befell and we showed symptoms of the pestilence—God have mercy upon us.

I did not look back at him as I passed into Cheapside but likely he was scratching his head, pulling at his earlobe and wondering at my unaccountably discourteous and most unfriendly behaviour. But what else might I have done to utterly deter him, he being a most persistent fellow when he has a mind?

Bess Chambers' apothecary's shop

I made my way, head down, towards Bishopsgate. I determined to avoid speech with anyone, most especially those I accounted friends, and kept my distance from folk, insofar as that was possible in London's busiest streets. In Poultry, I hastened into an alleyway when I saw Bennett Hepton, the wealthy fishmonger, coming along—he who be our friend Peronelle's husband. I would not want to pass on any contagion to that loving couple and their little daughter. He went by without noticing me, God be thanked, else he would have made conversation betwixt us, no doubt.

Bess's shop was busy as ever and my heart sank, not knowing how I might speak with her privily and, in such a crowd, neither could I avoid touching others. But as I stood in line, some at least of my questions were answered.

'Our neighbour across the way,' a plump woman at the front of the queue was saying loudly, 'Folk say he is dying of the pestilence and I spoke with his wife only last week, upon the Feast of St Barnabas or St Anthony or some other saint was it?

I can't quite recall. But of course, I'm that concerned now for my own health. How long does it take before... you know what I'm asking, Bess. When can I feel safe again?'

'In truth, Joan, few of us are safe once that dread disease is abroad but since it can make itself known within a day sometimes, or it may take as long as a se'en night, you'd likely be showing the tokens by now.'

'Well, I'm not, I can assure you...'

'Then you've almost certainly not been afflicted by your neighbour. Is his wife still well, do you know?'

'She was at church this morn, though I kept away from her. She looked hale enough when she was berating the churchwarden for his lacklustre ringing of the Angelus bell earlier.'

'Then it may be that her goodman doesn't have the pestilence at all. In which parish do you dwell? St Andrew's Undershaft, isn't it?'

'Aye, off Aldgate Street.'

'I've not heard of any other cases nearby that parish but, to be certain, I can recommend my remedy which is also a most excellent preventive...' Bess held out a glass bottle containing a cloudy greenish liquor. ''Tis well worth a groat to put your mind at rest, Joan. A spoonful night and morn and half that amount for the children will see you safe.'

This exchange had answered one or two of my questions but I wondered who this woman's neighbour might be. Sir Philip Allenby lived by the Crutched Friars off Hart Street in St Olave's parish, some little walk from Aldgate Street. Would she account him a neighbour? Nay, 'twas unlikely, I assured myself, not if he had been ill for some days but the days involved were not exactly clear. The Feast of St Barnabas was upon the eleventh day of June and St Anthony's two days after that but if 'twas the celebration of some other saint, Basil, for instance, or Saints Julitta and her son Cyricus... St Vitus' day and then St Richard of Chichester's translation was upon the sixteenth—Dickon's birth date, of course—and the feast day of Saints Gervase and

Protasius was but yesterday… With so many saints' days but lately passed, there was much possible confusion as to when this Joan had first encountered the sick man's wife.

At least I now knew that if we none of us showed tokens of the pestilence by Tuesday next coming, we were likely to have warded off the contagion in this instance. But I was shocked to realise that one of us might begin to fall ill at any moment and I prayed to the Blessed Virgin Mary, even as I waited to be served, that none at home were becoming unwell in my absence. And what of me? Did I feel hotter than the warmth of summer warranted? Was I sweating over much? Could a headache be threatening? Cease this foolish imagining, I reprimanded myself. There be naught amiss with you.

'God give you good day, Master Foxley.' Bess greeted me with a broad smile. I did my best to return it but failed, I realised, when she beckoned me through to the room behind the shop where her distilling was done. Pots bubbled over the fire and fragrant steam made the air muggy. 'Come into the garden, Seb, and tell me what's wrong, for I can see "trouble" writ clear upon your brow.'

'You can? Dear God in Heaven and I try so hard to conceal it. Likely, the whole of London must know since 'tis so plain.'

'Nay, master, only to me who knows your face so well.' She directed me to sit in the bower, surrounded by the perfume of roses and lavender and the humming of bees. A linnet sang from the pear tree and all seemed so joyous, taunting our woes. 'Now tell me.'

And thus I did as Bess bade me, recounting our great fears.

'I've heard no word concerning this Sir Philip Allenby and, as you know, ill-tidings travel quicker than lightning in this city. However, the man may not have sent for an apothecary nor a priest as yet but keeps to his bed along with his secret. Or, maybe, you mistook the token and a simple summer fever is all that ails him.'

'We made no mistake, Bess. Both Rose and I saw the lump

on his neck, so unless it may also betoken some lesser ill…'

She nodded.

'And he was sweating and his skin clammy?'

'Aye, and his hands shook as one with palsy and he groaned in pain as he collapsed. I fear he was *in extremis* ere they came to fetch him home and we have been stretched taut upon tenterhooks ever since. What can you advise to aid us, Bess, to ward off the pestilence? The cost matters not. Whatever you have, I shall purchase with the greatest alacrity.'

'Firstly, you need to take a large bottle of my preventive remedy: the one I sold to Joan Webster just now but enough for all your household. The children must have half a spoonful night and morn but they'll not like the taste, so I'll give you some honey and cinnamon pastilles for them to suck after. The rest of you must take a whole spoonful at the correct times when the Angelus sounds. If any of you show signs or feel unwell, take a spoonful at midday also, go to bed and drink plenty of my rosehip cordial and clear water from the conduit. In the meantime, take some of my scented candles. Burn one in each room of your house and workshop to dispel any foul miasmas and purify the airs.'

'I can ne'er thank you sufficiently, Bess…'

'And, of course, prayer would be advisable, too, Seb. Don't forget to pray to St Roche most fervently for protection from pestilence. All these things can but help and will do no harm. Oh, and I'll have Sarra attend you before you leave. Being a seventh daughter and sharing the nativity of Our Holy Mother, St Mary, upon the eighth day of September, my niece has skills little understood. Wait here and Sarra will come to you in a short while.'

'Twas some time before Sarra came and I had grown hot and thirsty even in the shady bower, watching the diligent bees, coming and going from the skeps, giving attention to every flower in turn. Their labouring in such heat was commendable.

At last, the lass appeared, beautiful as ever, bearing two cups of cordial. She handed me one containing a pale red liquid and sat beside me on the wooden bench.

'It's my aunt's rosehip cordial, Master Seb. She says you can't be too careful and it will fortify you against any ailment.' She sipped her own drink which was colourless. 'Mine is elderflower,' she explained, 'Since I'm not in any danger.'

'Did your aunt not warn you of the, er, possibility that I may carry the contagion upon my person?'

'Of course she did but I'm too well protected.' Sarra pulled a thong of white leather from 'neath her gown whence it encircled her slender neck. Suspended from the thong were two rough slivers of wood of about an inch long bound together with thin red cord to form a cross. 'It's rowan wood to ward off evil and the cord is red, dyed with dragon's blood, itself a sovereign remedy. I have been making amulets for everyone in your household to keep them safe from harm—that's what took me all this while of waiting.' She turned to face me. 'But you must wear this one constantly, Master Seb, close to your heart,' she said as she removed it from about her neck and put it around mine, murmuring words I could not make out. 'Also...' She took my head in her hands and kissed me upon the forehead, then each cheek, my throat and, lastly, upon my mouth. 'May the Five Wounds of Our Lord Christ protect you, Amen.'

'Amen,' I echoed as she gazed into my eyes and I plunged into the fathomless green, gold-flecked depths of hers. A thrill coursed through me, tingling along my limbs and raising the hairs on the back of my neck. I felt a brief surge of strength and elation but then she loosed her hold and all was as before, or nigh so, forwhy a sense, most pleasurable, yet lingered.

'Fear not, Seb Foxley, the Virgin Mother knows your name and favours you. Your days are not yet numbered.' Then she stood and business became foremost. 'Come, Aunt Bess will have all in readiness for you.'

Later, with bulging scrip and my purse a deal lighter, I departed the shop, wearing the rowan wood amulet tucked into my shirt, along with the hot memory of that kiss upon my lips and those green eyes. They were the colour of malachite dappled with flakes of gold leaf. How I should paint them would be a challenge indeed but one I could hardly resist. I knew not what powers Sarra possessed but they had affected me most deeply.

The Foxley Place, Paternoster Row

I returned home to find Rose, Meg and Nessie scrubbing floors, washing down walls and all our furnishings and hangings, coverlets and curtains standing out in the yard or draped along the hedge.

'What is this, Rose? I thought you did the Spring Clean afore Easter. Are things become grubby again so soon?'

'Not grubby but possibly tainted. We've cleansed the nursery from floor to ceiling, the parlour most especially and the hall and kitchen but you'll have to clear out the workshop and shop before we can give them a thorough scrubbing. Meg and Nessie are doing the bedchambers now.'

'Oh, a deal of work then. Have you told Adam of your intentions?' I wrinkled my nose as we entered the kitchen, for the smells of lye soap and lavender water were nigh overwhelming.

'Nay, not yet. He'll want to know the reason why, won't he? And I think we must tell everyone the truth. We can't expect them to keep away from other folk, swallow a preventive or take excessive care without knowing the reason why. Fortunately, Thaddeus hasn't come by this day. I hope he is well.'

'Aye, Thaddeus be well but I doubt he will call by for a while.' I did not say why that should be but my guilt lay like a stone in my belly. 'Where are the little ones?'

'Sorry, Seb, but I gave Kate leave from her desk to take them to collect eggs from the chickens, to make a thorough search and find every one. We couldn't clean and scrub properly with them underfoot and I know Adam wasn't best pleased to have her sent upon such a menial task but I was most firm about it.

I'm afraid I said you gave permission…'

'No matter. 'Tis of little import, I suppose, when who knows what may befall us upon the morrow.'

'Don't say that, Seb. Tell me what Bess advises whilst I find what I did with the ale jug,' Rose said. 'Oh, all is in such a confounded muddle, I hardly know what I'm about. Up is down and down is up. What a to-do!' She caught sight of our maid, about to empty a bucket out into the yard where our precious few pieces of furniture stood. 'No, Nessie, I said to scrub the stairs with that bucketful. Don't waste all the soapy water.' Rose sighed as the lass grimaced and lugged the heavy bucket back up the stair.

'Bess advises scented candles made with bees wax from her own skeps…,' I said as I commenced to empty my scrip. 'Sweet pastilles for the little ones… the sovereign remedy… more candles… rosehip cordial… and amulets. There, that be all she and Sarra say be needful for us, to keep us from harm.'

Rose stared, eyebrows raised, at the items now arrayed upon the kitchen board.

'She and *Sarra* advise all this? Why so many candles, Seb?'

'One for each room. They be perfumed to drive out any noxious airs. By the by, they will also deter moths, fleas and such like and I know our visitor last eve carried the latter upon his person and I shall be glad to be rid of them.'

The sound of smashing earthenware distracted us.

'Nessie! You foolish creature.' Meg's voice came shrill from upstairs. 'Look what you've done.'

Then came the great wails of which only Nessie was capable, the sobbing and shrieking. Souls suffering Hell's torments could not make a more horrendous noise than she.

'What now?' Rose muttered, resigned to accept whatever disaster had come to pass as she set a cup before me. 'I must go see…' There was no sign of the ale jug.

'Leave it, sweeting. Meg will deal with it. I must explain all to you afore the others come to eat dinner.'

'Dinner! Oh, Seb, I haven't prepared the fresh herrings. They need gutting, heading and de-scaling. Meg!' Rose called up the stair. 'Meg! I pray you, come help me, else dinner won't be ready. Seb, take those candles into the parlour, if you will. Put the remedy and the cordial up on that shelf, out of the way, and the pastilles, or the children will eat them afore we can say a Paternoster. And those, er, things, whatever they are.'

'Amulets, Rose. Here, let me put one about your neck.'

'I haven't time for that. I must see to the fish.'

'Indeed you have, wife. It will keep you safe. There. Tuck it 'neath your shift. See? I wear one also and so shall we all as soon as I explain after we have dined.'

We ate our hastily prepared meal surrounded by confusion and the scrubbed floor yet damp under our feet. Fried herrings, bread and ale were all and Adam sat frowning and staring at his sparse platter.

'What's going on, Seb? Rose? All this infernal cleaning and barely enough of a meal to get us to supper time... and after all your promises to the contrary, cousin, you've not done a stroke of work this morning. What about those Gospels? So urgent, you say, but then leave us to labour whilst you go dancing attendance on Thaddeus Turner or whoever... whatever...'

'I assure you, Adam, I have been about matters more urgent than the Gospels and naught to do with Thaddeus,' I said.

'Well, I'm tiring of this situation...' Adam made to leave the board.

'Nay, Adam, sit down. We have dire matters to speak of. Rose, if you would put the little ones in the nursery for their nap...'

'I'll do it,' Meg offered.

'You will not. This concerns you also, Meg.'

Rose ushered the children away to their beds, protesting as ever, Nicholas stamping up the stair, shouting that he was no babe and didn't want to sleep.

'Nick! Do as you're told,' Adam threatened, 'Or you'll feel my belt across your backside.'

For once, I let this pass without comment, there being more important things to speak of. I cleared my throat and began…

'As you all be aware, last eve, we received a visitor, Sir Philip Allenby.'

'Aye, and what's happening about his coat-of-arms?' my kinsman interrupted.' Are we doing with it or not?'

'Just hear what I have to say, for pity's sake.' I sighed afore I continued. 'Sir Philip, as you well know, was taken ill in the parlour and later carried home by his servants.'

'Is he recovered?'

'I know not, Kate. But as Rose and I attended him, we loosed his clothing about his neck and found… we found an ominous swelling there: we fear it may have been a bubo, a token of the pestilence…'

There were gasps of horror, questions were thrown at me like stones and Nessie began shrieking like a lost soul. I held up my hands for silence but Nessie continued with her monstrous racket.

'Go outside if you cannot sit quiet and harken to what I have to say.'

'We're all going to die,' she wailed.

'Be silent, I say! By all that be holy, do we not have enough troubles to contend with without your devilish din?'

'Shut your noise or I'll gag you with my napkin,' Adam shouted. 'You hear me, you stupid wench?'

Nessie buried her face in her apron, muffling the worst of her sobs as I reined in my temper and continued:

'It is by no means the case that any of us be about to die. Does anyone feel the least unwell?'

'I think I got a headache starting,' Nessie moaned.

'Hardly surprising,' Adam scoffed, throwing his soiled napkin at her.

'This morn, I visited Bess Chambers to ask advice. We now have a preventive medicine and we will each have a spoonful now. Meg, if you would take down that bottle from the shelf and a spoon… Aye, and we should take it night and morn but since we missed this morning's dose, we will have it now.'

Rose returned and aided Meg in pouring and passing round the spoon. There was much grimacing and shuddering as the green liquor was swallowed. It smelled of herbs and had a strong medicinal taste but, in truth, I had tasted worse.

'More pleasant than the ale they serve at the Green Dragon,' I jested. 'And think of the good it is doing us. And now I want you each to wear one of these rowan wood crosses to ward off evil. Do not remove them until the danger be passed.' I handed out the amulets and all put them on without demure.

'When will that be, Master Seb?' Hugh, silent until now, asked what we all were wondering as he examined the little rowan cross on its thong.

'According to Bess, if we all remain in good health for a week, then likely we be safe. But if any one of us should fall sick…'

At which Nessie recommenced her wretched wailing and Adam grabbed her, dragged her to the kitchen door and shoved her out into the yard.

Again, I let this pass as, of custom, I never would but I could withstand the din no longer.

'If anyone of us should become unwell, Bess has recommended a treatment of rosehips for us, so inform Rose or me straightway if you feel feverish or your throat be sore or any other sign. Meanwhile, scented candles will be lighted in every room, including the shop, and we all must pray right fervently. St Roche be the one who has special consideration for those afflicted by the pestilence, so address your prayers to him as well as to Our Lord, St Mary and any other you wish to call upon. Also, we must do all we may to protect our friends by keeping away from them. Sorry, Kate, I know you hoped to visit your father this Sunday coming but we must see him safe also.'

Kate nodded.

'Aye, master, I understand.'

'I believe I need say no more but ask Almighty God's

blessings and protection upon every one of us, in the Name of the Father and of the Son and of the Holy Spirit. Amen'

'Amen,' they repeated as we all made the Sign of the Cross.

'Back to work then,' I said. 'We have a living to earn.' I heard Adam's derisive snort as I went out to the yard to speak with Nessie, still snivelling.

'Do you truly have a headache? I asked her.

'Don't think so, master, but I hate that Adam. He's so horrible to me. Not like my Warin. He's kind to me.'

'Aye, well, get about the tasks Mistress Rose has set you. I think there are platters to wash and supper to be prepared—and quietly!'

I should have felt comforted, having taken so many precautions, yet my anxieties returned. Would our efforts prove sufficient? When would we know for certain? In truth, I felt like a condemned man with his head upon the block, wondering when or, indeed, if the axe would fall. 'Twas the not knowing which was so hard to bear, driving me to distraction. That afternoon, I hardly knew what I was about.

Intending to finish the title page to the Gospel of St Luke, the scene of the Nativity, I took great pains in mixing a batch of beautiful malachite pigment and sat at my desk. I uncovered the half-painted image, brush in hand, and stared in dismay. Green pigment? Why had I mixed green when the Nativity was a winter scene, and what little of that colour it required I had painted already? Malachite green… the colour of Sarra's bewitching eyes.

But the expensive pigment could not be wasted and the title page for St John's Gospel was to be bordered with summer flowers, so a deal of green was needed for that. I set aside the Nativity image and fetched a fresh sheet of finest vellum, measuring up the page and its borders in haste, afore the pigment dried hard. Of course, haste is ne'er advisable in such matters and I was studiously painting a spray of delicate fern leaves when I realised my ruled lines were all awry, laid out amiss, neither centred upon the page nor the sides running parallel.

What a mess. What a fearful waste of vellum and pigment. Cursing, I ripped it in half, screwed it up and threw it across the workshop. Gawain, startled from his dozing at my feet, whimpered.

Work ceased as they all stared at me.

Chapter 5

Thursday, the twenty-first day of June
Jude's house, Ave Maria Alley

MASTER WILLIAM Caxton's ledger book was all that Jude had hoped for: names of customers, details of what they'd ordered, how much they'd paid—or yet owed—dates and arrangements concerning delivery or collection, all noted in Caxton's neat script. Jack had done well to filch so valuable an item. Not that Jude would ever admit it. Rather he had complained about a few torn pages and water stains from the book's time in hiding by the City Ditch. But now he had it, he wasn't sure how to go about putting it to good use.

He could hardly visit each customer listed and offer his services, now that the Westminster printing press was destroyed, without explaining how he knew of their names and requirements. And if it were realised he had the ledger, it would be no work of genius to deduce who was responsible for the thievery and destruction at Caxton's house. Not that setting the place afire was Jude's idea. Nay, indeed, he was blameless on that account. It was Jack's doing, the young scoundrel, and he alone was guilty of arson and, maybe, murder too, for all Jude knew.

Thus, he must find some more subtle means of reaching out to Caxton's disappointed customers. So he sat, hunched over the galley, painstakingly compositing the reversed lead alloy letters and characters into words—backwards—to spell out his offer. The tiny letters were so fiddlesome; he needed tweezers to handle them and kept dropping the wretched things. Of course, if they fell to the floor, he had no way of retrieving them, being unable to bend at the knee, so there they remained, glinting dully, tormenting him. Yet the bills must be perfect to show would-be clients that they could expect the highest standards from Jude Foxley's printing press, as good, if not better than Caxton's at the Sign of the Red Pale. The trouble was, his rival had years of practice behind him and a half dozen skilled journeymen to aid him, whereas Jude had only himself, untaught, untried and learning by means of the mistakes he made.

But a man had to earn his livelihood somehow and King Edward's pension, paid to keep his silence and to avoid litigation, was being paid less frequently of late and in decreasing amounts. Jude could guess the reason why. No doubt but the king was tiring of his Italian mistress, Jude's own wife, Chesca—or Francesca-Antonia Baldesi-Foxley, as she liked to style herself— the strumpet, the hussy, the whore, Devil take the ungrateful, treacherous bitch. Had he not saved her from marriage to a foul old man, giving her his handsome, youthful self as a husband instead? And this was how she repaid him: by warming the royal bed, flaunting herself in silks and jewels, cuckolding him without a moment's thought as to his humiliation.

'Ungrateful bitch,' Jude muttered aloud, realising he had misspelt the word 'OFFER', putting in a long S instead of one of the Fs. 'Damn and curse it!'

'I hope you're not calling me an 'ungrateful bitch' or I'll take offence.' John Rykenor, as Eleanor, swept in, sumptuously clad in a low-cut, well-worn gown of amber brocade, bearing dented cups upon a battered tray. 'Ale, Jude?'

'Aye. I need it.' Jude stretched his back with a groan and then tried to ease his leg, wincing. 'I can't tell you, Ell, how bloody tedious and time-consuming this compositing business is. All morn I've spent, putting together four lines of type in the galley and it's still not right. It would be quicker to take up pen and bloody ink and write these by hand.'

'Then why don't you?' Eleanor sat upon a stool, spreading

her skirts in regal wise, showing off the tarnished silver braiding about the hem and flared sleeves as if it were bejewelled with pearls.

'Because that's the whole damned point, isn't it? These bills are to advertise my services as a printer, not as a bloody scribe. My brother can do that. And I need dozens of them, hundreds even, to spread about London and Westminster so Caxton's customers see that there is now another who can print books and pamphlets for them. Did you know he's printed stuff for the queen's brother and even the King's High-Bollocksness has placed an order? Now if I could get them on my order book...'

'You don't have an order book, Jude.'

'Stop splitting bloody hairs... and why are you wearing that gown again? I told you, it makes you look like a tuppenny trollop.'

'Why, thank you, kind sir.' Eleanor smiled, taking the insult as a compliment, as usual.

'You're a bloody fool, John. I don't know why you do it... this pretence...' Jude was shaking his head.

'Why not? It hurts no man and I'm more comfortable in ladies' attire. And I'm pretty, aren't I? And you like me this way, don't you, Jude?'

'Not especially. You'd be as much use in doublet and hose. Pick up those fallen pieces for me, then go play dress-up-the-duchess somewhere else; I'm busy.'

Eleanor swept together the type strewn across the floor, using the toes of her velvet slippers, then scooped them up and put them on Jude's desk in a dull metal heap. They were thoroughly muddled—upper case, lower case and punctuation characters all mixed up together—he would have to re-sort them before they could be of any use. This printing business was making his head ache, turning him cross-eyed and proving far more difficult than he'd ever thought it would be at the start. He glared at the press, the stubborn monster skulking there like a demon sent from Hell.

'Damn the bloody, infernal contraption,' he muttered,

deciding there had to be better ways of spending his sorry life than squinting at type all day and wrestling with mighty beams of oak. It was too much like hard work for Jude's liking but all that effort—not to mention the initial expense—could not be allowed to go to waste. As he sat brooding, bemoaning his lot, there came a moment of inspiration, bright as a candle flame in the darkness. He just might have a solution. He threw the galley aside, knocking over the wooden box with its multitude of sorted type, each in its own compartment, uncaring as the letters flew everywhere and yelled for Eleanor to find what he needed.

The first step was to resort to pen, ink and paper. A letter must be written.

The Foxley Place, Paternoster Row

In the workshop, we were all of us finding it difficult to keep our minds upon our tasks, although I determined to finish the two title pages for the Gospels of Saints Luke and John, having wasted that malachite pigment and a sheet of vellum yesterday, I needs must make amends.

'I have to go out,' Adam said, laying aside his pen.

'But you cannot. We discussed this, did we not? We all agreed that it was for the safety of other folk that we should remain at home as much as possible, so as not to spread infection. You consented to that last eve,' I reminded him.

'Can't be avoided, Seb. I have legal business concerning the guardianship of my lads. I told you I'd arranged to meet this lawyer fellow last week, before this happened.'

'Could you not delay it?'

'It's taken a year to get this far. You know how slow court cases are. I'm not putting it off again just because a customer fell sick. This is too important. The lads' futures are at stake here.'

'All our futures are at stake, Adam: every citizen's of London. You could carry the contagion to this lawyer and his household and thus spread it across the city.'

'You can't keep us imprisoned, cousin. We're none of us ill, in fact, and life must go on. Tell Rose I may be late for dinner. You never know how long these legal matters can drag on—all those "aforementioneds", "hereinafters" and "wheretofores".'

'Very well. I understand. But, I pray you, keep a safe distance betwixt you and whomsoever you may.'

'Oh, aye, and I forget about the "whomsoevers". There'll no doubt be many of them to wrestle with, too.'

'This be no matter for jesting, Adam.'

'I know.' With which, he departed and I said a silent prayer that the pestilence did not accompany him, riding invisible upon his person.

In the kitchen, when I went to fetch ale, Rose was sighing over a ruined dish of green peas fresh from our garden plot.

'I've added salt, not once, not twice but thrice! What a waste of good food. I just can't think what I'm about this morning.'

'I did likewise yesterday,' I admitted, 'Preparing a batch of fine pigment for which I had no use, then misruling a sheet of vellum. 'Tis no surprise we all be muddle-headed.'

'I'm not muddle-headed,' Nessie declared, she who be the worst offender even without any cause.

'The peas can be saved,' Meg said. 'My mother taught me this trick: just add milk and a little flour to save the dish. It'll be more of a sauce but it will temper the saltiness for certain. Here, let me do it for you, Rose.'

'Thank you, Meg.' Rose stepped away from the hearth and sat on the nearest stool. She looked weary, her cheek flushed. Of custom, the neatest of wives, her apron hung besmirched, and strands of corn-coloured hair escaped her cap.

Of a sudden, I felt afeared:

'Rose, are you quite well, dearest? Not fevered, I trust?'

'Just tired. I slept little last night, as did you, I know.'

'Aye, we shall all sleep more easily when this week be done.'

Then Julia began to cry and demanded attention. Rose took

her upon her lap, hushing and coddling her.

'That new tooth,' Rose said. 'Poor mite, it troubles her so.' She brushed the lass's soft, mousy curls away from her damp forehead.

Jesu Christ have mercy on us all, I prayed 'neath my breath. Let not my beloved wife and child be afflicted.

As if that was not sufficient to disturb me, the sounds of dissent came from the yard: squealing and shouting, then Gawain barking. Seeing the womenfolk occupied, I went out to discover what be amiss.

Nicholas was seated, fully clad, shoes and all, in the water trough beside the pump, splashing Dickon, Mundy and the dog, causing a merry chaos. The Lord be thanked that the little ones yet found reason to laugh.

'Did you fall in, Nick?' I asked, knowing the scamp to be capable of any mishap.

'No. I'm all hot, so I got in the water. Papa said we could.'

This last, I knew for a blatant lie: Adam had said no such thing but the nigh-five-year-old be as artful as any felon Thaddeus ever apprehended. I lifted him out, protesting vehemently, and received a wet-shoed kick in the belly for my trouble.

'Take off your shoes, Nick. We will leave them in the shade to dry off slowly, then find you some dry clouts.'

'No!' he roared and raced down the garden plot between the sage and lavender, leaving a dripping trail and snagging his sleeve on a rose bush. I heard the cloth rip asunder but he ran on, into what had once been our neighbours' garden but which now made our plot twice as large as it used to be.

'Nicholas. Come here and you shall have strawberry.' Bribery seemed the only recourse, though I be aware of the error in rewarding a child's misbehaviour. I would not threaten bodily punishment as Adam did.

'Don't want one,' he shouted back, squeezing into the tiny gap betwixt the fence and the henhouse, aware that it be too narrow for an adult to follow.

'Gawain wants a strawberry,' a small voice spoke behind me. Such was Dickon's way of making his wish known. 'And Mundy wants one, don't we, Mundy?' The little trio had followed me during the chase.

'Later, Dickon, once I have retrieved Nick.'

'Look, Papa,' Dickon pointed. 'There's, Nick.' And indeed, the scamp had come out from behind the henhouse and was running for our neighbours' side gate. I knew the gate to be in need of repair and the latch loose.

I ran, dodging raspberry and gooseberry bushes, sparrow-grass and fennel, attempting to reach the gate afore young Nick but he be nimble indeed and was on tip-toe, pulling on the latch. I saw it fall away, clattering to the ground, and the child was out into the street ere I caught up with him.

'Stay here,' I cried out to Dickon, 'All of you, stay here.' I followed Nick into Paternoster Row, expecting to see the lad standing perplexed by the bustle of folk. But there was no sign, neither to right nor left, no matter how I stretched my neck to see or crouched to look through the forest of legs. St Paul's gate into the Precinct lay across the way and I elbowed through the crowd. 'Have you seen a little lad, so high, tousled hair, soaking wet…' I asked the gatekeeper who yawned hugely and I realised the fellow had been dozing in the warm airs. 'No matter,' I said, peering through the gateway but Nick was not in sight.

Glancing back, I saw Dickon, Mundy and Gawain now stood at the far side gate from the garden, watching me. What to do? I could not risk them wandering the streets also but I had to find that errant scamp, else Adam would ne'er forgive me if aught befell him.

Returning to the gate that could no longer be secured, I ushered Dickon and Mundy into the street, then to our shop door, calling out for Kate to see them safe within, knowing Rose and Meg to be busy in the kitchen.

'Young Nick has gone a-wandering,' I explained to Kate who

was tidying cheap scholars' primers upon the shelf. 'I must find him in haste. Gawain, come, seek out Nick… good lad.'

We hunted along Paternoster Row and into Cheapside but the lad could have turned down by Bellhouse, making for his home in Distaff Lane by Friday Street, or gone back upon himself, along Bladder Street, or taken any number of other lanes and alleyways. London was a labyrinth and our frantic search was proving fruitless.

Fruit!

I had offered him a strawberry if he would behave but he refused, as was ever the youngster's way. But I knew Nick loved strawberries, raspberries and cherries—their bright colour attracting him as much as the taste. Thus, I led Gawain along Cheapside, paying especial heed to fruiterers with their woven willow baskets of gemlike sweetness up from Kent. But I discovered naught of the wayward child. I accosted every huckster, pedlar and stall-holder but none had seen him. Mayhap, I was mistaken in believing ripe fruits might tempt him and he had gone another way.

By Cheap Cross, an elderly man wearing a battered straw hat was crying his wares: 'Ripe strawberries! Kentish strawberries; farthing a punnet.'

I stopped, intending to describe Nick to the old fellow but Gawain had other ideas, barking at the cloth spread atop the baskets to protect the fruit from the sun's heat, pillaging birds, aye, and human thievery.

'What's amiss, master?' He removed his hat and wiped sweat from his face with his sleeve, 'Hey! Get your dog away: he's scaring off customers.'

'A moment be all I ask of you,' I said, stepping behind him to where a rounded shape propped up the cloth which I flung back to reveal Nick sitting cross-legged, gorging on strawberries. His mouth, cheeks and chin were smeared red as he stuffed his ill-gotten gains. I grabbed him by the scruff and hauled him up. 'The trouble you have caused me…'

'I haven't done anything,' he dared to protest when the evidence was painted crimson across his face and fingers.

'You are a thief and a mischief-maker, Nicholas Hutchinson.'

'What about my fruit he filched?' the old man demanded. 'You owe me for that. And look here: all squashed...' We surveyed the damage, forwhy the child had crushed and ruined far more than he could have eaten.

'How much?' I asked, unlatching my purse one-handed whilst keeping a firm grip on Nick's jerkin with the other.

'A shilling.'

'What? Sixpence.'

'Ten pence, then. He's spoiled all this.' The fellow made an expansive gesture which included half Cheapside.

'Nonsense. Eight pence.'

'Nine and I won't summon the beadle.'

'Done!' Without delay, despite my reluctance, I counted out the coin.

'And you can have those,' the fruiterer said, gesturing to a couple of punnets squelching juice. 'I can't sell them like that.'

'My thanks and I apologise for the trouble this one caused you... caused me also.'

'Your son needs a sound beating,' he called after me.

'The Lord be thanked, he is not my child,' I replied. 'Come, you little nuisance, afore I lose all patience with you.' I dragged him back to Paternoster Row with Gawain holding the lad's torn sleeve betwixt his teeth to ensure no further opportunity for escape.

'My belly hurts,' Nick was wailing by the time we reached home but I was right short on sympathy for him, thinking such suffering may serve well to teach him a lesson.

So much for my intention that, as responsible citizens, we should keep within doors so as not to risk spreading contagion abroad.

And the day's troubles continued for Nick was soon puking and violently emptying his bowels. Rose had him sit upon a chamber pot in a shaded corner of the yard where he whined and grizzled in his misery. She wore a worried frown quite alien to her countenance as she knelt beside the child, giving what comfort she might.

'I pray he's only suffering from a surfeit of fruit,' she said softly, 'And naught worse.'

I startled. Even in our present circumstance, the possibility had not occurred to me until she spoke.

'Nay. Strawberries may do that to a body when eaten to excess and so swiftly consumed.' I did my best to sound reassuring. 'The lad will be well by the morrow for certain.'

Rose nodded but I had failed to convince either of us. I watched as she straightened the neck of his little shirt. I knew she was looking for the dread tokens.

'I have work to do.' The return to my desk was made with due haste, eager to be away from the woeful child, but my anxiety concerning a possible alternative cause of his sickness set my heart thudding.

'How's little Nick?' Kate asked.

'Wretched but it shall pass in an hour or two.' I forced a smile. 'All will be well. The young recover quickly from such petty ailments. I hope he has learned his lesson but, knowing Nick, he will have forgotten it by the morn. Ralf,' I turned to my old journeyman, diligent as ever. 'How much of that poetry book be left to do?' When last I was in the workshop, Ralf was putting the gilding along the edges of an epic poem by Master Thomas Hoccleve, once a Clerk of the Privy Seal. The *Regiment of Princes* was a popular work and always sold readily.

''Tis done, Master Seb, stitched and ready for its binding. I'm now collating St Matthew's Gospel for the Prioress of Dartford...'

I sat at my desk and uncovered my title pages, laying aside the protective cloth: the Nativity scene for St Luke's Gospel nigh completed but that for St John's, with its garland of wild flowers, hardly begun. I required to prepare azurite pigment for the sky in both cases and sorted through my little casket of colours but, oddly, could discover no azurite. I was certain there had been a plentiful supply yesterday.

'By the by,' Ralf continued, 'Do you know when Adam will be back? I need to ask him about the arrangements we were making to meet up with friends.'

'I fear all such gatherings must be delayed, Ralf, at least until next week. We discussed this matter previously and 'twas agreed by us all. Has anyone been using the azurite?'

Kate and Hugh shook their heads.

'Aye, I know what we agreed—and, nay, I've not seen the azurite either—but… well, Adam's out and about e'en as we speak and young Meg went a-marketing and you've been wherever…'

'I be aware of that and, in each case, 'twas of necessity, not by choice.' I left my stool to search in the storeroom. 'The decision yet stands, Ralf, as best it may. Your consorting with friends will have to wait. Oh, where is that pigment when I need it?'

'Pity. 'Tis my Joanie's celebration, see? We planned to take her to see the menagerie at the Tower. You can hear them lions a-roaring from her house but she's ne'er seen the beasts, so Adam said, as we Norfolk men had ne'er seen them either, he'd arrange it with some of Joanie's gossips and we'd all go in company this Saturday after dinner. Have you e'er seen them, master? The lions, I mean.'

'Aye, and a sorry spectacle they were: moth-eaten and mangy and their keeper will charge you as much as he dare for the dubious privilege of gawping at them.' I began lifting reams of paper off the high shelf to look behind them. All I could imagine was that young Nick had been up to mischief again and hidden the pot of coloured pigment powder. In which case, why was I searching in a place he could not reach? 'Likely, Ralf, you will be gravely disappointed in the spectacle by all accounts. Spare yourself the effort; 'tis not worth the trouble nor cost.'

'But to see a great lion in the flesh, master… the King

of Beasts...'

'The King of Beasts, so-called, had but one eye and few teeth remaining, insofar as I recall, pacing to and fro, to and fro in his prison cage for all his remaining days. 'Twas hardly a marvel of God's Creation any longer, poor creature. I felt too sorrowful and uninspired to put charcoal to paper, though that was the purpose of my visit.'

Ralf nodded.

'It shall be as you wish, then, master.'

'Nay, 'tis not at all as I wish, Ralf. I would that we could all go about our daily round as usual but, of necessity, we cannot. You do understand that we must bear our responsibilities in this matter? We have not the right to risk spreading contagion amongst our fellow citizens.'

'Aye, I suppose, but Joanie will be right upset.'

'Oh, I admit defeat. I know not where the azurite may be. If Nick has hidden it, it could be anywhere. I shall use woad instead, though the colour may fade in time.'

'But, Master Seb, you always tell us we must only use the best for godly texts,' Kate said, looking shocked.

'I know...' I flexed my right arm. Mayhap, I had lifted down those reams of paper somewhat awkwardly and strained the muscle. In truth, I had not yet put them back on the shelf despite my insistence that the store be kept tidy at all times with everything in its rightful place. 'Perhaps the azurite will reappear...'

'Master, 'tis here.' Hugh had left his work to aid me in my quest. ''Twas here on your desk all the while, under the cloth beside your work.'

And thus it was: I had laid the cloth atop the pigment pot and failed to see it.

'My thanks, Hugh,' I said with a sigh as I resumed my seat. 'I know not what be amiss with my wits. Too little sleep, no doubt.'

'Aye, we're all suffering so, what with the worry,' Ralf said. 'Shall I fetch us some ale, master?'

Jude's house, Ave Maria Alley

Jude chewed the end of the quill, thinking how to word the letter to William Caxton if, indeed, the man was yet alive and not reduced to a pile of cinders in the blackened timbers of his home in Westminster.

'Ell! I need you to do something for me…'

'Don't you always?' She looked up from brushing the dried mud from Jude's hose after his recent fall and tossed her loose, curling locks. 'And when, pray, was the last time you ever did anything for me, eh?'

'Never mind that. This is important. Go out and talk to folk…'

'Who?'

'I don't bloody care. Anyone, everyone. I need to know if Caxton survived the fire at his place.'

'Why?'

'Because it's bloody pointless penning a letter to a corpse. That's why. Now stop asking foolish questions and do as I tell you… and don't spend two hours gossiping with your damned friends. I need to know now, not in a week's time. You hear me?'

'You're a heartless brute, Jude Foxley. I should leave you to fend for yourself as best you may whilst I find myself a true and gentle paramour. I don't know why I abide such mistreatment from you, ordering me about as if I were a lowly kitchen drab.'

Jude replied without looking up from the blank page before him, still frowning over the wording of the greeting: To whomsoever receives this missive… or To whom this may concern… or To the rightful executors of William Caxton…

'Because nobody but me would let you swan about like a trollop, wearing women's garments, doing as you please, spending money you never earned. That's why. Now go find out the tidings so I can write this bloody letter… and if Caxton survived, I have to know where he's living…'

With Eleanor gone about her quest, Jude leaned back on his

bench against the wall and his gaze fell upon the stolen ledger lying on the press. So important before, he'd almost forgotten about it. Now he foresaw another difficulty: explaining how that precious record of all Caxton's business dealings came to be in his possession. Rack his brains as he might, he couldn't contrive any legitimate means except to say that he'd found it and who would believe such a foolish tale and not know it for a lie? Better to say naught of it. Should he hide it away? Or, mayhap, it would be safer to destroy it? But what a waste of secret knowledge that would be. If he kept it safe, he could refer to it privily when needful and Caxton would be none the wiser. It might be to his advantage to know who owed money to the printer and collect such debts for himself.

Aye, that would bring in much-needed extra coin since the king's gratuities hadn't yet been paid this month and were becoming less reliable and more meagre—only five marks in May instead of the originally agreed fifteen. And, of course, the initial generous sum, buying Chesca's 'services' for as long as Edward desired, had long been spent on buying this great house and the accursed printing press, both of which he now regretted. For a man so lame, three floors and a cellar were fine to impress folk—especially his brother, as he'd intended—but otherwise of little use since the top floor and the cellar both required climbing ladders. Getting to the bedchamber above by means of a proper stair was burden enough for him and the damnable press took up most of the ground floor, where they used it as a buffet, a board and a coffer.

There it stood, gathering dust, draped in Eleanor's discarded gowns and mantle, adorned with spilt wine circles and dirty cups, hung about with the sharp odour of printer's ink from his one and only attempt at producing a page of type. It hadn't gone well but left him exhausted from the effort. What a waste of both room and money! Mayhap, he could persuade Caxton to buy the wretched contraption to replace that which Jack destroyed and be well rid of it.

Chapter 6

Friday, the twenty-second day of June
The Foxley Place, Paternoster Row

L AST NIGHT, deeply exhausted, I had slept a deal better than expected and awoke to a mist-shrouded morning, later than intended. The bed was empty beside me and I wondered, firstly, at the cause for Rose not being there and, secondly, what hour it might be. On both accounts, my heart beat frantically against my ribs even as I kicked aside the sheet and left the bed in haste.

'Rose! Rose! Be all well?' I called out as I pulled on my shirt and hose. 'Rose! Answer me, lass, for pity's sake.'

Footsteps came running up the stairs.

'What's amiss, Seb?' Rose asked as she arrived, breathless, at the chamber threshold. 'You're not taken sick, are you? Please, God, say you're not.'

'Nay, I be as well as ever but what of you, sweeting? Why have you risen at so early an hour? Has someone else fallen sick? Is it Julia? She was fretful last eve.'

'No, we are yet all well. Julia's new tooth is proving troublesome. But it's nigh the time for the Angelus bell. I let you sleep late since you plainly needed more rest, so deeply were you slumbering.'

I fastened my second shoe.

'By Heaven, Rose, you should not have let me sleep so long but 'tis blessed tidings indeed that all remain in fair health.' I finger-combed my hair as best I might and splashed water on my face at the laver bowl. Such half-hearted ablutions would have to serve for the present.

After hastening from hearing Low Mass in St Michael le Querne Church, wishing to avoid conversation with our neighbours and a rushed breakfast of pickled herrings, bread and ale—with young Nick's complaints about hating herrings and the yelp of Adam's cuffing him yet sounding in my ears—I hastened to work, having a dozen matters to attend to all at once.

But despite my best intentions, Dame Fortune, that fickle jade, would turn my day contrarywise.

Breakfast was done and I was unbarring the shop door with the front shutters lowered to serve as counter-boards and Kate was setting out our wares upon them for display when a liveried messenger arrived in haste.

'Is this Master Sebastian Foxley's place?' he demanded, pushing past me even as I stowed the door bar 'neath the counter.

'Who wants to know?' I could be as abrupt and discourteous as he, notwithstanding that I knew the answer in any case, forwhy I recognised the livery and cognisance he wore.

'William, Lord Hastings, the King's Chamberlain, has right urgent business with Sebastian Foxley.'

'Has he, indeed? And what business might that be, Master Messenger?'

'None of yours, unless you are this Foxley.'

I folded my arms and leant against the door jamb.

'Is it your custom to be so impolite? Or is it simply my misfortune that you come here upon an ill-starred day when your humours be all out of sorts?'

'I don't have time for this...'

'And neither do I. Good day to you.' I pushed upright and turned from him, making towards the workshop next door.

'But I come at Lord Hastings' bidding.' He lunged and grabbed my sleeve and I shook him off.

'In which case, Lord Hastings should see to it that his messengers are instructed in a few lessons in courtesy.'

The fellow stepped back, admonished, and bowed his head momentarily.

'I beg pardon,' he muttered then spoke up, 'Are you Master Foxley?'

'I am he.' I sighed, aware that my life was about to be disrupted by those who dwelt at Westminster—and not for the first time.

'Lord Hastings sends you this message.' He took a tight little roll of parchment, tied with a red ribbon, from the leather bag slung from his shoulder and gave it into my hand.

I saw 'twas of high-quality vellum and mourned the waste of it on so brief a missive. Mayhap, Lord Hastings thought to impress me.

'You are summoned to attend at Westminster by the Lord Chamberlain at ten of the clock this morning,' the messenger said as I read the exact same words. Hastings should have saved the vellum.

'For what purpose?'

'I'm not at liberty to say.'

'You mean, in truth, that you do not know. Lord Hastings did not divulge the reason to you.'

He nodded, shifting from foot to foot, frowning at the oak floorboards under his expensive Cordovan shoes.

'Forwhy,' I continued, enjoying and wishing to add to his discomfiture, 'He does not trust you sufficiently. And I heartily concur: I would not put my faith in one so ill-mannered either.'

'I need to know, Master Foxley, will you attend upon my lord at the hour specified?'

'Do you require an answer in writing?'

'Nay. I dare say your word will suffice.'

'Then you may inform Lord Hastings that I shall wait upon him at a half hour after eleven of the clock.'

'But the royal household will yet be at dinner...'

'And I dine at ten, so this will be at *my* convenience. I bid you good day, Master Messenger.'

As the fellow departed, I saw that Kate, who was there throughout this exchange, stood open-mouthed with raised eyebrows.

'I abhor discourtesy,' I said by way of explanation. 'Ah, our first customer approaches. Remember, Kate, do not stand too close nor breathe upon them.'

'Aye, Master Seb. I'll remember my manners also.'

'Good lass.'

In truth, as I went to my desk to commence working on the St John's title page, I, too, felt discomfited. I had been peremptory with the messenger as Lord Hastings' representative, which was ill-advised, but to then inform the chamberlain that I should come when the hour pleased *me* was utter madness. Whatever the reason for my summons—and doubtless it would not be for my pleasure and wellbeing—it did not do to put to inconvenience a man of status and authority afore we even met. I knew Lord Hastings from previous encounters and he was not one to take the least insult lightly. 'Twas not an auspicious beginning to the day.

And then Adam was outraged when I made it known I would be departing for Westminster after dinner, abandoning my rightful tasks yet again. When I said I was summoned by the Lord Chamberlain, he was somewhat mollified but, scowling, told me to make certain I breathed contagion on those "interfering no-goods who ever disrupt the lives of hard working, conscientious citizens". I know these last words were intended as a reminder for me that he would be labouring away whilst I took my ease, strolling along the Strand towards the king's palace. I would most eagerly have exchanged places with my cousin. Westminster ever meant one thing for me: trouble!

Westminster

Armed with my scrip against most eventualities, but having left faithful Gawain at home—much to his chagrin—I confess to having quite enjoyed my walk from Ludgate, along Fleet Street and the Strand, past the Charing Cross into Kings Street. I lingered a moment to watch the last of the early mist rising like a curtain to reveal the throng of river traffic to my left hand. An elegant pair of swans with downy cygnets sailed by upon deceptively sparkling waters and I made a hasty charcoal sketch, leaving the white of the paper below showing through to indicate the white birds—a kind of non-drawing, as you might say.

When I reached the Great Gate of Westminster Palace, I recognised the guard, Walter, from my time spent here as a scribe in the scriptorium two winters since, and he recalled me. We exchanged pleasantries—if addressing me as "you're the brother of that idle oaf, Jude Foxley, ain't you?"—may be termed a pleasantry. Clearly, my brother must have made a deeper impression upon the gatekeeper than I did.

I showed him the seal on Lord Hastings' letter and he directed me towards the gate into the Inner Courtyard, saying that I must know the way anyhow. The pointer upon the dial of the mighty Clock Tower was poised midway betwixt XI and XII.

I trod the once-familiar flagstone corridor and risked a glance through the open door of the scriptorium. The place was deserted; the clerks gone to dinner. Perhaps, 'twas as well forwhy, if I encountered any remembered face from my time here, I could afford no delay for merry conversation. It would not look well to arrive tardily at a time which was of my own choosing. My belly was drawing tighter with apprehension as I showed the letter to a servant at the entrance to the Great Hall, wondering, belatedly, the reason for my summons.

From within the hall, came laughter and loud voices, the clatter of knives and spoons on platters and dishes. Dinner at

Westminster was ever a noisy affair. My nose was assault
the mingled scents of roasted meats, exotic spices, unw:
courtiers, piss and excrement. As I knew right well, the lat ‗‗
in the Outer Court were reckoned too far for convenience by
most of the royal household, so alcoves, corners and fireplaces
more often served the need. Untrained dogs roamed the place
at will, relieving themselves upon door jambs and furniture in
lieu of trees and bushes. Naught had changed on that score.

Almost as though he would amend the ill-manners of Lord
Hastings' messenger earlier, the liveried servant who escorted
me to an inner chamber was obsequious to extreme, bowing
unnecessarily low each time he opened a door for me to pass
through, then scurrying ahead to open the next, begging my
pardon for the distance I must walk to reach it. The palace's
labyrinthine passages and corridors were confusing and lengthy
but hardly required such a profusion of apologies.

He showed me into a small chamber, begged me to take my
comfort as I wished and asked if I desired wine. With my belly
churning, I accepted the offer, hoping the wine would settle it.
As he scuttled off to fetch my drink, I surveyed the room in the
light of the solitary window of fly-spotted glass.

Like so much of Westminster, the furnishings, tapestries
and cushions and the giltware on display were all costly but
dust-laden and worn. A huge cobweb stretched betwixt a gilded
candelabra on the buffet and the padded arm of a brocade
settle. Gatherings of fluff, disturbed by my movements, hurried
away, out of sight, like mice seeking safety. My Rose would be
disgusted at such slovenly housekeeping. The tapestries showed
both the exquisite craft of the finest Flemish weavers and
decades of industry by generations of moths. Gold silk fringing
hung loose from a fancily carved day-bed and the faded velvet
cushions on the settle were worn thin and shabby. Though I
seated myself with due care, tucking my scrip beside me, a cloud
of dust arose, making me sneeze and revealing the cushion cloth
to be of a sage green hue, not grey. The room smelled mustily

of ancient beeswax with a hint of river damp.

The servant returned with the wine, heaping apologies for his tardiness and assuring me that he was utterly dedicated to my service if I required anything more. My drink was poured and the pewter cup proffered with a bent knee, as if I were an earl, born and bred. I was upon the verge of enquiring when Lord Hastings was likely to appear just as the door opened and two men entered. Neither was the King's Chamberlain.

The elder of the pair was portly and somewhat stooped, like a time-worn scribe, mayhap of three score years or more. His hair was sparse, close-cropped and grey, at odds with his unfashionable luxuriant beard which spread across his chest. His gown was of good cloth but a poor fit, straining 'neath his arms yet trailing on the floor behind him, sweeping up the dirt as he walked. Borrowed from someone taller but leaner, I thought. He frowned with worry or, mayhap, was short-sighted.

His skinny companion was far younger, closer to my age yet hairless, a black cap balanced upon his bald pate, kept in place by will power alone, so it seemed. His clothes hung on him as from a fripperer's hook and I noted that his front teeth overrode his nether lip.

I turned to the servant hovering uncertainly:

'Would you kindly fetch another two cups, if you will,' I said and more bowing and bobbing preceded his departure.

'Forgive the lack of any courteous introduction,' the elder man said, his voice deep, stepping forward, hand outstretched in greeting. 'Lord Hastings sends his compliments but has business elsewhere.'

Ah, so my insult was returned in kind. It served me right, I suppose.

'I am William Caxton, printer of Westminster. You may have heard of me as I have heard of you, if I have the honour of meeting Master Sebastian Foxley, stationer of Paternoster Row?'

'You do, Master Caxton, but the honour be all mine.' I shook his hand. His grip was firm and sure.

'And this is my indispensable assistant, Wynkyn de Worde,' he continued, pushing the younger man to the fore.

I wondered at a name so well suited to the craft of printing but, when he greeted me, I heard the alien way with my name, 'Voxley' and knew him for a foreigner. If he were of Flanders, as many in the book trade be, then 'de Worde' was likely a chosen name to spare our English tongues some unspeakable Flanderish contortions.

'Good day to you, Master de Worde.'

Caxton slowly eased down upon the day-bed whilst his assistant perched on an upholstered stool. Neither appeared the least intimidated by the surroundings but then, since the printer had royal patrons, I suppose a palace was naught strange to them. We discussed the recent hot weather, the cost of imported paper and the customs thus due. Had I had difficulty of late in purchasing supplies? And why did we English not make our own?

With the servant having returned with more cups and a dish of comfits, wine poured and introductions completed, we turned to the matter at hand—whatever it might be.

'Master Caxton,' I began. 'I was summoned here by Lord Hastings but to what purpose, I cannot imagine. Perhaps you will enlighten me if you know the reason.'

Caxton sipped his wine, puckered his lips and selected a sweetmeat for scrutiny.

'Indeed, Master Foxley, you are here upon King Edward's personal recommendation.' He popped the sweetmeat in his mouth and chewed, taking his time.

'The king recommended me? To what end? I do not see how I may be of any assistance to a printer unless you wish advice on page layout or stitching or cover design.'

'Naught of that kind is necessary, I assure you, but the king says you are most skilful in the art of unravelling mysteries. Apparently, you are famed for uncovering a nest of espiers here at Westminster not so long since and I would have you solve a most vicious mystery—a terrible felony, in truth—on my behalf. Will you oblige me in this, Master Foxley, for a proper consideration, of course?'

'I, er, well, indeed, Master Caxton, I was involved in oversetting some nefarious intentions at one time but, if I should agree to look into your mystery, I cannot make any promises as to solving it. I need to make that quite clear. Do you understand?'

'Of course. It goes without saying that your fee will be paid, no matter the outcome.'

'Nay, that was not quite what I meant. Rather that there may not be any outcome, as you term it. Some mysteries cannot be resolved by human effort.'

'Oh, come now, Master Foxley, I'm not asking you to explain the intricacies of God's Creation, simply to uncover the name of a wicked felon and, hopefully, retrieve certain of my irreplaceable possessions. In short, I want you to solve a crime which, as I've heard, you have done many times before.' He made it sound so easy, quick as shucking peas from the pod.

'Aye.' I nodded and sighed. The last thing I needed was some lengthy series of enquiries to distract me from my own business. On the other hand, something to keep my mind from brooding upon the possibility of the pestilence ravaging my family any day soon was to be welcomed. 'In which case,' I said. 'Afore I agree, perhaps I should hear of the nature of this crime.' I picked up my cup and drank some wine to brace my spirit for what was to come. It was blood red and tasted of vinegar. I set it aside. Mayhap, the purpose of the sweetmeats was to make the wine palatable.

'Wynkyn will tell you what came to pass, for I was upon business elsewhere at the time.'

Wynkyn took a mouthful of wine, winced, coughed, cleared his throat and began his woeful tale. In truth, it made for sorrowful hearing for one who could attest to the terrors of a house afire.

'Ja, Meneer Caxton. We were all of us sleeping, Meneer Voxley, the apprentices, Thomas, Jonas and Nathaniel, in the attic, myself and our journeyman, Hal Mathers, in a chamber on the upper floor. As fortune would have it, Meneer Caxton was in Kent, visiting Earl Rivers—the queen's brother and one of our most illustrious patrons—at his lordship's home of The Mote, near the town of Midstone, if you know of it?'

'The town is Maidstone, Wynkyn, not that it has any relevance whatever. Just get on with the story. You ramble worse than Homer in his *Odyssey* and what a deal of ink and paper went into that epic.'

'Ja. Neem me niet kwalijk.'

'Never mind your apologies. Master Foxley hasn't got all day to waste. He has a crime to solve for us. Now tell him… in God's own English, for Jesu's sake.' Caxton took another sweetmeat. 'Go on…'

'Ja, menneer. Mevrouw Maud and her serving maid were with her cousin, so we were all men at the house by the Almonry, Maandag…'

'He means Monday,' Caxton translated, becoming annoyed at his assistant's constant relapsing into his native tongue. 'When he becomes over-excited, he forgets no one else but me speaks his intolerable barbarian language. Is that not so, Wynkyn?'

'Ja. It was late in the night, Meneer Voxley, dark as ink, when a sound came to my ears: klink! Then, a soft thud. I thought a mouse in the eaves or a cat on the roof and turned back to my sleeping. But after a small while, I smelled the smoke and was set to coughing. I roused the others and we climbed from the upper window and jumped, all in safety.'

''Twas fortunate that you awoke or the consequences might have been grave indeed,' I said.

'Might have been?' Caxton repeated. 'Might have been? Why, the consequences were disastrous! I lost everything: my house, my livelihood, my possessions, my money… See?' He plucked at his ill-fitting gown. 'I have had to borrow this to appear half-decent at court, my clothes being naught but ashes except for the few belongings I had with me in Kent.'

'You have my most sincere commiserations, good master, but lives could also have been lost. For certain, they be of greater importance than gowns.'

'But what of my printing press, my stock of books and paper and all the paraphernalia of my craft? And my accounting ledger, order book and money...' Caxton looked and sounded close to tears.

'Could your coin not be saved once the fire was quenched? Or was it possible the flames proved so hot as to melt the silver? I cannot believe that.'

'And that is part of this accursed mystery, Master Foxley. It wasn't just the fire. I was robbed. Robbed, I tell you. The iron-studded coffer in which I kept my money and records of all business transactions was badly scorched but not burned away, yet it was nigh empty, a few loose coins being all that remained. The lock had been broken off. The fire had naught to do with that.'

'Perhaps a kindly neighbour risked his life to save your valuables,' I suggested.

'In which case, who has them? That is what I would pay you to find out. Someone set that fire for a purpose, either to ruin me or as a cover for their thievery or maybe both and I want them brought to account for their crimes.'

'A fire may start by mischance...' I suggested.

'Not this one, I know. Wynkyn, tell Master Foxley what you found among the charred timbers of my press yesterday.'

'Ja. I found cheese all melted.'

'Cheese? Are you certain?' Unaccountably, my thoughts leapt to Gawain, whose love of the stuff was legendary. 'There was melted cheese upon the printing press?'

'On or under it... the timbers were collapsed, Menneer Voxley, so I could not be certain where it was before the press burned.'

'I think someone hid under the press, waiting until Wynkyn and the others retired to bed before he began his evil work,' Caxton said. 'And he'd come prepared, bringing his cheese supper with him to eat whilst in hiding.'

'Well… 'tis a possibility to be considered, I suppose. In the meanwhile, Master Caxton, do you have any enemies who might desire to do you such harm: debtors, rivals in business, jealous kinsmen?'

'Of course not. How can I have business rivals when I'm the only printer in England? Mind you, I suppose those of your own craft—scribes—could be envious of my latest commission from King Edward himself, the first few folios of which are now but ashes, including the title page woodcut which will have to be carved anew. But what am I saying? Without a printing press, my whole livelihood is turned to ashes, all commissions void. And without my ledger, I don't have a full list of those to whom I must apologise for their disappointment, except for those names in my head. Ah, Her Grace, Queen Elizabeth… her copy of the *Fables of Aesop* was completed and awaiting delivery into her own hands. Now it's lost with all else, more is the pity.' Caxton sniffed and dabbed his eyes with the sleeve of his borrowed gown.

My sympathies for him were great, knowing what a loss it would be to me if my workshop was destroyed.

'If you do think of anyone so spiteful as to ill-wish you thus…' I said, reaching out to touch his liver-spotted hand, 'Tell me.' I almost added 'cheese-lover' to the description but that seemed fatuous with a matter of such gravity. 'As for the present, if you could take me to your house, that I may observe the scene of the crime for myself, that would be helpful and a reasonable place to begin my searching.'

'You accept the task, then, Master Foxley?'

'Aye, I suppose I do.'

'What a relief that is to me. But first, we must discuss terms: your fee and all. Wynkyn, have the servant fetch writing materials. All must be set down in proper fashion.'

'Can that not wait until I have viewed the scene? Then we may retire to a tavern to talk about such matters.' I raised my eyebrows questioningly, glancing at our wine cups, still nigh full. 'Besides, I have pen, ink and paper in my scrip here,' I said, retrieving it from beside me, brushing off the dust which had settled upon the leather even in so short a time.

Master Caxton, sharp of wit, construed my meaning straightway.

'Indeed, we shall have need of a jug of ale after you see my place for the smoke yet lingers and ash floats up at every step. We are done here,' he addressed the servant.

The elderly printer rose with some difficulty and both Wynkyn and the servant made to assist him. Wynkyn's withering scowl forced the servant to step back, bowing so low I wondered he did not topple on his face.

'We can find our own way out,' Caxton announced once standing. 'Come, Master Foxley, Wynkyn; no need to intrude upon the king's hospitality a moment longer.'

Caxton's Place, the Almonry, Westminster

Fire can be a fickle beast. Outwardly, Caxton's house at the Sign of the Red Pale, within the Almonry of Westminster Abbey, did not appear so badly damaged. Built of stone, like most of the abbey's older buildings, it yet stood tall. But closer observation showed the windows to be as gaping holes framed here and there with a few remnants of charred wood. The wall above each vacant square was soot-blackened, evidence of flames having escaped from within to lick the grey stones outside. The heavy oak door remained in its place but, as I mounted the stone step at the threshold and pushed it open, it felt strangely warm to my touch.

'Beware within. The stone floor was hot under Wynkyn's shoes earlier but we've sluiced it with buckets of water since,'

Caxton warned. 'Don't touch the walls either; they're hot as a potter's kiln even after three days.' He stood by the door, breathing heavily, recovering from the short walk from the palace, one arm braced against the wall. Already, his hand was besmirched with soot.

Inside, having left my scrip with Caxton, the place was stifling hot, the air hardly breathable. Ash floated up at every step despite the cooling water applied to the stone flags which had turned the soot upon the floor into rivulets of black mud. Likening it to a potter's kiln seemed an apt description—not that I, being of sound mind, had ever ventured so close as to enter one. I was glad of my foresight in leaving Gawain at home, elsewise blistered paws and singed fur might have resulted.

In the midst of this scene of dark chaos, 'neath a great ragged maw in the ceiling surrounded by upper floor joists protruding like rotten teeth, the stout timbers that had once been a printing press lay as huge sticks of charcoal. Had I not been familiar with the form of Jude's contraption, I might have failed to recognise it as such.

I tip-toed through the wreckage, realising the blizzard of black snowflakes that I disturbed was probably the remains of reams of paper, pamphlets and printed pages: Master Caxton's stock reduced to ashes. Behind the front door—that which had appeared hale and whole from the street but was, in truth, half burned through even its great thickness of wood on the inner side—I found the iron-studded coffer, the lid thrown back to reveal naught but emptiness. I examined the broken lock. It looked to have been hacked off with a stout blade, the wood around it deeply gouged. Afore the fire, that would have been, otherwise the fresh wounds should have shown pale, whereas they were soot-stained as all else and my examining fingers came away filthy.

Stepping over piles of burned timbers precariously heaped, despite my care, I stumbled as they gave way beneath me, pitching me forward. I grabbed at the nearest thing to save myself, only to dislodge a cascade of charred wood and ash, which set me choking as I fell with the sound of cracking and crunching underfoot and a final thud in a cloud of soot.

'Master Foxley! Are you hurt?' Caxton called from the doorway.

'Nay...' I coughed. 'I be well enough... I dare say.'

'I warned you to have a care, did I not?'

My hands and knees were grazed and 'twas hard to regain my feet forwhy the remnants of the blaze ever shifted under me but I achieved my goal, reaching what was left of the press. My movements now were tentative indeed. It took courage— or, mayhap, great foolishness—to crawl among the cock-eyed timbers, leaning this way and that, propped one against another like drunken Saturday-eve revellers and just as likely to topple over, crushing me 'neath their considerable weight.

And I found what I sought, as Wynkyn had described unto me: a patch, the size of a large platter, of something crisp and black. I broke off a piece, thin, brittle and hard. Aye, it might well be the remains of a melted cheese but its presence here seemed quite extraordinary. Prising it away from the stone floor with my penknife, I discovered wisps of woven straw which the cheese had covered and preserved from the flames. A basket, perhaps? It was hard to tell from so little evidence but it seemed a possibility. A broken dish, fire-charred, and a few burnt rags of cloth draped what had once been the flat surface of the press's platen, now pitted and flaked by the heat: unusable, though the mighty screw which raised and lowered it—as Jude had once explained to me—looked to have suffered somewhat less.

Having extricated myself from among the timbers without causing further slippage, I searched the part of the room farthest from the door. Here, the stairway to the upper floor was half collapsed, a number of the treads burned through. There would have been no escape from above stairs by this means. But beyond the stairs, the fire had done less damage. The small window there which opened onto a side alleyway, as I discovered, was yet intact. Its frame looked to be of recent construction but here I found the marks of a narrow blade around the catch and dirt scraped off on the window ledge.

There was no way of making further investigation of the upper chambers without a ladder. The stairs and floors were right dangerous and looking up through the huge hole above me, I realised I could glimpse daylight here and there through the roof tiles—the attic floor gone as well. The house had been gutted as thoroughly as a Lenten herring. Thus, I departed that cavernous darkness, having discovered what little I could.

Outside, in the bright sunshine, I looked in dismay at my attire. Vigorous brushing did naught to improve my appearance for my hands were as filthy as my clothes. My hose were rent at the knees from my fall.

'There's a conduit in the abbey precinct that we use. You can wash off the worst of it there,' Caxton said, frowning at my utter dishevelment.

'Ja, you cannot go to the tavern like that, Meneer Voxley,' Wynkyn said, stating the patently obvious. 'Neither can we lend you clean clouts, having none ourselves.'

'Did you discover anything?' Caxton wanted to know, even as they stood by, watching whilst I washed at the conduit. 'Anything worthwhile for your trouble and the ruination of your clothes?'

The cold water was right welcome and refreshing. I rinsed my hair in the trough, shaking it dry like a dog, and scrubbed at my face and neck. My hands felt sore, the left palm torn and bleeding a little. Soot was caked around my nails and in the creases of my knuckles. Soap would be required to get them clean. My clothing reeked of burnt wood and paper, its colours dulled and smeared with soot but what could I do to remedy that? Naught for the present. What I needed most desperately was a long, cool pot of ale to cleanse my parched throat and wash away the taste of smoke.

'One thing I can tell you for certain, Master Caxton,' I said as we made our way to the Fighting Cock Inn at a slow pace, such that the elderly printer might keep up. 'No kindly neighbour has saved your money on your behalf, nor opportunist thief, passing by since, taken it for his own purse. Your coffer was robbed afore the flames ever reached it.'

As we sat at our ale, myself having suffered the many suspicious looks and oft-wrinkled nose of the tapster, Caxton asked how I knew this to be so. I explained the evidence to him betwixt mouthfuls of ale—no salt-crusted mariner had ere been thirstier than I and the drink was good after the palace's vinegary offering. Despite this, Wynkyn was sipping his cup as if fearing the contents to be poisoned.

'Is aught amiss with your ale?' I asked him. Having paid for it in consideration of Caxton's recent losses, I felt I had to enquire the reason for his pained expression and grimacing.

'Your English ale is over sweet, meneer. I prefer Flaundrish beer, flavoured with bitter hops.'

'Oh?'

'I make my own. You should try it some time, Meneer Voxley. You will find it far more refreshing and pleasurable than this.' He tapped the jug with a dismissive finger.

'Even so,' I said, 'You must surely find this preferable to that ghastly wine we were served afore?'

Wynkyn looked doubtful, as was I concerning the possibility that I might partake of his bitter beer and enjoy it.

'What is more,' I continued, diverting the talk from the discussion of ale, 'I know how the felon gained entry to your premises.'

Chapter 7

Later that Friday
Jude's house, Ave Maria Alley

'I TOLD YOU. I don't know.' Eleanor's voice was strident.
'You were gone long enough to ask after Will Caxton's
entire bloody family, even to his most distant kinsmen. How
could you not discover his whereabouts?' Jude pushed himself
up from the bench. It was difficult to argue efficiently when
your opponent stood above you, hands on narrow, skirted hips.
'I'll wager you were too damned busy swilling ale and jawing
with your drunken cronies to make proper enquiries.'

'I found out that he survived the fire, didn't I?' Eleanor
stepped back, forced to look up at the taller man even as he
leant against the corner of the great printing press.

'I knew that anyway. Seb told me that much.'

'Maybe he's staying with friends but nobody seems to know
for certain. Perhaps the monks at the abbey have given him a
bed out of charity, or one of his wealthy patrons... but it's none
of your business. Why does it even concern you?'

'Of course it's my bloody business and concern out of, er,
Christian charity: he and I are fellow printers...'

Eleanor scoffed.

'Jude Foxley, you're no more a printer than my backside.'

The slap came hard and unexpected, leaving a hot red hand
print upon the cross-dresser's cheek and Jude nigh overbalanced
with the force of its delivery. Eleanor, shocked out of her comely,
ladylike role, reverted to his true self and it didn't take much of

a blow to send Jude sprawling.

'You're a useless scoundrel, Foxley, and a brute.' Rykenor said in his more manly voice, rubbing his bruised face. 'I'm done with you!' He took up the only stool and flung it across the room. One of its three legs snapped off as it hit the wall, 'And don't come crawling, begging me to come back and serve as your unpaid slave because it's over betwixt us. You can starve for all I care; lie in your own dirt; die of loneliness...' The litany of uncaring continued as he gathered up his belongings, making a heap of gowns, shifts and assorted womanly apparel by the door. Three trips above stairs to the bedchamber completed the task.

The last time, whilst Rykenor was upstairs and could not see him, Jude regained his bench by means of some undignified scrambling and cursing and now looked on, feigning indifference as his friend made ready to leave.

'Ell... I...' he began.

'Hold your tongue. I'm deaf to your pleas, so don't waste your breath.' Rykenor opened the street door then took up as much clothing as he could possibly carry in his arms. 'I'll send for the rest when I'm settled in new lodgings.' A linen shift fell from his grasp as he went out, preventing the door from slamming closed as he kicked it shut behind him.

'And good bloody riddance,' Jude muttered, though the sentiment was half-hearted. 'Can't even make a proper job of storming off in a huff,' he complained as he was forced to get up and retrieve the lost garment so that he could close the door, shutting out the damned miserable world before it could gawp and gloat at him in his difficulties. He threw the linen onto the remaining heap. It would have been most gratifying to kick it all out into the street, where he'd noticed a choice deposit of fresh horse shit, but such actions were no longer possible for him. His knee was throbbing from his fall and then he discovered the ale jug was dry. 'Bastard poxy bitch.' The day could get no worse, or so he thought, until he realised he hadn't had any dinner and the cook-shop would be left with no more than pasty crumbs by this hour and he couldn't be bothered to hobble so far, anyway. God rot everything and the Devil take it!

Bess Chambers' apothecary shop, Bishopsgate

A gaggle of goodwives clustered in sunlit Bishopsgate Street, the cobbles hot beneath their shoes and shade reduced to a thin strip under the eaves of the buildings but the heat of the day was an irrelevance. Some had just come from the apothecary's shop; others were intending to go in. In either case, the object of their gossip, their ever more embellished rumours, was the same: Sarra Shardlowe.

'With a family name like that, is it any wonder?' said Anneis Fuller, a stout matron, heavy basket in hand.

'Shardlowe? What's amiss with that?' asked a woman with a toddling pulling at her apron. 'Let be, Marky, Mam's talking. Be patient this once and you shall have a comfit. Later.'

'Well, in truth, Maud, 'tis not so far from 'Shadow', is it? And what an evil name that would be,' Anneis said, wagging her finger knowledgeably.

Others nodded agreement.

'After what she did to my goodman…' A third woman rolled her eyes skyward and threw up her hands. 'Those candles of hers… their scent made him randy as a bull. I haven't had an hour of peace since.'

'And you're complaining?' wondered a pretty young woman in a tawny gown. 'You can take mine, Frances. He does naught but mope since he first set eyes upon her and not a hand's turn of work has he done all week. I'm sure he's moonstruck and it's all her doing.'

'She's bewitched him. Put an enchantment on him, that's what,' concluded Anneis, setting down her basket for it was growing over-heavy and, clearly, this subject yet had a way to run.

'You think so?' Maud asked, looking shocked.

'Certainly. You need to go in there, Philippa,' Anneis pointed, directing the young woman's gaze towards the shop door, 'And confront Bess Chambers. That niece of hers is upsetting our men's humours and if she's not a witch, then I'm a... a... a tapster's droll.'

'Aye, a witch! That would explain all,' Maud and Frances agreed with enthusiasm. 'Go on, Philippa, tell Bess.'

'Why me? You go, Frances. Your man seems to have been most changed. Mine ever was an idle good-for-nothing. Besides, I must prepare supper and have errands to do before that.'

'I'm n-not so put out at my man's keenness for bed sport. Maybe we could all have a word with Mistress Chambers... tomorrow or Monday?'

'I have too much to do, caring for little Marky here,' said Maud. 'I don't have time for such things as witches. Why don't you see about this matter, Anneis, if it irks you so?'

'Then indeed I shall. Someone has to. But later will likely suffice. Or Monday next. Aye. That's settled then. Come Monday, we'll all speak to Bess Chambers together.'

With which dubious decision, the gossips of Bishopsgate dispersed about their own business. But the fateful word had been spoken; the seed planted and the poisonous weed among the sweet herbs could but flourish.

The Swan-on-the-Hoop Inn, Holbourne

Jack Tabor was living the high life. Caxton's coin was a fortune barely dreamt of in his days as a street urchin, stealing and begging just to survive, and now he would enjoy his ill-gotten wealth to the full as long as it lasted. After that, he'd let life take its course, as he ever had done before, and worry about the future when it arrived on his doorstep—not that he had such a thing as a doorstep or was ever likely to. That he'd just lost half a mark or more at a game of hazard was of little

THE COLOUR OF DARKNESS

account—almost certainly the dice were loaded against him forwhy no man's luck could be that bad. Later, he'd take his revenge on the cheating wretch.

Previously, he had thought to stow away on a ship bound for France but naught had come of that as yet. They spoke some alien tongue there, didn't they? He wouldn't even know how to ask for ale—if they even drank the stuff. Besides, good old England was where he belonged and why should he flee? Jude was just a bag of wind and spit, what with his empty threats. Nobody had any idea of what he'd done at Westminster and neither would they, so long as Jude kept his mouth shut. So he reckoned he was safe enough if he stayed out of the city, for the present, anyway. And with a comely and willing tavern wench on his knee, a brimming ale pot and a great oyster and onion pasty on the board before him all to himself, Jack was in Heaven. His idea of that Hallowed Place, leastwise.

The Foxley Place, Paternoster Row

Upon my return, Adam was embossing and gilding the leather binding of a prestigious copy of *The Arte and Play of Chess* for Alderman Verney. He being Kate's father, we had taken pains to make this volume somewhat special and I had permitted his daughter to decorate the initials and margins as she thought would be most pleasing to him—thus, dogs predominated, many of Gawain's kind forwhy my faithful friend had been bred by the alderman.

Our efforts would be worthwhile since a proud parent would wish to show the work to colleagues in the wealthy Grocers' Company and, having impressed them, we hoped, more commissions for fine books would come our way. A reputation for work of the highest quality was growing at the Sign of the Fox. Which reminded me: our sign was still in need of retouching after the frosts and icy blasts of last winter took their toll of the paintwork, fading its vibrant hues, causing flaking of certain less-weatherproof pigments and a shabby first impression would not serve to encourage prospective customers.

'Thought I'd best get on with this,' Adam said when I entered the workshop, 'Since I was absent much of yesterday, what with that lawyer and his legal conundrums and all the while my conscience was pricking me about this book.' My cousin gave me a look full of meaning. 'Others don't seem to have such a tender conscience as I do, in particular regard to our earning a living.'

In answer, I went straight to my desk, though I had thought to go to the kitchen for some elderflower cordial and a thorough wash following my ordeal and the hot walk home after.

'And how did matters proceed with the lawyer?' I asked as I uncovered those same title pages as yesterday and the day before and the day before that...

'You know lawyers, Seb: a snail could outmatch their pace of work. Not unlike you. Your rate of progress on those Gospel miniatures is not exactly rapid, is it? Your Julia is going to be a married woman before you're finished.'

'It cannot be helped. Other imperative tasks keep landing upon my platter. I could hardly refuse a summons to Westminster, could I?'

'What did Lord Hastings want?'

'Naught, as I discovered. 'Twas the king who suggested— nay, commanded—that I assist Master William Caxton in his hour of need.'

'Caxton!' Adam leapt to his feet. You mean that damned printer who's doing his best to ruin our business?'

'Aye. The same.'

'Seb, you can't help him. That's madness. Would a condemned man help the executioner sharpen the axe?'

'He might if he wanted a quick, clean death. But that be irrelevant. The king would have me solve a crime, not assist with any printing.'

'What crime? Don't you do enough unravelling of damned

mysteries for Thaddeus Turner?'

I did not respond to the accusation, despite its truth.

'You may have heard something of a serious fire at Westminster?'

Adam nodded.

'What of it?'

'It was Caxton's house and workshop…'

'How fortunate for us. That's one fewer rival for our business.'

''Twas an act of arson.'

'Then I commend the fire-raiser.'

'Adam! Do not say that. Lives could have been lost.'

'Were they?'

'Nay. As it came to pass, God be praised, all were safe but Caxton's livelihood, his possessions, his money be all gone.'

'Excellent. But why should the king want you involved?'

'Forwhy I uncovered that mystery of the Italian espier, so it seems, and His Grace was impressed. They want me to recover certain items which have disappeared.'

'Burned to cinders, no doubt. Even you can't recover them in that case.'

'You may think so but, as I discovered among the ashes of his place in the Almonry, I believe the fire was meant to destroy evidence of their theft. I found clear signs that Master Caxton's accounting ledger and cash were removed afore the blaze began.'

'That explains the state of you.' My cousin sat back at the board where the embossing tools were heating over a chafing dish and a sheet of gold leaf lay weighted down with a little bag of pounce powder, such that it would not blow away in the least draught. 'But I think you should change your clothes before you besmirch the work with soot. Look to your sleeve: all black.'

'Oh, no! I had not noticed that. You may have averted disaster, Adam. My thanks for it.'

'And Rose will be wrath with you when she sees the filth you've trampled across her scrubbed floors,' he said with a mischievous quirk of his mouth.

'Lord save us! I did not realise my boots be caked with ash.' In haste, I unlaced and removed the offending footwear but too late to avoid treading my pathway of mire and dirt all across the flagstones. Adam was correct: Rose would be displeased and rightly so.

'So, I suppose you'll be out and about, all over London and Westminster, poking your nose into every nook and crack instead of doing a proper day's work?'

'Probably.' As the fisherman says, I would not rise to the bait.

'And what of our decision to keep to ourselves, as far as we're able, to avoid spreading the contagion?'

''Tis not certain we have the contagion, is it? Besides, it cannot be helped. If I be contagious, likely I have already passed it to Master Caxton, Wynkyn de Worde and half the patrons at the Fighting Cock.'

'Who's this de Worde fellow? It's a strange name.' Adam pressed hard upon the little heated iron with its design of vine leaves, making the first of many indentations in the blue leather binding. Eventually, they would form a handsome gilded border on both front and back covers.

'He is Caxton's assistant from Flanders, so his master likely chose a more pronounceable name for him. A fair choice, though, for a printer, you must agree.'

'Would better suit a stationer... a scrivener like me. Adam de Worde? Aye, I like the sound of that. Maybe I'll change it when I buy my citizenship. On which matter, did I tell you? According to the lawyer, I have to become a citizen of this merry cesspool, according to the City Ordinances, before I can be appointed by the Lord Mayor as my lads' official guardian. I'll need your sponsorship, Seb, and testimony as to my irreproachably good character and upstanding reputation.'

'I would give both willingly, of course, but is it not the case that a kinsman be barred from giving testimony as to character for fear he may be biased? And you must have been resident in the city for at least three years.'

'The lawyer said naught about kinsmen…'

' No matter. I be certain my old master, Richard Collop, will oblige you. As Warden Master of the Stationers' Guild, his testimony will carry far more weight than mine as a mere Assistant Deputy. But three years, Adam? Have you been here so long?'

'I came back here with you and Emily from Foxley, just after Dickon was born, so, aye, a few weeks more will see my term of residency achieved, won't it?'

'In truth, Adam, you seem to have been here forever, yet no time at all but, as you say, Dickon was a newborn and now be three, indeed. But you have not mentioned the cost: your citizenship, lawyers' fees and guardianship… these things are not come by cheaply.'

My cousin blew out a long breath, causing the corner of the gold leaf to tremble.

'Well, aye. That. Aye. Can we talk of it later? Privily.' He added this last in a whisper as he glanced at Kate, Hugh and Ralf, so diligent at their work.

'That would be as well,' I said, picking up my pen. In truth, it occurred to me that the sum would likely be considerable—far more than Adam could have set aside in only three years, even on my generous wages, what with the expense of feeding and clothing his ever-hungry, ever-growing step-sons. I must discuss matters with Rose aforehand.

'Seb. Your mucky sleeves…' he reminded me and I set down my pen. Again.

'I can still smell smoke in your hair,' Rose said as we lay entwined in each other's arms that night. Fortunately, my dear one had forgiven me for the excess of dirt upon her clean floors and the unwarranted additions to next week's laundry, her forgiveness taking physical form: pleasures which we were able to enjoy to the full these days. The new nursery for the children was yet a marvel to us.

'I apologise, sweeting. I have washed it twice since: once at the Westminster conduit and here, using your fragrant lavender soap, yet the stink of smoke seems to cling. I shall wash it again upon the morrow.'

'And I'll rinse it thoroughly for you with rosewater.'

'I shall smell like a lady's bower.'

'Better that than a bonfire.'

'Aye, I suppose.' I kissed her smooth brow. 'Your hair smells of herbs.'

'Thyme for shine and gloss. Meg suggested it. Do you like it? The sheen on my hair, I mean?'

'It feels as warm silk,' I murmured. 'Molten gold.' In truth, I thought it felt as it always did, caressing my fingers as I stroked an escaping strand from her cheek. But, as I have learned, 'tis ever wise to approve a wife's efforts to make herself beautiful and more pleasing unto you, else why should she continue to do so for the future? Oftentimes, I admit, she was required to draw my attention to a new buckle on her girdle or a different way of braiding her hair 'neath her cap when I failed to observe the same. Yet I, as an artist, ought to see such details without her prompting. 'Twas remiss of me and familiarity with my beloved was no excuse. Thus was I proud of myself for having noticed the different scent.

'Seb?'

'Aye?'

'How is Adam progressing with this guardianship matter? He shrugged his shoulders when I asked and told me "well enough" but his expression said otherwise. Is there a problem with it?'

'More than one, I fear, but 'tis complicated and the hour grows late. You do not want to hear of the convolutions now.'

'But I do. I shall never get to sleep unless you tell me. I worry so about Adam and those lads. I want to see them all settled and content, as you do. Explain it to me, Seb, please.'

'Very well, if you insist, but I shall give you the bare bones of it only, else dawn will break afore we get any rest.' So I told Rose, in the briefest of terms, what was required of my cousin by the City Ordinances afore he could achieve his desire. When I ended my recital, I was surprised by her question—I know not why for 'twas the same that occurred to me:

'How will Adam afford all this when lawyers are renowned for charging a king's ransom for the composing of a few lines of Latin when, as a scribe and letter writer, you ask but a ha'penny for a morning's penmanship?'

'I write few letters for the illiterate these days…'

'Don't avoid answering my question, husband: where is the money to come from to pay Adam's costs? Has he robbed an Italian banker or a goldsmith? Please, God, don't say he's gone to a money-lender, else he'll never be out of debt. This matters to us all.'

'Indeed it does, my dear one, but I cannot tell that which I do not know. Earlier, Adam said he wished to speak privily upon the matter but the opportunity did not come to pass as yet. However, I foresee that his speech will concern money—or the lack thereof. Thus, since we now be treading this treacherous path of financial and pecuniary concerns, I would ask your advice.'

'Advice on what?'

'A moment, lass, and I shall set my—nay, our—dilemma afore you. I believe Adam will ask me to lend him the money he requires. I know not how large the sum may be but our coffer be well full and much of that by reason of Adam's hard work and excellent eye for business. Therefore, I think he deserves a fair share of our profits. Also, as you say, dear one, I would not see him living over his ears in debt for the rest of his days. Thus, I wish to make him a gift and a sizable one at that, such as he need never repay it.'

'How much can we afford, Seb? And supposing it's still not enough?'

'That be the matter upon which I would have your advice afore he asks me for a loan. And I suppose it would also be wise to enquire of Meg as our keeper of accounts… but if we determine the greatest sum we could possibly give without ruining ourselves and leaving naught for any possible unforeseen eventualities, then I shall know how generous we can afford to be. With your agreement, it goes without saying. And if his needs exceed that sum… well, we must pray that it does not.'

'Aye, ask Meg. She knows better than anyone the contents of our coffer. But, of course, you should gift the money to Adam.'

'My thanks for that, Rose. I knew you would understand. I shall speak with Meg in the morning and once we all three have decided what we can afford, I may inform Adam, spare him the embarrassment of begging a loan.' With a grateful sigh, I turned over in bed. 'Get some sleep now, sweeting…'

Saturday, the twenty-third day of June

A good morn should commence with a good breakfast but a mess of eggs from our hens and herbs from the garden plot must suffice. 'Twas my doing: insisting that marketing must be restricted to utter necessities in order to keep the chances of us infecting others as small as may be but my Christian responsibilities were becoming tiresome.

'I could have bought us a great pie from the cook-shop on our way here, if I'd known it would be eggs again,' Adam complained. 'So many damned eggs are binding up my guts more surely than glue.'

'I have a cure for that,' Rose assured him, reaching for a black pot high upon the kitchen shelf.

My cousin eyed it suspiciously and shook his head.

'Matters are not so bad.'

'If you should change your mind…' she offered.

'I won't. I took some of that stuff once before and I'm not foolish enough to take another dose.'

'My cousin be of a cowardly disposition,' I said. I rose from the board and kissed my dear one's smooth brow as I passed her by at the doorway.

'You don't know the half of it, Seb,' Adam continued as he made to follow me out. 'I spent two days in the privy last time and dared not leave.'

I gave him a sympathetic glance but no more than that.

'You go to the workshop, cousin,' I said. ''Tis Saturday, accounting day, and I must speak with Meg.'

'Upon our dwindling income, no doubt. We should all be at our desks…'

'Meg, may I ask you to leave your herb-chopping and join me in the parlour with the accounting book?'

Once in private, I explained as succinctly as I could my reasons and wishes.

The lass knitted her brows as she scoured the columns, tallying numbers. The way she kept glancing across at me, I believe she hoped I would change my mind about the gift.

'Five pounds in sterling,' she said after a deal of frowning and lip-chewing.

'Nonsense. A lawyer would hardly bother to put his gown and cap on for that. We can afford more.'

'Seven, maybe, if we all draw our girdles tighter at the board, especially Adam. He eats too much in any case.' That was Meg's way: she never minced her words.

'I hoped for twenty pounds at least. Twenty-five, if at all possible.' I sounded wistful, twiddling the lacings on my doublet, avoiding her gaze.

'What! You jest, master. You could purchase a whole street of tenements for that and gild the roofs with gold leaf. It's more than half a knight's fee.'

'I know. Likely, that be overly optimistic but Adam deserves a goodly sum.'

'You're not Croesus, you know. How much do you think we have in the coffer?'

I shrugged. In truth, I thought little of such matters. Meg and Adam were more concerned for these things. 'Twas, indeed, remiss of me, as head of the household, not to know more of our finances—*mea culpa*—but I never possessed the skill. Back in the days when I was doing the accounting and paying the wages every Saturday, the columns tallied as frequently as the sun shone blue.

'You currently possess fifteen pounds, eleven shillings and eight pence three farthings.'

'Is that all?'

'It is. And what about repayment of the money? You ought to draw up a proper contract.'

'Nay, did I not say? 'Tis to be a gift.'

'Don't be absurd. King Edward himself would hardly be so generous.'

'So I have heard from my brother. Tell me, then, how much might we afford at best?'

'Considering what's in the coffer now and if those customers who owe us could be encouraged to settle their debts promptly… ten pounds, perhaps, but only if we forego meat for a month, as though it were a second Lenten fasting, and nobody needs new clouts or shoes or any medicines… and I saw the state of your jerkin, hose and shirt last eve. It'll take the efforts of Hercules to get them halfway clean and respectable enough to wear again. Mistress Rose was saying she'd have to buy fine Holland cloth and stitch you some new shirts. I told her Holland cloth is too good for you, the way you spoil your clouts so often. If you gift Adam so much as this, you'll have to wear sackcloth for the foreseeable future.

'There! I've told you true, Master Seb. Do as you wish—at your peril, aye, and that of all of us in the household beside. What of Dickon and Julia?'

'What of them?' I came alert of a sudden, holding my breath, awaiting her words.

'Their inheritance. Don't forget that we are biding in the

shadow of the pestilence. What if you should die tomorrow and the coffer stands empty as a Smithfield beggar's bowl?'

'It will not come to that, Meg,' I assured her. 'We be earning money all the while.'

'Aye, and spending it as fast. Ten pounds, master. Not a penny more. And no giving of alms to beggars nor feeding a crowd on a Sunday as we are accustomed to.'

'We cannot do the latter upon this Lord's Day as it stands, what with our situation. 'Tis a relief to me each morn to find all present at the breakfast board with good appetite. Come Tuesday next, the threat should be passed, if Bess Chambers has the right of it and I pray to Our Saviour that it shall be so.'

'Mm.' Meg did not add the customary 'Amen', as others would have done. 'Well, if that's all you require of me, master, I was in the midst of chopping mint and parsley to prepare a sauce for our dinner of cheese and onions. And make the most of it for when the cheese is gone it'll be herrings salted, herrings dried and herrings pickled, boiled and fried from now on. I fear we shall all grow fins and gills before the summer's out.'

'My thanks, Meg.' I watched as she closed the ledger and departed the parlour, brisk and efficient as usual. I wondered how we had managed our business afore she came to us but 'twas disappointing to learn that I could give Adam no more than ten pounds and I doubted it would be sufficient for his needs.

I did not so much as rise from my seat afore Adam came in.

'Ah, I hoped I'd find you here,' he said. 'Now we can talk... unless you're rushing off to Westminster once more?'

'Family comes first; William Caxton can wait a while,' I said, smiling. I desired to make this as easy for him as possible.

'Aye, well, you'll recall our, er, discussion of yesterday...'

'Of course: your dealings with the lawyers, on which account, I would...'

'Hear me out, cousin, I pray you. As you just said, family comes first, and I want Simon, Mundy, aye, and even that knavish Nick... I would have Mercy's sons—God rest her innocent soul—to be my family. Thus, I wrote to my parents back home in Norfolk.'

I must have looked as shocked as I felt.

'I know, I know,' he continued, sounding contrite, holding up his hands in surrender, 'I should have told you.'

'But your parents disowned you.' Adam's father, Thomas Armitage, be my elder half-brother by twenty years or so, a man unknown to me until my brief sojourn in Foxley village. He had done naught to recommend himself to me, insofar as I knew, but blamed Adam for the demise of their deeply loved son, Noah. Noah and Adam—the despised son—were twins and I knew my cousin yet mourned the loss of his sibling.

'Aye, but I thought they might have mellowed in my absence. They only had Noah and me and with him gone, I knew my mother always prayed she'd be blessed with grandchildren. So I wrote, telling them about Mercy and the lads, though, I admit, I blurred the facts about their true parentage. I explained how they could have three fine Armitage grandsons but that it would cost a deal of money to make things legal.'

'And?'

'Well, to be honest, Seb, I never expected any answer, thinking my letter would go straight into the fire, unread. But yesterday, while you were at Westminster, a Norfolk carrier and friend of Ralf brought me a reply. And what a shock it was! Here, read it for yourself, cousin, and see what they sent…'

He took a fat, folded paper of excellent quality from his purse and spread it out before me, smoothing the creases. The hand was neat and clear, as was to be expected of a professional scrivener, the craft being handed down the generations of Armitages since the reign of the second King Richard:

From Thomas Armitage, Scrivener of Foxley in the County of Norfolk, greetings be unto you, dearest son.

"Dearest Son" was a hopeful and unexpected beginning.

Your mother and I heartily approve your intentions concerning our grandsons, Simon, Nicholas and Edmund and commiserate with you upon the loss of our daughter, Mercy, she whom we never had the joy of knowing.

I hereby enclose a purse, at your request, to cover the legal fees thus entailed and any money remaining shall hereafter be entrusted unto you for our grandsons' futures with one condition. That is to say, we desire you to visit us and bring the said children to Foxley. Your mother aforementioned is not in good health and desires to see them before her death. I bid you do not delay over long.

All blessings of God, His Holy Mother and All the Saints in Heaven be upon you and yours, Adam, our beloved and only son.

'Tis a fine letter though it reads in parts as a legal document.'

'That's my parent's way.'

'And to be addressed as 'beloved son' must please you mightily.'

'Huh, if I even believe the sentiment.' He dismissed this with a flick of his hand. 'What pleases me far more is the purse, my father being usually so parsimonious as to make a Jewish money-lender look charitable. He must have a guilty conscience, blaming me for poor Noah's death, and he regards money as the best cure for every problem. Besides, he's never done much else to aid me. But what do I care why he sends it? I now have the wherewithal to pay for my citizenship and all that follows.

'Forgive me for not telling you I was writing to your brother, Seb, but since I expected it to be naught but a waste of ink and I'd never receive any reply, I didn't want to mention it in the workshop nor anywhere with others to hear. To say honestly, Seb, I was worried that you might explode with anger at me for going behind your back in this way... wasn't sure you'd understand.'

Did my cousin truly think me a man of such ill-temper? I thought he knew me better than that. More likely, he did not want to suffer any embarrassment concerning a rude dismissal, if it came to that, nor to acknowledge his request for coin from his father, hardly daring to hope that he should receive anything by way of a purse.

'Fear not, Adam. I be delighted for you. Such marvellous tidings, except concerning your mother's health, of course.'

'My mother has been knocking at Death's door for as long as I can recall. According to her, she was never meant to make old bones.'

'Your father sounds concerned though.'

'Aye, wondering who'll cook his next meal, if she isn't there to do it.'

'You be so cynical, Adam. 'Tis most unchristian of you.'

'Well, you'd say the same if you had lived with them all those years as I did. If it wasn't for Noah, I would've run away by the age of seven. That's why I want my lads to have a good home and a father who cares about them and shows them affection, even though that's sometimes a hard task with Nick.'

'Will you take them to Foxley as your father asks?'

'I'll think on it, I suppose. A gift of fifty marks deserves some recompense, would you not agree?'

'Fifty!'

'Aye, well, he has never in his life spent so much as a farthing, if he might avoid it, so I dare say he can afford almost seventeen pounds without too much trouble.'

Chapter 8

Later on Saturday morning
Caxton's Place, the Almonry, Westminster

UPON THIS occasion of my return to Caxton's place, I took Gawain, hoping he might sniff out clues too faint for my nose. To me, the cheese had smelled simply burnt but maybe to Gawain, that canine connoisseur of the same, it would yet convey a hint of its original substance and I wondered if he might be able to follow its scent from whence it came. Likely, 'twas a vain hope but I would not know unless we made the attempt.

As a precaution and to avoid causing Rose any further anguish come Monday morn by adding more soot-stained clothing to the laundry, I wore yesterday's besmirched garments and ash-clagged boots, not having cleaned them as yet. It did not seem worth the trouble until my investigations here were completed.

The stink of smoke remained strong but when I put my hand to the stone floor, 'twas now cold and presented no danger to a dog's paws. At first, I allowed Gawain to sniff about as he pleased but when he, so concerned for a scent that he barged, unseeing, into a leaning timber and sent it crashing down in a cloud of ash, I decided to err upon the side of greater caution. When we recovered from coughing and sneezing, I led him to the spot where I discovered the crisped cheese previously. He had no difficulty in recognising the black crust for what it was. That it was be-sooted and set hard did not deter him and, afore

I knew it, he wolfed down a cheese cinder.

'Cease that, you foolish creature!' I did my best to wrestle another piece from his jaws but it broke off in my fingers and the rest was gone. 'What a greedy hound you be. You broke your fast as I did so do not pretend otherwise and go destroying evidence.' But Gawain only wagged his tail and went questing about for more. It seemed burnt cheese was quite a delicacy to my addle-pated dog.

He pursued the scent to that little window beyond the stairs as I hoped he would and leapt up with his front paws against the wall under the window, barking. Aye, the favoured scent was there for certain but elsewhere, in the shell of the house, all trace had been washed away by the efforts made to quench the fire with so much water, as Wynkyn de Worde had described to me at the Fighting Cock yesterday. There at the inn, Master Caxton and I had drawn up our contract, which Wynkyn and the tapster had witnessed, so all was made legal now. We each had our own indentured copy and mine was safe in our secret place, hid in the aumbry behind the framed painting of Our Lady in our bedchamber.

Therefore, with the scent of cheese in his nose, it made sense to begin Gawain's search from the other side of the window whence the perpetrator had gained entry and I led the dog outside and down the narrow alleyway. If we could not trace the evil-doer's escape then, mayhap, we could follow his course— and that of the cheese—to where it had commenced.

In the alleyway, nose down, Gawain turned circles, this way and that. It had not rained since before the fire, neither had water been required to sluice here where the fire never came. Thus, the alley must be a great confusion of scents to him, the one he sought overlain by a myriad others since. But he found it, eventually, and set off at such a pace back along the narrow passage to the front of the house and then pursuing a winding way amongst abbey buildings. The path opened onto a patch of dry grass and weeds, passing a midden and a pigsty, neither of which distracted him in the least from pursuit of his quarry. That cheese, afore it burned, must have been ripe indeed to have left so indelible a trail after four days.

'Hold, Gawain!' I called as I did my best upon two legs to keep up with his four. How fortunate it be that dogs do not comprehend the workings of a latch and a little postern gate in the precinct wall halted his enthusiastic chase. I paused to catch my breath and ease a stitch in my ribs whilst he barked his impatience at the gate and nosed the iron ring of the handle. 'Wait, wait. The scent has lasted this long; it will not fade in the next hour unless it rains.' The sky was cloudless. 'And I warn you, lad, there will not be the cheese you hope for at the end of it… though, mayhap, you will have earned some as a treat if we find the demon's lair.' I mopped my brow with a grubby sleeve—oh, how Rose had protested at my venturing abroad in such soiled attire until she realised the good sense of my decision.

'Here we go, then, lad,' I said, opening the gate once my stitch was eased. He shot through the gap afore ever I pushed it wide, knocking me aside in his onward rush. I had never known him so keen and keeping pace was impossible.

He crossed a dusty lane where great mullein grew tall along the margins and parched grass sprouted down the middle betwixt the deep wheel ruts, then disappeared into another alley across the way, decaying timber shacks on either hand. This part of Westminster beyond the abbey seemed little used. Barefoot, ragged urchins played amongst rotting wooden walls and towering stands of hogweed, shouting and laughing. Their efforts to persuade Gawain to join their game served to hinder his progress sufficiently for me to catch up afore he wrenched free of a skinny child's embrace and ran on.

This nether end of Westminster looked to be a likely place for a thief and fire-raiser to lurk but my hopes that Gawain's quest might be nearing its end were dashed when an overgrown way betwixt more affluent buildings led us out into Kings Street not far from the Charing Cross. The street was crowded indeed with folk a-marketing this midday and my dog lost the scent amongst the passage of so many feet and wheels. A pieman doing a deal of trade, crying his wares of coney pasties and baked crabs, distracted Gawain and, seeing the hour, I purchased a crab, the cooked flesh in its shell.

I sat on the steps of the famous cross, constructed in memory of a long-dead but much-loved queen—Eleanor, maybe it was— and ate my crab, scooping it from the corners with my knife. Gawain shared my dinner but his disappointment was plain that it was not cheese.

'I suppose the trail ends here then, lad,' I said, fondling his ears. 'And maybe we came close to finding the miscreant in that wasteland you discovered beyond the abbey. Who can say what a more thorough search might reveal? No matter. You did right well, better than any man's nose could do.'

In answer, Gawain put his nose to the ground, sniffing about. I laughed at him.

'Aye, you have proved your worth, my faithful assistant. Come, now, let us go home…'

But the dog had other intentions and raced off into the fields beyond the row of thatched cottages that faced the little church of St Martin. Was this some merry game of his, I wondered, as a flock of sheep scattered, bleating, as he ran amongst them? The shepherd yelled at him, waving his crook, yet Gawain kept his nose down all the way, having no interest in chasing the sheep. There certainly seemed a purpose to his quest. Was it possible that he continued to follow that same scent of cheese? Unlikely, as that seemed.

Gawain's path turned easterly towards the River Fleet and London beyond. He was far ahead but I could see him across the open fields, set upon a straight course. I called him back and he disobeyed me but at least he paused, tongue lolling and dripping, panting in the shade of some ancient elm trees, waiting for me.

I looked around, searching for landmarks, and realised that we were almost upon the road to Holbourne. Wearily, I climbed the wooden stile in the quick-thorn hedge whilst Gawain leapt it in a great bound and we were in Holbourne Lane. But instead of following the lane on its easterly way to the village, after a few yards he turned south, across open fields once more. And now his path became a devious one, from thicket to bush, from bramble patch to hedgerow. So my clever Gawain was continuing to follow the cheese! The culprit must have followed this way, furtively, keeping hidden, forwhy he was known in these parts. A Londoner, mayhap?

Our way ended abruptly at the Fleet Ditch. The banks here were steep but on this western side there were clear signs that someone had climbed down—or up—with clumps of thick grass torn out, the nettles trampled down and scuff marks in the fresh soil where weeds had been uprooted recently. On the bank opposite, willows overhung the ditch but it was probable that similar signs were hidden there amongst the graceful sweep of leaves.

But how Gawain had followed that solitary scent to this very place, I knew not. The stench from the murky ditch was so foul it overwhelmed all else. I turned away, my hands cupped over my nose and mouth, fighting the urge to retch on the stink. The sight of the rotting and bloated carcass of some animal or other—I could not say what kind—lying in that foetid water, a-swarm with flies, did naught to aid me.

Gawain stood on the bank's edge, uncertain. He looked down and then to me for guidance.

'Nay, lad. Not that way. We shall use the bridge as wise folk do. Come, now. Forget the scent. We can find this place from the other side. If Satan himself were at my heels, I would not go down into that ditch to save myself. In truth, I doubt even the Fallen One would stand so close as this. Come away.'

We retraced our steps a short way then turned south along Shoe Lane to where it joined Fleet Street. We crossed the bridge which led to Ludgate but left the street again to go north, passing the Fleet Prison. Here the stink grew even worse, the stench walled in by the prison and its odoriferous inmates on one side and the ditch upon the other. I felt dizzy, breathing in these foul miasmas, though Gawain seemed unperturbed such was his eagerness to catch the scent of cheese once more.

Beyond the prison, St George's Lane went east to The Bailey but we ignored it, continuing to follow the ditch through a wasteland of weeds and detritus in which feral cats hunted vermin and mangy curs patrolled like constables in their own ward, abandoned by man. Neither attracted my dog's attention in this instance. He was not tempted to chase the cats nor growl at the curs although he did put up a gang of crows, disturbing them from their feast of some gruesome mess.

At the stand of willows, Gawain barked his pleasure at finding the place and went in circles, nose down, searching out the scent. And there it was! We were once more upon the culprit's trail. Retracing our path, setting the crows flapping anew, we returned to St George's Lane and, this time, we did hasten east to The Bailey and then south, entering the city under Ludgate's moss-covered arch.

Along Bowyer Row and up Old Dean's Lane I followed Gawain and my heart was sinking. Whatever the cause of Gawain's excitement on the banks of the Fleet Ditch, it had all been to no purpose. Somewhere along the way, he had quite forgotten his quest and was now eager to go home. I warrant he had not, however, forgotten my mentioning a treat of cheese, hence his eagerness to get there. But then the creature surprised me.

To attain Paternoster Row, we needs must pass by my brother's door and, recalling the possibilities of spreading contagion, I had no intention of venturing into Jude's home, endangering his health, yet Gawain determined otherwise.

Jude's house, Ave Maria Alley

The dog went upon his hind legs, scratching at the door which was unlatched and his weight pushed it open. He bounded within afore I could detain him and I heard Jude bellowing his protests at the intrusion.

'Bloody dog! Get out, you greedy cur. Go on, get your great fat nose out of my things. Oh, it's you. Should've known you'd be two steps behind your damned dog. What do you want? Come to snoop have you, as usual?'

'And God's blessings be upon you, brother,' I said, forcing a smile despite my welcome. 'I come for no reason other than we were passing your door and Gawain, foolish dog, thinks you have cheese here for him.' I held the dog by his scruff to prevent his raiding the kitchen outhouse beyond Jude's untidy chamber.

'Well, I bloody don't, so go away.' My brother was seated sideways at one end of his bench such that his damaged leg rested along its length.

The place stank of stale piss, old food and mouldy bread— not as bad as the ditch but that my brother should live in this squalor was untenable. Unwashed nether clouts lay around, a full piss pot stood in the corner. Could he not empty that at least? By the door to the outhouse was a bucket stacked with food-stained platters and spoons in a few inches of cold, greasy water and dirty cups lay overturned upon the platen of the great press. I peeked through to what had once been a wife's proud domain. A knife and an ancient heel of bread were on the kitchen board.

'When did you last eat, Jude? That bread is blue with mould.'

'What do you care?'

'Of course, I care. When?'

'I don't know. Yesterday morn, I suppose. Don't bloody fuss me.' I saw as he used both hands to lift his leg into a more comfortable position on a broken stool that his knee remained badly swollen since his fall the other day.

'In the name of Heaven! Do you not know better than that how to treat a book, Jude?' I said, horrified to see the shattered leg of the stool propped upon a sizable work, the sharp ends gouging into the leather binding. The thick volume had clearly seen better days, stained and worn as it was, yet my stationer's instinct was to spare it any further insult and I looked around for something that might replace it. A half-log by the hearth might serve.

'Let that be, you interfering arse-wipe; get away from it. Don't touch the bloody stool. Can't you see my leg's a sodding agony to me?'

'But the book...'

'Damn it, it's only a book! Since the stool broke...'

I could well imagine how that came to pass: my brother's fiery temper, no doubt. With a sigh of defeat, I left the book to its fate.

'Upon my next visit, I shall bring you another stool from home and ask Stephen to mend this one. Mind, it may take a while since, with Jack's disappearance, there be none to aid him. Speaking of whom: have you heard any tidings of the lad?'

'No. You've asked me that before and I told you: I don't know where he is nor give a rat's arse about him. Besides, I haven't left this miserable house since I was at yours on Sunday for the roasted mutton dinner so how would I hear anything about anything?'

'I thought Eleanor might have heard something. And what of her? Has she gone a-marketing?'

'How in Hell's name do I know what that bitch does?'

'Ah, I understand now. What did you do to upset her, Jude?

'Why do you always blame me? Why should it be *my* fault? I didn't do anything.'

Aye, my brother reckoned himself blameless as ever.

'How can you abide this dirt and chaos?' I surveyed the place, throwing up my hands in despair.

'That's a woman's job, not mine.'

Shaking my head, I called to Gawain and we hastened from the ill-kept house to buy food and drink for Jude. I thought then how fortunate it was that Adam did not need our money for his lawyers' fees, elsewise, as Meg had explained, acts of charity such as this would be impossible. But, even had we been nigh penniless, I should have found some way to aid my brother who was plainly unable to fend for himself without Eleanor.

Returning to his door, I gave him an earthen pot of eels in jelly, a manchet loaf, a punnet of cherries and some honeyed wafers. Needless to say, he frowned at my offerings. A few steps behind me, a tapster's lad carried a jug of fresh ale. Having taken it from him, I paid him a penny and gave him the bucket of greasy water.

'Swill that out, lad, and refill it at the conduit, if you will, and you shall have another ha'penny.'

In the youngster's absence, I lit the fire in the hearth and set about putting matters to rights whilst Jude ate. I emptied the piss pot into the gutter outside and collected up the soiled linens, though what to do about those, I was uncertain.

'You're bloody fussing me again,' Jude complained, dropping his spoon with a clatter on the floor, having finished eating the eels, spitting the bones into the hearth, causing the flames to hiss. 'Why can't you leave me alone?'

'To starve?'

'I'd manage well enough without you. I have friends…'

I wondered if that were true forwhy none seemed to have come by to tend my brother's needs. Did anyone realise Eleanor had left him?

The lad returned with the water and I put some in a pot upon the hearth to heat.

'Do you know any washer-women around here?' I asked him. He shrugged.

'Mam takes in washing sometimes but only on Tuesdays when she does the bed sheets and napiery from the inn as well. She does ours on a Monday.'

'Do you think she might consider doing those linens in haste, if I pay more than her normal fee?'

'She might.'

'Hey!' Jude threw a squashed cherry at me. 'My bloody linen is my business, you pair of clods.'

'Of course, but who will do your laundry whilst Eleanor be elsewhere?' I gave the lad a groat and piled the linen in his arms.

Jude made no further objection. In truth, I think he was glad to have the unpleasant clouts gone.

'Rose could do it for free,' he said, munching wafers. 'And cook and clean for me... just for now, until I get things straight and my business thriving.'

'And when will that be? Rose has more than enough to do, caring for all of us and keeping Adam's house clean and well-ordered.'

'Oh, aye, so that's the way of it, is it? She'll work for that bloody cousin of yours but not for your brother. Jude Foxley is of no bloody account, as was ever the case!'

''Tis not like that, as you well know. Eleanor has dealt with such matters until now...'

'The pox-ridden whore.'

'...And one moment you demand that I get out and leave you be and the next you say I treat you as of no account, implying that I should do more for you.' I took the steaming pot from the fire with the hook for the purpose and tipped half the hot water into a dented laver bowl. 'Here, wash your face and hands, if you will,' I said but he laughed at me.

'Use it yourself. You complain to me about dirt when you're covered in filth. You look to have rolled in soot.'

'Aye, 'twas quite an unpleasant task this morn, raking through ashes,' I told him as I put the platters, spoons and cups to soak in the rest of the water.

'Women's work looks to suit you, little brother. You can keep house for me since you've naught else to do but interfere in my life.'

126

On my knees beside the bucket—something my brother could do no longer—I ignored his sneering tone, scrubbing at the dried-on food with my fingernails for want of scouring sand and putting the clean platters and cups on the hearthstone to dry.

'I know not what to do for the best with you, Jude, in truth, I do not. But, there, 'tis done. I bid you good day, brother, and ask Our Lord's blessings upon you.'

'Blessings? Huh! It would be of more use if He sent me a miraculous pasty once in a while, or just emptied the piss pot occasionally. That's not too much to ask, is it? If He's not too busy saving souls?'

The Foxley Place in Paternoster Row

I decided not to tell of my unintended visit to Jude. After all, it had been agreed that we should avoid family and friends until the threat of contagion passed. In the meanwhile, I prayed I had not done the very thing I dreaded, endangering Jude. 'Twas of much concern to me also that, in this time of his sudden need, we were constrained by our own situation, the responsibilities resulting and, therefore, were afeared to aid him as we should.

I was pondering upon these matters as I entered the shop with Gawain at heel. (By the by, I had contented him with the purchase of cheese when I bought the food for Jude.) Despite it being Saturday when 'twas the custom to cease work and close the shop at midday, Meg was serving a customer, wrapping a cheap primer and a more expensive volume of *Piers Plowman* in a square of linen and accepting the coin, keeping at arm's length from the well-clad woman in a fur-trimmed kirtle. We each bade a courteous farewell to her as she departed, looking well pleased with her purchases.

'She's also bought a ream of fine paper and a box of pens for her husband's counting-house,' Meg explained. 'She'll send a servant to collect those later. I think you did right, master, not to close early since we need the coin.'

'Aye, and you have done well, lass, but what of Kate? Is this not her task for the afternoon?'

'Aye, but she said she was in the midst of some detailed work and asked would I serve here that she might finish it. I hope I did right, master?' she added, seeing my frown of puzzlement. 'They all decided to work this afternoon as they cannot go out and about. Ralf is yet chagrined that he and Adam can't go visit the menagerie at the Tower.'

'It cannot be helped, Meg, as you well know and 'twas a kindness, indeed, on your part, taking on Kate's task.' I spoke true but, rack my brain as I might, I could not think what piece of such detail concerned Kate. The book on which she had worked for her father was in Adam's hands now and her allotted task this morning had been to stitch a stack of pamphlets for Ralf. I knew this to be a tedious occupation but felt she would benefit from the practice, it being some weeks since she had last done stitching, apart from darning the children's hose with Rose.

Boots removed and sooty garments exchanged for clean, I went to the workshop. Two scented candles burned there, as was now our custom. Kate was at her desk, so engrossed in her work that she did not look up as I entered in order to greet me as others did. She kept her eyes downcast upon her desk, her unruly curls escaping her coif, as they ever did, concealing her face and whatever it was that occupied all her attention. Such diligence was to be commended and I felt obliged to follow my apprentice's fine example.

Mayhap, an hour passed without my noticing but, God be praised, the Nativity miniature for St Luke's Gospel was complete at last, every detail delineated and painted to my satisfaction. I set the page aside to dry and took up the title page for St John's Gospel upon which a deal of work had yet to be done. But inspiration was with me and the batch of fine kermes pigment I had prepared for the shadows of the angel's gown in the Nativity was but half-used. Mixed with a ground of white lead, it made the perfect hue for the wild rosebuds in the garland border of this next title page. I set to, doing my utmost to paint the perfect flowers, petal by petal, in imitation of Almighty God's creations.

'Master Seb.'

'Aye?' I looked up from my work to find Hugh standing by my desk like a scholar expecting chastisement. 'What is it, Hugh?' I dipped my brush.

''Tis Kate, master,' he whispered. 'I fear she's not well.'

Oh, Sweet Lord Jesu. Was the worst befallen? Brush abandoned, unwashed, I said naught but went to the lass, easing her upright that I might see her face.

'I'm so very sorry,' she murmured. Tears or sweat or, mayhap, a mingling of both, ran down her flushed cheeks. She looked at me, her eyes deep, dark wells of misery.

'You have done naught for which to apologise, lass, 'tis no fault of yours. Fear not, Kate, all will be well,' I assured her even as my heart plunged into my belly to lodge there as a leaden lump. 'Fetch Mistress Rose,' I told Hugh as I held the lass against me, feeling her heat through her clothes and mine. 'May Our Lord Saviour and St Roche protect us all,' I prayed.

Rose and Hugh took Kate to her bed. In the workshop, we sat: Adam, Ralf, Simon and I, each alone as an island in a sea of dismal thoughts.

'Is it…?' Adam broke the silence at last.

'I cannot tell,' I said. 'She has a fever for certain but…'

'It may be…' Ralf added his piece to our conversation of unfinished sentences.

Simon began weeping and went into Adam's arms.

How strange it seemed that beyond this room I could hear children laughing, folk calling out greetings, jesting, one with another, whilst here we sat, of a sudden incapable of doing aught but await our doom.

Then it came to me: the laughter was Dickon's and Mundy's; the greetings Meg's. How joyous were they in their unknowing but I must go to them and turn their bright day the colour of darkness.

The household was subdued indeed—barely a word was spoken.

Meg and Nessie prepared supper but it went nigh untouched. Even Adam gave up after a few mouthfuls, having not the heart for eating. Rose and Hugh did not so much as sit at the board but trudged up and down the stair with this and that: anything that might aid Kate's comfort.

I said grace in thanks for the meal but gave more attention to adding a lengthy prayer, beseeching her swift recovery and our continued health. We made certain to dust off the amulets and wear them conspicuously and our evening doses of the herbal sovereign remedy were swallowed without complaint, even by young Nick. The youngsters seemed to comprehend somewhat the dire solemnity that had descended upon us and the sweet pastilles to follow cheered them little.

The decision was made that Adam and his sons should stay here forwhy, if they too did sicken, all could be cared for 'neath the one roof.

Meg put the young ones to bed in the nursery, all but Julia fractious and fretting—she not yet of an age to be downcast for long.

Adam sat rehearsing the lengthy list of lawyers, secretaries and clerks he might have infected at Guildhall, bemoaning some but declaring that others rightly deserved it.

I could have done likewise but Jude lay heaviest upon my conscience. If only Gawain had not gone to his door... My brother had troubles enough and would he send word—if indeed he was able—if he fell ill? The thought of him lying alone with none to succour him or give comfort... or summon a priest, if the worst befell, was unbearable to me, yet another visit might only serve to do harm, if 'twas not done already.

'The sweet Christ Jesu be thanked that we need not open the

shop upon the morrow,' I said, 'It being the Lord's Day.'

No one made comment. The silence hung like a pall.

Each time Rose came down the stair for more cold water, fresh clouts or whatever was required, we all looked to her, expectant, fearful that she might pronounce the dread word, the sentence of death upon us, but she did not. And thus, the eve dragged by, slower than a martyr's funeral cortege.

Rose and Hugh watched at Kate's bedside throughout the long hours of the night. None of us retired to our beds. There seemed no point in lying awake, alone with our fears. If our days were numbered, we may as well spend them in company with those we loved who shared our anxieties for what the morrow might bring.

At long last, young Simon fell to sleeping around the time that the bell of St Martin-le-Grand rang to summon the brothers there to Matins and Lauds in the small hours. The lad lay with his head resting upon his folded arms at the board. Ralf did likewise, the ageing journeyman's snores a rhythmic, rumbling backdrop to my unquiet thoughts. Adam leaned back against the wall, eyes closed, but I knew he was not asleep forwhy, every now and then, one eye would open to look to Simon's slumbering form, that all was well with the lad. Meg sat upon a stool by the dying hearth, as did Nessie, whose head rested against Meg's shoulder. When Nessie whimpered in her sleep, Meg would pat her and shush her in her bad dreams.

And thus we passed the night.

Chapter 9

Sunday, the twenty-fourth day of June, the Feast Day of St John the Baptist
The Foxley Place, Paternoster Row

SINCE WE did not attend St Michael's for Mass, still determined not to afflict our fellow parishioners with any contagion, I made much of our household prayers afore we should eat. I begged Our Lord Christ in His mercy to see Kate improve this day and to keep the rest of us in good health. Especially, I beseeched Him to give us strength, naming no names but knowing He would understand that I was asking more particularly on behalf of Rose and Hugh, both worn and weary, to be aided in their exhaustive care of the lass. In truth, I feared that even if they did not take the sickness upon themselves, they might fall ill of such an excess of toil and lack of rest. I had ne'er seen my Rose looking so pale and wan.

No matter that it was the Lord's Day, beyond our house, Paternoster Row and, indeed, the rest of the city was full of folk hurrying about the streets, preparing to celebrate Midsummer and the Feast Day of St John the Baptist. Despite it being one of the Quarter Days when rents come due and debts must be paid, far more attention was given to the building of the bonfires on street corners, in readiness for the evening. The largest fire would burn at Smithfield with torchlit processions through the streets to the open ground, lighting the smaller fires as they went.

'Twas ever an eve of hazard, requiring watchfulness on the

part of all the constables and beadles, for fear of an unattended fire spreading to thatched buildings but, for all that, none in authority dared to suggest the celebrations should be prevented. In the past, riots had ensued following such efforts to forbid the bonfires, resulting in worse and less predictable damage across the city. All the same, Thaddeus Turner would likely have a busy night.

Meanwhile, there were merry sports to pursue at Smithfield: archery contests, horse racing, bowling at skittles to win a piglet, Moorish dancing, music, acrobats and fire-eaters. Most importantly, the city's Guilds and Companies would perform the series of Mystery Plays throughout the day, relating the Bible Story from Genesis to the Last Judgement. The Guild of Stationers would re-enact the Sermon on the Mount. He who played Our Lord Jesu would read aloud the lengthy list of the Beatitudes from a gilded vellum scroll nigh unto a hundred years in age and as exquisite as ever—a testament to the skills of an unnamed scribe of long ago.

Adam and I were allotted parts, he being one of 'the crowd' who harkened to the sermon and I the disciple, St Bartholomew. I doubted we would be much missed and sent word, by means of a passing urchin, to Warden Master Richard Collop with our apologies, citing 'unforeseen circumstances' as the reason for our absence. I did not wish to say more for the present, praying that would be all the guild should ever require to know.

But, for the folk at the Sign of the Fox, the joys of St John's Day were far distant. Our shop stood shuttered as sleep-heavy eyes, our doors barred. Yesterday's bread and ale and the remains of last eve's cold supper would have to serve for our celebration feast. Instead, to while away the hours—may the Lord God forgive me—I spent a few hours at my desk, working upon the title page for St John's Gospel. I expected to have difficulty directing my mind to such a task but, strangely, it seemed my thoughts were eager for some other matter to occupy them and the painting progressed apace.

With none to interrupt me, the page was completed, the garland of wild flowers, roses, poppies, meadowsweet and cornflowers encircled the title: 'Here beginneth the Gospel of Saint John the Evangelist', the letters inscribed in golden yellow orpiment, shadowed with black, so they appeared to stand out from the page. Orpiment be a poisonous pigment, as I well knew, but what did that matter now, when the fateful Sword of Damocles might fall upon us at any moment?

By the time Adam came to find me out, I had collated the fourth Gospel, matching up catchphrases so the pages were correctly ordered and ready for stitching. 'Twas a job well done and I felt pleased with my accomplishments but, with it completed, I was snatched back to our unhappy reality.

'It's Sunday, Seb; a day of rest, for pity's sake,' Adam said. 'Come, join us in the garden. Who knows how many more fine days we'll have… afore it rains, I mean, not…' He left the sentence unfinished.

'Aye, I shall come. Is the gate yet firmly tied?' Yesterday, despite all, I had the forethought of tying shut the gate with the broken latch. It must serve for now to prevent the children—Nick in particular—from running out into the street.

'I fixed it properly earlier.'

'Upon a Sunday?' I grinned at him wearily and he grinned back.

'Aye, well, needs must. Can't have Nick getting lost among the crowds today. We'd never find the lad.'

As Adam and I were about to leave the workshop, Hugh, tired and dishevelled, came downstairs. For him and Rose, Kate was their sole concern. He looked gaunt and hollow-eyed and I feared he was ailing likewise.

'Nay, Master Seb, I am well enough… or I will be when my dearest Kate recovers. Mistress Rose told me to take a turn around the garden and breathe in the sweet fresh airs, else I would not leave her bedside.'

'How does she fare?' I asked, wary of the lad's reply.

'Mistress Rose says she's doing as well as we can expect. Likely, the fever will run its course in three or four days...'

'"Tis just a summer fever then, such as Dickon and Mundy suffered back in May? Or an ague, mayhap?'

'I pray so, master, I truly do with all my heart.'

I saw then how exhausted Hugh was, swaying on his feet, his hand steadying him against the door jamb.

'Sit at your desk, lad, not to work but lest you fall down. I shall fetch you some ale and bread from the kitchen. And what of Rose? She must be in need of rest also.'

By the time I had collected bread, a wedge of cheese, hard-boiled eggs and ale and returned to the workshop, Adam signed to me, his finger pressed to his lips and nodded towards Hugh. The lad was sound asleep at his desk, so I left the food and drink for him.

Young Nick came running from the garden with Dickon a few steps behind.

'Trumpets, Papa!' he cried as he collided with Adam's desk, dislodging a sheaf of collated pages which slid to the floor, all out of order. 'I want to go see. Now!'

'Hush, lad,' Adam grabbed the youngster. 'Hugh is sleeping and look at what you've done! What've I told you about running in the workshop, Nick? Get out, unless you want another beating, you clumsy pup.'

Dickon pulled at my sleeve, dancing with excitement. The youngsters had sharp ears, indeed, for I had to listen hard to make out the fanfares of the City Waits which led the procession as it wound its way from Aldgate in the east to Newgate in the west and thence, without the city walls to Smithfield.

'Me, too. Gawain likes trumpets. Please, Papa.'

'Aye, I know, my little one.' What could I say to quell their eagerness and lessen the disappointment? We might have watched the procession from our bedchamber window but, unfortunately, the usual route from Cheapside was along Bladder Street and the Shambles which afforded wider passage for the pageant wagons, rather than Paternoster Row which required a tight turn at the end into Dean's Lane. Then I had a thought… 'When the trumpets come near, we shall all be in the back garden and you shall climb the apple tree—just this once, mind—and, mayhap, you will see the procession as it enters the Shambles.' In truth, 'twould be a brief and obscured view but better than naught.

'Now?'

'Nay, Dickon, not yet. The procession moves slow as a snail as the guilds perform their plays in Aldgate Street, at the Standard in Cornhill and again by the Cheap Cross. The Genesis Pageant, the first play, will likely pass by our garden close unto dinner time.'

'Can we see the plays?' Nick wanted to know.

'I fear not. The last performance afore Smithfield will be at the Grey Friars—too far for us to see the actions but you will likely be able to hear the music.'

'I want to see them,' Nick demanded, stamping his foot and turning crimson of face.

'Well, you can't and that's an end to it,' Adam told him, 'Now cease your tantrum.'

'Unless…' I said, 'Suppose your father and I put on a pageant especially for you? What say you, Adam? We could cobble some story together and all play a part, could we not? Simon and Ralf, Meg and Nessie and the little ones can join in.'

'Not Mundy or Julia; they're too small,' Nick said. 'But me and Dickon can, can't we, Papa?'

'We'll see,' Adam said, sounding dubious, 'But only if you behave yourself. Understand?'

Nick nodded solemnly.

'We'll behave sooo good. Won't we, Dickon?'

Aye, I thought, and if that truly came to pass upon Nick's part, all our efforts would be well worthwhile.

After a dinner of eggs—our hens now providing much of our sustenance—with herbs and flat breads and a meagre few mouthfuls of ale as we did our best to stretch what remained in the barrel, we prepared for our Mystery Play.

In truth, 'twas a motley mix of various Mummers' Plays, as well as the more lavish performances put on by the guilds. Ralf, garbed in a white sheet and assisted to a perch upon the pigsty wall, had the part of God Almighty, thundering out stage directions as he saw fit:

'Do this; go there; now Simon—sorry, St George—you fight the dragon!'

Adam was the dragon with a blanket over his head, tied about the neck with a red ribbon supplied by Meg to represent his fiery breath. And he made such a fearful roaring and commotion that the hens scattered, clucking, to hide amongst the roses, fearing a fox come upon them.

Simon played St George, armed with a pot-lid buckler and a pea-stick sword. Dickon, similarly armed, was the knight's trusty squire, mounted upon his precious hobby horse and insisting he be accompanied by his fine dragon-scenting dog, Gawain. Attempting to keep his horse in check without dropping both sword and buckler proved no easy matter and, at length, the pot-lid had to be abandoned.

Of course, there be no such thing as a surfeit of gallant heroes so Nick, resplendent in a green kerchief and carrying a curved stick with string tied to each end, was Robin Hood. We were not so foolish as to furnish him with anything that might serve as an arrow else eyes were too likely to be put out. Little Mundy trotted behind his brother as the sole Merry Man, though he preferred collecting chicken feathers and finding beetles amidst the cabbages to righting the wrongs of poor folk.

Meg, Nessie and Julia were the king's beautiful daughters, each in turn captured by Adam's dragon and requiring to be rescued by the heroes. The play, such as it was, took an original turn here for in seizing Princess Julia, the dragon swung her up high and round and round. Chuckling and squealing in delight, the youngest of our fair maidens refused to be rescued, returning to her captor repeatedly, arms raised, wanting to be swung high again.

For myself, I played multiple parts. As God's messenger and narrator of the tale, the Angel Gabriel, I fluttered napkins in each hand to represent wings and wore a circlet of golden honeysuckle, fashioned by Meg, for my halo. It served well enough for my kingly crown also as I pleaded with both St George and Robin Hood to rescue my daughters. I was also the physician, summoned to administer a reviving strawberry to the casualties of battle, although Nick refused such a remedy— not surprising after what had happened yesterday following his sojourn in Cheapside.

The hours passed in merriment in the garden. At last, Dickon and Mundy tired of the play and sat in the shade of the old apple tree, counting twigs and straws, laying them out in lines and patterns until Mundy fell asleep. Adam shed his hot costume and deferred abducting maidens until another time, much to Julia's grave disappointment. I assisted Ralf down from his 'heavenly' seat on the pigsty wall from whence, at one time, laughing so heartily, he had nigh toppled into the pit of pig dung. Only Nick determined to continue the play, racing around the garden, swiping at bushes with his stick which had previously served for a bow.

'For the love of Our Lady, Nick, will you cease your noise and be still?' Adam pleaded. 'Be quiet and Uncle Ralf will tell you a tale of Norfolk folk.'

'I will?' the old man queried, quirking as eyebrow.

'Aye, tell us about the time you visited Norwich Castle… with the one-eyed merchant… That's a merry story but keep it decent and clean for the lads and for Seb's innocent ears, of course.'

We sat upon the small patch of grass, taking our ease, lulled by the sound of Ralf's Norfolk burr, the humming of bees and the heady scent of lavender and mint, roses and honeysuckle, whilst Meg and Nessie argued half-heartedly about who should fetch the elderflower cordial.

'Seb! Seb!' I turned to see Rose hastening down the path from the kitchen.

'What be amiss?' I leapt to my feet. 'Is it Kate?'

'Did none of you hear someone banging at the street door? Sweet Lord Jesu but you must all be stone deaf.' She wiped her damp face upon her apron hem. 'I told him to wait in the shop, Seb, thinking that to be safest. I know not what opinion he must have of me, all amiss and bedraggled as I am, that I had to unbar the door to him wearing a grubby apron, sleeves unlaced, cap askew and without offering him refreshment.'

'Did he give a name?'

'Who?'

'Our visitor.'

'Oh, aye. William, er, Caxton. From Westminster, he said.'

'Ah. *Mea culpa*. I promised to report my findings to him yesterday at the Fighting Cock but forgot it utterly.'

'Is this about the fire he suffered?'

'I expect so. I shall tell him what little I discovered, excuse our lack of hospitality and send him on his way. I be sorry, lass, that you were disturbed from your ministering at the sickbed. How does Kate fare?'

'She's sleeping now but all your noise out here greatly unsettled her. She needs quiet, Seb, not shrieking and shouting.'

'Forgive us. I never thought. We wanted to recompense the little ones in that they could not see the parade so we devised an interlude, a jape was all.'

Rose gave a tired smile.

'Seb, go attend Master Caxton before his patience runs out.'

I straightened my attire, discarding my 'angel's wings' in the kitchen and went through to the shop. With the shutters closed, the place was in gloom so I opened the street door a few inches to give us light.

'I crave pardon, Master Caxton, for my failing to come to you yesterday and the lack of a proper Christian welcome in my house. If you can forgive us…'

'I suppose St John's Day takes precedence. I see you've been celebrating.' He looked and gestured to my head.

I felt for my cap to make proper greeting and discovered the wreath of honeysuckle.

'My undeserved halo,' I said as I removed it. 'I must explain unto you, master, that we have a case of summer fever in the house and are keeping to ourselves out of courtesy to others. We be somewhat in disarray. 'Tis the reason I forgot to come to you and why I have not invited you to enter into the parlour nor offered ale. In truth, what little ale we have remaining be upon the verge of turning sour in the heat and we wish to avoid the tavern to fetch more. Also, my goodwife—who opened the door to you—has not time to bake wafers whilst attending to my ailing apprentice.'

'A summer fever? Are you sure that's all it is, what with so much caution?'

'For certain, but even so, 'tis best to have a care.' I crossed my fingers behind my back.

'Aye, I suppose.' Caxton stroked his lush beard. 'So, since I can't expect a drink, if you'd make your report brief, I'd appreciate it.'

'I can oblige upon that score for certain. All I discovered—or, in truth, my dog discovered—was that a trail led betwixt your house and Ludgate. I suspect the culprit ventured forth from Ludgate carrying the cheese… you must understand that my dog has such a love of the stuff, he would likely follow its scent to the end of the earth, if he were able but, once within the city, he lost the trail, it being overwhelmed by so many other smells.'

'So why couldn't the trail have been left by the villain returning to London after committing the crime? Aye, and bringing my book and coin with him.'

'I suppose 'tis possible, if he followed the exact same path which went through fields and over a stile, even crossing the Fleet Ditch, but since the cheese remained at your house to become a cinder and did not return with him... the dog can recognise the scent of cheese but not of a stranger he has never met. Even so, I think the perpetrator most likely came from London and be a man of some height, forwhy the window whereby he gained entry to your house was high up.'

'Unless he found something to climb on.'

'Mayhap, though I found no sign that he did so.'

'And thus we have it, Master Foxley: our villain is a tall, cheese-eating Londoner! That narrows the possibilities so considerably I imagine his apprehension could happen within the hour and my properties regained upon the morrow at the latest. In which case, I'll bid you good day.'

And, with a touch to his cap, William Caxton departed, much aggrieved at my lack of progress in solving his mystery.

As I watched the bearded printer hobbling away along Paternoster Row towards Amen Lane, the street was now devoid of folk—a thing rarely known—all gone to the festivities, no doubt. Yet there was Old Symkyn across the street at his preferred perch by the gate into St Paul's Precinct, the begging bowl beside his stool. It looked to have few coins within this day and I was, of a sudden, concerned for his not having had a decent dinner this day.

'Be you well, Symkyn?' I called out from my doorstep, not wanting to go too close to my friend.

'Well enough, Master Seb, I thank you. And you and yours? Are you all in good health? I wonder that you're not enjoying the day at Smithfield.'

'Not this year, I fear, forwhy we have a case of fever in the house and would not want to spread it abroad.'

'Who is sick?'

'Young Kate only, at present, and we pray it remains thus.'

'Aye, indeed, and I'll add my prayers to yours, master.'

I was glad of his kind offer forwhy a poor man's prayers be the more worthy in the eyes—or ears—of Almighty God. Seeing but a meagre few farthings in his bowl, I unlatched my purse, stood in the midst of the empty street, as near as I dared, and tossed in a couple of groats.

'No need to pay for my prayers; you shall have them for nothing as my good friend. You do more than enough for me, Master Seb, seeing to it that I ne'er go hungry.'

Since 'twas our custom to have Symkyn share our dinner upon the Lord's Day, along with family and friends, he and they had all had been disappointed on this occasion and must have fended for themselves without the benefits and pleasures of the cookery skills of Rose and Meg.

'I apologise that 'tis not the case this day: no hearty meal for any of us, what with the pantry and buttery unreplenished and none to be welcomed at our board for fear of the fever. Thus, the coin be to buy you a goodly supper, Symkyn. Mayhap, Our Lord Jesu willing, Sunday next will see matters set aright once more. In the meanwhile, I beseech God's blessings upon you and may He keep you from harm, my dear friend.' With which prayer I returned withindoors.

Later, as we harkened to the distant sounds of revelry from Smithfield carried upon the warm summer airs, the earlier noise of knocking upon our street door was repeated, though with far more gentle courtesy than Master Caxton's thunderous thumping.

I opened the door, standing well back from the threshold, but no one stood there. Across the way, beside Old Symkyn, I espied our loving friend, Peronelle Hepton, her little daughter, Alice, in her arms. Pen waved and gestured to our front step, pointing to a covered basket.

'We're all praying for you and yours, Master Seb, and for Kate especially,' she called out afore turning away and hastening toward Cheapside.

I shouted my thanks but knew not if she heard. The basket proved heavy. I wondered that she had managed to carry both it and her child but then recalled that the little lass could toddle a few yards these days.

In the kitchen, I set our unwarranted benevolence on the board and removed the cloth covering. I lifted out a flagon of ale; a flask of primrose wine, neatly labelled; fresh-baked bread; a dozen small pasties, still warm; a covered platter of bacon collops sprinkled with chopped herbs and pepper, ready for the pan; a pot of soft cheese; a linen bag, stained red, containing a dish of raspberries; a little jug of cream and a bunch of fresh, feathery dill. This last did not grow so well in our garden this season but, since 'tis a sure remedy for belly ache, Pen must believe it would prove useful in a house of sickness. Her generosity summoned tears to my eyes as I called to the others to witness this act of great kindness.

'Tis to be acknowledged that tidings can outrun a king's messenger through London's streets, even when they seem empty of folk to convey the words. Naught remains a secret for long in this city and now that Symkyn knew of it all would hear of our misfortune. In truth, I hoped Jude learnt of it and did not struggle to our place in hope of a welcome he would not receive. If he should come, I wondered what he might say if I told him to go or, at best, threw him a coin to purchase a dinner or supper elsewhere.

We ate a fine supper of chicken and mushroom pasties, raspberries and cream—saving the bacon collops to break our fast upon the morrow—and drank sparingly of the ale and but a sip each of the wine. Unlike the rest of London, celebrating the feast of the Baptist, we at least would not suffer thick heads come the morn but were all of us heartened to learn that Kate seemed somewhat improved and no tokens of pestilence had appeared thus far.

Monday, the twenty-fifth day of June

After a good breakfast of eggs from our chickens and Peronelle's generosity of bacon collops, we each settled to our work for the day. I examined Lady Howard's sorry-looking Psalter book. It appeared to be nigh a century in age and, to judge by its condition, had been in use daily over all that time. 'Twas of fine vellum, the ink as bold as the day it was first penned but the stitchery had failed utterly. I must disassemble the gatherings and begin anew, re-stitching them afore making a sturdy new spine betwixt the ancient fraying covers. New leather was required for it and we had naught of that deep dragon's blood hue. Thus, the cover must await repair until we were released from our self-imposed confinement and I might go purchase some suitable leather from Giles Honeywell at his stall in St Paul's nave.

Dinner consisted of the remaining bread, the soft cheese and yet more eggs—'twas as well that our hens be fine layers through the summer—with a vegetable pottage. Meg and Nessie had little ado to prepare our meal, save peeling and chopping a few onions and chives, shucking fresh peas from the garden plot and washing my favoured alexanders, the last of the season, sadly.

After our brief meal, Rose took a piece of sewing upstairs to stitch whilst keeping vigil at Kate's bedside. Likewise, Hugh took a book to read from amongst our exemplars. Adam, Simon and Ralf returned to the workshop whilst Meg shooed the little ones out into the sunlit garden.

Thinking 'twould be wise not to leave them unwatched at their merry play, I did not return with the others to my desk. Yesterday, in the midst of our Mummers' Play, I had espied a scene in the garden which might suffice as a goodly miniature or decoration for a margin. I had my sketching board upon my knee as I sat with my back against the pigsty wall, watching a pair of redbreasts feeding their brood of speckled chicks lined along a branch like household servants awaiting instruction.

Except that they were giving the command with gaping beaks and fluttering wings, constantly demanding food. The diligent parents brought a continuous round of caterpillars, flies and other pests, doing our vegetables a fine service in removing so many. I drew the little family in painstaking detail. Fluttering feathers be a challenge to depict with charcoal and chalks upon paper but a little judicious smudging with my finger produced the blurring effect of beating wings and I was pleased with it. I wondered how the like might be produced in paint.

I then turned my attention—and charcoal—to the apple tree where green fruits the size of hazelnuts were already apparent, waiting to swell and ripen in the weeks to come. It occurred to me then—I know not why—that this would come to pass whether or not we would all be here to witness it. I suppose Nature continues her seasonal round regardless of man.

And then the side gate from our kitchen yard banged open, causing me to startle and drop my charcoal in the grass.

Jude hobbled in, leaning more heavily than usual upon his staff, his hair plastered across his brow with sweat and an expression of such ill-temper I was already fearing the consequences of this unfortunate visit.

'Ah, Jude…' I began.

'Don't you give me any of your "good day" bloody nonsense because it isn't. Where's the ale jug?' He slung a small bundle off his shoulder and dropped it beside a lavender bush. 'I'm parched.'

'Er, we have very little, I fear. Brother, I must warn you, there be fever in the house and I would not want you to…'

'Fever? What do I care about that? One more bloody trouble to add to my burden, it'll hardly notice. What's for dinner?'

'You be too tardy for that. We ate pottage, eggs, a little bread and cheese…'

'Call that a Sunday dinner?'

'Jude, 'tis Monday,' I said but he seemed not to hear. 'And closer to suppertime.'

'Gutter rats eat better. What's amiss with you all, eh?' His frown grew darker. 'It's not Rose who's sick, is it?' Was that a note of sincere concern for the woman he was once supposed to wed?

'Nay, not Rose. 'Tis young Kate, though Rose be nursing the lass constantly.'

'Good because my best hose are in that bundle and in need of mending.'

'Eleanor has not returned then?'

'She couldn't use a bloody needle to stitch a cabbage sack, never mind fine woollen hose, the useless bitch. Where's my ale? You've forgotten your manners, little brother. Come on, play the host, as you should instead of sitting about, doing naught… If it is a bloody Monday, as you say, shouldn't you be working?'

'I was working.'

'A bit of sketching? You call that work?'

I nigh spoke my mind at that. When all be said and done, when had my brother last done a day's labour? But I would refrain from provoking an argument.

'Aye, you had best come within doors, if you care not about the fever,' I said with a sigh, collecting up my drawing stuff and calling to the little ones. 'We have some primrose wine, if that will suit you?'

'Primrose wine? What sort of drink is that for a man? Sounds more suitable for bloody convent nuns and village idiots.'

''Tis stronger than you might think. Adam and I drank some of it last eve and it seemed quite potent.'

'No doubt it did to a pair of lily-livered noddies like you two but I may as well give you my opinion on it—a man's opinion, that is.'

As we entered the kitchen, Meg was holding a basket, smiling broadly:

'Look, Master Seb, another gift left upon our doorstep. I know not who… they were gone ere I opened the door to their knocking.

''Tis not from Peronelle this time,' I said, seeing a frayed hem to the cloth which covered it. 'Pen be neatness personified in

146

all things.'

'Never mind that,' Jude said, using his staff to bar my way. 'What's in it? A decent dinner, if there's any justice in this miserable bloody world.' He snatched away the cloth to reveal a jumble of items. Fresh peas in their fat green pods were strewn within, all haphazard, about a cracked platter of fat slices of smoked ham. A wedge of hard cheese, a pot of cherry and quince curd, a folded napkin of wafers and, much to Jude's obvious pleasure, a flagon of ale completed this anonymous offering of kindness.

Anonymous, maybe, but the moment I saw the wafers and attempted to break one, I knew the donor. Our friend, Beatrice Thatcher, be infamous for her teeth-shattering wafers. Although a fine spinster of silk, she had little renown in other housewifely skills but her man, Harry, and their ever-increasing brood of children seemed content enough. We were grateful for such Christian generosity, knowing the Thatchers had few pennies to spare.

'Not much ham here,' Jude complained, 'Not enough for everyone but Kate won't need any, nor your offspring, though I suppose your damned cousin'll expect a share.'

'*Our* cousin deserves the same as anyone else. He works hard indeed. Do not begrudge him his share.'

'He's a bloody pinch-penny scoundrel.'

'You know not the half of Adam's labours which keep this business thriving. Without him, it may have foundered long ago. He puts bread upon our board as much as I do—more so, in truth. But for his work, there would be insufficient to spare to feed you for charity's sake.' The moment the words left my tongue, I regretted them.

'Charity's sake! Is that all I am to you? Am I, your own brother... to be cast aside in favour of a distant kinsman of doubtful lineage?'

'Adam be our nephew by blood so hardly a distant kinsman and his lineage stands beyond question.'

'So you and he claim. I've not seen any bloody proof of it. I've never met this mysterious so-called elder brother of ours. His mother was probably a tavern whore, if he even exists.'

'Thomas Armitage was born to our father's first wife a score or more of years afore he wed our mother.'

'A previous wife of whom he never spoke. I wonder why. Could it be because she never was?'

'Jude, our father was old when we were born. Our mother young, as he described. Do you truly believe he ne'er had a wife before her, in his days of youth? Why would he not?'

'Then why would he not mention her, pay for prayers to be said for her soul as he did for our mother's, eh?'

Meg rapped the board with a ladle.

'Shall I serve the food as an early supper, masters, or do we wait upon your ending of this argument? Nessie, go call the others to come wash their hands.'

As everyone took their places at the board, apart from a first exchange of fearsome scowls, Jude and Adam ignored each other's presence, mercifully, until Adam poured out Beatrice's ale—of tavern quality, far better than her wafers—and failed to fill my brother's cup quite as full as his own by a mere hair's breadth. A tirade of insults and venomous name-calling ensued. I did my best to quiet the pair, reminding them that young ears were listening when Meg made use of the ladle once more, clouting both men upon the arm.

'Still your tongues! You're worse than squabbling novices. Street urchins have more courteous speech than you. Can you not give a thought to the sick lass above stair?' Meg's brave outburst met with greater success than my objections had, mayhap forwhy 'twas utterly unexpected from one so recently escaped from a convent.

After that, we ate in silence for a while, including the rightfully admonished offenders against peace and etiquette.

'Jude,' I said as we shared the last of the cheese whilst the little ones spooned up the cherry and quince curd, making a mess as

148

usual—apart from Julia, neat as ever, despite being the youngest. 'Jude, I have had a thought during recent sleepless nights…'

'God help us all: another one? That always means trouble.'

'Nay, not upon this occasion but rather it may be of help to you. I hardly dare mention his name but, I pray you, hear me out, brother: it concerns Master Caxton's printing press —'

'Don't talk to me of that bloody wretch… my competitor in trade. Wherever the bastard is, I hope he rots.'

'He bides at the Fighting Cock which, no doubt, you frequented during your time living at Westminster. And, if you but listen this once, Jude, this be my suggestion: since you have a press standing unused and his has been reduced to cinders, as I have seen with my own eyes…'

'It's not unused! I…'

'Why do you not offer the use of yours to Master Caxton? Either let him pay you a rent on it or share the profits made from production? I be certain you could come to an agreement satisfactory to both parties and, all the while, you would be able to observe the processes of printing and learn so much from Caxton's previous experience. Might that be a plan to aid you, Jude, temporarily, of course?'

'Of course it bloody wouldn't. I refuse to let that devil anywhere near my press. Why should I aid the scoundrel who would deny me a living, if he could? You're the worst kind of fool, little brother: one who believes he's doing good. Well, you're not! Don't you dare mention that man to me again and keep your idiot's thoughts to yourself.'

'I crave pardon then. I hoped such a plan might be of benefit to you.'

'It won't. Do something useful instead and pour me some more ale.'

Chapter 10

Tuesday, the twenty-sixth day of June
The Foxley Place

UPON TUESDAY morn, though I intended the shop to remain closed, we had another unexpected visitor right early: Sarra Shardlowe, Bess Chambers' niece. Her smile lit up the threshold.

'God give you good day, Sarra. I would invite you within but…'

Yet she was over the doorstep afore I could warn her, lugging a weighty basket wedged against her hip. I made to aid her with it but she shrugged me off.

'Aye, we know, Master Seb. When we heard how you were shutting yourselves away, we thought we knew the reason. Aunt Bess said you told her Sir Philip Allenby came to you and took sick so we made enquiries of our fellow apothecaries, to see how the man fared. Shall I take this to the kitchen?'

I nodded and led the way along the hall. Adam, Ralf, Simon and the youngsters were about to abandon a board yet arrayed with dirty dishes and empty cups after our breakfast of eggs and griddled bread but upon sight of our visitor, the menfolk tarried. Adam's eyes were as large as platters forwhy he had not met the beauteous Sarra until now.

'This be Sarra, Bess Chambers' niece of whom you have heard,' I said.

'What a delight and honour it is to welcome such loveliness to Paternoster Row,' Adam said. 'Welcome to our humble place made gladsome by your presence…'

'And the tidings I bring will be most welcome to you and yours, Master Seb,' Sarra continued, ignoring my cousin's over-effusive pleasantries as she put the basket on the floor. 'Sir Philip is quite recovered from his ague. It wasn't the pestilence after all, so you need not keep apart from others any longer.'

'God be praised!' I groped for a stool, my knees gone weak with relief. 'Be you certain? What of the great token upon his neck? I saw it, as did Rose.'

'Aye. He has suffered with a goitre these five years past, so we learned. It has naught to do with his fever and is in no way contagious.'

'That's marvellous news,' my cousin put in, determined to have a part in the conversation.

'Merciful Heaven,' I said. 'And because of it, we nigh shunned the poor man. In truth, we could not send him from our door fast enough. I shall write unto him, giving my apologies but, meanwhile, we should celebrate our release from imprisonment.'

'Then 'tis as well that Aunt Bess has sent you a jug full of her fresh brewed ale, flavoured with honey from our hives and meadowsweet to give you all strength and easement for whoever has fallen sick among you.'

'Let me aid you with that.' Adam elbowed Ralf aside to take the stoppered jug that Sarra lifted out of the basket. 'By the by, I'm Adam Armitage, Seb's kinsman. To all intents and purposes, I run this place, well, practically.' He removed the greased stopper and sniffed the jug's contents appreciatively. 'Aye, this'll put us all to rights. Line up the cups, Simon, and a clean one for our esteemed visitor. Sit you down, Sarra.' He set a stool for her.

She accepted the seat even as she gave my cousin an arched look but continued to speak to me:

'We did not know who was ill or what else might be needful so I brought you these small loaves spiced with cinnamon, fennel and anise with a pot of thyme butter…' She put the items on

151

the crowded board.

'Nessie, I pray you remove the breakfast stuff,' I said, seeing her standing idle by the hearth, picking her nose. 'And cease that disgusting habit.'

She huffed and scowled and obeyed with ill grace. Without Rose or Meg to command her, our maid was of less use than a broken quill pen.

'Meg told me to wait upon the water heating fer the wash tub outside. We're all be'ind with the week's washin'. Should've been done yesterday and it ain't my fault. It's Kate's fer layin' abed and everyone rushin' about, waitin' on her. It ain't fair, master.'

I paid her tirade no heed, watching as Sarra continued to produce treasures from the basket.

'...And a cooling calf's foot jelly of gooseberries and borage flowers, a feverfew tisane, cowslip wine to balance the melancholic humours and more rosehip cordial... the jelly and tisane be especially good for treating fevers.'

''Tis Kate, my young apprentice, who has the fever,' I explained. 'She became unwell upon Saturday last and we feared the worst, as you may suppose. Hugh, her betrothed— my journeyman—be beside himself with worry for her and he and Rose have hardly left the lass's bedside these three days. They are with her now and be that weary... as are we all from lack of sleep.'

'Then the wine and cordial will put you all in good heart.'

As Sarra straightened her back, having put the last item on the board, I saw her face crease of a sudden, a sharp wince as if in pain. She pressed her hand to her ribs for the briefest moment afore the accustomed smile returned to her lips as though naught was amiss. But, having seen this, I regarded the lass with a more discerning eye. As she brushed a lustrous lock of copper hair from her cheek, did I not observe a bruise beneath? 'Twas artfully concealed with a tinted powder of some kind but, even so, did not escape my artist's eye. Someone had recently mistreated this comely lass and I could not imagine that kindly

Bess Chambers might be to blame. Nay. Some other had hurt Sarra Shardlowe.

Rose came into the kitchen then, laden with fever-stained sheets for washing.

'Sweeting,' I said, hastening to unburden her, passing the mountain of stained linen to Nessie. 'Sarra has brought us glad tidings indeed: Sir Philip Allenby was suffering an ague. Kate does not have the pestilence but simply a summer fever, as you suspected.'

'Then I'm right glad of it.' Despite her words, Rose's voice was flat, toneless with exhaustion, and I realised that, whatever name belonged to Kate's ailment, the work involved in caring for her was no less.

'Here, drink this,' I said, passing her my cup of Bess's ale, ''Twill fortify you.'

'A night's sleep would serve me better,' she said but drank it all the same. 'Aye, that's a fine brewing.'

'Sarra brought it.' I gestured to our guest.

'Oh, forgive me,' my wife said, 'I didn't see you there… God give you good day, Sarra, and my thanks for the ale.'

'The cowslip wine may cheer you even better, Mistress Foxley.'

'Mm, maybe later. We have all this washing to do first before I can think of taking my ease with a cup of wine—excellent, as I'm certain it is. Thank your aunt for her great kindness, won't you? And your good self for bringing it… Oh, Seb… spare me your stool for a moment… I'm that wearisome…'

'Rose? You are not sickening, sweeting, are you?' I took her hand in mine as she sat in my place, leaning her elbow upon the board. Her skin felt cool enough but I also touched her forehead to be certain. It was dry and likewise cool.

'Don't fuss me, husband.' She batted my hand aside. 'Can a body not be worn out without you leaping to the worst conclusions? I am quite well, and before you ask, so is young Hugh, despite his being tired to the bone. You won't make the lad work this day, will you, Seb? He needs rest and sleep but the tidings about Sir Philip's ailment will bring him much relief.'

'Tell Hugh he may spend the whole day abed, if he feels it needful to do so. In truth, we be well in advance with all our work forwhy this time of isolation has seen us with little else to do. The Gospel Book for the Prioress of Dartford be complete at last, Alderman Verney's *The Arte and Play of Chess* awaits delivery, Hoccleve's epic poem, *The Regiment of Princes,* stands ready for sale as does a stack of little Primers and I be repairing Lady Howard's Psalter. We have not wasted our time these few days. It has been better to keep working than to brood upon our worst fears.'

'Which brings to mind the other reason for my coming,' Sarra said, once more delving into her basket and lifting out a volume of considerable size and age which she gave to me. Its cover was coming adrift from the damaged spine, its gilding long since worn away and the vellum pages stained, well-fingered and foxed. No wonder her basket weighed so heavy. 'Aunt Bess would have you repair it and then make another copy for me, if you would. She says she's willing to pay you a reasonable sum and knows it won't be cheap but the new copy can be upon paper with a simple binding. Only I shall use it, so no need for any expensive decoration either.'

With due care for the book's fragile condition, I leafed through a few pages.

'These diagrams will require a deal of labour to ensure they be correct,' I said, considering, 'Some be of great complexity, it seems to me... and Greek lettering in parts... and this looks to be the script of Araby or Hebrew, maybe? I have no knowledge of either.'

'But you can copy it, can't you? That's all we require.'

''Tis easier to copy a text if the scribe can read the words but, aye, as my brother always says: you can copy from a book by way of the eye to the hand without a mote of understanding, the words ne'er touching your mind. 'Tis not a method I like to employ but it can be done.' Then I turned to the title page, its top right-hand corner torn away, but sufficient remained for me to learn the name of the work: *The Ars Notoria*, 'The Notorious Art'. The title gave me pause. I had heard of it: its contents questionable, its morality suspect and its reproduction discouraged by the Stationers' Guild. For all I knew, 'twas likely condemned, if not forbidden, by the Church as well. In truth, I should not touch this devilish creation and yet my thirst for knowledge, my curiosity, was urging me on.

'It's to aid my studies. Aunt Bess says it has instructions telling how I may learn more quickly and remember far more upon a single reading and I have so much to learn of the apothecary's art.'

'Aye, I dare say you have. But give me leave to consider... the cost, that is. I shall come to Bishopsgate later with my offer or...'

'Or?'

'Or bring the book to return it, if it be beyond repair and impossible to copy.'

'Oh.' Sarra sounded disappointed, unsurprisingly, but Adam's face reflected his shock at my possible refusal of a contract. 'Twas a thing nigh unknown at the Sign of the Fox. But then he had not seen the title.

Jude's house, Ave Maria Alley

Jude was cursing his brother: Devil damn the interference of family in his affairs. The letter he'd finally written to that bastard Caxton the other day yet lay there before him, awaiting a means of delivery to the old printer staying at the Fighting Cock. At least Seb had inadvertently told him where the man was living, what with his house turned to ashes by that bloody idiot Jack, but what was the use now?

The letter set out terms by which Caxton might have use of the printing press looming there across the chamber, garnering cobwebs by the hour, but Jude couldn't possibly send it, not now. How could he when Seb would believe—quite wrongly—that *his* idea had been taken up? Insufferably arrogant as he was, he would never credit that Jude had the idea first without any prompting from *him*.

But, then again… suppose he did send the letter and Caxton accepted the offer? What with the way of the world, in Jude's experience leastwise, matters were sure to go as awry as humanly possible and then it would all be Seb's fault. He could take the blame, aye, and compensate both parties for whatever chaos resulted. Now that wasn't such a bad plan. Perhaps he should send the letter after all.

The Fighting Cock, Westminster

I had naught to add to the hasty report I had given to William Caxton two days previously but I thought it a matter of courtesy to visit him in his temporary refuge. At the least, I could reassure him that the case of fever in our household had not spread amongst us and the patient now seemed upon the mend. Also, I felt obliged to introduce my Gawain to the elderly printer since the creature had discovered most of what little evidence we possessed concerning the crime.

Accompanied by Gawain, I entered the taproom of the inn, where we had taken ale together and made our contract, squinting into the gloom, hoping to espy Master Caxton or his assistant. There was no sign of either man so I made enquiry of the plump serving wench. She fluttered her eyelashes at me, wiggled her hips and thrust forth her generous assets but could have spared herself the effort. I had no interest in such matters, having bed-sport aplenty at home if I felt thus inclined, though not of late, admittedly. But then who turns their thoughts in that wise when sickness rules our lives? Thinking on it, I realised the lass was but attempting to earn her living, as my Rose was forced to do when first she came to London, so I took pity upon her and gave her a penny.

With a nod of thanks and a faint smile, she directed me to

climb the stair and go to the far end of the gallery forwhy I should find the men I sought in their chamber with the surgeon and the priest. Such words did not bode well. Despite all our cautious endeavours, had Caxton come back from our house, bringing the contagion with him? Were matters so desperate that a priest was summoned to the sickbed? God forbid, I prayed, my humours turning cold in my veins at these possibilities.

The inn was ancient, the stairs creaked and I be certain the gallery swayed 'neath my feet. I reached the far chamber and knocked softly upon the door, not wanting to cause any disturbance to those within, and waited. None bade me enter so I knocked again, a little louder this time. Gawain whined, sensing my trepidation.

'Hush, lad. No need for you to come within.' At which, he sat down beside the gallery rail to observe the comings and goings in the courtyard below. When he barked at a cat crossing the cobbles, I told him to hush and he gave me a sorrowful look afore returning his attention to the mouser, a low growling rumbling in his throat.

'Twas Master Caxton in person who eventually opened the door and a wave of relief flooded over me to see him well.

'Oh. Master Foxley. Now is not a good time. Come back upon the morrow. I bid you good day.' He made to close the door.

'Good Master Caxton, if someone lies sick, I would offer my aid. Others have been so generous to us of late…'

'There is naught to be done now for my journeyman, Hal Mathers. The surgeon says he swallowed an excess of smoke. He has grown worse each day since the fire, coughing and spitting up black phlegm, and now his lungs have turned morbid. He is dying, Master Foxley. I bid you pray for his soul and as to your aiding us: go, find whosoever set my house afire for the crime will shortly become an act of murder!'

He closed the door and I stood there, stunned, as I began to comprehend the meaning of those words. Seeking to discover the felon was, of a sudden, of far greater importance and urgency.

But where to begin, I knew not.

At a loss, I returned with Gawain to the scene of the crime in the Almonry. A web of stout timbers now shored up the gutted building and the rivulets of sooty mud were dried and grey upon the cobbles but the taint of smoke yet lingered, trapped within the very walls, clinging to the remains of plaster and lurking in the crevices of cracked stones like secret spiders. The place felt more dismal than ever, knowing now that a short journey unto death had set forth from here.

Quite what I hoped to find, I could not have said, but I concentrated my search around the window by which means the felon had gained entry, as I believed. A few threads were caught upon a splinter in the side of the casement frame. They could have been blown there since the fire or been left by somebody intent on scavenging what little remained of Caxton's business. If the latter, I dare say they must have been gravely disappointed forwhy naught remained of any value to be looted, unless a considerable supply of charcoal and ashes was their objective. Nonetheless, I folded the threads within a paper and put them safe in my scrip.

I continued along the narrow alleyway, eyes fixed upon the ground in one direction and then raised higher as I returned to the window. The alley went a little beyond the window, towards a straggling thicket of brambles. The way was enclosed, such that the sun ne'er shone here and the brambles stretched thin and pale of leaf in their desperate quest for light. As my eyes adjusted to the gloom, I saw that the stems were broken down close to the wall of the neighbouring building. In fact, upon closer examination, a way had been hacked through. Another few days and this gap would have become overgrown anew and I might not have found it. As it stood, 'twas no longer passable.

Gawain barked, attracting my attention. He was sniffing in the tangle of undergrowth about the thicket and barked again. And there it was, whether a clue or not, a torn piece of dark leather strap, an inch or so in length, with the metal tag end still attached. It hung, snagged, upon the thorns, the tag still shiny so it had not been lost too long since. Observing it more closely in sunlight, I saw that the leather was frayed so thin it could easily have been pulled off but did it belong to the felon? Who else would trouble to escape by way of chopping a path through the brambles? No man in his right mind, for certain. It looked to be the end of a boot or shoe strap and if I should ever happen across an item of footwear appropriately damaged, or its partner with a matching strap, then mayhap... 'Twas what the archers call 'a long shot' or, more likely, an impossible one. Even so, I also wrapped this in paper and tucked it in my scrip.

Something white, deep amidst the thorns, caught my eye but 'twas no easy task to retrieve it. I pulled my jerkin sleeve over my hand to guard against the sharp spines and, even so, was scratched and scored for my pains. Yet it seemed worth the trouble forwhy I now held a half page, mayhap from a book, neatly written. With no rain having fallen since the fire and the dousing of flames not required here, the paper had remained dry enough that most of the ink was yet legible.

'Twas an accounting of expenses, noting monies paid for the mending of a stool and a broken catch, tapers, candles and wax... but then I read of four bobbins of linen binding thread, cloth tape of two ells length and a pot of rabbit-skin glue. These things be needful for stitching books and setting them firmly within their covers. My own accounts listed such items oftentimes, such that I did not doubt this to have come from Master Caxton's workshop. All the same, at a more opportune time, I should show it to him, nigh certain he would claim the script for his own hand.

Upon the other side of the page were inscribed four lines but here the writing was blotched by some sooty finger marks and I must make out the words when I had a little time to spare.

As I walked back home, my mind was awhirl with questions: Why would anyone want another man's accounting book? To whom would it be of the least use? And I began to wonder if someone suspected Caxton of swindling him or of being otherwise involved in dubious practices, perhaps concerning money. Might the printer act the money-lender as an adjunct to his respectable business? Somebody most definitely wanted his workshop to founder and who among our guild members most feared the arrival of printed books? I suppose we all did to some degree, if such a method should have lasting success and did not fail for lack of custom. But with the king as its patron, was that likely? Even so, Caxton was the lone printer in England (though I had heard rumours of one set up in Cambridge for the university, or was it in Oxford? I could not quite recall); how much of a threat to our craft could the man possibly pose?

I discounted my brother's efforts since he had yet to print a solitary page upon that great contraption of his and I had my doubts that he would do so within the twelvemonth. As for producing an entire book, I believed that two score and ten years hence were unlikely to prove time enough for Jude to achieve such an endeavour, producing a volume of saleable quality. Not that I would ere express my thoughts to him concerning this.

Thus, I arrived home in time for dinner with a few scraps of possible evidence in my scrip, my belly empty but my head full of unanswered queries. Mayhap, I could talk them through with Adam who ever saw things otherwise than I did. A new view from a differing slant might prove an illumination upon the matter.

Dinner was a more lively affair than of late as Hugh joined us at meat, smiling, forwhy Kate was much improved though she would rest abed for a few days yet to regain her strength. Rose remained at her bedside, feeding her a nourishing broth but apart from those two, we were all at the board, enjoying Meg's cooking.

'Master Seb, will you grant me leave to go to Walbrook and tell Kate's father the good tidings? He must be that worried for her.' Hugh was grinning as he helped himself to more morsels of pork in a sage sauce. 'Twas good to see his appetite returned, having had so little interest in food whilst his betrothed lay sick that I had feared for his own health.

'Aye, Hugh, I should be glad of it and you can inform him that his book be completed. Take it with you, if you will, since I have a deal of work to attend to this afternoon,' I said, mopping up meat juices and sauce with my bread.

'Nay, master. I think Kate should take it when she's mended. She did most of the marginalia after all—so many dogs!' Hugh chuckled. I had not heard that sound in days and it cheered me greatly to see the lad happy once more.

'For another thing, Seb, you need to hire a reliable carrier to take the Gospel Book to Dartford now that it's finished at last,' Adam reminded me. 'You said you know someone...'

'A friend of Thaddeus, aye.'

'Can we trust him to return with our hard-earned payment?'

'I hope so...'

'Else I could take it in person when this business with the lawyers is done. Simon could come with me. I've been thinking on it and an adventure into Kent would do us both good after being imprisoned here all this while.'

'Barely a se'ennight, Adam, in truth.'

'Well, it seemed like a month, didn't it, Simon? I'm sure you could spare us for a few days, perhaps from Thursday next as I'm embroiled with the lawyers tomorrow. Again. Though that should see all prepared, ready for me to apply for citizenship, unless those cunning devils find yet more reason to delay, in which case I'll kick their skinny backsides as far as

Christmastide.'

'I be certain that will help matters mightily, cousin,' I laughed. 'But of course you may go, if you wish, both of you. At this time of the year, there will be many parties travelling the Watling Street, whether merchants on business, soldiers bound for the Calais garrison or pilgrims journeying to Canterbury, as we did last leaf-fall, so you shall not lack for company. Go with my blessings. But, afore that, there be a matter I would discuss with you.'

I saw Adam's face fall, devolving into a frown.

'Fear not,' I said in haste, 'It concerns a conundrum upon which I would value your thoughts. Naught to cause any anxiety—not to us, leastwise. 'Tis Master Caxton's trouble which confuses me. The crimes of theft and arson—which now may include that of murder—make no sense.'

'Murder? Has it now come to that?'

'I fear so. The printer's journeyman be dying of the morbid lung caused by the smoke, so they say.'

'Then the felon deserves to burn in Hell, whoever he is. Do you think you'll discover the rogue, Seb?'

'I know not, Adam. I suspect him to be a Londoner and somewhat tall but that reduces the possible suspects hardly at all. Oh, and there may be some connection with cheese.'

'Cheese? A cheesemonger or a dairy wife, then?'

'Do you know of any dairy wives who stand two yards in height or thereabouts?'

'Can't say that I do.' Adam scratched his stubbled chin in thought. 'So, a cheesemonger then… but what does the stuff have to do with arson and murder?'

''Tis all part of the mystery. I found a cheese melted and turned black and burnt 'neath the remains of Caxton's printing press. It seemed to have been in a basket. He cannot account for it so we assume the felon brought it with him. But why?'

'Because he was hungry?' Simon suggested.

'Some cheeses are greasy and might burn well?' Hugh said

as he swallowed the last morsel of pork.

'Perhaps he set the fire on his way home from market? Or from St Paul's, where the cheesemongers keep their wares cool in this hot weather?' Meg contributed.

Adam shook his head.

'What manner of felon would encumber himself with a cheese whilst committing his crime?'

'A mad man,' Ralf said. 'Anyone who sets a fire has to be mad.'

We all agreed with that.

'Mayhap, Caxton or one of his household did put it there but has forgotten doing so in all the panic? That was my first assumption.'

'Aye, that seems most likely, Seb, don't you think? Unless...'

'Unless what, Adam?' I asked.

'Unless the cheese was put there of a purpose to mislead you?'

'Who could know that I would be asked to enquire concerning this crime? No one.' I answered my own question.

'Well, not you in person but whoever delved into this matter... if anyone was asked to do so.'

''Tis too far-fetched...'

'I hate cheese. It stinks. Pooh!' Nick shouted, holding his nose but determined to add his pennyworth.

'Gawain likes cheese,' my son said. 'Is there cheese, Papa? I like cheese, too.'

'Aye, likely Meg may find you a small piece, if you will, Meg? Just for you.'

'And Gawain.'

'Gawain also...'

'And me!' Nick insisted.

'No, not for you,' Adam told him. 'You just said you hate cheese.'

'Only the stinky stuff. I want cheese, now!'

'I said no. And you'll suffer my hand on your backside, if you don't quiet your tongue, you ill-mannered pup.'

'I shall leave you to your disputations,' I said, draining my ale and leaving the board before I might have to witness the little lad's punishment. 'I must visit Bess Chambers to discuss the book she would have us repair and copy.' I did not add that I had grave reservations concerning this possible commission and wished to persuade Bess against having a copy made. Repairing a book was one thing and did not require us to read the text. But making a precise and accurate copy of a work suspected to be dangerous, if not heretical, by the Church, was another matter entirely and I would not put our workshop at risk.

I was upon my way, threading a winding path through the crowds of housewives in search of after-dinner bargains of sun-spoilt soft fruits, wilting worts and melting butter along Cheapside, when Stephen Appleyard came hastening from his carpenter's shop.

'Master Seb! Wait, lad…' Hot, flustered and breathless, a wood plane still in his hand and shavings bespeckling his thinning hair and clinging to his leather apron, he caught at my jerkin. 'Not so fast,' he panted. 'I can't run as I used to in my youth… Ah, what news, eh?'

'News? And good day to you, Master Appleyard.' I greeted my onetime father-by-marriage in proper wise, such that he might catch his breath. 'What news?'

'What indeed. Have you heard of our Jack?'

'Jack? What of him? Has he come home?' In truth, Jack Tabor's disappearance had flown from my mind quite utterly. I had not given him a thought in days.

'Nay, that's why I'm asking. Have you found any sign of him or heard any word? I'm that worried for the foolish lad. You know how he draws trouble to himself as a lodestone draws iron. I fear he may be fallen in the river and washed away or set upon by rogues in some dark alley or lying sick of the pestilence somewhere. Oh, Seb, is there no news of him at all?'

'Not that I have heard.' My reply was honest but I did not admit the reason for my hearing naught of Jack was that I had made little effort to discover or enquire concerning him this week past. 'Thaddeus, as City Bailiff, would have informed you, if they had found any such signs, I be certain, so take heart from that. If anyone can survive, Jack can.'

'But, Seb, I know that as you do, so why does he not return to his own bed and board? I don't work him over hard and we were merry enough that morn. He gave no hint that he felt discontented in any way. Why would he choose to leave? That's why I fear he cannot return for some reason: that he may be imprisoned whether by the authorities or some other or that he might be… if the worst has befallen him… He's a rascal, I know, but I have a great affection for him. If you can't bring the lad home, Seb, I beg you, at least discover if he's still living, if you may. I want to know—whether good or bad tidings—that I may pray for his safe-keeping or for his doughty young soul. He had a hard life before you took him in and deserves whatever help we may continue to give him.'

There were tears in the old carpenter's eyes. For all the lad's legion faults, Stephen loved him like a son and I had neglected them both. No wonder guilt pierced my conscience sharp as a joiner's bradawl. Thus, I determined to visit my friend Thaddeus, to whom I must also tender my apologies, as I recalled, and to ask him concerning Jack before I should attend upon Bess Chambers regarding the *Ars Notoria*. A busy afternoon awaited.

Bess Chambers' shop, Bishopsgate

Having gone to Guildhall only to discover that Thaddeus was elsewhere, conducting his business as City Bailiff and not expected back for an hour or more, I continued to Bishopsgate. The apothecary's shop was a-bustle with customers amidst the scents of rosemary and gillyflowers hanging in the heavy airs, wreathed about with less pleasing odours, such as brimstone and tallow. A bunch of shed vipers' skins hung from a peg, swaying and rustling in the draught. I shuddered to think what purpose they might serve for I had not seen them in Bess Chambers' shop afore but, mayhap, they were intended for some powerful new remedy against the pestilence.

From what I heard of the customers' conversations, our Kate was by no means alone in being afflicted by the summer fever. Both Bess and Sarra were dispensing the same medicaments they had lately prescribed for us.

'Indeed, mistress, see that your son takes the remedy thrice daily and oftentimes drinks of my rosehip cordial. The fever will abate in three days or so,' Bess was saying. 'That'll be five pence ha'penny, if you please.'

Anneis Fuller, plump and healthy, grunted in annoyance and turned away, leaving the items on the counter, greeting her fellow gossipmongers by the door.

'Five pence ha'penny, indeed!' I heard her mutter. 'I'll not waste so much upon my layabout son. He's not worth it. What say you, Maud?'

'Your John's a good enough lad,' Maud protested.

'Work-shy and shiftless, that's what he is. He'd lie abed 'til noon if I didn't kick him out and I swear he spends more coin in the tavern than he ever earns as a cutler. And now he has the summer fever as a further excuse to do naught.'

'Aye, and my man's no more keen to do a day's work,' their friend Frances put in, 'And neither is Philippa's. We saw the pair of them playing dice behind the stables when they were supposed to be mending the roof. Isn't that so, Philippa?'

Philippa nodded as they all moved aside, allowing passage to a sparse-looking woman encumbered with a toddling and a squalling babe, Bess's next customer for whom I, too, stepped away that she might be served afore me.

''Tis the same as last time and the time before, Mistress Chambers,' the woman explained. 'I need some of your ginger. It saves my life, I'm sure of it.' She was wan and worn, struggling to keep a hold upon the squirming babe as it wailed and shrieked in her arms. ''Tis all I can do to suckle this one. She's ever hungry.'

'Sarra, measure out four ounces of candied ginger. Aye, now, well, you suck upon this for the nausea,' Bess instructed, 'And this rose syrup electuary will give you strength. Shall I put it on your account?'

'I suppose, if you will. I can't believe I'm with child again… after so short a space,' the woman was saying with a sigh, 'And this 'un not yet eight months in age. But the sickness every morn is a sure sign and I need to be about my work. I haven't the time to waste with my head bent over a bucket.'

Bess was shaking her head sorrowfully as the woman departed.

'Have a care, Mistress Goulden,' she called after her.

'That's Mary Goulden. She'll not last long, that one,' Anneis Fuller said, not troubling to lower her voice. 'The rate at which her good-for-nothing man gets her in the family way, seems to me his pizzle is the only bit of him that ever does any work. Poor woman. Mark my words, she'll not make old bones unless he dies first, in which case, it most surely won't be from overwork, I can tell you. That Tom Goulden is an idle wretch and he beats her. I know forwhy I've seen the bruises on her arms when she pushes up her sleeves on washday.'

'Mistress Goulden has a hard life, indeed,' Maud commented, 'But we can't always choose, can we?'

'Well, I wouldn't have chosen *him*. Why did she?' Anneis demanded to know. 'He's always been known for a lazy knave with a foul temper.'

'Her father chose, so I heard,' said Frances. 'Owed Tom Goulden gambling debts, he did, and paid him off with his daughter's hand.'

'Dear sweet Christ! So she has to pay the price?' Anneis shifted her basket to her other arm. 'Then her father deserves hanging, if you ask me.'

Maud disagreed.

'Nay, not hanging. Why should he have a quick death when

that poor skinny lass is condemned to suffer all her days, be they ever so few?'

'Men! We'd be better off without them, I swear,' said Anneis '... No more filthy clouts to wash, no more dinners demanded, no more running about at his beck and call... life would be so easy.'

'Aye, and no more marital obligations, as my Reynold calls them,' added Frances. 'No more child-bearing... what a relief that would be. Let's be done with menfolk, eh?'

'In which case, mankind would soon be no more,' Philippa pointed out, ever the thoughtful one.

'I wish the Lord God hadn't created Adam... just Eve and that would've suited me well,' said Frances. 'Come, Philippa, since He *did* mistakenly make Adam, I suppose we must go prepare supper for his wretched descendants.' With which comment, the goodwives of Bishopsgate departed, much to my relief. My business with the apothecary was not for their ears nor for their wagging tongues thereafter.

When, at length, I stepped forth to the counter-board—the last customer in the shop—I took out the account I had drawn up earlier for the repair of the *Ars Notoria*.

'Good day to you, Mistress Chambers, and a busy one, I see.'

'And to you, Master Foxley. How is young Kate faring?'

'On the mend, Bess, the Lord Christ be praised for His mercy and thanks to you also for your kindness... and to Sarra. Kate hopes to arise from her bed upon the morrow for an hour or two.'

'And Rose and the children?'

'In good health. We be blessed indeed.'

'In which case, delighted as I am to hear this, how may I aid you, Seb?'

'I have brought you a list of costs involved in making repairs to the book you sent, Bess. I fear, 'tis quite a sum—one shilling and tuppence three farthings—but you be aware that the book's spine be broken and falling apart, pages loose and the cover damaged. The whole thing must be unpicked, stitched anew and rebound.'

'Aye, it has been much used down the years but it will be worth the cost to be able to turn the pages once more without them falling out. And what of a cheap copy for Sarra? Have you come to a price for that?'

'Er, not as yet and I wonder concerning it, whether 'tis wise to make a copy of this particular text known to the authorities as being suspect in nature. The Church disapproves of it. Mending it be one thing but producing a new volume of a heretical text...'

'Psht. It's no more heretical than Geoffrey Chaucer's tales, simply an excellent aid to learning which will serve Sarra well in her quest for knowledge of the apothecary's art. You're not going to disappoint us, are you, Seb?'

'Please, Master Foxley...' Sarra touched my hand upon the counter board, sending tingling sensations up my arm which were by no means unpleasant. Her gold-flecked malachite eyes beseeched me and I could not look away.

'Or would you have me take the book to some other stationer...' Bess went on, 'Or even that printer fellow at Westminster?'

'Master Caxton cannot help you,' I said, able to drag my gaze back to the older woman as Sarra withdrew her hand from mine, 'Forwhy his press was but lately destroyed and his business with it. As for other stationers making a copy for you, the *Ars Notoria* be on the guild's list of dangerous texts and to do so would be to risk a charge of... witchcraft,' I whispered. 'I think you know that.'

'All nonsense, of course, young master. What if I paid you double the cost?'

''Tis not the money, Bess, but the risk to our reputations— yours and mine—and even our livelihoods, if we be found out.'

'Ah. *If* we be found out... What are the chances of that? Small, indeed, I should say, if you make the copy in secret? None need know of it. Don't enter it in your accounting but

I'll pay you well...'

'Please, Master Seb.' This time, Sarra took my hand and held it to her heart. 'Do it for me,' she pleaded softly, even as my senses swam and my better judgement melted away like mist upon a summer morn.

'Oh, er, I-I suppose it might be possible.' I blinked and shook my head, hoping to clear both my vision and my mind. 'N-not an easy t-task.' Even my words were failing me. 'B-but if I do it, none else in my workshop must learn of it and quite how I may achieve that, I-I know not.'

'You'll find a way, Seb. I know you will.' Sarra's voice came from afar, echoing long after inside my head.

I returned to Paternoster Row, bemused and somewhat in a daze, recalling naught of my walk home. I could not seem to set my mind to a single sensible thought.

What had I done?

Chapter 11

Wednesday, the twenty-seventh day of June
The Foxley Place

BAD DREAMS had plagued my sleep although I could not have described them; they made no sense but left me with an air of foreboding that I could not shake off. Thus, even after attending Low Mass, I was distracted and of uncertain temper at breakfast.

'Is something amiss with your herrings, Seb?' Rose asked, bringing me out of my reverie.

'What?'

'Your herrings… they're going cold.'

'Oh, nay, naught amiss with them.' I took up my spoon and ate a mouthful.

'You don't seem quite yourself, husband. You're not coming down with the fever, are you?'

'Nay. All be well with me… a great deal to think upon is all. I intended to visit Thaddeus yesterday. Stephen begged me to enquire after Jack but, somehow, the matter quite slipped my mind.'

'That's most unlike you, Seb.'

'Getting forgetful in your old age, cousin,' Adam laughed in jest, forwhy he be my elder by some months. 'I think this morning I shall make a start on repairing the book for Bess Chambers. The stitches need all unpicking…'

'Nay! I mean… she said there be no need for haste with it. I can attend to it in odd moments… that will be soon enough.'

My explanation sounded weak even to my ears.

'But we have little else to do at present now the Gospel Book is on its way to Dartford.' Adam saw my guilty look. 'You haven't arranged that either, have you? Are you waiting upon me and Simon to take it, in which case it may be a week or two until my business with the wretched lawyers is done? I can't go before then.'

'I intended to make arrangements...'

'It seems to me that you intend many things of late which don't get done at all.' Adam huffed in frustration, as well he might. 'What's happened to you? You never used to be this way. Are you sick? Is your mind failing? I'm truly worried for you, Seb.'

I looked at the other faces gathered about the board: to judge by their expressions, it seemed Adam was not alone in fearing for my health.

Rose left her stool and came to me, putting her arms about my shoulders.

'We are all of us concerned for you, dearest. You're so distracted of late yet now we are spared the pestilence, we know not why. If we can help, you need but say.'

'I be aware of my faults recently but all is well with me, in truth. 'Tis just that I have matters to think on... too many... what with Master Caxton's mystery to solve, Kate's fever, my brother's surliness, young Jack gone missing and Sarra...'

'Sarra? What has she to do with anything?' Rose sounded perplexed.

'Naught at all... merely a slip of the tongue. I meant to say...' Well, what did I mean to say?

'That lass has bewitched you, husband, like half the men in this city. Turn your thoughts to more wholesome matters and tend your work as you should. Do some drawings over by the Horse Pool. I'm certain that's the cure for your troubles. It usually puts you to rights.

'Now, Meg, Nessie, we have chores to do and Kate will need

aid in her washing and dressing later. Dickon, don't let Gawain chew your napkin like that, he'll make holes in it, and Nick, you'll get no dinner if you put one more finger-full of fish in Julia's hair. What a troublesome brood you are this day! Mundy, I've told you before not to bring your toy to the board whilst we eat and leave that else…'

Afore Rose finished speaking, a great clatter betokened the chafing dish with the remains of herrings and herbs, spoons, knives, platters and cups tumbling to the floor, smashing earthenware and denting pewter. Little Mundy, staring, shocked at what he'd done, burst into tears. The table cloth was caught upon his favoured possession: a carven figure which once had looked like a dog when Adam first whittled it from an apple log but was now splintered and lacking three legs, mostly due to Nick's rough play in teasing his younger brother. Worse yet, it had now lost its fourth leg during the mishap, caught in the tablecloth—a cause for further tears and anguish.

I knelt to assist in picking up the broken pots but Simon stepped back, slipped in the spilt ale, knocking me aside and we tumbled over, adding to the chaos.

'Pardon, master, I lost my footing. I…'

'No matter, lad,' I said, using an overturned bench to right myself afore setting that straight. 'We be all of us in a turmoil this morn.' Looking down, I realised I was smearing blood wherever I touched, including Simon's fresh-laundered shirt sleeve. 'Ah, me, what a mess.' I took Dickon's dog-chewed napkin to blot my hand, cut upon a pot shard, and made a token gesture to clean Simon's sleeve. I only made it worse. *Mea culpa.*

'Out! All of you!' Rose ordered, pointing towards the workshop. 'Go to your work or whatever you will but get you from my kitchen. By the Sweet Virgin, you men are worse than the children. Shoo! You also, Ralf and Hugh, you're of little use either. Mind that!' Rose cried out—too late—as Hugh stood upon a piece of pot, crushing it to dust underfoot. The powdered clay began to mix with the spilt ale, turning to mud.

'Out. And don't dare show your faces until dinnertime.'

Thus, were we menfolk dismissed.

I considered taking my drawing stuff to the Horse Pool at Smithfield, as Rose suggested but, upon my first peering from the window, as I opened the shutter in the workshop, it seemed the days of fine weather were ending. Lowering clouds, the colour of dirty fleeces, threatened rain afore too long, riding upon a sullen, fitful wind. 'Twas not to be begrudged forwhy the earth was in need of it after a fortnight of drought but it precluded drawing out of doors.

Since I must forego that pleasure, I decided a visit to Thaddeus was long overdue, both to make my apologies for keeping him from my door and to enquire of any tidings concerning Jack. Privily, whatever Stephen feared, I thought it most likely the lad, ever wayward at heart, had simply determined upon some adventure. That he had not seen fit to bid his master farewell was simply Jack's disobliging nature and lack of concern for others. It probably ne'er occurred to him that Stephen or we might care about him sufficiently to be the least anxious for his safety.

Afore I should walk to Guildhall, I went to the storeroom to find that suspect book of Bess's, the *Ars Notoria,* yet lying in full view upon the shelf. It would not do. I dare not risk the others deciding to work upon it. That dubious task must be mine alone, whatever Adam intended. Thus, I wrapped it in an oddment of leather, too misshapen to use as a binding, and wedged it behind the coffer on the floor in which we locked our most expensive pigments and gold leaf. It must serve until I thought of a better place. In truth, I regretted having consented to mend it, never mind make a copy. Whatever had possessed me to agree? 'Twas certainly not common sense. What a fool I was.

With my hooded mantle over my arm—'twas too warm to wear it unless a downpour ensued—and my scrip over my shoulder, I called to Gawain and we departed.

Guildhall

Thaddeus was in the tiny cell—it could hardly be called a chamber—which he used as City Bailiff to conduct official business. A high, narrow window allowed the early morning sun to cast a horizontal bar of light along the floor. One chair and two stools were all the furniture and there was no room for more. Many was the time I had sat with my drawing board resting on my knees with my inkwell beside me, noting down what some felon was saying as Thaddeus questioned him. My friend would be in comfort upon the chair; the prisoner crouched on the low stool for the greatest discomfort.

In theory at least, my friend now had a clerk to scribe for him but no concession had been made for him either: no writing desk nor proper table could be fitted in. Thaddeus, as ever, was lounging in his chair, munching a pie, though whether as a belated breakfast or an early dinner mattered not.

'God give you good day, Thaddeus.'

'And you, my friend. Sorry, but you're too late for pie.' He brushed crumbs from his jerkin which Gawain wasted not a moment in recovering, and swallowed the last mouthful. 'However, Parker has gone to fetch ale.'

'Ah! Your new clerk. And how does he fare in his task?' I sat on a stool and Gawain, having searched out the last pie crumb, circled thrice afore flopping at my feet to sleep.

'You'd serve me better, Seb.' Thaddeus pulled a face. 'I swear his scrawl is no better than mine. Oftentimes, I can hardly read it. The wretch invents his own abbreviations; I may as well try to read Dutch. And he complains whenever I send him out for food or drink. I tell him to get the good ale at The Bull but I'm sure he's too lazy to walk that little way because it always tastes like dyer's piss. Either that or—it has just occurred to me—maybe he drinks half the jug of decent ale and then refills it with his own piss. Aye, that's likely why it tastes so bad.'

'The two of you are not content together in your work, then?'

'Content? We hate the sight of each other.'

'How unfortunate for you both.' I changed the subject to a matter more pleasing. 'But I come to make my apologies to you for this week past, forbidding your welcome at our board but it had to be. Now the problem be past, we shall be most heartily delighted to see you there once more.'

'Aye, I heard you had a case of fever and feared the worst. I should account you a most honourable and considerate citizen for thinking of others' health, were it not that I've nigh starved for want of your wife's good cooking. How is the invalid?'

'Kate be recovering well now, so you will be welcome to break your fast with us upon the morrow. But what of Parker?'

'What of him?'

'Should I not invite him to eat with us also?'

'Damn it, Seb! Would you put me off my food? The sight of his miserable countenance across the board would quite spoil my appetite. Don't ask him, I pray you. He finds fault with everything and would complain about even Rose's joyous dishes. He'll ruin any meal for everyone.'

'Very well, then. I shall not mention it to the clerk. But I have another matter to enquire of you: have you heard any tidings of Jack Tabor? Any word at all?'

'No, nothing. We had a likely corpse wash up against the starlings of London Bridge on Saturday last: a young fellow, well-built, dark of hair… It quite gave me a start when I was first called to see but—thanks be to Our Lord Christ—he wasn't your Jack.'

We both made the Sign of the Cross and asked blessings upon the unknown soul.

'Whoever he was, 'Thaddeus continued, 'He had but half an arm, either amputated long since or, mayhap, born that way. It would've been useful to have you sketch his likeness that his family might know him but he had to be buried, nameless. It couldn't wait in this hot weather.'

'Perhaps the description of his arm alone will serve to discover a name. In truth, I am relieved that it was not Jack for I have done my best to reassure Stephen Appleyard that the lad can fend for himself and will keep safe.'

'Do you believe that yourself, Seb?'

'Mm, you know me too well, Thaddeus. I do try. I hope. But as the days pass without any word or sign… I cannot tell if that be good or bad. I be unsure what I believe any longer. Jack is hardy, capable… but also reckless and foolish. In all honesty, I suppose I do fear for him… aye. Leaving of a sudden as he did, I feel he has become embroiled in trouble of some kind and fled the city.'

'In which case, we may never hear of him again.'

'A situation that will be of little comfort to Stephen or any of us.'

'Better than finding him lifeless in an alley.'

'I suppose.' I shrugged and sighed. 'Oh, well… I shall take my leave of you, my friend, until you join us for breakfast in the morn. I shall advise Rose to fry extra bacon for you…'

'Excellent. My belly's rumbling already.' The bailiff patted his paunch which seemed to grow daily despite his not sharing our meals of late.

'As it ever does, Thaddeus,' I said, laughing. 'Oh, upon another matter entirely afore I forget… your friend, the trusty carrier who journeys into Kent oftentimes…'

'Aye. Cobb. What of him?'

'A book for Dartford Priory be ready for delivery…'

'He leaves at sunrise every Thursday, so you're in luck, from the stables beside St Lawrence Jewry where he keeps his horse and cart. He'll be glad of the extra coin, having lost business when his beast went lame a few weeks back. You'll needs be prompt; he doesn't waste time.'

'I shall be there. Thank you.'

'You won't wait upon Parker bringing the ale?'

'Not if he adds that vile ingredient to it, as you suspect.'

'Wise, indeed, Seb, wise indeed. Until tomorrow, then.'

'Aye. Come, Gawain, you idle creature, bestir your bones.'

Bess Chambers' shop, Bishopsgate

I had no reason to go there but could not keep away, striding along Catte Street and Lothbury as though with much purpose, Gawain trailing along behind, tongue lolling. For me, 'twas as though invisible bonds drew me to the apothecary's shop. I should wish to say that I could not resist the scent of flowers and herbs, the enticement of cinnamon and cloves, Bess's garden of birdsong and bees. But it was none of those things. 'Twas a pair of green-gold eyes.

The local gossip-mongers were by the shop door, as usual, and I wondered when they attended to their housewifely chores, if indeed they did. Mind, thinking on it, this might reflect upon me in likewise and perhaps they also wondered if I ere did a day's work. However, since their gossiping took all their attention, mayhap they did not notice me at all.

As I waited, I overheard their conversation most clearly since they made no effort to speak privily but squawked loudly as chickens with a fox in their midst. The allusion made me smile.

'If my Reynald doesn't get off his fat backside and do a hand's turn and get mending a few roofs, I don't know how I'm supposed to put food upon the board next week,' one woman was complaining. I heard the others address her as Frances. 'Oh, how marvellous life would be if we had money to throw about as some folk do instead of counting every farthing as I have to.'

'Aye, that Lady Allenby fritters away coin as though it were but fallen leaves,' Anneis Fuller was telling them. 'Why, only yesterday, at a goldsmith's shop in Cheapside, I saw her trying on a pendant. She didn't buy it, not then and there, leastwise, but when I enquired the price it was ten shillings! All for a useless pendant. It was pretty though... amethysts.'

'So you went into the goldsmith's place just to find out the cost?' Maud looked stunned by her friend's daring.

'Well, I had to know, didn't I? It's the neighbourly thing to do. And it would look very fine about my neck... better than around her scrawny throat. And last week she bought new gloves... another pair, as if she needs them! I swear she has a score or more already and there's me with but two and one of them nigh worn through and hardly fit for church-going.'

'You're jealous, Anneis.'

'And why wouldn't any woman be? I'll wager you'd like to have more money than you can count, if you speak true, Maud.'

'Aye, I suppose and some folk have all the good fortune... more than they should.' Maud beckoned her fellows closer. 'My sister, she who lives out at Holbourne way, she's friends with the local taverner's wife who told her about this youth who was throwing his coin about like a king giving largesse.'

'A wealthy lordling or merchant's son...'

'Certainly not! Only the commonest sort drink at the Swan-on-the-Hoop and there he is, this lad, buying ale for all, swiving every pretty lass and eating meat enough for an army, claiming he won the money at dice which nobody believes. My sister says the taverner reckons the lad got it by thievery.'

'Then he should tell the beadle or a constable,' put in Philippa, the quiet one.

'But he won't do that forwhy he doesn't care, so long as it goes into *his* coin box.' Maud folded her arms as if that was the end of the matter but, as ever, Anneis had to have the last word:

'And no wonder. I would welcome some crafty rogue putting money in my purse, so long as he was handsome-looking and young enough...'

I left the gossips, intent upon my business at the apothecary's counter-board but, for some reason I could not explain, the words 'crafty rogue' lodged in my thoughts. Where had I heard them afore?

'God give you good day, Master Foxley,' Bess greeted me. 'Back again so soon?'

'And also to you, Mistress Chambers. I, er...' My eyes searched for movement in the gloom; my ears strained for some sound of activity from the still-room at the back of the shop.

'If you're hoping to see Sarra, she has gone upon an errand for me.'

'Oh, nay, that was not my purpose, Bess. Rather, I came to ask concerning whether you wish a leather or parchment cover upon the book you commissioned.' But I could tell she was not fooled by my denial.

'So you've finished copying it in a single day and 'tis but awaiting its binding. How swiftly you work, Seb... such dedication to a task is to be commended.'

''Tis not quite so advanced as yet,' I said, feeling my cheeks burn. 'I need to know, is all... for the accounting and, er, what I must purchase aforehand...'

'Oh, well, it's good to hear that the work is coming on apace. I shall look forward to receiving it very soon.'

'And the cover?'

'Leather, I think, for the book will be much used. Was there anything else, Seb? I have a new batch of lizards' tongues to treat sore eyes or ravens' talons for the gout... or would you be in need of maidens' milk to quell the flushing of the face?' She was jesting with me, teasing me.

'Nay, mistress, that w-was all,' I said and hastened away, stumbling over Gawain who had lain down behind me. I felt an utter fool, behaving like a love-lorn youth at my age of six-and-twenty.

As I stepped out into Bishopsgate, the skies opened and the clouds released their burden of rain which was soon sluicing down the streets in torrents. Ah, me! This morn seemed to be faring worse by the hour. Folk dashed for shelter but I could not face returning to the apothecary shop and suffering Bess's keen eye upon me and even keener wit.

Instead, I made for the inn next door.

The Bull Inn, Bishopsgate

The inn was full of folk escaping a soaking but I squeezed myself and Gawain into a corner left vacant for the simple reason that a larger man would not find it the least comfortable. As it was, Gawain was forced to lie wound about my ankles, his heavy head using my right boot as a pillow and his great haunches wedged 'neath the stool, nigh tilting my seat as he breathed. I caught the tapster's eye and held aloft one finger: ale for one.

Whilst awaiting my drink, two fellows at the nearest board were laughing, waving their cups about. It seemed they had been there some time forwhy their words were drink-edged, their boots dry, unlike most folk crowding in now.

'What d'yer think o' that buxom piece in the shop next door?' The bearded fellow nodded towards Bess's place and since I was yet musing on the same—God forgive my inquisitiveness—I harkened to their conversation. In truth, their loud voices made it hard not to overhear.

'Aye, ripe for plucking, I reckon,' said the one in the blue cap, grinning lecherously, showing a broken tooth. 'But my wife and her cronies—bitches all, o' course—they reckon she's a witch. I heard some o' them threw stones at the wench the other day. Be a pity to spoil such a pretty face.'

'Well, the lass bewitched me; set me up proper, she did. One sight o' her and I rushed home and got my wife to bed in such haste, she couldn't catch her breath.' They sniggered over their ale as the tapster edged past them to serve me in my corner.

'Have a care, Reynald. Too much o' that'll have you in an early grave,' blue cap warned.

'Fie! I've got the strength of a stallion. Twice before dinner and thrice after does me no harm. Just because you're worn out if you sally forth once a month…'

'Shut yer mouth, Reynald. I'm as good as you any day but this is a serious matter. Did you hear that Tom Goulden was taken with a seizure last eve? My wife says that Sarra put a curse on him. Now the poor bugger lies helpless in his bed and the surgeon—not that he knows any more than my arse about anything—says he won't last the week. They sent fer the priest an' all.'

'Why would the lass curse Tom? He has a wife t' do that, don't he?' Reynald chuckled and wiped his mouth with the back of his hand.

'What, that little mouse? Mary Goulden wouldn't curse the Devil if he shat on her doorstep. My Philippa reckons Sarra heard them saying how Tom beats his wife. Aye, the insolence of it, denouncing a man for exercising his marital rights when Holy Church fully approves but that's wives for you... damn but my cup's empty again. Tapster! Now, what was I saying?'

'That the lass heard 'em talkin' of Tom... wot they had no right t' do...'

'Oh, aye, well, that Fuller woman and the other busy-bodies reckon Sarra thought to release Tom's wife from her marriage by cursing him and making a widow of her. Though how that'll help put bread on her board and pay the rent, I don't know.'

'D'yer b'lieve she cursed him?' Reynold raised his brows in question.

The fellow in the blue cap, whose name I had not heard, gave a great shrug.

'How would I know? It's all women's talk, that's all and I reckon the world would be a better place if they put their tongues to some other use.'

'I can think of a few,' Reynald said, licking his lips.

At which point I would have ceased to listen, not wanting to hear Reynald's filthy ideas but, of a sudden, I saw him nudge his companion and gesture towards the door where a bedraggled youth pushed his way inside, dripping, boots squelching.

'Say no more, my friend. John Fuller's just come in. Looks right sickly to me, don't he?' the blue cap muttered. 'It's his mother who's saying them women next door are witches. My wife said she's making out the lass has cursed her son, that's why he can't do no work.'

'To my knowing, John Fuller never did a proper day's work in his life, bewitched or not, the idle jackanapes.' And the fellows guffawed right heartily.

I was much concerned to hear Sarra's innocent name spoken of along with 'witch' and 'curses'. And who had dared throw stones at her? I saw for myself the bruises on her fair cheek and the way she held her ribs. I felt I should warn Bess of this as soon as the rain ceased and my ale was finished but I knew she would tell me to pay no heed to rumours nor to the chatter of fellows in their cups. And mayhap she would be correct. Besides, her wit had already got the better of me once this morn and I would not risk her knowing eye a second time.

But then again, it occurred to me of a sudden, I could return there upon some legitimate business. Bess be as skilled as any physician in the casting of horoscopes and reading the stars, both of which be excellent methods of foretelling the whereabouts of lost things. So inspired was I by this sudden notion, I drained my cup, called to Gawain to extricate himself from under my stool and shoved my way to the door through the crush of folk.

Outside, the rain still fell as from an overflowing conduit but it mattered not; I should be within the shelter of Bess's shop in no more than a few strides and avail myself of her knowledge and cunning. The cobbles were slick and treacherous underfoot, the rain having turned weeks' worth of dust to a skim of mud but I arrived whole if soaked anew.

Bess Chambers' shop—once again

Two wet customers huddled inside, waiting out the weather, but since they showed no sign of intending to make any purchases, Bess, leaning on the counter-board, beckoned me forward.

'Again, Seb?' Bess puckered her lips and tilted her head. 'Twice in one morn? How may I assist you this time? Surely you have medicaments and pigments enough for a twelve-month and we settled upon a leather cover for the book earlier.'

'Indeed we did, good mistress, but now I would have you aid me in finding that which be lost.'

'A favoured book, maybe, knowing you? Or I'm good at searching out keys, if Rose has mislaid them, or jewellery, lost dogs... I even found a will one time and a stolen gown, filched from a coffer, uncovering the thief in that case.'

'None of those, Bess, but a lad, gone missing. Can the stars help with finding my one-time apprentice, Jack Tabor?'

'Mm. Well, his horoscope will certainly tell if he yet lives and may suggest whether he has journeyed elsewhere or remains close. But first, a few indisputable facts are essential... let me fetch pen and ink...'

'I have all necessities here in my scrip and can write down whatever you need to know.' I got out my things and set them out upon her counter-board.

'What is the lad's proper name?'

'Jack Tabor.'

'Is Jack short for John?'

'Jack be all I know him by,' I said, shrugging.

'And Tabor is definitely his family name... with an 'o' or 'ou' spelling?'

'In truth, I cannot say. We wrote T.A.B.O.R. on his indenture of apprenticeship.'

'Then that must suffice. When was he born?'

'I have no idea. Likely, he be seventeen or eighteen years or so but, being a lad of large proportions, he may look older than his true age.'

'Do you know where he was born?'

I shook my head.

'We took him in as an urchin off the street.'

'Ah, me,' Bess said, frowning in thought. 'This isn't helping us, Seb, so instead of drawing up the lad's horoscope, let's discover the stars' alignments at the moment he went missing.'

'Will that work?'

'It can tell us the likely outcome of his disappearance. When was this? And you'll need to be as precise as you can.'

''Twas upon the morn of Tuesday, the nineteenth day of June... more than a week since that was. We were at breakfast when his present master, Stephen Appleyard, came hastening to tell me the lad was gone, he knew not where.'

'Are you saying he disappeared during the night?'

'Aye, I suppose he must have.'

'Then it could have been upon the Monday eve before midnight?'

'It may have been, aye. That might easily be the case.' I sighed, seeing the page before me had naught but Jack's name upon it with a query mark beside it. All else was blank. I had known the lad for six years yet, in truth, I knew him not at all.

'I must tell you, this is not enough for a horoscope of any kind, Seb.'

'Then I fear you cannot aid me and I have troubled you to no purpose. Forgive me.'

But Bess smiled and wagged an admonishing finger at me.

'Don't give up so easily. We might try another way if you have something which belongs to the lad.'

'I have naught, though Stephen must have some item... but wait... I know not if it will serve... Gawain! Come hither...' I patted his head and bade him sit afore telling the tale. 'Some years since, Jack had a little dog, a scruffy thing, but he loved it most dearly. When it died, thinking to console the lad, I acquired Gawain here without realising 'twas too early, what with Jack's grief so new and raw, to consider replacing his dog. But, for the space of a few days, Gawain here was regarded as belonging to the lad. Might that be of help?'

'Sarra!'

The lass came through from the still-room at the back: a vision of beauty emerging from the gloom and my heart sped up. The women conferred in whispers and I saw doubt writ large on Sarra's lovely face. She turned to me.

'I'm not sure this will work, Master Foxley, but come through to the still-room and bring the dog. It's worth trying and who can say what may be unveiled to us? It can be a fickle art.'

'My niece, like my sister, has the art of scrying,' Bess explained in an undertone so the customers—yet browsing the shelves—should not hear. I nodded, pretending knowledge but without any idea of what this scrying might entail.

'Twas dark in the back room, what with the door to the garden and the window shutters closed against the rain. Myriad scents assaulted my nose and I kept hold of Gawain's scruff for fear he might investigate these new smells and cause havoc, sending glassware and pots crashing to the floor. I had had sufficient of such mishaps earlier in our own kitchen. Here, who could know what precious vials or poisonous mixtures could be spilt if my dog went barging about in the darkness?

As my eyes became used to the dimness, I saw charcoal glowing in a brazier dish over which a small iron pot bubbled, emitting steam pungent with herbs. Another larger pot was set aside to cool, giving off less pleasant vapours as a draught wafted them towards me and the odour of brimstone, like rotten eggs, wrinkled my nose. Gawain sneezed and shook his head as if to dispel the stink.

Sarra moved this pot to a high shelf, out of harm's way and cleared a space upon the cluttered work-board amidst bunches of fresh thyme and savoury, a dish of red sandalwood powder, a wedge of cheese and half a loaf of bread. I wondered at this place: was it an alchemist's cave or a woman's kitchen? It seemed somewhat dangerous to combine the two.

The lass took a spotless white napkin and spread it out as if in lieu of a proper table cloth for which there was not room enough. The stub of a beeswax candle in a gnarled wooden candlestick carven with strange devices was next set there. Sarra took a spill to the brazier afore using it to light the candle. As the flame flared, danced and settled, she brought out a silken bag, threads a-gleam, evidence of a costly cloth and took from it a dome-shaped crystal of a size to sit in the palm of her hand. Perfectly smooth and clear, it shone eerily in the candlelight as she held it up in some act of reverence, murmuring words I did not comprehend.

'My scrying crystal,' she said without further explanation as she put it at the centre of the cloth. 'Now, my fine lad…' She bent to fondle Gawain's soft ears, something he relished, if not quite so much as a piece of the cheese for which his snout was questing along the board. 'After, you shall have cheese,' she said, reading my dog's thoughts though they had not met before. 'But first, you must give me a gift…' In that moment, he gazed at her adoringly, willing to give her everything in exchange for cheese. 'There!' Sarra had plucked a few hairs from his scruff and he never knew.

She arranged the glossy black hairs upon the napkin then put the flat bottom of the scrying crystal atop them and moved the candle closer, such that it was fully illuminated. She closed her eyes, breathing deeply whilst I sat in silence, watching. Swaying back and forth, she intoned some kind of chant, soft and rhythmic, and I realised I, too, was swaying and could not prevent it; nay, I did not wish to stop it. Then Sarra became still—as did I—and opened her eyes, leaning close to the crystal, staring intently into its pristine depths. I also looked but could see naught but glimmering reflections of candlelight but then I did not possess this strange art of scrying.

'I see a white bird upon holy water,' she said at last. 'Does that have any meaning for this Jack whom you seek?'

'A seagull on the Thames, mayhap?' I suggested. 'Can the Thames be accounted holy? Would that mean Jack drowned in it?' God forbid, I thought, and felt I should cross myself but my hand refused to oblige.

'No, I do not sense that at all. It's a lesser body of water… a stream maybe.'

'A holy stream?' I mused aloud. 'Could be… Clerkenwell

has a spring that was once believed holy by the ancients. Or what of a conduit supplying some religious house or other? St Martin's le Grand has one and the house be a sanctuary for those in trouble...'

'The white bird,' Sarra continued as though she had not heard my suggestions, 'I see it more clearly now... it's a goose... no, a swan. Aye, a swan for certain.'

'Oh, but what of Jack? Did you scry anything of him or whatever term you use?'

Sarra sat back, blew out a breath and mopped her brow with her apron. She looked weary, those matchless green eyes tired.

'No. The picture has gone. Besides, a few hairs from a dog he did not love may not be enough to conjure the truth from the crystal. I don't know what it means, Master Foxley. It may mean nothing at all.'

'I be grateful for your efforts, lass. How much do I owe for this scrying?'

'Naught at all for I cannot be certain that it worked but there may be something of truth in it. However, I promised your dog a reward for his aid.' She cut a generous chunk of cheese from the wedge and, without prompting, Gawain sat to receive it. In truth, it took more time for the lass to take up her knife and cut it than it did for him to eat it. I doubt he tasted it at all but Sarra was, henceforth, my dog's most beloved friend for life.

And all I had was the vaguest possibility of a swan in holy water to guide my searching—if, indeed, it had any relevance whatsoever.

Back in the shop, the customers were gone and Bess and I were alone for a few moments.

'Bess, I would warn you, as a good friend, that I have heard rumours concerning your niece. They include words the lass should not hear.'

'There are always rumours, Seb, to accompany our craft. It is simply the way of things. Folk believe women to be ignorant creatures and can't understand how we can have such knowledge without recourse to unholy means. I pay them no heed and neither should you. Rest assured, the rumours are groundless.'

'I know that but malicious tongues yet wag amongst the goodwives and their menfolk in the tavern.'

'Those gossipmongers, Mistress Fuller and her ilk, do you mean? They're a trial to me yet they buy my wares so I can't complain.'

'Aye, the very same. And I heard tell that stones were thrown.'

'Mercy me! Whatever next? Sarra didn't mention any such happenstance.'

'But she wears a bruise…'

'She said she bumped into a door but I'll enquire… And, by the by, your serving wench, Agnes, came by again yesterday…'

'Nessie?' I had ne'er heard her addressed by her proper name afore. 'What did she purchase?'

'Another of Sarra's love philtres. I thought you should know of it.'

'Another? Has she then bought one previously?' I was incredulous. Why would Nessie want a love philtre?

'Three. And she says they work well but the effect wears off after a week or so. But I know little of such things. Love potions and philtres are in my sister's realm of cunning and Sarra has learnt much from her mother.'

'Then there be all the more reason why you must have a care, Bess, and I pray you, keep Sarra safe.' With which warning and plea, I departed the shop, Gawain at my heel, into a day now bright with sunshine, dazzling as it reflected off wet cobbles. Dazzling as a pair of green-gold eyes and likewise nigh blinding me to the way ahead in every sense.

Nessie! Love philtres? Such things were beyond my comprehension.

Chapter 12

Later that Wednesday
The Foxley Place

I RETURNED HOME to enticing smells which dragged me from confusing thoughts and set my mouth to watering. The kitchen had been restored to perfect order and a most wondrous meal was set upon the board: thick, succulent slices of roasted pork loin—on a Wednesday; a day of fast!

'It won't keep until the Lord's Day in this warm weather,' Rose explained, smiling with pleasure at being able to present so fine a repast. 'And what of it if we must do a penance? Nessie got such a bargain at Fattyng's butcher's stall, we dare not risk it spoiling, so eat up and enjoy. There's plenty for second helpings, Adam, fear not, and enough for cold cuts at supper. Serve yourselves with buttered worts, seared onions with hazelnuts and a thyme and verjuice sauce. The bread is fresh-baked, and there's ale aplenty. Oh, and I had to buy two new ale cups to replace what was broken earlier, so a penny ha'penny needs to go into the accounting, Meg. I forgot that, what with cleaning, tidying, marketing and cooking...'

'You have worked a small miracle here, sweeting, after the mess we left you to amend earlier.' I kissed her and whispered, 'Dearest of wives,' in her ear, knowing what a fortunate man I was.

I was also delighted to see Kate joining us. Looking somewhat pale with shadows like bruises below her eyes; nevertheless, she managed smiles for us all which was right heartening.

With everyone seated, knives ready and tongues drooling, I said a hasty grace and we began. For a while, all was quiet apart from the occasional clatter of cutlery as we relished our unexpectedly lavish dinner. Even young Nick could find naught to complain about as he chewed the tender meat Rose had cut into small pieces for the little ones. This once, the imp forgot about daubing Dickon, Julia or Mundy—this last his most frequent victim—with sauce or sprinkling crumbs in their hair and, thus, Adam had no cause to threaten punishment for any mischief. 'Twas a marvellously peaceful meal and I was so enjoying mine that I nigh forgot Gawain 'neath the table, patiently hoping for another reward. I dropped him a succulent morsel and a piece of crisp crackling to keep him content for a few moments at least. The sound of sharp teeth crunching could be heard in the quietness, the shuffle of a shoe, old Ralf's soft fart.

When the dishes and platters were empty, none rushed to leave the board, so replete were we with fine food.

'How did we come to earn such a dinner?' Adam leaned back against the wall, belched and loosened his belt a notch—hardly surprising after the number of times he had replenished his platter. 'Even the penance we'll have to do for eating meat on a Wednesday can't spoil my enjoyment of that fine meal, Rose.'

'It was Nessie's doing,' Rose said, patting the maid's plump hand. 'She should take the credit for buying such an excellent joint of meat for a mere two pence. Her powers of persuasion must be incredible.'

'He loves me, that's why, though he forgot me whilst we were shut up here. I needed another potion to remind him.' Nessie looked smug—a rare thing indeed—patting her cap and hair and dusting off invisible flecks from her sleeves.

'Remind who?' Adam asked, looking bemused at the possibility of Nessie being loved.

'My Warin, o' course.'

Adam frowned.

'Who?'

'Warin Fattyng from the Shambles,' Nessie explained.

'Oh, it's that knock-kneed, pimply apprentice with the braying laugh. How could I forget? And even he requires a potion before he can see your merits.'

'Nay, Adam, I pray you, do not taunt the lass so cruelly,' I said, turning to Nessie who was now crimson of face and looked to be upon the verge of either bursting into a flood of weeping or throwing a dirty platter at Adam or storming off in a temper. I knew not which—perhaps all three. The fit of tears came and she flounced out of the kitchen, racing up the stairs to her room in the attic, fortunately, without the flinging of any tableware.

'Love potions! Such nonsense,' Adam declared.

'They seem to have worked,' Rose said, 'And now you've upset her, Adam. Fie on you.'

'It's all foolishness. Only you women folk believe in magickal spells, charms and what-not.'

'You were eager enough, cousin, to wear the rowan wood amulet to ward off the pestilence,' I reminded him. 'And I see you wear it still,' I added, noting the thong tucked about his neck within his shirt.

'That's different,' he said, putting his hand to his chest, fingering the amulet through the cloth. 'A matter of keeping in good health… a sensible precaution.'

I said naught but my wayward thoughts slipped back to dwell upon the lass with bewitching green eyes, she who had made the amulets. I reprimanded myself silently for such transgressions. Being a contented husband with a perfect wife, I should know better and count the marvellous blessings bestowed upon me, instead of constantly musing on pretty Sarra. It occurred to me—right foolishly—that mayhap I was also the unsuspecting victim of some love philtre or other such potion but realised, if that was true, so were half the men of London.

'To work,' I said after a while. I would not waste the entire afternoon. 'I have a new project in mind for us. Having completed the Gospel Book, which should be upon its way to Dartford Priory first thing in the morn, what say you to the idea of producing each gospel as a separate work? Not so lavishly done as that for the nuns and smaller but yet beautifully decorated with marginalia that should attract customers to buy them. We can repeat the images we used previously since we know they look well with the texts.'

'Aye, maybe, since we have little else to do at present beside cheap primers,' Adam said, considering. 'But what of the illuminated title pages, Seb? Each of those took you an age to finish and all that gold and ultramarine cost a fortune. Would you repeat that?'

'Nay, I think not. I shall simplify them and use orpiment instead of gold leaf and azurite instead of lapis lazuli. That will save both time and expense and I hope to be less distracted in future.'

'I doubt that,' Adam said. 'You're constantly going off on spurious errands and I believe Master Caxton's mystery and Jack's whereabouts have yet to be resolved?'

'Aye. I fear 'tis true in both cases.'

'Well, then, I dare say you'll be as distracted as ever, cousin. Why not let Hugh try his talents using the sketches you made for the Dartford book?'

Hugh looked up from his examination of Kate's pale hand in his, released his hold of it and leapt to his feet.

'Oh, could I, Master Seb? Let me do the title pages, please, I beg of you. I'll not let you down, I swear upon my life.' His earnest face, such eagerness, how could I refuse? Besides, I had the *Ars Notoria* to copy and that, being a difficult text with strange diagrams, would take time. As yet, I knew not how I might achieve that in secret-wise.

'Mm, I suppose... perhaps you might begin with St Matthew's Gospel and we shall see how you fare...' In truth, I felt somewhat reluctant. 'I shall go find my sketches to aid you. I put them in the storeroom for safe keeping.'

Illuminated miniatures were what I excelled at and to give this special task and privilege to our young journeyman seemed a step beyond. As I went to the workshop and the others followed me, I wondered if I was afeared that Hugh might produce something as good—or better—than my work. That was a foolish fear. Journeymen are supposed to aspire to be as good as their masters, if not exceed them, eventually; otherwise the craft would gradually diminish down the years. Searching out the sketches in the storeroom, I had to own that Hugh, despite being cack-handed, was a fine artist and likely capable of producing a piece as good as anything I could do. Mayhap, I felt envious of his youth combined with his skills, aware that I had come to my talents some few years later than he.

As everyone settled to their tasks—except Kate who was resting in the parlour—I took out my scrying glass. Sarra's use of hers that morn reminded me of those threads, the strap end and the scrap of paper I had discovered in the bramble patch beside Master Caxton's place. Just as she had done, I spread a clean napkin on my desk and put the objects upon it.

The strap end was just that and no more. The metal tag had once been patterned but that was nigh worn smooth for the most part and impossible to make out. The torn paper was, indeed, as I had made out yesterday, an accounting of items purchased including book-binding materials. But the reverse, besmirched with soot as it was, nevertheless, 'neath my scrying glass, revealed something or other which I could not make out, followed by "for the Queen's Grace a book..." and then "Fables". At least, I thought that to be the word and recalled Master Caxton's lament that his finished copy of *Aesop's Fables,* made for Elizabeth Woodville, was among the works destroyed in the fire. That confirmed, to my satisfaction, leastwise, the page as having come from the stolen ledger.

Lastly, I used my glass to magnify the threads I discovered upon a splinter in the window frame whence the culprit had gained entry and escaped from the premises. It required a good light and a deal of squinting but I made out that the threads were of a greyish brown homespun by the look of them: the kind of cloth worn by the common sort, labourers, apprentices and such like. In truth, the most ordinary cloth in London. Yet, what was that caught betwixt the threads? A tiny curl of pale wood, a shaving no larger than a nail paring from a child's finger. Hardly a clue at all.

Thursday, the twenty-eighth day of June
Beside St Lawrence Church, Jewry Street

First light saw me and Gawain hastening to Jewry Street, close by Guildhall, where Cobb the Carrier stabled his horse and cart. Thaddeus had warned me to be early forwhy the fellow departed promptly at sunrise yet there was no sign of him. I stood by the church lych gate, clutching 'neath my arm the precious Gospel Book in its bag of waxed leather to keep it dry, cooling my heels, as they say. I began to wonder if he was gone already and I had missed him when a man came from the stable yard, leading a sturdy mare ready harnessed to a stout cart. It was loaded with bales of blanket cloth and barrels of pitch, to judge from the harsh smell and black staining on the barrel rims. The horse appeared lively, ready for a day's labour, prancing and tossing her mane.

The same could not be said of her master. Leaden-footed and bleary of eye, he looked more in need of his bed.

'Cobb the Carrier?' I asked.

A grunt was all my reply.

'Good day to you and God's blessings be upon you,' I said cheerily for 'twas a fine morn with the newly risen sun golden on the rooftops, the warmth dispelling the wisps of mist from shadowed alleyways and courtyards. 'Are you bound for Kent this day?'

'Mebbe. Depends, don't it.'

'Depends upon what?'

'If me 'ead holds t'gether long enough. I'd curse me bruvver but 'twas in a good cause.'

'A good cause?'

'Wettin' the babe's 'ead. Got hisself a son at long last. Potent stuff… the ale wot they serve at the Swan-on-the-'oop over 'olbourne way. Ain't use to it am I? An' 'twas quite some ado there, a young fella throwin' coin about like he wos castin' corn seed abroad at sowin' time. Bought drinks fer everybody thrice times over he did. Ain't no wonder me 'ead's splittin' in two this morn.'

'He sounds most generous, this young fellow… Must be wealthy, indeed.'

'Aye, but everybody reckons the coin is ill-gotten gains cos he weren't no lord nor merchant, not in them raggedy-arse clouts. Mind, he wore new boots wot must've cost a fair bit. I envied 'em meself, so did me bruvver. And who wouldn't envy a young lad like that: built like an oak tree, a lovesome coppery-haired, green-eyed wench upon his knee and a bottomless purse? Lucky sod. An' all I got is a sore 'ead poundin' like the devil an' a long journey to do. Woe is me. Any 'ow, wot d'you want?'

'I would have you take a precious object to Dartford Priory for me. City Bailiff Turner recommended your services; he said you be the most trustworthy carrier in London.' This was not entirely true. Thaddeus had told me Cobb was the man to ask if I needed a delivery made into Kent but a little flattery ne'er did any harm. 'How much will you charge to take it?'

'Precious, you say? Am I likely to fall prey to robbers, if they sees it?'

''Tis a Gospel Book, well concealed in its bag.' I showed it to him.

'To Dartford?'

'For the prioress herself.'

'Seven pence should do it.'

'Two groats now and two more when you return with the

coin the prioress will pay you. That will be a penny extra for your trouble and, I pray you, have a care with it.' I gave the book into his calloused hands where he tested its weight as though it were a sack of onions instead of a holy book before putting it in the cart under the driver's bench.

'Where do I take the money when she gives it me?'

'Leave it with City Bailiff Turner at Guildhall. He will count it and give you the two groats owing on my account. I shall arrange it thus. When do you expect to return?'

'I'm goin' beyond Dartford to the market in Maidstone and then on to Sutton Valence, so I'll not be back 'til Monday sometime most like.'

'Very well. And I advise meadowsweet for your headaches in future.'

'No need. I can't afford drinkin' so much in one wettin'. If it weren't fer that Jude Foxley plyin' us wi' strong ale..,'

'Who!' I felt as if he had struck me with a club and staggered back a step. 'Who did you say?'

'Jude Foxley. That's wot the rich fella said his name wos. Mind, he laughed like a king's fool when he said it, so wos prob'ly a lie.'

'A moment more of your time, my good man,' I said, taking out my drawing stuff from my scrip.

'I ain't got time t' waste, being late startin' cos o' me 'ead.'

But I was sketching swiftly.

'There.' I showed him my charcoal drawing. 'Is that the fellow who called himself Jude Foxley?'

'Aye. Might've been.' He squinted at it. 'Aye, he looked much like that. Why? D'you know him?'

'Indeed, I believe I do. And you were at the Swan-on-the-Hoop in Holbourne last eve?'

'That's the place.'

'You have my most sincere thanks, Cobb. Fare you well and keep the book safe and dry.'

The Swan-on-the-Hoop in Holbourne village? I knew of

197

the place, having painted its inn sign a few years ago. A white bird on holy water, Sarra had said after staring into her scrying crystal in an attempt to discover Jack's whereabouts. Dame Ellen, I recalled, had once said that she remembered folk of old naming the village as being beside the holy bourne or stream and a swan was certainly a white bird. Sarra had not failed me but as for Jack... such impertinence! Taking my brother's name in vain, how dare he? And how did he come by so much wealth of a sudden? Ill-gotten gains, Cobb had said, and I feared he might well be correct.

Breakfast would have to wait. I must visit Jude and warn him directly.

Jude's house, Ave Maria Alley

I hammered upon the door. No response. I knew my brother was unlikely to be from his bed at so early an hour and he could not hasten down the stairs. I must curb my impatience. Even so, I rapped on the window shutters for good measure and shouted out to Jude. Gawain barked loudly, pawing at the door timbers.

Other doors and windows opened in Ave Maria Alley and Amen Lane, the house being at the corner betwixt the two. Neighbours berated me, shouting curses; someone threw out last night's soil, piss pot and all, which landed close to my feet, denting the pewter and splashing my boots.

At last, the sound of my brother's door being unbarred, the portal opening an inch or two.

'Bloody hell! I should've known it would be you, you and that damned dog. What in the Devil's name do you want now, at this hour?'

I pushed past him into the house without awaiting an invitation. This matter could not wait.

'What do you know of Jack?' I demanded, turning to face Jude as he closed the door on a small group of gawpers which had so swiftly assembled in the street.

'By Christ's bollocks, Seb! How many times have I told you? I know nothing of that young rogue and neither do I care one jot about him. He's a bloody useless rascal. Why are you so bothered about him?'

'Jude, harken to me. You must needs be bothered about him also forwhy he be taking your name in vain, calling himself Jude Foxley.'

'The poxy knave!' My brother balled his fists. 'I'll gut him like a Friday fish for this when I get a hold on the bastard. Wait until I catch him…' Jude limped to his usual seat upon the padded bench and began running his fingers through his thinning fair hair.

I noted, belatedly, the blanket on the floor, the dented pillow on the bench, the rumpled clothes he wore and realised he had slept the night here rather than in his bed chamber. The air smelled stale. Did he have such difficulty climbing stairs these days that he now lived here in this one room, night and day? I should have to think on this… later.

'And I do not believe you to be entirely ignorant of his recent activities either,' I continued.

'Are you calling me a liar?' he snarled. 'Because if you are… you're not so high and mighty that I can't box your bloody ears, *little* brother.'

'Do not waste your breath on idle threats, Jude. Tell me the truth about you and Jack. I know you two have been embroiled in some nefarious activity. I suspect that it resulted in this latest damage to your knee, the day you were besmirched in mud, head to toe. What have you done?'

'I'm not guilty of anything.' He flung his arms wide. 'You accuse me unjustly. Where's your bloody evidence, eh? You're always so keen on evidence, so show it to me. What have you got to prove it, eh? Nothing. That's what. Because I haven't done anything!'

Jude was lying, I knew. The greater his vehemence in denying his guilt, the less I believed him. I glanced around the dusty shelves, the cobweb-draped printing press and then I saw it. 'Twas not the first time I had espied it but only now did I understand its relevance.

'This,' I said, lifting down the tattered book from off the platen of the press, that which he had previously been at such pains to keep from me.

'Put that down. It's none of your bloody business,' he screeched, attempting, and failing to wrest it from my grasp as I retreated beyond his reach.

I flicked through a few torn, soot-stained pages and recognised the neat scribal hand, the way the columns of monetary amounts were set down—had I not seen them afore upon that scrap of paper I found in the bushes beside the burnt-out house in Westminster? That scrap was back in my scrip and I took it out to compare it to the pages in the book. There could be no doubt: the paper, the ink, the script were the same. I could even match the piece to a torn page.

'Indeed, I think this be very much my business since Master Caxton hired me to find it for him. This is his book, is it not?'

'You can't accuse me of stealing it. How would I manage that with my bloody knee, eh? Why would I want it?'

'You do not, then, deny that this is Master Caxton's accounting and order book?'

Jude only shrugged and stared at the floor. He said naught.

'I am not accusing you of the theft itself. I suspect Jack did that. But you planned it. Jack would not have thought of stealing a book. The money—aye, he would take that for certain—but words and numbers be of no use to him. Oh, Jude, why did you have him set the place alight? What has Caxton ever done against you that you would destroy his home and workshop so utterly?'

'I didn't! I'm bloody telling you. I had naught to do with setting the place ablaze. It wasn't my doing but Jack's own idea, the infernal fool. I told him to get the book and make the press unusable. I never mentioned fire.'

'Are you aware that a man has since died from the smoke in his lungs? Caxton's journeyman be dead. Thus, the crime is now one of murder, not only arson and theft.'

I saw the colour fade from my brother's cheek so recently suffused red with self-righteous anger. Although 'twas common fame throughout the city, he did not know of the death until now forwhy he hardly left his house of late on account of his lameness.

'No. I didn't know. Bloody Jack! When does he not make matters worse than they need be? Wait until I get my hands on his fat carcass...'

'Aye, I know: "you will gut him like a Friday fish", as you said. But he lies beyond your reach, in Holbourne, as I heard tell, where he be enjoying life to the full at Caxton's expense and misusing your good name.' In truth, I was unsure whether the name of my brother was one of good repute any longer. If it yet was at present, likely it would not remain thus for many more days, once the tale of his crimes spread abroad.

But who would spread the ignoble tale? I alone knew of it beside the guilty parties. Justice should be served but how could I betray my brother; my own flesh and blood?

'Tell me what came to pass,' I said, sitting upon a stool beside his bench and bidding Gawain to lie down. 'I would have the whole sorry story, Jude. And what in the name of heaven does cheese have to do with it?'

'Cheese? Oh, that.' Jude gave a great sigh and looked about to reveal all but then shook his head. 'Nay, I'll say no more until I've had some ale. I can't tell you on an empty belly and...' He inspected the flagon stood by his feet. 'There isn't any. You'll have to go buy some.'

And thus I did as he required, running to the Sunne in Splendour tavern and returning in haste with a brimming jug.

But I returned to an empty house. Lame or not, Jude was gone.

I could well imagine where my brother would go: to Holbourne, although, fortunately, I had not mentioned the

Swan-on-the-Hoop. However, if I recalled aright, the village was not so large with but two taverns and the inn. It would not take Jude much effort to find out where Jack had been flinging largesse to the commons like some great lord. But I had time in hand, so I hoped, forwhy, lame as he was, my brother would not be there for some while.

Thus, leaving the ale for Jude to drink later but taking Master Caxton's accounting book with me, I went home for a belated breakfast.

Stephen Appleyard's carpentry workshop, off Cheapside

Having gulped down a dish of bacon collops, a heel of fresh bread and a cup of ale at home, leaving the others—including Thaddeus who made a welcome return to our board—to break their fast in leisurely wise, I made straight to Stephen's workshop. The carpenter was planing a timber, ready for use, surrounded by curling shavings and the fresh, tart scent of newly-exposed oak. He looked up as I entered, the light of hope brightening in his face when he saw me.

'Jack?' was all he said, putting down the plane.

'Aye, the lad be whole and intact, safe last eve, leastwise.'

'May the Lord God and all the Saints in Heaven be praised for that.' He crossed himself and smiled, relieved. 'I've been so afeared for him. Where is he? Where did you find him?'

'I have not seen him as yet but he was biding at Holbourne last night... but, Stephen, I fear 'tis not all good tidings concerning him.'

'Oh, I thought that might be the case.'

'Though yet at large, insofar as I know, Jack be in serious trouble...'

A customer came in then and Stephen took orders for a new joint stool of ash and a replacement beech wood handle for a garden rake. Business must take precedence. He leaned the broken rake in the corner and noted down the customer's requirements regarding the stool before we were alone once more and I could continue my report.

'Tell me, Seb. Come through to the back room where we won't be disturbed, then you can tell me the worst of it.' Stephen was already wringing his hands and shaking his head. He knew Jack as well as I did—better, mayhap—and was well aware of the lad's recklessness and casual disregard for the law when it suited him.

I explained about the crimes of wilful damage, arson and theft at Westminster.

'Aye, I heard about the fire at William Caxton's place… and you say that was all Jack's doing?'

'I fear so and a man has since died of the smoke. I be sorry, Stephen, that this news comes so shocking and dire…' And now was I at the point of my great dilemma: should I reveal my brother's part in this pother of crime? Somehow, I ploughed on, though my voice was no more than a hoarse whisper as I stumbled over the words:

'"Twas the lad's doing, indeed, but not entirely his idea,' I said. 'Another be to blame for that… Oh, Stephen, I can hardly bear to name the originator of this chaos.' I hung my head, biting my lip to keep from speaking the name aloud. '"Twas… 'twas Jude. My own brother. And I know not how to proceed with this fearful matter. I beg you, Stephen: advise me. Help me. Tell me what I should do…'

The carpenter sat silent for so long, I wondered if he had heard what I said.

'Aye, a hard decision for you, Seb,' he said at last. 'But let's not be over-hasty. We should hear Jack's side of the tale first. Where may we find the young rapscallion?'

'Holbourne. Last eve, he was at the inn there, the Swan-on-the-Hoop, if you know of it.' I admit, my spirit felt somewhat lighter at having shared my burden and relieved that Stephen was not in haste to inform the law.

'Aye. Well then, we must go there straightway and discover my wayward apprentice who thinks to abandon his labours and indenture without my leave. Come, Seb, we be bound for Holbourne.' The carpenter girded his purse to his belt, straightened his cap and fetched a stout stave from the workshop.

As we walked towards Newgate, I explained about Jack using Jude's name as he spent the stolen coins, as Cobb the Carrier had told me earlier that morn. I also mentioned that my brother was likely upon the same errand as ourselves but I hoped we should discover the lad afore he did, for fear another course of mayhem, even murder—Heaven forefend—might ensue. Who could hazard a guess as to what Jude would do to Jack or, more likely, the other way around, what with Jack having strength, agility and youth upon his side.

The Swan-on-the-Hoop, Holbourne

Stephen, burly and strong despite being nigh two-score-and-ten, kept up a goodly pace I could but match with no small effort, Gawain loping alongside. I suppose a carpenter's work made a man hearty as a stationer's did not. Or, mayhap, his eagerness to find Jack far exceeded mine and gave wings to his feet. In truth, I did not relish confronting the lad nor my brother, come to that. And most certainly not in public where there could be no knowing what might be said or done that should be much regretted after.

I hardly recall our walk past the Saracen's Head on Cow Lane, nor crossing the bridge over the Fleet Ditch and climbing Holbourne Hill forwhy my thoughts were in turmoil.

The inn yard looked well ordered as we ducked 'neath the archway at the Sign of the Swan. An ostler was grooming a horse, talking to the beast as he curry-combed it. A maid carried a pitcher of water into the kitchen range, singing as she went, and another came down the outside stair from the upper gallery bearing an armful of sheets for laundering.

I was grateful for this scene of calm which eased my mind somewhat, though not by so much.

'We deserve a pot of ale after that walk, do we not, Seb?' Stephen said, forcing his merry tone and the smile which accompanied it was unconvincing. I dare say mine was no better but I had worked up an honest thirst on so warm a day.

'Aye. The taproom be this way,' I said, remembering its whereabouts from the day I had delivered the new painted sign which still swung outside. I wondered if the innkeeper would recall me and hoped he would not, assuring myself that he must have seen a thousand other faces since then. Thinking further to avoid any chance of recognition, I made for the darkest corner, away from the light, and let Stephen order our drink from the tap-boy.

The taproom was gloomy after the sunshine and my eyes took a while to adjust. I had thought at first that the place was nigh empty but I gradually made out, as shadows became solid forms, that we were not the only customers.

A trio of gaudily clad fellows with musical instruments beside them were playing dice by the empty hearth—no need for a fire at this height of summer—likely awaiting a larger audience around dinnertime.

A pair of pilgrims sat at ease by the door in a patch of sun, sipping their ale as the light glinted on their badges of Palms from Jerusalem, Scallop-shells from Compostella in Spain and the Three Kings from Cologne. Well-travelled were they. I wondered, idly, where next they might be bound.

A roar went up from the minstrels at someone's loss or gain upon the fall of dice, I could not tell which.

But of Jack there was no sign as yet. Mayhap, after a night of carousing, he remained abed despite the hour, he being ever the idle sort if not prodded to work.

As the tap-boy brought our ale, cool and refreshing, and I took my first most welcome sip, a familiar voice came out of the dimmest corner by the cellar stair.

'Couldn't bloody stay out of my business, could you? I knew you'd come, sooner or later, sticking your damned long nose where it doesn't belong... as bloody usual.'

'Jude, I did not expect you here,' I said, doing my best to conceal my dismay.

'Thought I couldn't walk so far, did you?'

'Nay, of course not,' I muttered the half-truth as Jude struggled from his stool to join us. I went to aid him but his fierce look of utter determination kept me on my seat. He leaned heavily on his staff yet still required to steady himself against the wall or furniture, each in turn, even grabbing at the shoulder of one of the minstrels who shrugged him off so forcibly he staggered and would have fallen if a pilgrim had not leant a hand. With my brother's approval or not, Stephen and I fetched him to our table-board, having thanked the pilgrim for his timely help. The minstrel made his apologies also, saying he had been caught unaware and never meant to fling aside such a 'poor, helpless old cripple'.

Dear Lord, if the musician had seen the expression of fury on Jude's face as he heard this description, the fellow should have cowered in fear. A wounded bear can be greatly more dangerous than one unscathed.

We helped Jude to a bench and I gave him my cup of ale whilst Stephen went to fetch another. The light was feeble but, even so, I could see enough to know Jude was haggard with pain, his face deeply etched and grey. The effort of coming to Holbourne had been too much for him and he looked most unwell.

Stephen was twitching with impatience, twirling his cup by the stem, fidgeting with the laces on his jerkin which were perfectly tied and in no way needing adjustment.

'Well?' the carpenter said at last, addressing Jude. 'Have you found Jack? Tell me true, for pity's sake. I must know if he's safe.'

Jude shrugged.

'Why ask me?'

'Stephen knows all,' I confessed in a whisper.

'You bloody fool… you slack-jawed betrayer.' Jude's tone was a snarl.

'I had to, Jude. Stephen has the right, Jack being in breach of his apprenticeship.'

'I forced him to tell me,' Stephen told him. 'I held a chisel to his neck. Would've used it, too, if he stayed stubborn and silent.'

I glanced at the carpenter, surprised at his words but the merest shake of his head warned me not to contradict.

'Well, I haven't seen the bastard knave so I know no more than you do. There. Are you satisfied now?'

'Maybe this will help,' I said, taking from my scrip the sketch I had made earlier to show the carrier. I beckoned the tap-boy.

'More ale, masters?' he asked with a broad grin.

'Nay, not as…' I began.

'Aye. A flagon will do,' Jude butted in. 'He's paying.' He pointed at me.

I sighed as I unbuckled my purse and found the coins appropriate for a large flagon.

'And bread and whatever they're eating.' My brother nodded towards the pilgrims who were now dipping wedges of bread into a steaming bowl.

'Pottage with mutton and oysters?' the tap-boy said. 'For three?'

'Aye, and no stinting. I'm bloody starving.'

It occurred to me then that Jude had most likely eaten naught this day and who knew when he last consumed a decent meal. Thus, I paid over the extra money without complaint.

'Afore you take our order to the kitchen…' I caught the lad's sleeve to detain him. 'Do you know this fellow?' I showed him the likeness of Jack.

'Oh, aye,' he said after the briefest of glances. He lowered his voice, speaking from behind his hand. 'He was a good sort. Gave me these boots, he did.' The lad glanced down at his footwear:

well-scuffed and missing a buckle strap on one. I realised its partner yet lay within in my scrip. 'But don't let the master see the picture, else he'll fly into a rage, I know.'

'Why would that be?' I asked, likewise in a low tone.

'That fellow has been staying here since last week sometime, the coin flowing right merrily and readily, especially last eve when it was the merriest of all. Master's been well pleased with all the coin spent and the extra custom of folk who came to join the celebrations. Then this morn, the fellow came from his chamber, as usual, and ordered a huge breakfast—as always. Master served him hisself, seeing he was a wealthy patron but then, when Master gave him the reckoning for last night's bed and board and breakfast this morn, the fellow took out his coin bag... I could see how thin it was and so could Master. A penny farthing was all he had left. I thought there would be a fight and so did everyone else, 'less the fellow had another bag of coin. We gathered to watch. There wasn't any more coin and Master and the fellow looked to be quite a fair match. Have you seen Master?'

'I have upon another occasion, aye.'

'Then you know he's of a size and more to match most men and so was this Jude Foxley...'

I felt my brother tense and put my hand upon his arm to prevent any unwarranted excess of reaction.

'But then the fight never happened. Master boxed the fellow's ears and kicked him out into the street. I saw him running off like a beaten cur.' The tap-boy shrugged in disappointment. 'We was all hoping for a good wrestling match but it wasn't to be, so Master hasn't vented his wrath proper, as yet, about the loss of coin. So I'm treading warily and, I pray you, don't show him that.' He pointed at the drawing. 'Put it out of sight, I beg you.'

I did as he asked, folding the paper and returning it to my scrip.

'In which direction did the fellow depart?' I asked.

'Easterly. But before he reached the bridge, I saw him turn

north, disappearing behind the walls of the Bishop of Ely's place. He'll be far away by now at the pace he ran.'

'You have our grateful thanks, lad, and here is an extra tuppence for you.' I pressed two pennies into his hand, sticky with ale. 'Now away to the kitchen with our order, if you will.' I returned my attention to Jude and Stephen. 'I fear we are too late. Jack be gone but leastwise we know he be in good health and whole.'

'And with hardly a farthing to his name,' Stephen said, looking downcast indeed. 'It bodes ill, does it not? He'll have to turn again to thievery if he's not to starve?'

'May God rot the rogue's skinny bollocks!' Jude added maliciously.

Unfortunately, there was naught I might say against Stephen's conclusions and, privily, though I would not speak the words aloud, I thought that if we ever saw Jack again, he would most likely be dangling at the end of the hangman's rope.

Chapter 13

Later that Thursday
The Foxley Place

I DETERMINED THAT I was done with Jack; I would pursue him no further.

I sat at my desk in the workshop after we had dined on a coney pasty with mustard sauce. This was not a matter of greed, partaking of a second dinner, but because my portion of the mutton and oyster pottage at the Swan-on-the-Hoop had been entirely consumed by Jude who looked so greatly in need of the additional sustenance. When he had eaten all he might, I paid a friendly carter to oblige by taking my brother home. I could not bear to think of his walking—or rather limping and staggering—all the way back to Ave Maria Alley. Apparently, some other carter had done him similar service in the opposite direction, thus enabling him to reach Holbourne before Stephen and me.

Now must I compose a letter to William Caxton, explaining right carefully what had come to pass. The old printer's money was gone, as was the miscreant who caused so much chaos and loss, but at least I could return his accounting and order book which I had brought from Jude's house this morn. I should gloss over where and how I had come by it. Also, whilst enjoying the ale and pottage in Holbourne, my brother, being then of a far more amenable humour, seemed willing to consider my previous proposal—rejected out of hand last time—the possibility of renting his unused printing press to Caxton. This, too, I would mention in my cautiously worded letter.

With constant reference to the contract lying before me, agreed betwixt myself and William Caxton and witnessed by the tapster at the Fighting Cock and Wynkyn de Worde, I wrote as follows:

From Master Sebastian Foxley of Paternoster Row in the City of London to Master William Caxton at the Fighting Cock in Westminster.

Greetings be unto you, good master, from your humble servant.

Wherefore I have pursued with diligence the enquiries you required of me in regard to the crimes of malicious damage, arson and theft committed against your person at the premises at the Sign of the Red Pale by the Almonry in the Abbey of Westminster upon the night of the eighteenth and nineteenth of June in the twenty-first year of the reign of King Edward, the fourth of that name since the Conquest, and in the year of Our Lord Jesu 1481, I now make my report as here followeth.

As pertaining to our contract, I have ascertained that the perpetrator of the crimes aforesaid has since departed from both Westminster and the City of London, beyond the jurisdiction, authority and apprehension of the above, taking his ill-gotten gains with him. Thus, both the miscreant and the aforementioned ill-gotten gains, namely, an amount of legal coin of the realm, value unspecified, are now gone beyond retrieval. I would hazard but cannot prove that the coin is now spent.

However, with regard to a certain book of accounting and orders relating to the business conducted at the aforesaid premises at the Sign of the Red Pale, this I have been able to recover and shall return it unto you, in person, at your convenience. Kindly send word to us at the Sign of the Fox in Paternoster Row as to the time and place most convenient unto you for this transaction upon which occasion I shall also present my account of expenses ensuing from the aforementioned enquiries.

Written at the Sign of the Fox in Paternoster Row in the City of London this twenty-eighth day of June in the year abovesaid.

Post Scriptum. I may be in a position to suggest unto you a means whereby your printing business could be resumed within a short space, without obligation on either part, if you permit me to speak of the matter when next we meet.

I omitted any reference to the death of the journeyman forwhy that had not come to pass when first I was summoned to Westminster to assist Master Caxton and was, therefore, not mentioned in my original instructions concerning the investigation. The contract stipulated that I should make enquiries regarding the fire and the theft of valuables; naught else. And in this instance, I would not venture an inch beyond what was specified. It was the safest outcome for us all.

I signed the letter, folded it and sealed it with red wax, using my signet of the fox's head. Deciding against trusting my missive to an urchin, I asked Hugh if he would oblige me by taking it to the Fighting Cock at Westminster. Master Caxton's 'humble servant' I might well be but a respectable citizen does not deliver his own correspondence.

With Hugh gone upon his errand, Kate resting, regaining her strength, sitting in the garden 'neath the apple tree, Ralf busy stitching another primer and Adam preparing pages for the individual Gospels which were to be our next rightwise project, I saw the opportunity to begin my own secret work.

I took the *Ars Notoria* from its place of concealment in the storeroom, covered it in a piece of leather, not only to hide its recognisable binding, such as it was, but to hold its broken spine together, and carried the suspect text to my desk. I should begin the much-needed repairs and, whenever my colleagues were otherwise engrossed in their own tasks—as now—I would also make a copy of the text. And so it began: my association with the ill-starred book.

And the world commenced to go awry from the writing of the first word. The ink, perfectly usable when I wrote the letter to Master Caxton, seemed to have curdled, watery and lumpy by turns. I had never known the like afore. Two pens broke in quick succession as they scratched and caught on the paper's surface, leaving blobs of ink like black buboes, and a draught from nowhere kept flapping the pages as I attempted to copy them. I prepared more quills, trimming the nibs with great care. It made little by way of improvement.

By mid-afternoon, I had produced four pages with script of a standard the newest apprentice should be ashamed of, blotted, smudged and replete with minor errors too numerous to count. I abandoned them, disgusted at my lack of skill in simple copying, and turned to another task.

In order to prove to myself that I was not at fault in my scribing, I began a new gathering for Ralf's primer upon the conjugation of irregular Latin verbs using the same ink, the same pen and all was well. The ink had uncurdled—if such was even possible—and now flowed evenly as the pen glided over the paper. No blots; no mistakes.

Again, I would try with the *Ars Notoria* and took a scrap of waste paper to pen from memory the opening line. Just as before, I could not write without the ink dribbling where it would, the nib grating upon the page and errors appearing which I swear were not of my making. The book seemed cursed. I could think of no other reason for my sudden difficulties.

Instead of making a copy, at least for the present, I determined to work upon the other part of Bess's commission: the repair and rebinding of the book. 'Twas so badly damaged, the text would have to be taken apart completely, the whole stitched anew and rebound. I could but hope the curse would not extend to preventing my efforts on this account.

I detached the cover boards which took no effort whatsoever as they fell off in my hands. I cut through the few remaining stitches with my blade for the purpose, sharp as a surgeon's fleam, though a blunt edge would have sufficed on the worn and frayed thread. The gatherings were now separate and I needed to mend the torn parchment as best I might. Sheets of vellum, so fine they be nigh invisible, must be cut to size and glued over the tears and to make good any missing corners, of which there were many. Such vellum be right costly but enabled the text beneath to be read through it and I had agreed its use with Bess beforehand.

By suppertime and the end of work, half the damaged folios were repaired and spread to dry on the board in the storeroom. This task went well and I could have done more but the board was covered in pages with not an inch to spare and I must leave it, making certain that I closed the door firmly. I dare not risk Gawain or Grayling, our mouser, or one of the little ones disturbing the order of the folios which the ancient scribe had not thought to number for my future convenience.

At supper, we ate a pottage made with scraps of various meats, tasty, cheap and nutritious. The meal was good and the company merry. I did not tell of my walk to Holbourne with Stephen forwhy none should know of Jack's crimes nor Jude's but I said I had tidings of Jack, that he was well but gone from London upon some venture of his own devising. That seemed to content most although Rose mouthed to me: 'Tell me later' and it was clear she knew there was more to the tale.

All the while, I noted Nessie was not her usual morose self. She smiled constantly, swishing her skirts as if about to dance and she flew about the kitchen, serving, tidying and cleaning even whilst we ate our meal.

'Nessie,' I said as I set aside my empty bowl which she instantly whisked away to be washed. 'Dare I ask why you be of so cheerful a countenance this eve?'

''Tis naught,' she said, smiling ever more broadly, showing the gap betwixt her front teeth.

'There's nothing amiss with being joyous,' Rose said. 'Is that not so, Nessie?'

'She's up to no good,' Adam concluded. 'What have you

done, eh, you foolish wench?' He helped himself to more pottage, having to grab his bowl to prevent her from taking it to wash. Such efficiency was unheard of 'til now.

Nessie drew herself upright, what little height she had, then head in the air and defiant she said:

'Don't call me a foolish wench, Adam Armitage. I'm Mistress Agnes Fattyng now an' if yer don't give me the proper respect wot I deserve as a married goodwife, my husband'll come an' take yer all t' task. So there!'

A stunned silence followed this pronouncement. I looked to Rose but she appeared as shocked as the rest of us. Only the children and Gawain continued with supper. Then we all spoke at once:

'Don't talk such ridiculous nonsense.' (Adam)

'What? But why would you?' (Meg, who has little time for men in general, God in particular.)

'You can't be. I wouldn't miss your wedding for anything.' (Kate)

'That was sudden.' (Hugh)

'Truly?' (Simon)

'Did I miss something?' (Ralf, who accepts whatever life throws at him.)

'How come?' (My erudite contribution.)

'Nessie...' Rose began.

'It's Agnes now!'

'Very well, Agnes... I pray you tell us how and when this... your marriage came to pass,' Rose said. 'And whom did you wed? Do we know him?'

'She can't be wed without Seb's consent so what does it matter who the damned fool happens to be?' Adam said, returning to his food, stirring his pottage with his spoon afore taking a hearty mouthful.

'I can and I did!' Nessie retorted. 'An' yer can't do nothin' about it. I'm wed good an' proper an' God Hisself knows it.'

Oh, by all the Saints in Heaven, I thought, 'tis one of those behind-the-tavern, under-the-hedge exchanges of vows the Church recognises as a true marriage if both parties consent and consummate the union. Lord save us!

'Who got wedded, then?' Ralf asked.

'Me an' Warin Fattyng, o' course... my true love... we plighted our troths—or whatever it is—this mornin' in the alley off the Shambles betwixt his mother's butcher stall and the Grey Friars yard. He kissed me an' everything an' called me his goody... his wife... so now we're wedded.'

'He kissed you? Is that all he did?' Adam asked, wiping his bowl with the last of the bread and finally setting down his spoon.

'What else should he do?' Nessie was frowning. 'We plighted our troths, like I said. He's my husband now.'

'But did he swive you?'

'I think that be sufficient interrogation in front of the little ones,' Rose said brusquely. 'Later, we may discuss the matter properly. Meg, I pray you, help me put the children to bed. Nessie... er, Agnes, serve more ale and attend to the dirty dishes...'

'But I...'

'All new wives must practise their housewifery skills. Come, Dickon, Julia.'

'Rose? Will you see Nick and Mundy abed also?' Adam said. 'I can't go back to Friday Street and miss this, er, discussion. After all, it's a matter which concerns us, too, doesn't it, Simon?' In truth, my cousin seemed gleeful at this sudden turn of events, and the possibility of a scandalous outcome amused him greatly, whereas I felt naught but dismay at this disastrous happenstance.

I shall not relate every twist and turn of that eve's conversation for, in truth, 'twas convoluted and an entanglement of uncertainties. Nessie became right angry and tearful by turns, saying we did not believe her and, amidst the tears and protests at our lack of belief, her telling of events became ever more muddled and bewildering.

By nine o' the clock by St Paul's bell, we were all us of wearied by our attempts to unravel the truth as to whether Nessie was wed or not. A quick kiss in an alleyway and the use of the term 'goody', meaning 'goodwife', did not constitute a marriage agreement in anyone's mind but hers. As for having 'plighted their troths' each to the other, the lass was so vague as to the meaning of the term that we knew not what she meant by it. Likewise, she seemed to think the kiss was an act of consummation and Adam's blatant description of the word's true meaning brought forth such cries of distress that we knew not whether they confirmed the lack or simply the acute shame of public acknowledgement.

According to the law, Nessie required my consent to marry, as Adam had said. As for Warin Fattyng, as an apprentice—if he be indentured officially through the Guildhall—the terms would forbid his marrying until the apprenticeship was completed. However, if the lad was but his mother's help at the butcher's stall, his parent's consent would suffice. But Nessie had no idea of Warin's situation nor his age. His mother, Matilda, was a widow and, according to Nessie, would not prevent her precious son from doing anything he wished. If he were already of age at one-and-twenty then he could please himself as to marrying.

But was all this immaterial? Had the couple done sufficient concerning the exchange of vows and intimacy for Holy Church to validate their union? We did not know.

As we retired to bed, I admit to being none the wiser as to Nessie's wedded state. But what was now made obvious was that I must needs speak with Matilda Fattyng and her son in due haste upon the morrow. If they were as vague as Nessie as to the facts, I knew not what should be done.

But, in any case, my thoughts had gone beyond this to more practical matters if, indeed, they were proven to be man and wife. Where would they live? What of making a living… a dowry for Nessie? Little wonder, then, that I hardly slept at all.

Friday, the twenty-ninth day of June
The Shambles by the Grey Friars' Church

Friday was a fish day but, all the same, the stench of butchery, even so early in the morn, already assaulted my senses. By midday, as the sun's heat increased, it would become untenable. Noisome heaps of yesterday's unsold offal accumulated in the gutter, reeking and fly-blown, despite the city ordinances which forbade such filth being left in the street. It seemed the gong-farmers had not troubled to bring their carts here last night, condemning the good citizens to suffer this appalling stink and black clouds of flies which rose and then descended as before at my passing. Needless to say, I had come to the Shambles alone, without Gawain, for obvious reasons, but other mangy curs growled and fought over the leavings.

Despite Nessie's fervent insistence that she ought, by rights, accompany me, I intended that my talk with the butcheress and her lad should be dignified and sensible, whereas I knew, if she came, Nessie's emotions would gain the upper hand and cause the discussion to fall into either a heated exchange or a puddle of tears. I had not the heart to deal with argument nor lamentation.

I approached the stall, stepping around a pile of still-steaming chitterlings which had slithered from a newly slaughtered carcass, having to bury my nose in my sleeve, struggling not to cast up my breakfast. Yet Matilda Fattyng appeared immune to the vileness, jointing the pig, cutting out the blood-engorged liver, dripping gore down her canvas apron stiff as a battle shield with old blood. I determined that plain bread and ale would suffice me for dinner, if I even had the courage to face that.

Despite my squeamish belly, goodwives thronged, bargaining and quarrelling over the best cuts whilst they were fresh, though they should be saved until the morrow. I held back, observing. Coming betwixt a trader and her proper customers—and she ready armed with a clattering cleaver and a rasping bone saw—

would in no way be conducive to amiable conversation. I saw that neither Fattyng, mother nor son, was a fair advertisement for their wares, both being skinny, the woman gaunt as a cadaver although her arms looked well muscled from wrestling with unwilling porcine victims. Their family name was an utter misnomer for not an ounce of fat sat on their bones all put together.

Although I thought calm consideration of the facts was required and an outcome, fair and reasonable as possible, must be decided upon, matters did not begin well. The son, Warin, recognised me—I walked this way to Newgate often enough—and squared his narrow shoulders in defiant stance, so, mayhap, he guessed the likely reason for my coming. I did not have the look of a customer, being without a basket for my purchases, and few men concerned themselves with marketing, that being a womanly task in the main. We men be too easily persuaded of a bargain that is no such thing, being ignorant of the appropriate price for many household necessaries and provisions. I knew not the cost of soap nor laces, of cabbages nor onions.

'We're busy,' Warin said, his voice high-pitched and as thin as he was.

'As I can see. I shall wait.'

My wait was lengthy as the sun shone directly along the Shambles and the heat grew in its intensity, turning the fresh meat darker in colour, accompanied by hordes of flies and the stink becoming worse as an hour passed and the morn progressed. I sought a patch of shade in an alleyway—likely the very one where Nessie claimed the couple had 'plighted their troths'—even as sweat dampened my shirt and glued my hair to my brow. Patience be a saintly thing, I reminded myself as three more goodwives came to discuss the virtues, or lack thereof, of each cut of meat in turn and haggled over the price.

At last, as a goodwife, babe in arms, finally decided upon the piece of pork belly she would purchase and moved away from the stall, I seized my opportunity.

'Good day to you, Mistress Fattyng. I am Sebastian Foxley of Paternoster Row. I believe my wife, Mistress Rose Foxley, be well-known to you as a customer of yours, along with our serving wench, Nessie by name—Agnes, if you will. I come to discuss a heavy matter regarding the standing of the wench and your son.'

Matilda Fattyng pulled herself upright, being of middling height for a woman, and wiped her gore-smeared hands on her filthy apron before folding her arms and bracing herself.

'Standing? What do you mean by this?' Her eyes glittered with maternal ferocity. 'My Warin has naught to do with wenches.'

Like a toddling, the youngster stood half-hidden behind his mother's skirts. I could see from his reddening cheek and wayward glance that what Matilda said was untrue, whatever his mother thought.

'Nessie claims that she and your son have plighted their troths, either to other, and thus stand wedded in the eyes of God and Holy Church. Is this true?' I turned and spoke directly to the lad. 'Well? What do you have to say in this matter?'

He stared at the crimson-stained sawdust strewn about the stall to soak up the blood, kicking at an unnameable piece of offal with the toe of his shoe afore burying it in wood shavings and an accompanying swarm of flies.

'Warin! Answer the man.' Matilda reached out a strong arm, grabbed her son by the arm and shook him. 'Tell him you've done naught so foolish as that. Go on; tell him or I'll box your ears.'

An incomprehensible mumbling was the only response as his cheeks and neck turned darker than the liver on the slab.

'What? Speak plain, you dolt.' Matilda slapped him.

'I might've said some'at like...' his voice trailed away. He looked to his mother and then burst into tears like a little child. And this was the one Nessie would call 'husband'? It did not bear thinking on.

'What age have you?' I asked him but 'twas his mother who answered:

'He's seen eighteen summers, if you can believe that? Snivelling like a babe. You disgust me, Warin. I married a fine man all those years since. How did he ever beget you upon me? What did I do to deserve you, you puling wretch? Now shut your noise before I give you a thrashing you'll not forget, you whinging ninny.' She took up a well-bloodied broom from behind the stall and smote him across the backside. The ensuing howl set the local dogs a-barking.

The Foxley Place

I summoned the household to the kitchen without delay. 'Twas time to put this nonsense to rest. Everyone stood ranged before me as though I were a Roman orator or the like.

'I have been to the Shambles and had speech with Matilda Fattyng and her son Warin. Now harken well, all of you...'

'But master, I...' Nessie said, moving forward.

'Hold your peace. You have had your say previously. Now hear me. Warin Fattyng admits taking you aside into an alleyway and whispering blandishments in your ear.'

'It weren't no blandishies... he said he'd marry me...'

'Nessie, that lad be half witless. He cries like a babe; he is but a child despite his eighteen years. I don't doubt he spoke sweet words unto you but he does not understand the meaning of plighting his troth and I am in some doubt that you know any better than he.'

'But we love each other!'

'Love be one thing, lass. Marriage is quite another. He could ne'er take responsibility for a wife... or children or put a roof o'er your head and bread upon the board.'

'We would have plenty of meat to eat.'

'Aye, I dare say you might but...'

'An' you could let us live in one o' your houses in Friday

Street or Distaff Lane like Adam... an' I'll come here each day t' work like Adam does, an' Warin would help his Mam in the Shambles like he does now. I planned ev'rything, master.'

'Nessie, a man and a woman must both fully understand the meaning and responsibilities involved in making a vow of marriage. Warin does not. Declaring that he loves you and kissing your cheek—which he admits he did—does not constitute a marriage. I consulted Father Thomas at St Michael's on my way home and he confirms this.'

'But he gave us stakys of beef and a whole leg of pork...'

'Indeed, whilst his mother's attention was elsewhere and she has beaten him soundly for his foolishness. They cannot afford such generosity.'

'But I love him... he loves me...' Nessie wept quietly—not her usual noisy wailing—and I realised this once the tears were genuine.

'I be sorry, lass,' was all I could think to say as I patted the back of her hand. I ne'er knew what to do with a weeping woman and was relieved when Rose and Meg took my place. 'Now, the rest of us have work to do in the shop!'

Rose looked at me over Nessie's bowed head.

'A word with you, husband, before you set to work.'

My heart clenched. Neither her voice nor countenance seemed to be of good cheer and I wondered what else could be amiss as she bade Meg to deal with Nessie and beckoned me to follow her out into the garden. We paused 'neath the apple tree in its verdant shade, surrounded by the perfume of roses, lavender and other flowering herbs. A blackbird sang lustily and bees hummed. Yet it was clear my love had other things upon her mind than the beauties of summer. Her face was troubled.

'I would not have the others learn of this nor you to hear it by means of the gossipmongers. Seb, I know you have a considerable liking for Bess Chambers' pretty niece...'

'You be mistaken, sweeting. I feel naught for her...'

Rose put up her hand to stop my protest.

'You like her, Seb, I know that and must warn you to stay away, not because I'm a jealous wife—I trust you as I trust the Lord Jesu—but tales are abroad.' She wrung her hands and seemed to have difficulty finding the words. 'In short…a man called Thomas Goulden has lately died and they say that Sarra Shardlowe cursed him and has used witchcraft to bring about his death. There. So now you know.'

'Where did you come by such nonsense, Rose? You should pay no heed to rumours.' I broke off a sprig of mint, twirled it betwixt my fingers afore inhaling its clean scent and chewing the top, tender, folded leaflets.

'I visited Bess's shop whilst you were at the Shambles. Fever still stalks the streets. There are a few cases of pestilence now in Vintry Ward and Kate yet needs to regain her full strength so I went to buy more medicines. A crowd of folk had gathered outside the apothecary's shop and was shouting out Sarra's supposed crimes, crying "Murder!" and yelling for the bailiff and the beadle to come and take the witch away from among them. Bess barred the door and shuttered the windows but I saw them hammering on the woodwork fit to break it through.

'Oh, Seb, those poor women… poor Bess. What has she ever done but help folk? Now they're imprisoned in their own home, afraid of their neighbours.'

'Thaddeus must be told of this straightway.'

'But he must know of it already for the accusers themselves had sent for him. But matters were getting hotter, the crowd becoming impatient, threatening to hang both aunt and niece if the bailiff did not come in haste to do his duty. Coward that I am, I came home. I knew not what else to do, Seb. There were so many of them: a mob, in truth, chanting "Witch, witch, witch!" And none spoke out to support Bess's cause. Mayhap, like me, they did not dare for fear of being accounted likewise a witch. Oh, Seb, I felt so helpless.'

'You did right to come away, lass.' I embraced her tightly, relieved that she had the good sense to depart the place. I would

have failed as a husband if aught harmed her and could ne'er
have forgiven myself for it. 'There was naught you could have
done, sweeting: one woman against so many, all with their
blood a-boil. But I will go. Thaddeus should be informed of
the whole tale and not be prejudiced by the crazed mob. He and
his constables may need the aid of reasonable citizens.'

'Then take Adam with you. An extra pair of strong arms
cannot come amiss. Take your old staff, too, it may be of use.
And Seb, have a care, I pray you.' She kissed me then as one
might a lover who would not return.

'All will be well. Fear not.' I made to walk away but turned
back. She watched me from the tree's dappled shade: those
adored hazel eyes, that kissable mouth. 'I love you, Rose, with
all my heart and soul,' I added afore going within doors to
collect Adam and my trusty staff which had seen me safe so
many times in the past.

Bishopsgate

We arrived, breathless, in Bishopsgate Street. The place was
in uproar with Bess Chambers' shop at the centre of the mêlée.
Men and women were throwing stones, mouldy worts and
insults at the innocent doorway. From the edge of the crowd,
Adam and I craned our necks, trying to espy Thaddeus Turner,
certain he must be somewhere in the unruly throng, attempting
to restore order. But we could not see the City Bailiff nor his
constables.

Despite the noise, a woman's strident voice shouted louder
than the rest:

'Give us the murdering witch, Bess, and we'll leave you in
peace.' I recognised Anneis Fuller, the local gossipmonger-in-
chief. I was unsurprised that she stood at the centre of the strife
if, indeed, she was not the instigator and primary cause thereof.
'You know full well she cursed Master Goulden and now he's
dead by her bewitchment. Hand her over, Bess, or suffer the

consequences along with her.'

There were shouts of agreement and 'Give us the witch!' I saw a fellow with an axe muscling his way through the throng. Folk moved aside when they realised his intent, opening a path directly to the shop door.

'Adam, we must stop this,' I said.

He nodded and we, too, pushed our way through the crowd. He carried a cudgel and I my staff and, just as for the axe-wielder, we were given clear passage to the shop. Obviously, they mistook our purpose for one of aiding him in breaking down the door. The wretch leant his axe against the door jamb whilst he spat on his palms, preparing for the effort required. He took it up again and practised hefting it—once, twice, thrice— enjoying being at the centre of the crowd's attention. This delay gave us leave to reach Bess's threshold. Just as he braced himself, took a firm stance, feet apart and raised the axe a fourth time, aiming to strike at the painted oak timbers, Adam swung his cudgel and hit the fellow across the back. He pitched forward with a squawk of pain. The axe fell from his grasp and clattered upon the cobbles. I fended off another who attempted to retrieve the axe, jabbing him in the belly with my staff.

'Stay back, all of you!' I shouted. 'Whatever crime you think has been committed, 'tis the business of the proper authorities to see justice done.'

'We are the proper authorities,' Mistress Fuller yelled back. 'We are the hue-and-cry in rightful pursuit of a felon.'

'Then you must have proof of guilt. Did any one of you witness the crime?' I looked about the crowd but none met my eye.

'No, but I heard her curse Tom Goulden with my own ears and now he's dead of it,' Anneis Fuller declared. 'So, as a dutiful citizen, I called up the hue-and-cry as I should and we're here to apprehend the felon. We all know the murderous witch is hiding in there. Come on!' she called out to the crowd. 'Ignore these puling milksops. Break the door down.' With which she shoved me aside and grabbed up the axe. I could have used my staff upon her but, she being a woman, I hesitated.

Adam had no such qualms and pulled her back, flinging her aside.

'Keep away, you malicious bitch,' he growled. 'Get that bloody axe, Seb, before anybody else thinks to use it.'

I attempted to do as my kinsman said for it seemed most prudent to do so but, of a sudden, hands grasped at me, my clothing, my limbs, and wrestled me to the cobbles. I was struck here, there and all about. I was kicked and boots trampled upon me. I felt bones crack; a blow to my head set my senses reeling, a shaft of pain lanced through my shoulder and for a moment darkness overwhelmed me.

Then Adam was laying about us with his cudgel.

'Get up, Seb. On your feet, if you can. Go to, you harpy! Stand away, knave! Let him be, I say.' I heard the thud of stoutest oak thwacking flesh and bone; the howls of the injured. 'Get up, cousin. I can keep them at bay no longer.'

I obeyed, slower than oozing treacle, pausing time and again so the pain and dizziness might subside. Once my feet were beneath me, Adam grabbed my arm to lead me away but I cried out as a flaming torrent of agony ripped through me. He loosed his hold and took my other hand, pulling me into the alley beside the Bull Inn next door. I sagged against the coolness of the plastered wall, sweat dripping.

'What came to pass?' I asked, my voice shaking.

'Never mind that now. Let me look at you.' He touched my left shoulder, feeling with his fingertips. Despite his care, I gasped. 'Your shoulder is all out of joint. We'll get you to the surgeon straightway. Come now, can you walk so far or must I carry you?'

'I can walk,' I assured him though I felt unsteady as a St John's Eve drunkard, swaying on my feet. He took a firm grip upon my good right arm, still carrying both his cudgel and my staff, but none bothered us once we left Bishopsgate.

The journey seemed endless to Surgeon Dagvyle's place by St Mary-le-Bow Church at the end of Bread Street. I had to stop frequently to rest and steady myself. At one point, sick with pain, Adam propped me against some convenient wall and left me, returning shortly with a ladle of cool water, after which blessing I felt somewhat restore and staggered onwards.

Mercifully, the surgeon was at home and none other was there before me, demanding his attention. Likely, more customers would arrive shortly, my cousin having made right readily with his cudgel, there would be lumps and bruises aplenty requiring a surgeon's skills. My condition was not difficult to assess forwhy Adam told him what was amiss. Even so, an age of probing and manipulating followed as I bit my nether lip and drew blood in my effort not to cry aloud.

Only after that—why not before?—did Mistress Dagvyle give me some bitter cup to drink to dull the pain, so she said, whilst the surgeon set up a tortuous-looking device of straps and pulleys with a great winding handle on the side. I dared not think upon its purpose.

'Tis a new invention of mine,' Dagvyle told me cheerily. 'I had the idea quite a few years since, after I was called to the Tower of London to attend a poor wretch who'd suffered at the hands of that appalling rogue, the king's brother-in-law. You know the one I mean? Exeter, aye, that's him: mad as a bear and vicious as a serpent. I was right glad when I heard he was drowned.' Dagvyle paused to mop his brow as he wrestled with some disobliging piece of the apparatus and I watched, further disconcerted by the minute. 'Anyhow, the duke had this damnable device to rend a man's limbs, pulling them from their sockets, and so proud of it was he that he called it "his daughter", as if it were a benevolent thing. Aye, "the Duke of Exeter's daughter", that was it.

'Now, having seen it, I thought how the cursed thing might be used for good—to undo the damage it did and return a man's joint to its rightful place—with just a few adjustments, of course. And here it stands, built to my own specifications. I've not used it before but yours is the perfect case to try it out.'

Feeling anything but reassured by the surgeon's tale, I wanted to leave but he and his wife guided me towards it and sat me down in a chair in the midst of the contraption.

'Now, see, we strap you in firmly... thus, so your body can't move.'

So I cannot flee and escape its devilish ministrations, I thought. Not that I could have run anywhere had God Almighty Himself ordered me to do so.

'All will be well in no time, Seb,' Adam told me, standing well back, though neither his tone of voice nor his doubtful countenance as he eyed the device were convincing.

Then—and agonisingly—the surgeon pulled my left arm out straight to the side and fastened another strap above the elbow and a second about the wrist. Tears ran down my face and I wiped them away with my free hand but then that, too, was fixed in place. Only my legs below the knee remained unbound now.

'I'll make a few more adjustments here... and here,' the surgeon was saying. 'That should suffice, I think. Let's give the handle a few turns and see what happens. If it works, I'll call it "Dagvyle's daughter" Aye, that sounds very well. And you can advise your friends of its benefits, if they ere have a need: come see Surgeon Dagvyle's child.'

'Lord Jesu, save me,' I prayed under my breath and began reciting the *Pater Noster*. The handle turned, ropes tightened, pulleys squeaked and my arm began to twist. I cried out as bones grated but the surgeon continued my torture.

I had suffered the like some years before. Crippled in shoulder and hip from childhood, a fiend I shall not name once hung me up by my wrists and left me to die in a fire. I had wrenched my joints so hard in the struggle to be free, I called it a miracle from Almighty God when my body was pulled straight. But I suppose I yet had a weakness and my shoulder dislocated more readily than it should.

A great crack like a cannon shot from the Tower seemed to rip through my body but then I must have swooned forwhy I do not recall the straps being undone nor my release from that hellish device.

The next I knew I was sitting on a settle, propped about with cushions and a blanket over me. I was naked from the waist upwards and Surgeon Dagvyle was binding my shoulder firmly in place. It ached severely but the worst fires of pain were quenched. Mistress Dagvyle assisted me in getting dressed and once decently clad in shirt and doublet, the surgeon returned with a wide leather strap. I shrank back, half expecting further torture, but he arranged the leather into a loop about my neck in which he settled my arm.

'Rest that limb and keep the bindings tight for a fortnight at the least. The bones and sinews need to regain their strength in their rightful positions. You'll know when they've reset themselves for the pain will subside though the bruises will take longer to fade. Have a care, Master Foxley.'

'My wife spoke those very words to me but a few hours since,' I said.

'Well, you should've heeded her wise advice. Now, as to the reckoning: poppy juice for the pain, two pence; ointment for bruising, a penny; bindings, another penny; the use of my marvellous new "Dagvyle's daughter" you may have half price because I had not tried it before and 'twas by way of an experiment, as you might say, so five pence for that. With my skills and knowledge and my wife's services in addition... shall we say one shilling in all and cheap at the price?'

'A shilling? That's robbery and naught else,' Adam declared, folding his arms. 'We're not paying you more than six pence. You could've put my cousin's arm back in its socket by brute force alone. I've seen it done: a pull and a twist and it clicks into place, good as new in a few moments without all that fuss and prolonging his suffering.'

'It is what it is,' the surgeon said. 'Progress is needed in medicine as with any other craft. Look to your own, Master Armitage: scribing is being replaced by the new printing press.'

'Not if we have any say in the matter, it isn't. Cursed contraptions… the world's bane.'

Wearily, I eased myself off the settle, feeling bruised and battered as a pig's bladder in a game of foot ball.

'Here, take my purse, Adam; pay the man his due. I have not the heart to argue. Let us go home.'

The Lord alone knew what Rose would say when she saw me.

Chapter 14

Saturday, the thirtieth day of June
The Foxley Place

DAYLIGHT, TOO bright to bear at first, streamed through the glass panes of the window. I hurt; every part of me. Each bone, muscle and sinew, every inch of skin throbbed, from the hairs on my head to my toenails. One great black mass of pain radiated from my left shoulder. How came that to be? At first, I could not recall and briefly imagined I was back in Canterbury, having suffered that dire fall. But, nay, this was my own bedchamber at home.

Ah! Bishopsgate. That I now remembered. Trampled by the mob... my shoulder out of joint. How could I forget the surgeon's new device of torture? But what of Bess Chambers and her niece? Their safety had been our purpose in going to Bishopsgate, had it not? How had they fared after we abandoned them to their neighbours? There were so many questions to which I must have answers.

'Ah, Seb, the Lord Jesu be thanked, you are awake at last.' Rose stood beside the bed.

'What hour is it? I must go to Bishopsgate...'

'You're going nowhere this day but resting abed.'

'Where be Adam?'

'He lingers at the board, as usual, hoping for an extra helping. Where else would he be? Now drink this remedy. It will ease your hurts.'

'Very well but then...'

TONI MOUNT

'Then you'll lie back and sleep.'

'I am no invalid to waste the day.'

'You have more bruises and lesions than I have hairs on my head. Rest, husband! And that is my final word on the matter.'

'But what of Bess Chambers and Sarra?'

'Never you mind.'

'I must know. Are they safe?'

'Safe enough for the present.'

'Where?'

'In Thaddeus Turner's care at Guildhall and he's downstairs having breakfast, too, if you would speak with him. I'll send him up to you later… Now cease your fretting.'

'What, both women? But they be innocent.'

'Sarra is in his custody as much for her own safety as any other reason. Bess is with friends.'

'Who?'

Rose sighed as she straightened the sheets and propped my aching arm upon a cushion like some holy relic.

'With us, if you must know. She prepared this strong remedy for your easement but you must drink it whilst it's still hot for the best effect.'

'Bess is here? What of her shop?' I sipped the potion. It scalded my tongue; even so I tasted bitterness 'neath honey and mint.

'Her shop was wrecked, Seb. They smashed everything, pulled up or chopped down all the plants in her lovely garden, overturned the bee skeps. Her business is ruined. And atop all these concerns, Sarra stands accused of witchcraft. It's so unfair. I invited Bess to stay with us as long as is needful for I could think of no other way to help her.'

'You did right, Rose, but the greatest aid would be to resolve this foolish accusation against her niece and I cannot do that whilst lying abed. I pray you, help me to dress, lass. 'Tis difficult with my arm bound up like a babe in swaddling and twice as useless.'

'Drink Bess's remedy, I pray you, then, maybe…'

I would not be dissuaded but, as I had said, getting clad for the day was not a task easily nor swiftly accomplished. However, at last, I descended the stairs and, belatedly, gave 'good day' to one and all and joined the company in the kitchen to break my fast.

'How's the shoulder?' Adam asked, wiping the last of the buttery juices from his platter with a wedge of bread.

'As well as I might hope after my encounter with the surgeon's dreadful contraption.'

'I'm sure it would've been far less trouble just to pull the arm back into place by brute force. That's what they did when I fell out of a tree as a lad and put mine out of joint. Mind, it took three grown men to do it: two to hold me down whilst the third did the deed. I screamed, I can tell you, but not half so loud as you did yesterday. What a weed-sop you are, cousin.'

'*Deo gratias. Amen.*' I murmured a brief grace over my platter of pigeon breast in a butter and parsley sauce as Meg set it before me, ignoring my cousin's insult. I ate alone and one-handed as the others departed to their daily tasks, to the workshop or market, until only Thaddeus and Bess remained.

'I must thank you, Master Seb,' Bess began. 'You did your best for us and it gained you naught but injury for which I'm greatly sorry. And now you give me succour in my time of need for which I'm beholden unto you also. If there are any means by which I may repay your kindness...' She used her apron to dab at her eyes.

I put down my spoon to touch her hand with mine.

'We but did as any Christian would,' I said.

'Aye, but a great many so-called Christians didn't. In truth, they were calling for Sarra to be dealt with in the name of Our Lord Christ, saying she slew Thomas Goulden by using the black arts and invoking the name of the Horned One. All lies! That Anneis Fuller should be ashamed of herself, spreading such malice and she having been aided by Sarra in easing her painful joints and the removing of warts.'

233

Thaddeus shifted on his stool, a troubled look in his eye.

'I have apologies to make, too, in that an accident with an overturned wain and a flock of sheep on London Bridge took all my attention when you both needed me,' he said.

'A man cannot be in two places at one time; 'tis no fault of yours, my friend.' I finished my meat and passed the soiled dish to Nessie for washing. She snatched it from me with ill grace. I had not been forgiven for undoing her would-be marriage to the butcheress's lad, yesterday. I sipped my ale afore asking: 'What of Sarra? Is she safe?'

'Aye, safe from the mob for the present,' Thaddeus said. 'She has a bed and food and drink supplied.'

'Not in gaol, God forefend!'

'No. In my chamber at Guildhall but it can only be temporary. As you know, Seb, it's cramped as it is without a truckle bed and a necessary bucket as well and I need a place to work. But, for the present, she has food, drink and blankets.'

'Who is guarding her safety whilst you are here? Guildhall is a public building; anyone could enter and harm her.'

'Not with young Constable Tom Hardacre standing at the door. He's smitten, you know… with Sarra, I mean. He'd ward off a Saracen horde to protect her.'

I nodded but was not reassured.

'I know the lass can enchant men, Thaddeus, having felt beguiled myself, and might not folk think the young constable has fallen under her spell also? If he goes to any length to keep her safe, it could be said that she has enthralled him likewise in her web of magick and what then? 'Twould be another accusation to make against her. Have a care in this regard, I beg of you. Set old Angus the Scot to watch over her instead.'

'I can't. Angus has the summer fever upon him and lies abed.'

'Oh, no. That, too, could be accounted her doing in such wise as to ensure her guardian be in her power.'

'Now, Seb,' Bess said, 'Don't go making more of this than there is. Nobody has said anything in that regard about young

Thomas Hardacre and Alfred so don't even suggest it. My niece is in more than sufficient trouble as it stands without you adding to it. Somehow, I have to prove her innocent of these ungodly charges.'

'You are not alone, Bess. Thaddeus and I will do all we can on that account, will we not, my friend?'

'Aye, I suppose so.' The bailiff did not sound keen, and sat, fiddling with his sauce-stained napkin. I think he had much other business upon his mind and legion duties to carry out.

'I shall come with you to Guildhall and we can begin our enquiries to prove Sarra's innocence straightway.'

'But you're injured,' he said, as though I needed reminding.

'There be naught amiss with my legs to get me there nor my mouth and ears to ask questions and hear answers. My eyes and mind also be fit enough for the task, I assure you.'

'All the same, I shall also be keeping a watch on you as we make our way,' Bess told me, wagging her finger at my bold words. 'I have to go to my shop.'

'You intend to return to Bishopsgate, Bess? Be that wise?'

'As wise as your decision in your wounded state. Besides, where else should I go? It's my home and I have a livelihood to repair and amend.'

Bishopsgate

As it came to pass, we went not to Guildhall in the first instance but to Bess's home and shop to see what might be salvaged afore looters and other ne'er-do-wells made matters worse than they were already.

We three arrived at a scene of devastation which had so lately been a thriving apothecary's shop. The door hung askew, one of the leather hinges ripped asunder. The shutters had been smashed, leaving the windows as empty eye-sockets and, within, not a pot nor vial, neither counter-board nor shelves: naught remained undamaged. Thaddeus and I stood staring at the wreckage, disbelieving that the hands of neighbours and customers—those whom Bess had aided down the years—could have done this. Poor Bess. She stood in the doorway, shocked beyond measure, silent tears coursing down her cheeks. I wanted to offer words of comfort but what could I say?

Thaddeus bent to pick up a bunch of dried lavender, pulled from its peg in the rafters like all the other herbs. He sniffed it before he handed it to Bess. She breathed in its perfume and managed a smile. Some things could not be destroyed: Nature's gifts for one; a woman's determination for another. But the garden out the back nigh undid her resolve.

The bee skeps were broken apart, leaving the creatures homeless. The rose bushes were hacked down; their lovely blossoms trampled into the dirt. Every other plant had been uprooted. Marigolds and white comfrey lay strewn and wilted; feverfew and woundwort, gone; Our Lady's lilies pulled up in their purity.

Bess righted the garden bench, where we used to sit and drink her elderflower cordial, and would have sat upon it except that its fourth leg now poked from the earth, having been employed to dig out the rosemary and lavender. Instead, she eased down onto the back step and buried her face in her apron.

I left her to her sorrow. I knew not how her garden might be saved but I could attend her books in the still room, if they might yet be salvaged. Having passed from the shop directly through to the garden, I had taken little heed of the still room previously, but, in truth, I now saw that it had suffered the worst damage of all. At every step, broken glass or smashed earthenware crunched 'neath my boots. I took up a broom, intending to commence sweeping a path through the debris, but swiftly discovered that using a besom one-handed was no easy task. I left it leaning in the corner as I had found it.

Books lay tumbled under the broken shelves on which they once lay. A greenish liquid had been poured over them—a herbal tisane of some kind, to judge by the smell of it. Pages were torn asunder, others soaked in oak-gall ink, obliterating forever the knowledge therein. Such a loss! I straightened pages where I could and set the volumes to one side upon the floor to dry. The workbench at which Bess distilled her remedies and concocted her medications had been thrown off its trestles and chopped to firewood with an axe. The trestles were, likewise, broken beyond mending.

Bess came in, red of eye but calm, and took up the discarded broom. Swift and efficient, she swept the detritus of her life into the front shop and then out into Bishopsgate Street in a defiant mound for all to see and be inconvenienced by. Mistress Chambers was not to be cowed by her neighbours.

'You can't leave that there, blocking the way, Bess, it's against the City Ordinances,' Thaddeus told her.

'So? Fine me, Sir Bailiff, as if I care what you do. I haven't a clipped farthing to pay a fine nor the scawagers to remove it, so it will have to stay where it is, won't it?' She marched back to her still room, holding her broom like a staff of office.

Thaddeus sighed and shook his head but said no more of it. Instead, he returned to the shop, retrieving whatever he could from the mess as he went. A linen bag of shed snake skins was brushed off and restored to a peg, out of harm's way. He lifted bunches of thyme and marjoram and blew away the dust.

'Watch out for that!' I warned him, pointing into the gloom where a pair of beady eyes stared at us.

'Good God defend us!' My friend jumped back, startled.

'Fear not,' I said, laughing. ''Tis dead as a stone.' Awkwardly, I lifted a stuffed, scaly thing from under a clutter of torn cloths and broken pots. 'Bess says 'tis a young crocodile—whatever that be—and serves no purpose other than to attract custom.' I saw that its tail was snapped off but its teeth appeared fearsome as ever.

'To attract custom? Is that true, Seb? The Lord knows it would scare me away.'

'Children are intrigued by it, apparently. Most believe it to be a dragon's chick.'

'Ah! Bailiff Turner. Well met, indeed. I've been to Guildhall, looking for you.'

We left the strange beast and turned to see Mistress Anneis Fuller on the threshold.

'Shop's closed… for obvious reasons,' Thaddeus said.

Mistress Fuller straightened her shoulders and stood tall as she might, oozing self-importance.

'As if I shall ever seek any remedy or ointment here again. Never trust a witch, I say.'

'There be no evidence of any such…' I began.

'Indeed there is. I have the proof. Look here, Bailiff. Is this not proof enough to condemn those two, both aunt and niece?' She folded back a napkin which covered her willow basket and took out an object about as long as my hand and gave it to Thaddeus. My friend's eyes widened in horror and he looked about frantically, desperate for somewhere to put it other than flinging it to the floor.

I took it from him but swiftly regretted doing so.

'Where did you come by this… thing?' I asked.

'Here, of course. Well, in the still room, hid behind the books on the shelf in secret-wise. It's how that witch did curse Thomas Goulden to death. No doubt about that.'

In my hand lay a poppet; a doll made of wax; a mannequin. It had a lock of black hair with a few grey affixed to the head by pressing it in whilst the wax was yet warm and malleable. Otherwise, the poppet was naked but possessed of exaggerated male parts. But that was not the worst of it: rusty-tipped pins— it could have been blood, or was that simply my imagining— pierced it: one through the head, a second through the groin from front to back and the third skewered a tiny heart-shape of red cloth through its breast.

A cry of dismay came from the still room and Thaddeus and I hastened to see what was amiss, Anneis Fuller bustling in our wake most eagerly.

Bess stood, staring down at the flagstone floor, now swept clear of debris. One hand covered her mouth.

'Oh, aye, and I was about to tell you of this.' Mistress Fuller pointed at the stones whereon was drawn a chalk star-shape of five points, now somewhat smeared by the action of sweeping but clear enough all the same. 'We found this too: a device used by witches for the conjuring of demons,' she explained. 'It's called a pentangle, a wicked thing invented by the Devil to aid his acolytes.'

'It wasn't here before,' Bess cried. 'It's not of my doing nor Sarra's. I swear this upon the Gospels.'

'Don't you dare misuse Holy Writ to try to deny what I know…' Mistress Fuller shook her fist at Bess as Thaddeus pulled her back. '…what we all know… that you are in league with Satan, his filthy minions, his worshippers. It wouldn't surprise me if they find more of these wax dolls about the place… in that cauldron, I shouldn't wonder, or upstairs in the linen coffer or hid in the chimney. Aye, that's where witches hide such things, the evil bitches, but I'm wise to your wicked ways, Widow Chambers, and I'll see you both hang yet.'

Bess turned away and went out to the garden. I followed her as she climbed the outside stair to the room above the shop. This, too, had been ransacked; the featherbed, sheets and coverlet lay ripped asunder, feathers everywhere. Bess could not suppress a sob, wiping her tears away with the back of her hand, but she said naught. She lifted the lid of the linen coffer—or what remained of it—to reveal a tangle of shredded garments. And there, in the midst of the chaos of cloth, quite undamaged, lay another mannequin of wax, just as Anneis Fuller had foretold.

'Look to the chimney, Bess,' I said and, indeed, another similar image lay, soot-covered, behind the ready-laid fire in the hearth.

'She put them there,' Bess said. 'How else would she know? But how can we prove it, Master Seb, when all will blame us?'

I took the mannequin from the hearth to the doorway where

the light was brightest, blew away the worst of the soot and examined the thing with close care. I wished I had my scrying glass to hand, the better to observe the detail but, even so…

'I think there may be a way, Bess. Do not despair.'

'Truly?'

'I make no promises but I can try. I used such evidence once before, some years ago, to prove my brother, Jude, innocent of murder… well, it helped, leastwise… and I believe the same may aid us in this instance.'

'Oh, please try, I beg of you.' Bess held my good arm, imploring me.

'What I require is beeswax and a means of heating it.'

'Use the wretched poppet; melt that down straightway.'

'Nay. This be part of the evidence we needs must preserve. Do you have any good candles? It matters not if they be broken or merely stubs.'

'I had some of best beeswax which I made from last year's hives. They were in the still room but are gone now. They would fetch a good price, no doubt.'

I looked at the mannequin in my hand and wondered.

'Do you not also use wax to seal your vials and bottles?'

'Aye, I do, and I keep some spare for the purpose…' Bess hurried out and down the stair, back to the still room. 'It's here,' she called out, 'There is some left.'

As I arrived behind her, Thaddeus stepped forward, holding another wax image, a small thing, swaddled as a babe.

'It was in the cauldron, as Mistress Fuller said was likely,' he told us, his face grave.

'And you know Mistress Goulden lost the child she was carrying?' Anneis Fuller declared, her face suffused with triumph. 'They say it was because of the shock of her husband dying so sudden but I think otherwise and there you have the truth of it in your hand, Bailiff. She and her niece killed the babe in her womb!' An accusatory finger pointed at Bess. 'I demand that you lock her up and leave her to dwindle and rot

THE COLOUR OF DARKNESS

away like those she's cursed.'

'Be not so swift to accuse, mistress,' I said. 'How was it that you knew precisely where the mannequins were hid?'

'I saw them when...'

'When you wilfully destroyed all Widow Chambers' linen above stairs and poked about in her fireplace? And when you flung her precious books from the shelf and nosed into her cauldron afore tipping the contents thereof over the books?' This was guesswork on my part but her expression betrayed that my suppositions fell close to the mark. 'Or, mayhap, that was when you seized the opportunity to hide the images in those places?'

'How dare you suggest...'

'Oh, indeed, Mistress Fuller, I dare a great deal when I see grave injustice done.'

'You can't prove anything... any of you.' With which words, the woman stormed out of the shop.

'Not yet,' I murmured, 'But I will.'

'Bailiff! Bailiff Turner!' Constable Tom Hardacre burst over the threshold, having narrowly avoided colliding with Mistress Fuller. 'Thank God, I've found you.' The fellow paused, leaning against the door to catch his breath but it promptly collapsed and fell from its only remaining hinge, depositing him on the front step. 'Damnation! I—I'm so sorry. I...'

'No matter, Hardacre,' Thaddeus said, helping his constable to his feet. 'What's so urgent?'

'I've been searching everywhere for you...'

'And now you've found me.'

'And for her... she's gone, sir!'

'Who's gone?'

'She... Sarra's gone... magicked herself away. She wasn't there when I took her food... gone... through a locked door and all and nobody saw... I'm so sorry, sir.'

'Ill-tidings, indeed,' I muttered as gloom descended like a pall upon us. 'Fleeing will not aid her case in the least and neither will your accounting her escape as being by means of magick, constable. Do not speak thus of her disappearance, I pray you. Magick had naught to do with it.'

'How can you know?' Hardacre insisted. 'You weren't there when I unlocked the door and found her gone. Unless she was there all the while but had made herself invisible or turned into a mouse by witchery and escaped as I opened the door... that could be it. Aye, that makes sense.'

'Listen here, constable,' Thaddeus shook him roughly by the shoulder. 'That makes *no* sense whatever and Master Foxley is right: you are to say naught of magick. The lass has escaped our custody, where she was safe. That is foolishness, not witchery, you hear?' He turned to me. 'But how in the Holy Name of Christ Jesu did she do it?'

Guildhall

We crowded into the City Bailiff's cramped place of work: Thaddeus, Bess, Tom Hardacre and myself. 'Twas all too true. Sarra was gone.

Parker, Thaddeus' useless and generally idle clerk had, this once, so it appeared, made the effort to tidy the little chamber. Gone was the truckle bed and slop bucket and an empty cup and platter were on a stool. Unfortunately for him, the clerk arrived just as we surveyed his handiwork.

'You damned fool, Parker. What have you done here?' Thaddeus scolded him ere he could squeeze in the doorway.

'I put the place t-to rights, sir. I thought with the wench gone, there was no reason...'

'There may have been clues to her means of escape and you've destroyed them! I should relieve you of your post this instant, you incompetent idiot. You never tidy anything, so why now, for pity's sake? The one time you should have left all as it was... and who ate her breakfast, eh? Go on; get out of my sight, Parker. Your presence offends me mightily.' Thaddeus slumped down in his chair, pulling at his earlobe in frustration as the clerk scurried out. 'Now what do we do? Any ideas, Seb?'

'Aye. One or two and you can dismiss any notion of magick. See this? The plaster be badly scraped 'neath the window, which I do not recall having seen afore, and, I warrant, one of the stools was here until Parker moved it. Sarra climbed out of the window and attempted to get a purchase for her feet against the wall.'

'But she couldn't,' Hardacre interrupted. 'It's high and so narrow and the window shutters were yet barred from the outside as well as from within. They're made that way in case we need to keep prisoners in, as well as keeping folks out. I saw that the bar outside was still in place when I opened the shutters first thing this morn.'

'Sarra had an accomplice,' I said. 'What say you, Bess?'

'It wasn't me. I stayed at your house all night. Ask Meg. I shared her bed.'

'Indeed, I ne'er supposed otherwise but can you think of anyone who might have aided your niece in her escape?'

'I'm the only family she has in London and I've not yet written to my sister concerning these recent calamities, so none else in the family know. In truth, I'm not sure I dare to tell her.'

'What of friends? A lovely lass like Sarra must have made friends here in the city.'

'I think not. We work long hours at this time of year—or we did until...'

'I know how hard this must be for you, Bess,'

'Aye, Seb, it is. But Sarra was busy, learning the apothecary's art, tending the garden... the loss of Our Lady's lilies, which she nurtured so carefully, will break her heart when she learns of it.' Bess sniffed and dried her eyes on her apron. 'Apart from running a few errands and occasionally delivering remedies to customers at home, she hardly went out... except for a few times, after sunset. You know, I did wonder...'

'Wonder concerning what?' I encouraged her.

She forced a laugh and shook her head.

'Foolish, I know, but I wondered if she might have found herself a lad.'

'In the case of such a pretty lass, that seems more than likely,' Thaddeus said.

'Aye, but if she did, it must have ended forwhy there haven't been any twilight assignations of recent evenings. If there ever was a lad, I expect the golden light of love has since turned to dross, as it ever does.' She sighed and wept anew. 'My dear Sarra, what have I done? I should've kept a closer watch upon her, made her stay at home. Oh, where is she now? 'Tis all my fault.'

'Nay, Bess. You could not have foreseen any of this. Besides, you be her aunt, not her gaoler.' I drew her close with my good arm. ''Tis none of your doing. We will find her and turn aside all this nonsense which has been stirred up by Mistress Fuller and her ilk, if I be not mistaken.'

The Foxley Place

Bess and I returned to Paternoster Row. For the present, there was little to be done at Bishopsgate and Guildhall but we visited Stephen's carpenter's shop and arranged for him to go repair the door and shutters of Bess's place to deter further damage and thievery. He said he would do his best that afternoon but, being without Jack to assist him, he needs must ask aid of another carpenter. Therefore, until he had assessed the work and materials required and persuaded some other to labour with him, he could not name a price. I gave him twelve pence on account and we agreed I should settle the reckoning when the task was done.

Bess looked utterly forlorn.

'I'll never be able to repay you, Master Seb,' she said as we continued past St Michael's.

'Indeed you will,' I said, smiling. 'Once your business be refounded, a supply of flower waters, cordials and a few fine candles will cover the cost soon enough.'

'You think my neighbours in Bishopsgate will allow me to continue there?'

'Once winter takes a hold and cold, phlegmy humours prevail again, they will be as eager as ever for your remedies.'

'I'm not so sure.'

'In which case, you could set up shop elsewhere in the city. This ward of Farringdon Within does not have an apothecary so, mayhap, you could open a shop hereabouts. We would most certainly appreciate that.'

At least Bess looked somewhat less downhearted as we arrived home. 'Twas nigh unto dinnertime and I thought everyone would be assembled, waiting in the kitchen. Meanwhile, I made haste to the store room in the workshop with my scrip. It now contained the four fearsome mannequins and I wanted none else to set eyes upon those terrible things afore I had time to deal with them. I would hide them behind the rolls of unused parchment for the present. But I was not alone.

'A letter came for you whilst you were gone,' Adam spoke behind me, causing me to jump and I dropped one of the wax poppets. 'What's this?' He picked it up. 'Dear sweet Christ!' He crossed himself and put the image, supposedly of Thomas Goulden, the one pierced by pins, on the shelf. 'Why do you bring such a devilish thing here? For pity's sake, Seb, get rid of it.' He looked on in horror as I took the other three from my scrip and placed them beside the first.

'They are evidence,' I said simply. 'And this letter you mentioned?'

'What? Oh, aye.' He cast a wary glance at the mannequins. 'It's on your desk.'

'Lock the storeroom door, cousin, if it makes you feel easier in your mind.'

And he did so.

The letter was from Master Caxton. In truth, I had utterly forgotten having written to him previously, except that he made reference to my earlier correspondence. So many things had come to pass in only two days that it seemed impossible 'twas so short a time since I wrote.

A good dinner of ham hock in a coffin served with a sharp verjuice sauce, crisp fried shallots and fresh white bread awaited us at the board. Having said grace, I realised how hungry I was and set to, one-handed, of course. When I wished to pull my heel of bread in two, I nudged Adam to ask his aid and saw him frowning in the direction of the workshop. His platter was hardly touched.

'You locked them in, Adam,' I whispered. 'And there they will stay. Eat your meal and fear them not.'

'I don't like being under the same roof with them,' he whispered back. 'There was a witch in Norwich caused such harm with the like of those wretched things. Can't you leave them somewhere else? Shouldn't Thaddeus have the keeping of them?'

'I have work to do upon them. Forget them; pay them no mind. Now, please, break my bread for me, if you will.'

'Mm, there. So... what was the letter concerning? Anything of interest?' He finally picked up his spoon and began to eat.

'Master Caxton wishes to conclude our business as soon as may be.' I used my bread to scoop up a plump, succulent gobbet of ham dripping with sauce. Delicious. 'But, afore then, I must draw up my reckoning of expenses and speak with Jude. I made a tentative proposition in my correspondence the other day that, mayhap, my brother could rent out his printing press to Caxton. After all, it does naught but gather cobwebs at present and such an arrangement would be of advantage to them both. Previously, Jude utterly opposed such a plan but, upon Thursday last, he seemed prepared to consider it. I needs must discover whether he remains in favour of it. We all know Jude well enough: he could have changed his mind a half dozen times since then.'

'Are you mad, Seb?' Adam was aghast and dropped his spoon, splashing sauce across the board. 'Why would you aid a damned printer in his business? He'll rob us of custom. Can't you see that? Bad enough that your own brother thought to rival us—but failed through his own incompetence, God be thanked—so now you'll help a stranger do the same and one who knows how to use the accursed press. He's our enemy and yet you would serve him our livelihoods upon a gilded platter.'

'I think you overrate what one man with one printing press may do but, either way, is it not better to make a friend of your would-be enemy?'

'No! Not in this case. You betray our guild if you do and I'll not be a part of this.' Adam stood and kicked aside his stool afore departing, leaving his dinner but half eaten. I know not which was more shocking: his accusation of betrayal or the abandonment of his food.

Chapter 15

Later that Saturday afternoon
Jude's house, Ave Maria Alley

WHEN I called out to my brother, somewhat surprisingly, he bade me enter with good grace but his words of greeting as I walked in were not so encouraging.

'Christ on the bloody Cross, Seb, what have you done this time? Wrestled a bear and lost by the look of it.' He chuckled but then had second thoughts: 'Wasn't a bloody bear, was it?'

'Nay, a London mob was all,' I said, making light of my obvious hurts—the bruises were blacker than thunder by now and I kept my aching arm in its sling.

'You might have fared better against a bear.'

'Aye, I know it.'

'You want ale? Ell bought it fresh this morning.'

'Eleanor has returned? That is good news, indeed. I did not like to think of you living alone, Jude.'

'Well, now you can cease fussing me like a bloody mother hen, can't you? What do you want, anyway? Have you come to tell me that scurvy rogue has been caught, damn him?'

'Jack? Nay, none has seen him since he departed Holbourne insofar as I have heard.'

'Good. The farther he runs, the better I like it. Cathay would serve best where he can be run down by Tartar horsemen, enslaved by the dog-headed heathens or eaten by a basilisk. I don't care so long as he's as far from me as the breadth of the world allows. So why are you here? Fallen foul of your wife, have you? I suppose it was only a matter of time.' He poured ale for us both. To my relief, I saw that the cups were clean.

'Rose is as much in accord with me as I could wish but...'

Jude wrinkled his nose.

'Well, you've fallen out with somebody. I can bloody smell it. That fat turd of a cousin of yours, I suppose.'

'Adam be as much your kinsman as mine, as you well know.'

'It was him, then... that you've had a fight with. Did he break your arm?'

'We did not fight and I told you 'twas a mob that did me injury. And my shoulder was put out of joint, not broken.'

'So what of your bloody cousin?'

'We disagreed upon a business matter. But what I would discuss with you concerns Master Caxton... amongst other things.'

'Other things? Such as...'

'Never mind. I shall come to those later.'

'Always supposing I let you stay.' He let the words hang betwixt us.

'Aye, well, it is about your press... when we were at Holbourne, it seemed to me you were inclined to reconsider my suggestion that you might allow Caxton the use of it, for a fee, of course.'

Jude growled and muttered into his cup but I could comprehend no words so I continued:

'I had reason to write to the printer to conclude my business with him...'

'You took my bloody book, didn't you? You're a thieving knave and no better than Jack. You had no right...'

'It is Caxton's property, as you be full aware, and he employed me to seek out and return whatever of his possessions I was able to retrieve, which I shall do as soon as possible. I know not why or how his accounting book came to be here and, for your sake, I shall not ask. However, in my letter to him, written upon Thursday last, in order to be of aid to you, I took the liberty of mentioning that my brother has a printing press, standing idle and unused, and...'

'You did what! How dare you, you interfering bloody arse wipe, you treacherous toad, you conniving cur... My business is none of yours. How dare you assume...'

'Forgive me but I thought...'

'That's your trouble, isn't it? Always bloody thinking you know best, sticking your snout in everybody else's trough. What I do with my press—*my* property—has naught to do with you, so get that through your thick skull. You hear me, *little* brother?'

'Aye, I hear you but I inform you of what I wrote for courtesy's sake only, since Caxton gave no response to my suggestion. Mayhap, he has acquired another press elsewhere or is shipping in a new one from Burgundy.'

'Or maybe we're perfectly capable of making our own arrangements without your interference.'

'We? Do you mean you and Caxton?'

'He came to inspect it this morn. I got Ell to dust it off first. We shook hands on the bargain and his people are coming on Monday to dismantle the bloody ugly thing and I'll be rid of it at last. I'm sick of looking at it.'

'So you took up my idea? Oh, Jude, I...'

'I did no such thing, so you can wipe that bloody smirk of triumph off your face. I thought of it long before you did and wrote to him weeks since.'

'Weeks since? But his own press was yet useable then.'

Jude shrugged off his mistake.

'Aye, well, he might've had reason to want a second press, being so busy and all. I suggested an arrangement to suit us both. We don't need you as our go-betwixt. The deal is done and no thanks to you.'

'I be right gladdened to hear it, Jude,'

'You are?'

'Aye, to know you have not given in to despair and melancholy. I feared for you of late. You seemed despondent and weary of life.'

'Weary of you, more like. When you're not here, bloody annoying me, all is well, so you're wrong, again. In future, I'll live my life how I see fit. I don't need you and I don't want your damned advice at every turn.'

'I understand. In which case, I shall take my leave but you will dine with us upon the Lord's Day tomorrow, will you not? Eleanor be welcome also and I promise not to offer you any advice on any matter whatsoever.'

'You swear?'

'I so swear. But you remain my beloved brother. If ere you be in need…'

'Of a good meal, aye. Of all else, nay.'

'Indeed.'

'So what of these "other things" you spoke of before we meandered off into this Caxton nonsense.'

'Other things? Oh, they concern a charge of witchcraft.'

'Witchcraft! Christ's bloody bollocks, Seb. What are you doing dabbling in witchcraft, you damned fool? This time, you must take my advice and leave well alone.'

'I am not dabbling in anything. Four dubious waxen mannequins have come into my possession as evidence in a case I am attempting to unravel. Being but one-handed at present, I need assistance in uncovering who made the images. I do not want Rose or the children or anyone else in our household to know of them, except that Adam saw them and is of such doubt concerning them, I cannot ask him.'

'Why don't you ask your friend, the bloody bailiff?'

'Thaddeus will not touch them.'

'But you suppose I will? And in desperate need, where else would my little brother turn but to his obliging elder? Oh, very well, show me the damned things.'

'Damned is what they are, I fear.'

'A bit of wax?' Of a sudden, Jude was turned courageous. 'You wouldn't fear a melting candle, would you?'

I took the horrid images from my scrip and laid them out for his examination. He looked but did not touch. I think he would have recoiled, as did Thaddeus and Adam, but now determined to wear a bold face.

'Who made these?' he asked, venturing to turn over one of them with his penknife. 'It's supposed to be a babe, isn't it? And this is some poor bugger with a pin through his bollocks, God help him.'

'I know not who made them but rumour runs that it was Bess Chambers, the apothecary, you may recall, and her niece, Sarra. I be certain that is untrue and I need to prove it.'

'You speak of Sarra Shardlowe. I've heard of her from... well, never mind who told me. Though I've not laid eyes on the wench myself—more's the pity—she's a fine piece, so they say, and handsome... and willing.'

'I do not believe that. Sarra is a respectable lass, hard-working and diligent.'

'She has poor taste in men; I know that for a fact.'

'How can you know?'

'Many a tale reaches my ear. You'd be surprised.'

'Eleanor told you.'

'No, not Ell. Not that jackanapes in skirts. A young buck in tight hose showing a neat arse—now that the idiot would notice—but he wouldn't notice a pretty woman if she fell on him from out the sky.'

'In which case, have you heard also that, somehow, Sarra has escaped custody this morn and disappeared? I believe she had assistance. I doubt you know aught of this?' I asked but an idle question yet Jude denied it right vehemently which set the germ of an idea sprouting in my mind. I would think more upon it when I had the leisure.

'So, what do you want of me with these bloody horrible things?' he asked, poking at them. 'That poor bugger for one... you ought to remove those pins; they make me feel uncomfortable. Who's it supposed to be, anyway?'

'A man named Thomas Goulden.'

'Never heard of him.'

'He died.'

'Ah. No wonder folk account it witchcraft.'

'That is how it be intended to appear but this is the malice of others, not Bess nor Sarra, and I would uncover the culprit.'

'How?'

I took from my trusty scrip all the things required for my experiment: a couple of extra sticks of charcoal, an oyster shell in which I usually mixed my egg tempera, a small earthen bowl, a fine painting brush, my precious scrying glass, the spare beeswax which Bess had given me, pens, a lidded pot of ink, paper and my drawing board. I spread the items along the bench in lieu of a table board.

'If you would take your penknife and scrape away at this charcoal into the shell, Jude… I need it to be as fine a powder as possible. I cannot do it so well myself, one-handed, and Adam refuses to aid me in this.'

He took the charcoal—misshapen bits unsuited to drawing—and obliged me, frowning, either in concentration or, mayhap, forwhy he was quite mystified as to my intent. After a little, he looked up and showed me the shell half filled with black powder.

'Will that suffice?'

'Aye, 'tis fine enough, I hope. May I light a taper? I need to warm some of this wax.'

'You're not going to fashion another horror, are you? Because if you are, you can bugger off now. I don't want any more of these things in my house.'

'Nay, fear not. I need but to soften this waste wax somewhat is all and then I shall demonstrate my purpose unto you. The idea came to me when Bess found one of the mannequins in the hearth, soot-covered.'

The afternoon passed as we worked together. 'Twas like times years afore, when we had been but journeymen, toiling on some project in progress for our then master, Matthew Bowen. I wished we might be joined in such peace, amity and purpose more often. But, at length, the Angelus bell rang, denoting the supper hour at home and I must depart.

'Thank you for your help, Jude. I could not have done without your aid,' I said as I packed everything back in my scrip.

'O' course not. I'm a bloody wonder. Mind, you're not such a lackwit as you look, are you, little brother? Clever… what you did, I grant you. Let me know what comes of it.'

'Of course. Shall you and Eleanor come share our Lord's Day dinner on the morrow?'

The Foxley Place

That eve, after supper and Vespers at St Michael's, with Adam and his lads gone home, the household sat in the garden, enjoying the cool of a long summer's eve. Swallows flew across the pearl blue sky, squealing and darting as the sinking sun began to turn the few wisps of cloud to gold in the west. Sleepy little ones were already abed, the day's chores completed and this was a time of tranquillity as the streets round about fell quiet. The scent of honeysuckle was strong, attracting ghost-like, pale-winged moths. A thrush sang his last repeated refrains afore seeking rest for a few hours.

My Rose, never idle, was tying in a pea plant that had grown unruly but the others took their ease. Meg sat reading a copy of *Aesop's Fables* which I had made for the household's enjoyment, rather than for sale. Ralf was whittling something or other from a scrap of kindling wood with his dinner knife and Nessie was plucking at straws from a bundle by the pigsty, still sulking over her unmarried state, whilst Kate and Hugh stole kisses behind the apple tree, thinking we did not notice.

Bess was yet staying with us, her own house still unliveable, with neither doors nor window shutters, until Stephen had a chance to make necessary repairs.

'Come to the workshop, Bess, if you will,' I bade her. 'I apologise for interrupting this peaceful hour.'

'Is it about my book? Have you made the copy and rebound it so soon?' she asked eagerly.

'Er, nay, and that be another matter I wish to discuss with you but, firstly, I would show you what I have done with those mannequins.'

'Oh, Seb, must you? I don't want to see them ever again.'

'I think you may find my conclusions to be somewhat of a relief, in part, at least.'

In the workshop, I lit two candles afore setting everything from my scrip out upon my desk, much as I had at Jude's house.

'The wax poppets look so grubby now. I know the one from my hearth was soot-besmirched but now they all are. What have you done with them?'

'Ah, permit me to explain. It may aid you to use my scrying glass, the better to make out what I describe unto you. Here, Bess, upon the image made somewhat in the semblance of a babe... can you make out an indentation upon its head?'

'Aye. You've put soot here.'

'I used powdered charcoal, brushing it on with the lightest touch. Do you see how the black picks out raised lines in the indentation? I have drawn the patterns thus revealed.' I showed her the relevant images I had made with pen and ink at Jude's house.

'I see them but what do they mean?'

'It may aid your understanding, Bess, if you come closer to the candle and observe the ball of your own thumb through the glass. Do you see a similar pattern of lines there?'

'Well, I never did! Indeed, I do. I've not noticed that before.'

'Few folk do notice such designs but we all of us have them. Now, I shall soften the spare wax you gave me in this dish above the candle flame... but not so much that it melts. I discovered the reciting of three *Paternosters* gave sufficient time to warm it...

255

'And, if you will, Bess, I pray you, press your thumb into the wax smartly without moving it about: in and off. Perfect. And now comes the moment of truth. I brush the mark lightly with the charcoal dust. See how it clings to the raised pattern? I did this with my brother's thumb mark and my own this afternoon.'

Looking through the scrying glass—mine which served simply to magnify, not to foretell the future as Sarra's crystal did—I took pen, ink and paper and drew a much-enlarged image of the pattern Bess's thumb had made in the softened wax—no easy thing to do one-handed but what with my practising earlier, I achieved a fair representation. I showed Bess the result.

'That's most interesting, Seb, but what of it? It looks much like the others you showed me.'

'Much like, most certainly, but *not* the same. That be the important part. Here. See for yourself. This image represents the thumb mark we saw on the babe-like mannequin. Look how the lines swirl on your mark but, on this, the loops breaks here... and here.'

'How does that aid us... if it does at all?'

'It proves, Bess, that the hand which shaped this thing was not yours.'

'But I knew that anyway.'

'Of course you did but 'twas only your word against those of Mistress Fuller. Now I have evidence to prove it.'

'Didn't you believe me before? Oh, Seb...'

'I did believe you without any doubt whatsoever but we must convince others, Bailiff Turner especially.'

'But what of Sarra's thumb mark? We must find her and get her to make her mark and prove she didn't form these horrible things.'

'We certainly must find the lass. However, I do not think we require her thumb mark to prove her innocence.'

'How so?'

'Rather, we search out the person whose mark be a match for

those upon the mannequins, imprinted during the moulding and making of them. All bear the same marks as I discovered earlier this afternoon.'

'But there are thousands of folk in the city. You can't get them all to press marks into warm wax. It will take until Judgement Day.'

'Ah, but I know with whom we shall begin and I trust our search will be swiftly concluded.'

Bess gave me a doubtful look then shrugged and shook her head.

'You know best, Seb. But you spoke of my book? The *Ars Notoria*?'

'Aye, I have to confess to there being difficulties...' I retrieved the book from the store room, still in its separated gatherings although the damaged pages were now made good with the finest vellum. 'The repairs are done and the whole now awaits re-stitching. I can have it done by Tuesday.'

'I know not how I'll pay you now...'

'No matter. We can leave such considerations for the future. My problems concern the copying of the text.' I showed Bess the few pages of blotched script, numerous errors and atrocious penmanship.

'Mm. Who wrote this? If I may be so bold as to say, 'tis not of the best workmanship, is it?'

'Nay, in truth, 'tis of the worst. A 'prentice in his first few months could do better yet, I admit, my own hand did this.'

'Yours? You made all these mistakes? I don't believe it. Why would you?'

'I cannot say, Bess. I think there be a curse upon the book against copying. Neither pen nor ink would work as they should. I know they say an unskilled craftsman blames his tools but that was not all. Words which I attempted to copy went awry betwixt my eye reading and my hand writing and I could do naught to prevent it. Errors seemed to appear of their own making. I apologise, Bess, but I be unable to make a copy for you.'

'A curse, you say?'

'I can think of no other cause for my ineptitude.'

'Ah, me. The copy was meant to aid Sarra in her studies but, as matters stand and with the lass gone away, who knows where, likely she won't have a use for it anyway. I'm sorry to have put you to so much trouble.'

'Then I shall be well content to destroy these pages.' I tore them in half and held them to the candle flame. 'I cannot tell you how relieved I be to do this,' I said as the papers glowed at the edges, blackened and then flared up afore crumbling to ash upon my desk. I did not speak of the terrible self-doubt which had come upon me during my attempts at copying, moments when I feared my precious skills were, of a sudden, quite lost to me. I was truly glad to watch them burn and my heart seemed lighter of a sudden. I smiled at Bess and she returned my smile, be it a half-hearted effort.

'Master Seb?'

'Aye?' I swept the ash fragments to the floor and returned the repaired gatherings to the store room for safe keeping. The glue was dried now and I stacked them in order, ready for stitching.

'Do you think Sarra is safe?' Bess was winding her apron strings around her hands distractedly.

'You know her better than I. What be your thoughts upon this?'

'She's a hardy lass and capable... and if somebody aided her to escape, mayhap, she's not alone out there... I pray she isn't fallen into the clutches of a rascally rogue.' Realising what her hands were doing, she let go the strings and straightened her attire.

'Bess, why do you not draw up her horoscope? I know you understand the stars as well as any physician and I've seen the astrological charts in this book of yours. Mayhap, you can discover her whereabouts?'

'All that you say is true but...'

'But? You be afeared of what the stars might reveal. Is that the difficulty for you?'

'Aye. Supposing she is lost to me? I promised my sister I'd take good care of her, keep her safe... yet I have failed most grievously on both accounts. Oh, Seb, I don't know what to do. Should I write to my sister and admit my faults... warn her of what may have befallen the lass? She will ne'er forgive me, I know. Sarra is her dearest and youngest child.'

'Well, then, there may be another way. Do you have anything belonging to Sarra—a comb, a kerchief, a garter?'

Bess eyed my scrying glass upon the desk.

'If you think I have the art of seeing in the glass, that is Sarra's skill, not mine,' she said. 'And you know the mob smashed hers... I'm not sure this little thing would work anyway, even if I knew how.'

'Nay, not the glass... Gawain! To me, lad.' My dog came bounding in at my call and I fondled his soft ears. 'Here we have the best nose in London. I should have thought of it afore. He traced Jack all the way from Westminster to... aye, well, pay no mind to that... but he may be able to follow Sarra's scent likewise. He loves her for giving him cheese in the past and would pursue her right readily if any scent of her remains. Do you have something of hers that might serve to remind Gawain of her smell?'

Bess shook her head.

'I fear all was lost when everything was wrecked. They even slashed all our bedding. I suppose there could be some scent of her upon the shredded sheets although it'll be mixed with mine as we shared the bed. The linen in the coffer was also destroyed—as you saw—but I might be able to find a piece that was more certainly hers. One of her shifts had embroidery about the neck but I fear that was freshly laundered so won't help even if I recognise a piece of it for certain.'

'Bedding! Thaddeus said he supplied Sarra with a truckle bed. The blankets may yet harbour her scent sufficiently to remind Gawain of his friend. Upon the morrow, first thing, we shall go to Guildhall, I promise you.'

Later, as the daylight faded, afore we retired for the night, with Rose and me alone in the kitchen, I watched as she swept the last of the day's dirt out into the yard and recalled another experiment I wanted to set in progress. I fetched a stick of chalk from the workshop and, on hands and knees, began drawing on the flagstone floor of the kitchen.

'Oh, Seb! I've just swept and you watched me do it. Now see the mess you've made. What are you about?'

'Forgive me, sweeting, this be to aid Bess and I promise to wash the floor myself once I have proved my point.'

'Which is?' She regarded me, hands on hips, as I drew the outline of a swan. It happened to be the first thing that leapt to mind. 'How will a swan aid Bess? And I'd like to see you washing my floor with but one hand. And how are we supposed to work here, cooking meals and doing our daily tasks without stepping on it and spoiling it? It's quite a handsome bird, I'll grant you that.'

'You may ignore it, Rose, tread upon it as you will. My intention be to discover how long such a drawing may withstand feet coming and going upon it in haphazard wise.'

'Why?'

'Forwhy, there was a chalk drawing upon Bess's stone floor 'neath all the mess. A woman claimed Bess had drawn it but a mob had trampled there and, to my eye, it yet looked fresh, the chalk hardly smudged. I do not believe the drawing could have been put there until after the shop was wrecked: it was too clearly defined which suggests...'

'Neither Bess nor Sarra drew it.'

'Aye, in which case someone else must have done it.'

In bed that night, with Rose breathing softly beside me, I tried to put my thoughts in order. 'Twas no easy task when so much had come to pass of late and yet required resolution of some kind. I rehearsed in my mind what I would say to Master Caxton upon Monday morn next coming. Adam's disgust that I should do anything to assist a would-be competitor against our craft gave me pause: was printing truly a threat to our livelihood? If it were, I could turn my hand to portraiture, heraldic and sign painting but the others in the workshop were less fortunate. How would they make a living if not by scribing, illuminating and book-binding?

And what of little Dickon? I had said naught of such hopes to anyone, not even to Rose, but a father cannot help but have ambitions for his son. I dreamt of Dickon taking on the workshop at the Sign of the Fox one day, a respected and accomplished craftsman, even that he might become Warden Master of the Stationers' Guild eventually. Would printing deny us that possibility?

My thoughts moved on, briefly, to Jack, whereabouts unknown, but now another was gone missing also. Where was Sarra? I recalled how, that afternoon, when I put the question to Jude, in jest, that he might have some knowledge of her escape from Guildhall, his denial had been right vehement, more so than my suggestion warranted. Did he know more of her disappearance than he would admit? Nay. My brother could not have aided her. He could barely aid himself. Besides, how could he know the lass was in custody at Guildhall? But someone did and words spoken at some point recently bothered me: 'copper-haired'. Where had I heard that?

And Adam. We were at such cross-purposes of late about the mannequins, Caxton and I knew not what else. He, too, had much to think on. Belatedly, it occurred to me that his business with the lawyers concerning his citizenship and the guardianship of Simon, Nick and little Mundy must be nearing the point of the Lord Mayor's final decision, yet my cousin had not spoken of it for days and more... or, mayhap, he had and I was not paying any heed to him. Little wonder then if he was angry with me. I must ask him at breakfast, come what may, and show Thaddeus the thumb marks... with Gawain also... and Bess, of course... and 'copper-haired'...

Chapter 16

Sunday, the first day of July
The Foxley Place

AT BREAKFAST, after Low Mass, I remembered to ask Adam how his business with the lawyers was progressing concerning his citizenship and the guardianship of his lads. If I thought to hear that the Lord Mayor's decisions were imminent, my hopes were brought to naught.

'Oh, the excuses continue,' Adam said with a sigh, 'You know how it is with the law: slower than a legless donkey and just as stubborn. I doubt the situation will be confirmed by this mayor and I'll have to begin anew when the next takes office at the end of October. In truth, Seb, I tire of the whole mess. If it wasn't to the benefit of the lads to have a legal father, I'd drop the proceedings and save myself a deal of time, trouble, heartache and expense. But I have to do it for their sakes.'

My cousin sounded so disconsolate, I gripped his arm firmly.

'Of course you do, Adam, because you love them as their blood-father ne'er did. If I may aid you in any way, you need but ask. My offer of money yet stands if funds fall short.'

'Aye. It may come to that if matters drag on for much longer. The damned men of law are eating away at the money my father sent like ravenous wolves at a carcass.'

'Father, I'll do odd jobs to earn coin to help,' Simon put in, his young face so troubled. 'I'll take gentlemen's horses to the water trough at the Panyer Inn and hold the stirrup when they remount. I could carry baskets home for women a-marketing or doing laundry. I could…'

'I know you would, Simon,' Adam smiled and ruffled the lad's hair. 'But you have your 'prentice's work to do here. That's most important.'

'But I want to be your son proper-like. And so would Nick and Mundy if they were old enough to understand. You won't give up on us, will you, Papa Adam?' Tears glinted and one escaped, trickling down the youngster's cheek. He cuffed it away in haste lest we should remark upon it.

'Rest assured, I'll never give up on you, not even scrape-grace Nick.' Adam looked fondly at five-year-old Nicholas busy crumbling his bread and flicking the crumbs at his little brother, Mundy. The youngest of the three simply ignored the nuisance and continued to eat his black pudding and eggs, being, mayhap, more mature at two-years or else grown bored by Nick's everlasting antics. This once, my cousin did not reprimand the miscreant and let the misbehaviour pass unpunished. I think his feelings ran so high at the moment that love overwhelmed anger.

'I must go to Guildhall after breakfast,' I said in order to change the subject as I mopped up my egg with a heel of bread. 'To show Thaddeus the thumb marks on those mannequins.'

'Damnable things…' Adam muttered. 'Will you go now? It's the Lord's Day.'

'The bailiff's work does not cease even so and, oftentimes, what with an excess of drinking and revelry upon Saturday eve, Thaddeus has more miscreants to deal with of a Sunday morn than any other.'

'I pray these mannequins truly will prove that Sarra and I are innocent,' Bess said. 'I shall come with you, Seb, to show I have naught to hide nor be afeared of.'

Guildhall

The mannequins were not my sole business at Guildhall. Something else was more urgent—the mounting clouds behind us determined it thus—as Bess and I went with Gawain, hastening to meet Thaddeus. Fortunately, the storm was yet afar and I hoped it would remain so.

I carried those hateful mannequins in my scrip along with all that was needful for making further thumb marks. Then I should be heartily glad to be rid of them though I prayed they would first serve my purpose as intended.

On the way along Cheapside, we stopped at Stephen Appleyard's carpentry shop but he was elsewhere, mayhap at Bess's place, making repairs. Despite it being the Lord's Day, such work could be deemed necessary, especially with ill weather approaching. However, I saw a greasy cap hanging upon a hook—not Stephen's, I knew for certain—and borrowed it, tucking it into my bulging scrip.

'Why do you want that grubby thing?' Bess wanted to know but I would not say.

At Guildhall, Thaddeus was in his little chamber, drinking ale and frowning over a document.

'Ah! My prayer is answered. You're just the fellow I need, Seb. Read that for me, will you? I can't make out what that idiot Parker wrote.'

'I thought you dismissed him.'

'I did but he wrote this some weeks ago and now the court case is pending and I have to state the circumstances of the crime and must recall all the details…'

I took the document to the window where the light was best and studied the clerk's execrable scrawl. It was a disgrace to the scribe's craft and even with my years of practice, copying some truly dreadful penmanship, I could hardly make out what was written.

'I shall do my best, later, to make a legible copy for you,'

I said with a sigh, knowing that was what Thaddeus hoped I would say. 'But first, I have something to show you. I know you have no liking for the mannequins we found at Bess's place but I think they may bear witness as to their creator and it was not Bess for certain. And I suspect it was not Sarra either.'

For the third time, I explained about the thumb marks, how they were made visible with charcoal dust and, since it seemed no two person's marks were the same—at least I hoped that was the case—the maker of the mannequins might be unmasked.

Thaddeus was not convinced.

'You can't take the marks of everybody in London to compare, Seb.'

'That's what I told him,' Bess put in.

'It couldn't be used as evidence in court anyway, so what's the purpose?'

'If we can prove who made them to our satisfaction,' I explained. 'Then we shall know where to look for evidence that *would* be acceptable in court—if it comes to law—or clear Bess's name and Sarra's at the least.'

'You're convinced this would work?'

'It did some years back, afore your time as bailiff. I proved that my brother was not the one who held the knife which killed a man. The bloodied finger mark upon the handle had been made by another.'

'And the court agreed?'

'Nay, the Duke of Gloucester agreed and that was sufficient to stop the hanging until the king granted a royal pardon.'

My friend puffed his cheeks and blew out a breath.

'Then I suppose if your method holds merit enough to satisfy royalty, then who am I to dispute it? But I still don't see how you can test the marks of every man.'

'I propose that we begin not with any man but with a woman. Who has cried loudest of Bess's guilt? Whose accusations of witchcraft against Sarra have been the most vehement? Who led the mob and brought their blood to the boil that they would wreck the shop?'

'Mistress Anneis Fuller,' Thaddeus and Bess said together.

'Aye, so let us begin with her. However, she will keep for the present; her thumb mark will not change in the meantime. Of greater urgency, taking account of the possibility of a coming storm and the reason why I brought my loyal Gawain—I thought we might allow his nose to guide us in attempting to follow Sarra's trail. If it rains, the scent may be washed away.'

'Then I should go home and fetch the shred of Sarra's clothing I told you of,' Bess said.

'Unless, Thaddeus, you have the blankets upon which the lass slept yesterday?' I said, hopefully.

'I fear not. I borrowed them from the innkeeper's wife across the way at the Green Dragon, and have returned them since. Anyhow, it seemed to me they smelled more of sour ale, other folks' sweat and mildew than of her.'

'Well, a dog's nose might conclude otherwise but—though you may think me quite mad…' I noted my friend's dubious expression as if he thought that to be the case already. '…I brought this for Gawain to sniff.' I took out the greasy cap I had borrowed from Stephen's carpentry shop.

'But that isn't Sarra's. How will it serve?' Bess asked.

'I know not if it will but 'tis worth trying.'

'Whose cap is it?' Thaddeus wanted to know.

'It belongs to Jack Tabor.'

'But you've been searching London for him all this while.'

'I shall explain if needs be but, first, let us see if my supposition bears fruit. Come, Gawain.' I led the way outside and around the narrow passage betwixt the bailiff's chamber and the building adjacent until we stood below the high window by means of which Sarra had made her escape. I covered my dog's nose with Jack's cap for a few moments that he might inhale the scent of it right thoroughly. 'Go, seek, Gawain.'

The dog went in circles, sniffing the ground. He took so long about it that I began to fear I was quite mistaken. Indeed, my assumption was a bold one with little basis in fact. The passing mention of a wench who was 'copper-haired' being seen in Jack's company at the Swan-on-the-Hoop in Holbourne and Bess's vague thoughts that Sarra might have a lad whom she may have visited at twilight were hardly grounds enough for a tentative guess yet I was acting upon these scant possibilities.

In truth, what had put the foolish idea into my head in the beginning was the similarity of the configuration, shape and position of the window here at Guildhall in comparison with that at Caxton's place in Westminster. Knowing Jack had gained entrance and made his escape through just such an aperture once before had made me think, seeing its like again through Jack's eyes, could he have aided Sarra's escape? But perhaps I should rather have considered whether the two even knew of each other.

And then Gawain was off, nose down, following a scent for certain. I prayed it was the correct trail, else we were on a chase to no purpose whatsoever but if Jack had been here, I was right on that account at least.

We wound our way to the north of Guildhall, through noisome alleys, passages made dark tunnels by overhanging buildings and debris-filled courts surrounded by dilapidated tenements reeking of human and animal waste, fly-ridden hovels all. How Gawain could distinguish betwixt the scent he was following and all these other stinks, I knew not. Right swiftly, I lost all sense of direction.

Mangy dogs barked at us, ragged wives cursed us, babes howled and filthy, shoeless urchins threw stones—and worse—at us. Trust Jack to have come by the most vile and disreputable of ways. During his childhood days spent upon the streets, such places were, no doubt, familiar to him and I became ever more convinced that we were, indeed, upon his trail.

'Have a care!' I shoved Thaddeus aside as a bucket of slops was emptied from an upper window precisely in his path.

'Bitch!' He shook his fist at the woman above as she leaned

out. 'I'm the City Bailiff and I'll send my constables later to arrest you on a charge of nuisance.'

She cackled, showing toothless gums, afore closing the shutter.

'Will you do that?' I asked.

'Nay, but I had to say something. Besides, how can I direct Hardacre to come here when I've no idea where we are in this hellish midden? I didn't know my own city was so disgusting... thought I'd seen the worst of it but this... folks shouldn't have to live like rats in a latrine pit. I must speak with Lord Mayor Browne about this place. It's an insult to our fine city, like a festering carbuncle upon the face of a beautiful woman.'

'Come, Gawain be leaving us behind,' I encouraged him and Bess.

'And the sooner he leads us somewhere wholesome, the better. I need a drink to wash away the taste of it. Where do you think he's going?'

A monstrous rat, the size of which made a lady's lap-dog seem as a mouse, scuttled along before us, turned and stared at us right boldly, showing no fear of humankind. This was its realm, where vermin was king. It then made its way through a hole in the wall and disappeared from sight.

'If we be following Jack's path, I truly cannot say but I suspect we now be walking west. Do you see those ominous storm clouds be ahead of us beyond that roof-top? I pray the rain holds off a while yet.'

The passages became wider and less befouled. Doors were painted and walls lime-washed, front steps swept and paths devoid of weeds, wives wore clean aprons and Sunday veils and children made way for us. I recognised the squat tower of St Alban's Church betwixt the gables as Gawain crossed a street to which I could put a name: Wood Street. But then we were returned to winding back alleys once again until we came to Foster Lane where I had lived as a child with my father and Jude. And now I knew Jack's destination forwhy the westerly side of Foster Lane backed on to the Precinct of St Martin-le-Grand which abbey held the privilege of sanctuary. Jack, ne'er renowned for his wisdom, had yet done a wise thing if he brought Sarra here.

'How did you know?' Bess asked as, having knocked at the porter's lodge, we stood by St Martin's gatehouse, attempting to puzzle out our next step. Thaddeus' writ as City Bailiff held no authority on Church property. 'About Sarra and Jack, I mean.'

'I did not, in truth, know aught of them, whether they ere so much as set eyes upon each other. But a lovely lass and a lad who—for all his headstrong and ill-conceived notions—be handsome enough in an unkempt way, well-built and, likely, of an age with your niece... then the one being accused of witchcraft and the other forever a misfit rogue... their situations might have drawn them together. I admit, 'twas naught but a fortunate arrow loosed in the dark. Besides, as yet, we know not whether they be here or no.'

'And what of your chalk drawing on the kitchen floor this morn?' Bess continued. 'A fine swan but Rose said you wouldn't explain your purpose when you made it last eve.'

'You remember the pentangle chalked on your still room floor? How clearly it was delineated?'

'Aye.'

'Yet the swan, during the time we took over breakfast, was nigh obliterated by the passage of our feet.'

'True but what of it?'

'A mob had rampaged through your house. How well do you suppose a chalk drawing would have survived so many feet trampling upon it?'

'Hardly at all.'

'Precisely. Thus, the pentangle was freshly drawn *after* the mob departed. And who was it that revealed it to us?'

'Anneis Fuller. She must have drawn it and strewn my dried herbs all about to conceal it. Wretched woman. Why would she do this to Sarra and me? That's what I can't understand.'

'We can ask her later,' Thaddeus said as the porter bestirred himself, at last, to open his little window on the world.

'Who knocks upon St Martin's door?' A tonsured head and jowled face pushed forth.

Thaddeus announced each of us by name, giving our professions also.

'You have no authority here, Bailiff, so what's your business?'

'We seek two young, er, relatives who may be here.'

'If they've sought sanctuary, there's naught I can do to aid you. Go with God's blessings.' He made to close the window.

'No. Wait. We only want to know if they're here and safe,' Thaddeus insisted.

'Names?' The monk relented.

'I told you our names.'

'Not yours; theirs.'

'Oh, of course. Sarra Shardlowe and Jack Tabor.'

'I'll make enquiries on the morrow. This day is the Lord's Day and such business must wait. Come back tomorrow.' With which instruction, he closed the shutter.

'Damn it!' Thaddeus cursed. 'Why are we frustrated at every turn?'

'We did our best, thanks to your clever Gawain, Seb,' Bess said, making much of the dog, patting him and rubbing his ears. He would suffer thus for hours without complaint.

'Let us go home—you also, Thaddeus—I believe we have earned a good dinner and 'tis nigh the hour. Besides...' I held out my hand, palm uppermost. 'The rain begins. We should make haste to avoid a drenching.'

'Aye, Mistress Fuller can also wait until the morrow. My belly's needs are more important,' my friend decided.

Chapter 17

Sunday

OUR DINNER was well advanced, overseen by Meg, when we returned home. Rose and the others of our household were lately returned from High Mass at St Michael's. Jude and Eleanor, Stephen and Thaddeus, our friends Peronelle and her husband, Bennett Hepton, with their baby daughter Alice were already served with ale in the parlour—not Jack, of course—and Rose was divesting the little ones of their Sunday best fore-smocks for fear of soiling them at the board. Julia's linen might survive unscathed but Dickon was by no means a trencherman renowned for neatness. 'Twould be quite a gathering, as was our custom to celebrate the Lord's Day, with Kate and Hugh, Ralf and his beloved Jeanie, Adam and his lads, Bess who must stay a little longer until she had a bed to sleep in at home, Nessie and Old Symkyn as our usual guest. I was glad that Eleanor had accompanied Jude, that they were friends again forwhy I might have need of her support later.

We had barely taken our seats to commence dinner when the storm burst upon us. The first flash of lightning and crash of thunder drowned out my recitation of grace for the meal. We were served with braised beef in a mustard sauce and sliced new carrots in a honey dressing; a sweet cheese and rosewater curd with elderflowers and rose petals; fried pork gobbets in a crisp breadcrumb coating flavoured with shallots and sage and a cherry pottage with almond wafers. 'Twas a meal befitting royalty, indeed, excellent as we all expected. As rain lashed down, bouncing off the cobbles of the yard, 'twas as well to be within doors. But, whilst we ate, the storm passed over, less severe than it had threatened.

The sun returned and grass and plants dried and, thus, our meal done, we menfolk were able to retire to the garden with our ale whilst the women cleared away the dishes, Eleanor— accounting herself a man in this instance, probably to avoid the washing and scouring of bowls and pans—commented upon how well my shoulder looked to be mending such that the sling was discarded. In truth, I had but left it off in order to eat my dinner in more comely wise but I realised that she had presented me with the perfect opportunity to make my suggestion to Jude, one which had but lately occurred to me. As we sat upon an old sail-cloth in the shade of the apple tree, watching the children and Gawain chase butterflies among the herbs, I seized my chance:

'Jude, I have been thinking...' I began. A poor choice of words.

'Oh, Christ aid us, not again, little brother. Your thinking always means trouble for somebody—usually me. Can we not enjoy this afternoon in peace?' Whilst the rest of us lay upon the grass, Jude required a stool and kept his staff to hand. Even so, I saw him wince as he shifted his leg about in an attempt to ease the pain.

'About your knee...'

'Bloody thing. I'm trying not to think about it.'

'As Eleanor said, my shoulder be now returned to its rightful position and is so greatly improved... Jude, do you not think it might be worthwhile visiting Surgeon Dagvyle? He has this new contraption which looks to be a device of torture, I admit, but it set my bones as they should be. Mayhap, it could do as much for your knee?'

'No! Definitely not.'

'You could discuss the possibilities with him, at least.'

'I said no, damn it. I'm not letting that sawbones quack tamper with my knee. He splinted it awry in the first place, if I remember it rightly.'

'Your shin bone was broken. He explained that he could not pull your knee cap back straight without risking the broken bone piercing your flesh—an injury which would likely prove fatal. But now that your shin bone be mended, maybe his contraption could untwist your knee cap. Jude,' I said in a whisper, 'You recall that the Lord Christ once granted me a miracle of this kind and I did pilgrimage to Canterbury to request the like for you…'

'Aye, well, it was risking life and bloody limb to save you that got me into this wretched state.'

'I have not forgotten your sacrifice nor ever will. You know that. But mayhap Dagvyle's device is the answer to my pleas and yours. Mayhap, God had the surgeon invent it to perform the very miracle we have prayed for.'

'And where was God when that bloody horse and cart came hurtling down the hill and I pushed you aside, eh? He could've spared everybody so much pain and suffering and trouble by stopping the runaway in the first place. But He didn't. Why should He go to the effort of putting matters to rights now? Eighteen months of my life have been blighted. I know because I count the bloody days, every agonising one. You've had your so-called miracle. There won't be another for me. The Devil shat on me that day and there's no undoing it.'

'Eleanor, can you not persuade him to at least speak with the surgeon? It can do no harm to consider it.'

'Don't bring Ell into this. I've said no and I mean it. Now shut up and fetch me some more ale.'

I shrugged—an action now far less painless, God be thanked—and did as he bade me, fetching a jug full from the barrel kept in a shadowy corner of our yard where the sun ne'er reached. I replenished everyone's cup as the womenfolk joined us at our leisure. Simon instigated a make-shift game of pitch-and-toss with pebbles aimed at an upturned pot which occupied the little lads whilst Meg showed Julia the intricacies of making a daisy chain. Peace reigned but, of course, in our household such a perfect situation could not last.

Unexpectedly, someone came through our side gate into the garden: a woman, dark hair uncovered. For the first few moments, I hardly knew her for my brother's lawful wife, so changed was she. Her once plump and pretty face was drawn and shadowed as she struggled with a weighty basket.

'Chesca! God give you good day, sister. Have you eaten?' Rose was retying young Nick's shoe so he should not trip upon it but now hastened to greet our visitor. 'We yet have bread and meat aplenty left from dinner, if you are hungry?'

I glanced at Jude whose look of utter astonishment was swiftly replaced by the fiercest scowl.

'The whore's not staying,' he snarled, rising awkwardly from the stool. 'Bugger off, you treacherous bitch. You're not welcome here.'

I could not have Christian hospitality thus disregarded in my house. I went to her and took her hand. I noticed her attire was costly but wrinkled, the braid hanging loose and frayed.

'Chesca, lass, let us go within… give me your basket…'

'No, Seb.' She set the basket down on the grass and pulled away. 'I no staying here. I leaving this safe with you. I knowing you taking care for me.' Her English was as odd as ever, she being Italian. 'My Eduardo—he yours now. The king, his godfather, sending this.' She held aloft a bulging money bag.

'That's more like it.' Jude grinned. 'That whore-mongering oaf owes me. He hasn't paid me for your services for bloody months…'

'Is not for you, Jude. I not being with the king. He not liking me fat.' She turned to me. 'Is for his caring. If it pleasing you, Seb… my bambino Eduardo…'

'But Chesca, we ne'er knew you were with child,' I said. 'When? Be you quite recovered?'

'Bambino coming last Christmastide, the feast of the Holy Innocents and he baptising on Epiphany—Kings' Day is fitting, no? I well now. The king, he wanting me back and I needing to look best. He not wanting me with bambino but he paying money for it.'

Rose peered into the basket and reached in. She lifted out a blanket-swathed bundle.

'My little Edward,' she murmured, holding the babe close against her.

'The king's fucking misbegotten bastard!' Jude roared. 'Take it away. It's not mine and no man can say it is.' My brother folded his arms, a clear gesture we all understood. To claim fatherhood under the law, a man must take a babe in his arms and hold it high, that all should recognise the fact. Jude had no such intention of standing parent to a child sired by another, even the king.

'Oh, Seb… my prayers are answered.' Tears flooded Rose's cheeks. 'I, a barren wife, am blessed. My dearest Edward, once lost, is now returned to me. Oh, Seb… my babe has come home.'

I knew not what to say to her words of joy. Taken aback, sensible thought failed me but everyone was watching me. I was slow to realise why: such a momentous decision should be pondered upon, considered deeply, not rushed at like a bull at a gate. They waited to see if I would do as Jude would not.

I wrestled with my thoughts: why should I take responsibility for a royal by-blow born of my sister-by-marriage? As matters stood, I already treated Julia as my own whilst knowing my then-wife, Emily, had conceived by another man's seed. My daughter's mismatched eyes told the truth of that betrayal— only Gabriel Widowson, once my journeyman, then a heretic and now a sea captain—could be her true father. Why should I burden myself, my household, with another child not of my blood nor of Rose's?

But seeing my sweeting's anxious, hopeful, pleading countenance made the decision for me. I had no choice: Rose had already taken the babe to her heart. I led her a little aside.

'Rose, 'tis no light matter, lass,' I said softly. 'We should think on it for a while, a week, a few days at least…'

'But I am barren…' She stroked the babe's tuft of pale hair.

'Nay, dear one. Barren is a harsh and empty desert. You be loving, caring, gentle and kind. Such cannot be named barren.'

'But I didn't care for my first babe and he dwindled away. My love didn't suffice and now I'm punished with barrenness.'

'You were but a misused child yourself. You had no choice in the matter. You are not being punished.'

'Then why have I not conceived in all this time?'

'Mayhap, the fault be mine…'

'But neither did I conceive by all those men at the Pewter Pot. I should've known I couldn't have another babe. I married you in false guise, promising to bear you children.'

'Rose.' I spoke sternly. 'Enough of this. You be overwrought. Now put the babe down in his basket and fetch wine to serve us all. I think the occasion merits wine as befitting and would have you calm and quiet of mind afore we consider the matter fully.'

'You will not let me keep him.'

'I have not said that.' In truth, my answer was as certain as the morrow was Monday but I would not be seen to plunge into a seething cauldron of new responsibilities without at least some semblance of proper consideration.

Our gathering in the garden fell so quiet that I could hear the fledgling redbreasts chirping in their nest amid the ivy. A breeze soughed softly through the apple and elder trees and whispered amongst the lavender. Even the children sat in silence, awaiting they knew not what.

Rose served wine, wiping away tears every now and then and avoiding my eye. When her task was done—filling my cup last of all—'twas as if he knew the moment had come. The babe stirred and began to whimper. She set down the jug and made to pick him up.

'Leave him, Rose,' I said. I sipped my wine to fortify myself then handed the cup to Ralf who happened to be closest at hand. I went forward to the basket. I looked to Rose: 'You be certain of this, lass?'

She nodded.

I stooped, took a firm hold of the babe and raised him up. He was a fair weight and my shoulder protested greatly but I held fast.

'Behold this, my son, Edward Foxley!' I announced as I turned full circle that all might witness my acknowledgement. Within the space of one hour, I had conceived, borne and claimed fatherhood of another child. I could hardly credit what I had done. Was I quite mad? I laid him back in the basket afore I should drop him and eased my throbbing shoulder.

Then everything happened at once. Most congratulated me, wetting the babe's head, as they say, drinking to his good health and future prosperity. But Chesca slipped away without any farewells. Jude departed, dragging Eleanor with him, cursing me for a bloody fool and condemning him to seeing this bastard child whenever he should visit. I did not note until later that the money bag went also. Adam muttered that he wished legal parenthood could be so readily achieved for his step-sons.

But all that was truly of importance to me was the joyful face of my Rose as she discussed more practical matters with the womenfolk: in the main, how to come by milk to feed the now lustily wailing babe. They passed the child around betwixt them, admiring and assessing, though how they could attend to it, smiling and laughing, when its cries were quite deafening, be beyond the comprehension of a mere man.

'Twas Peronelle who saved our ears, mercifully. Her little lass, Alice, at nine months of age, was yet at the breast and Pen, apparently, had milk enough to spare for the unexpected new arrival. Fresh tail-clouts were fetched from our linen chest and, if we knew not before, we swiftly learned that royal babes smell no better than humble ones.

'Pooh! It stinks,' was Nick's comment as the tail-clout was changed. An honest assessment.

The children soon lost interest and returned to their games. The menfolk dispersed except for Bennett who required to know whether his goodwife and her child were to stay the night with us, in order to keep both babes fed until other arrangements could be made upon the morrow.

Adam and Ralf, as fellow Norfolkmen, took Hugh, Simon and Ralf's beloved Joanie to the Panyer Inn to enjoy 'peace and sanity', as Adam described it.

Thaddeus went off to check on his constables and the Marching Watch who would patrol after dark.

Old Symkyn came to bless the newcomer afore departing to his place of repose in a quiet corner of Paul's Precinct.

Thus Bennett and I remained under the apple tree. Once, years ago, we had been competitors for the hand of Emily Appleyard in marriage. I had won but our youthful rivalry was long since forgotten and we were become friends.

'Have you done the right thing, Seb?' he asked, sitting cross-legged like a tailor upon the sail-cloth, chewing a sprig of mint plucked from a clump in the herb bed.

'I know not, Ben; in truth, I do not. But Rose's smiling face tells me I have. What would you have done?'

'You know I'd not deny Pen anything but would I take on another man's bastard just to please her… and a king's at that?' He shook his head and sighed. 'It's quite an undertaking, a huge responsibility. A rash act, indeed, my friend.'

'Aye, 'tis a great deal to have done for the sake of a wife's smile but she longs for a babe of which there be no sign despite fervent prayers, a pilgrimage, various amulets and potions and I know not what else. Mayhap, this be the Lord Christ's answer to her prayers, as she believes.'

'But a king's son, Seb, could be a dangerous thing to possess in times to come.'

I frowned, thinking on Ben's words.

'Nay. The world will know him as plain Ned Foxley, a child of no note to any but his loving family. To us.'

'Can you love another man's begetting?'

'Of course. I love Julia. Adam loves his step-sons. Children be innocents. Their parents' faults are not theirs. They should not suffer for the sins of their forebears.'

'But many do.'

'Not 'neath my roof, Ben, as God be my witness.'

Sunday eve, Vespers
St Paul's Cathedral

In the presence of the Bishop of London, I sang with the cathedral's choristers. We were celebrating the feast of St Thomas the Apostle, this being the nearest Sunday to the third day of July and St Thomas being Thomas Kempe's, the bishop's, own chosen patron saint.

Unfortunately, Rose did not come to hear my best efforts. She had the new babe to attend and, as yet, we were not determined upon a plausible tale as to how the Foxleys of Paternoster Row had so suddenly come by an infant of six months in age. Tongues would wag; rumour would spread like a contagion. This we knew and must decide how best to deal with it. Also, our parish church of St Michael must be informed of a new family member.

But everyone else, including Adam, had come to harken to our singing, apart from Meg who no longer found it in her heart to acknowledge the Lord God. Her mistreatment and her sister's death at the convert had turned her utterly from the Church, though we all prayed constantly that she would return one day soon.

The Precentor had composed a new anthem for the occasion to be sung at Vespers with myself to sing the solo parts. Mercifully, the anthem went well. It must have forewhy the Precentor nigh smiled at me when it ended with a spectacularly difficult *Gloria*. I think he enjoyed forcing me to work so hard to reach the highest notes and then receiving the plaudits himself from the bishop when the office was done. I suppose he deserved them for having composed a piece so exquisite. The choristers received no thanks at all. We never did.

Chapter 18

Monday, the second day of July
The Foxley Place

SLEEP HAD eluded me for most of the night. Rose was from bed twice each hour to go down to the parlour where a feather bed was laid to serve for Peronelle, her little Alice and our incomer—Ned, I must recall to use his name—to be certain all was well with them. She need not have troubled for Ned slept until wakened by dawn light and only then demanded to be fed, rousing the household with lusty cries that likely could be heard in St Paul's belfry.

But 'twas not so much Rose's nocturnal activities which denied me peaceful slumbers. In truth, Ben's warnings of yestereve disturbed me more. What had I done? Was a moment's rashness going to haunt our future? Would we all come to regret my decision? Why had I not taken time to consider thoroughly the implications instead of rushing headlong into the mire? 'Twas thoughts such as these that had me writhing in a turmoil of doubt.

Not that others would know my true feelings forwhy I determined to show naught but confidence in and contentment with my new chosen situation as father to a second son. And a fine little lad he looked to be. Large for his six months, so the women agreed, and I could see he neither lacked a pound weight nor an inch compared to Alice who was half as old again. I suppose his size was unsurprising since the king who sired him stood six feet and a hand-span in height and was broad and hearty in every dimension.

Breakfast was a cobbled-together affair of yesterday's leftovers, the women more concerned for settling in young Ned. Whilst he slept oblivious to the chaos created on his behalf, they sorted out babe's linens—fortunately, he was past the age for those leagues-lengths of cloth required for swaddling—washed down the crib Stephen had first constructed for Dickon, aired small blankets in the sunshine and, most important, Meg was sent in search of an endless supply of goat's milk to feed him. Peronelle could not serve for his wet nurse for more than a day or two. Besides, milk intended for a girl child was not suitable for a boy; all medical knowledge agreed upon that. So, goat's milk it must be. Julia and Edmund had done well enough upon it after Mercy Hutchinson—God rest her poor soul—was rudely taken and no longer nursed her and Mundy. I had no doubt that Ned would thrive no less than they.

But Bess and I had business elsewhere and were to meet with Thaddeus at St Martin-le-Grand's gatehouse at seven of the clock, an hour after Prime.

'Oh, Seb, I have been praying that Sarra will be there, safe within,' Bess said as we hastened along Paternoster Row, 'Now we can prove our innocence. I prayed for your Jack also, of course.'

'I hope likewise,' I said, not adding that Jack's presence, he being known for a rogue and a knave, could make matters far worse than they need have been.

The Abbey of St Martin-le-Grand

Thaddeus awaited us by the gatehouse. The abbey was built like a fortress with high walls and few points of entry. Its Rites of Sanctuary were fervently enforced by the brothers to the extent that the abbey's precinct served as a haven for miscreants. The accepted forty days of grace and safety awarded to any who begged sanctuary were impossible to police with so many mischief-makers to keep account of. 'Twas common knowledge that some had been harboured here for months— years even—making the abbey their home and place of business whilst using the postern gate at the northern end to come and go at will. At night, the Marching Watch kept a close eye there, occasionally catching ne'er-do-wells as they departed upon their nocturnal forays of crime, thievery and assaults or returned with their spoils. Others, more wily, scaled the aged walls elsewhere, avoiding discovery.

I suspected nimble Jack would be one of the latter and thus, possibly, his arrival and departure had passed unknown to the good brothers. In which case, I feared the porter at the gate would have no intelligence for us.

'God give you good day, Thaddeus,' I greeted him. 'You did not come to us for breakfast.'

'Aye, well, a new babe and all… no doubt there was a deal of confusion…'

'That you wished to avoid? In truth, 'twas not so bad. Bess will tell you: the womenfolk be well organised in the main. Be that not so?'

Bess agreed.

'Seb speaks true, Master Turner, and it's a comely little lad, fair of hair, blue of eye, not a bit like his mother but very like…'

'Best not say more, Bess,' I warned.

'Nay, indeed.'

As upon our previous visit, Thaddeus rapped on the shuttered window in the great gate and we stood back to await a response which was slow to come. We arrived at such an hour that the Office of Prime was done and that of Terce two hours hence, so we should not interrupt the brethrens' daily round of prayer but, of course, the monks had other duties also, apart from the *Opus Dei*—the Work of God.

At length, the shutter slid sideways and the porter's jowly visage was thrust forward, filling the aperture.

'Who are you? What business brings you here?'

'I'm Thaddeus Turner, City Bailiff. I come...'

'I told you before: your office holds no authority here. Go away.'

'You also told me to return this day and you would make enquiries concerning...'

'Our Chapter Meeting begins in five minutes. I don't have time to waste on enquiring about anything.'

'Good brother,' I said, pushing forward afore he closed the shutter, 'I am Master Sebastian Foxley of Paternoster Row. I realise your duties must be onerous indeed but we come in search of Mistress Chambers' young niece. We have reason to believe she may be within. If she sought sanctuary here, in truth, she had no need. 'Twas but a grave misunderstanding is all. We know she be entirely innocent and can prove the same. We wish to inform her of this.

'If you have not the time to spare to seek out the guiltless lass, allow us entry and we will find her—if she be here. Please, good brother, we ask this for sweet charity's sake. She does not deserve to be here with other law-breakers. What say you? May we come within? We shall spare you the task that you can attend Chapter with a clear conscience.'

'There's naught amiss with my conscience but how do I know you've not come to drag out some who have rightfully sought sanctuary? You break our rite and God and the Dean will have me doing penance for the rest of my days. No. I'm not letting you in.' He made to close the shutter.

'Hold! One moment, I pray you...' I turned to Thaddeus, balled my fist and thumped him in the gut, pushing him backwards. 'See, now, I have assaulted an Officer of the Law. I beg you, give me sanctuary else he will arrest me.'

The shutter closed anyway.

'What an imbecile you are,' my friend gasped, struggling to catch his breath and nursing his belly.

'I apologise most sincerely. I held back from striking you with any force. I could not think what else to do.'

'You could've missed, damn it.'

Missed so significant a target? Unlikely, I thought. But I held my tongue.

'And I suffer to no purpose whatever,' he added just as the door opened silently on well-greased hinges.

'You'd better come in, then,' the porter said, sighing at the trouble caused, 'You alone, not the bailiff. And if you do anything untoward, I'll throw you back into the street myself, you hear me?'

Once through the door, I saw the gatekeeper from head to foot for the first time and realised his threat was not an empty one forwhy he was built four-square as the Tower of London's keep. He would have no difficulty expelling a fellow lean as myself.

'I must attend Chapter,' he said. 'None will deal with you until after our meeting when I'll expect you in the church, on your knees as a penitent before the Rood Screen. If the Dean likes the look of you, he'll allow you to approach the High Altar, there to grasp and kiss the cloth to claim sanctuary for forty days. Understand?'

'Aye, I do, brother.' As he hastened away, I wondered how long the meeting might last. Would I have time to find Sarra afore then and depart together?

The precinct did not look as I expected of the domain of contemplative monks but the cloister was on the far side of the church. Here, 'twas as busy as anywhere beyond the walls, elsewhere in the city. A farrier was shoeing a horse; a cooper mending a barrel; two women were draping the Monday laundry over a bush and a bare-foot child playing with a small dog. A group of elderly fellows sat at their ale in the shade as at a tavern. One of them, I realised, lacked a leg—mayhap, an old soldier. Most looked so respectable except the cooper's face bore an ugly scar across one cheek. But a scar did not make a villain. Were all these folk truly here to seek sanctuary from the law?

I approached the women arranging shirts and shifts on the

bushes to dry.

'Good women,' I greeted them. 'God give you good day.' At first, I thought they would ignore me as I received their sideways glances but no word.

'Comely fellow, ain't he?' one remarked to the other as they worked.

'Wonder why he's here? Wot crime did he do, eh?'

'I struck the City Bailiff,' I told them.

'That all? Yer'll only get a fine fer that.'

'If that's all he did.' The pair laughed together.

'Looks like he can afford the fine, anyway, in them good clouts. Reckon those boots will fetch a good price down Dowgate way. What say you, Margery? Shall we take 'em?'

'What! Nay, I pray you, good women…' But 'twas too late as they wrestled me to the ground. One sat on my chest whilst the other unlaced my boots. I was nigh overwhelmed by her stink of sour sweat and attempted to hold my breath. Other women came to join the fray—a merry game to them—all laughing wildly. Despite my loud protests and best efforts, my leather jerkin was removed, my good shirt and my hose. By the time they released me, naught but my nether shirt and drawers remained to me and my shoulder—much abused of late—throbbed like the very devil.

'Let's leave him his dignity, eh?' They delighted in the jest.

'I don't know. I want to see what he keeps hidden down there. I ain't seen a clean prick in months.'

'Go to, then, Dorcas,' they cried. 'Strip him! See what he's got.'

'Leave the poor bugger in peace, you poxy whores,' the farrier told them, striding over. 'Play your filthy games with some other. Can't you see he's innocent as a lamb? He ain't used to your kind. And give him back his clothes… and them boots.'

'I owe you my thanks,' I told him as the women returned to their laundry; their sport ended, and I began to dress. 'How glad I am to see a worthy Christian.' I brushed dirt off my hose afore pulling them on, finding a rent in one. Rose would be displeased with me and I wondered if I should tell her how the damage was wrought by a bevy of disreputable women. My shirt sleeve was likewise torn.

'A worthy Christian, you say? Aye, well, I only deliver the wrath of God upon them what deserve it. Five o' the king's tax-collectors so far I've relieved o' their takings and two what objected of their miserable lives an' all. You ain't a tax-collector, are you?'

'Certainly not.' I laced my jerkin and adjusted my belt over it. About to put on my boots, I saw that a lace was broken, hardly of sufficient length now to tie. Ah, me.

'Just as well then… Are you unhurt? They don't mean no harm, them jades. Why are you here? You ain't no rapscallion, either, I can see that.'

'My friend's niece may be here. Sarra by name. She was wrongly accused of a crime but the matter has been put to rights now. I believe she may have come here upon Saturday night last, possibly with the lad who aided her escape. Sarra has a wealth of red hair…'

'Sarra, is it? That's not the name she told us but few use their true names here. Dorcas and Margery are no more those bawds' names than mine's John the Baptiser. But your lass is safe in my hut over there. I kept her away from those flea-bitten jades. Fear not! I didn't ruin her reputation either. My wife made sure o' that.'

'You live here with your wife?'

'Aye, we've been here years. I ply my trade as a farrier, looking after the Dean's stable and my wife washes the church linen, repairs vestments and altar clothes. We do well enough. We got wedded here after she was accused of poisoning her first husband—a vicious sot. Was an accident, o' course. How was she to know she'd picked the wrong sort o' mushrooms when she don't eat them? Mind, I won't eat them either, not if she's cooked 'em.' The farrier chuckled and winked his eye. 'Now you're decent and fit to be seen, I'll fetch the lass. Be sorry to see her go, though, but it'll remove temptation, wont it? Wouldn't want such a beauty leading astray a worthy Christian like me.' He laughed out loud as he crossed the precinct to his hut.

I made to follow him, wary of Margery, Dorcas and their fellow laundresses but he came from his hut with a plump woman and... Sarra. God be praised!

Upon seeing me, Sarra ran across the cobbles and flew into my arms, all propriety abandoned. 'Twas quite unseemly, I knew, yet my heart leapt to feel her pressed against me. *Mea culpa*. I rejoiced in holding her close and, to make my sin worse than ever, 'twas in a monastery upon holy ground. We must depart in haste.

'Oh, Master Seb,' she cried. 'I knew you would come for me when you could prove me innocent. You can, can't you?'

'Aye. We know that whosoever be guilty of witchery 'tis not your aunt and she vouches for your innocence. Be you safe and unharmed, lass?'

'Quite safe, master. John and Mary kept me from harm.'

The farrier and his wife were watching. I went to my purse to give them a few coins in gratitude but, little wonder, it was not upon my belt. No matter. I embraced Sarra closely. I could not help myself, so relieved was I at her finding.

'Your niece, you say?' the farrier muttered.

'Nay, the niece of a friend,' I corrected him.

'Mm. I've heard the like of that before. Well, good fortune to the pair of you.' He slapped me upon my back and chuckled. 'You're a lucky rogue.'

Realising the direction of his thoughts, I made to protest but it did not seem worth the trouble.

'Come now, lass; your aunt awaits us outside. Let us go now.' I did not add that I wished to avoid explaining matters to the porter. Just before we reached the gate, I stopped and asked her straight: 'But where be Jack? Is he here with you?'

'Jack?' She looked askance, not meeting my eye. 'I

know no Jack.'

Outside, I stood back whilst Bess and Sarra rejoiced in their reunion. There were tears and smiles aplenty as aunt examined niece for the slightest sign of injury. A torn, muddied skirt was all that proved amiss. But then the lass espied Thaddeus standing across the way in the shade.

'M-master Bailiff, I can explain,' she began hesitantly, clinging to Bess's arm.

'Later will suffice,' he said. 'I suggest, Bess, that you take your lass to Paternoster Row to get her cleaned up and fed. Foxley, here, and I have matters to discuss.' His use of my family name foretold his displeasure. 'Come, you, we're going to the tavern and you're buying.' He pulled me by the sleeve towards the Sunne in Splendour.

'I think not.' I pointed out the lack of my purse.

'Where is it?'

'I lost it.'

'Careless fool. How did you lose it?'

'There were but a few groats within.' I shrugged, determined to make little of it.

'But you lost the purse itself… of good leather, too. You were robbed, weren't you, in that den of thieves and murderers?'

'Call it a charitable donation.'

Thaddeus shook his head and tutted.

'You're out of my sight for the time it takes to recite a *Pater* and an *Ave* and look at the trouble you land in. I see your hose are ripped… how you've survived this long is quite a mystery to me.'

Our visit to the tavern was of short duration. Firstly, Thaddeus berated me soundly for striking him earlier and then demanded to hear what had befallen within the precinct. I described but the barest bones of the incident with the women, dwelling rather upon Sarra being in the care of the farrier and his wife. I admit, I withheld the truth, implying rather that my purse must have come loose from my belt, yet I could tell he did not believe me. By which time our cups were empty and my friend refused to waste another farthing upon refilling them.

Thus, we parted: he to Guildhall, having reminded me I had still to transcribe Parker's illegible document for him and now a report to write regarding the retrieval of an escapee from custody, though I was to ensure it laid no blame at the Bailiff's door. We also agreed to meet after dinner to complete—as we both fervently hoped—the matter of the mannequins.

I went home to face Rose's dismay at the damage done to my attire.

The Foxley Place

Sarra was bathed and her hair yet damp. Kate had leant her a gown of tawny linen which jolted the senses, somewhat, alongside her coppery locks.

I was warned that dinner would be much delayed, forwhy the water heated in readiness for Monday's washing had first been used in Sarra's bath. Meg was gone longer than expected upon her quest for goat's milk to feed young Ned and Rose was as disorganised as I had e'er seen her, attending the babe, soaking the laundry and attempting to prepare food for dinner. Bess was trying to aid with the washing whilst insisting that Sarra should rest and Nessie was of even less use than normal, getting in everyone's way and achieving naught. At least Kate was in her rightful place at her desk in the workshop.

The children, sensing turmoil, were fractious and quarrelsome and I arrived at the very moment when Nick tipped a bowl of dried oats—destined for the pottage pot—over Julia's head. She set to wailing; Dickon shouted his protests at his sister's mistreatment; Mundy wept in sympathy; Gawain barked furiously, adding to the din, and Ned began howling to be fed from his cradle in the corner.

St Martin's had been but a peaceful interlude in comparison. 'All you children,' I said, employing my most stern voice,

'Outside, now. Come, play in the garden.'

'It's too hot out there,' Nick whined.

'Not as hot as it is in this kitchen. Your Mam-Rose and Meg have enough work to do without you making matters worse. Out you go.' I watched as the sullen child led the other little lads outside. Bess was consoling Julia and brushing oats from her mousy braids, wiping her eyes. 'Will you come also, Sarra?' I said. 'There be matters of which we must speak.'

Sarra did as I asked but with a worried countenance. We set the children to picking caterpillars from the cabbages—a task they always enjoyed with an element of competition as to who could find the largest.

'You be content now, Sarra?' I asked as we watched the little ones at their task.

'Aye. Aunt Bess told me about those mannequins, how you proved she did not make them. I didn't know of them. Aunt said they were hid about our house, in the chimney and amongst the linen. And how our house now lies in ruins.'

'Stephen Appleyard makes great progress in repairing it. Soon, you may return there.' I hastened to step aside as one of our hens mistook my only remaining long bootlace for a worm and pecked at it. I shooed it away. 'Earlier, I asked you about Jack.'

'And I told you: I don't know him.'

'Indeed you did. But you *do* know him, whether he calls himself Jack or by some other name. You spent time with him at that inn in Holbourne and then he aided your escape from Guildhall and guided you to St Martin's. I be certain of it forwhy Gawain followed Jack's scent to that place, not yours. Nick! Put that stick down afore you poke Mundy in the eye. Now, I say!' Disaster averted, I asked Sarra: 'How did you meet him?' But Gawain intervened.

'How fares my dear friend Gawain?' she said, making much of the dog.

'Do not change the subject, lass. What of Jack? Tell me, I

pray you.'

'You're right, master,' she admitted with a sigh, 'I do know him. He came to the shop some while since. A whitlow on his thumb needed removing. It required daily treatments of a hot poultice. We got talking and liked each other and spent evenings together. Then he said his uncle had died and left him some money… told me to meet him at the Swan in Holbourne. That wasn't true, was it? About his uncle?'

I shook my head.

'He stole the money, didn't he, master?'

'I fear so.'

'Is he in terrible trouble?'

'Not from me. I have kept his name from Bailiff Turner and everyone else.'

'You would do that for Jack?'

'I have done so. The lad had a poor beginning in life and has suffered for it ever since, in one way or another. I did my best to guide him upon a righteous path—so, too, has Stephen—but 'twas too late to undo what was done in his childhood. Do you know where he be, Sarra?'

'He isn't at St Martin's, I swear it.'

'In all honesty?'

She nodded and crossed herself.

'Upon my very soul. He was there but didn't stay. He said you would find me when the time was right.'

'Jack said that?'

'Aye, told me he used to work for you. Is that true?'

'He did but he could not learn the scribe's art. He does better working wood with Stephen.'

'He said you were clever and would prove I never did witchcraft.'

'I be glad of it, indeed, lass. Hearing you wrongly accused hurt my heart. However, I oftentimes uncover secrets because I see them in folks' eyes. The eyes, being the windows of the soul, cannot lie. And in yours, I see but a single lie: you know where

Jack has gone, do you not? I be his friend and yours, so why not tell me? None else shall learn of it from me.'

'He made me promise I wouldn't tell his secret... not to anyone.'

'Ah, and a promise must be kept. I understand. In which case, I shall not press you but, I beg of you, answer me this: has Jack left London and gone from the authorities here? If he has, then I may breathe easy once more.'

'Indeed, Master Seb, Jack will soon be far away... and I miss him so.' And then she wept.

It filled me with sorrow to realise that Jack, so long unloved, had found the love of a comely maiden only to have to flee for his life without her. The world be ever unfair. But then what sort of a husband would the rascal have made? Hardly a reliable and respected one so, mayhap, 'twas just as well for Sarra's sake that he was gone. She would find another.

Since dinner was so delayed, I determined that I had time enough to conclude my business with Master Caxton at Westminster. Thus, I changed my torn attire and replaced the lace in my boot afore setting out to walk the two miles and a little more to the Fighting Cock.

The Fighting Cock Inn at Westminster

Gawain and I reached Westminster. The day was hot and a brassy sun hung in a bleached sky. My shoulder ached and my fresh clouts were swiftly sweat-soaked. I removed my jerkin and splashed my face with cool water at the conduit by Charing Cross. But it made little difference.

I found the elderly printer alone at dinner in the inn's refectory.

'God give you good day, Master Caxton,' I said in greeting, doffing my cap.

'And to you, Master Foxley.' He gestured with his spoon to the platter before him. 'Doesn't seem much point in rushing meals these days with no work to do. Will you join me?'

'My thanks but nay. I dined at home.' My belly rumbled, disproving my words, and I hoped Caxton could not hear it. His food smelled good.

'Did you see my assistant, Wynkyn de Worde? You surely passed him on your way here. He is gone to dismantle an unused press near St Paul's. I have purchased it from a Master Jude Foxley. Here, help yourself to ale after your walk for 'tis a hot day.' He handed me a jug and a spare cup. 'Is he any relation to you?'

'Aye. My brother.' I poured ale and drank it gratefully. Gawain had already availed himself of a long drink at the horse trough outside, water droplets yet clung to his whiskery chops.

'A strange fellow...' Caxton added, 'If you'll forgive my saying.'

'Jude has his ways. Life has not been so kind to him.'

'And even stranger: that creature who cares for him. I know not whether to say he or she.'

'She prefers to be addressed as Eleanor when in womanly attire and as John when clad in doublet and hose. We have become used to her—a good sort in truth.'

'I'll take your word for it. Now, your report, if you will, good master.'

I set my cup upon the board and took the smoke-besmirched accounting book from my scrip. Even in its battered condition, Caxton's eyes lit up at sight of it.

'Ah! The record of so many years of work lie within these covers. You cannot imagine how much this book means to me and my business.'

'I fear it has not come through unscathed. Some pages are torn or missing...'

'No matter...,' he leafed through the book. 'A few of last year's accounts are lacking but my future orders and commissions here at the back are nigh intact, God be praised. You have done well, Master Foxley, but I'm mystified as to why anyone would steal it in the first place and how you succeeded in finding it.'

'Dame Fortune smiled upon my endeavours,' I replied vaguely as I set forth my reckoning of expenses, placing the neatly written list beside the printer's empty dinner bowl, eager to depart afore he asked questions I dare not answer.

'But no sign of the thief and fire-setter who ruined my life and ended that of my poor journeyman?'

'I fear not.'

'And no clue as to who he is?'

I crossed my fingers behind my back and shook my head. I would not put my tongue to the lie.

'I hope he is gone far from Westminster and London then, whosoever he is. I wouldn't want him troubling me again when the new press is set up. It's costing me a deal of borrowed coin to have my house and workshop repaired. The bedchambers are yet blackened husks but the roof is now whole, the floors re-laid and my workshop usable once more.' Caxton wiped his greasy fingers on a napkin afore picking up my reckoning. He squinted at the neatly written paper, each expense itemised for clarity. 'And now you want me to pay your expenses?'

'I have my copy of our contract here…' I took the paper from my scrip, unfolded it and began to read. 'We agreed…'

'Aye, aye, I know what we agreed—my wits are sharp as yours—but I expected you to recover my money which you've singularly failed to do… not so much as a farthing. In which case, where do you suppose I shall find coin enough to pay you? I refuse to borrow any more from my creditors simply for the purpose of satisfying your greed.'

'My greed? But I pared down my expenses to the least amount reasonable. I have not charged you for…'

'I don't care. It's too much. Besides, how can I be certain you didn't find my money and decide to keep it for yourself?'

For a few moments, I could not respond so shocked was I at his words. I had been accused of many sins in the past but none had ever impugned my honesty until now.

'Y-you think I be a thief no better than the felon I sought on your behalf?'

'For all I know, you could be in collusion with the wretch… or are you the felon in question? You're a stationer. Do you fear I'll take your customers? Was it you who destroyed my livelihood and stole every penny I had?' Caxton was becoming crimson in the face, his eyes glazed with ire as he worked himself up into a frenzy. 'What have you done with my money?' The printer was on his feet, shouting and shaking his fists at me, spraying spittle.

Other customers at the inn abandoned their privy conversations to harken to ours.

'Give me back my money,' he screeched, coming around the table and grabbing me by my lately injured shoulder.

I winced and pushed him away. Gawain's hackles stood on end and he showed his teeth, growling, ready to leap to my defence. I held out my hand to him, palm downwards: a sign he understood to indicate that he should back away and rest easy.

'I do not have your money but, if you want to know where it is, go to Holbourne, to the Swan-on-the-Hoop. Enquire of the innkeeper there and the tap-boy where your money has gone and who spent it for 'twas not me.'

'You and they could all be conspiring together against me…'

'You be overwrought, making these wild accusations. We have a contract drawn up, signed and witnessed in this very place…'

'I declare it null and void!'

'You cannot do that. The law states…'

'And don't think to make an issue of it at law because the king is my patron. You'd lose your case. Now get out of my sight. If I ever see you again, you foul rascal…'

I departed, knowing not what else I could do. Those unfounded accusations hurt me raw. Adam was correct: the printer be our enemy—now, if not afore. Thus, I was not in the best of humours when I reached my brother's house.

Jude's house, Ave Maria Alley

The door was open and I heard voices within, the sounds of hammering and curses. As I pushed my way in, Jude was seated upon the stairs, out of harm's way, whilst two hired men dismantled the printing press under the direction of Wynkyn de Worde.

'Hold!' I cried. 'Step away from the press. Put down your tools, I say.'

The men obeyed, much to Jude's disgust.

'What? Are you bloody interfering in my life again?' He pushed himself up off the stair and limped towards me. 'This has naught to do with you. Get out of my way, Seb, and the rest of you get on with your job.'

'Has Caxton paid you for the press?' I demanded.

'None of your blasted business.'

'Well, he has not paid me and says he possesses not so much as a farthing, so unless he paid you aforehand...' I let the words hang: Jude could draw his own conclusion.

'All will be well, Master Voxley,' Wynkyn put in. 'Meneer Caxton will pay you right soon.'

'Soon!' Jude bellowed. 'We agreed payment before delivery. We shook hands on it. Where's my bloody money? I need it now, not next week nor next year, whenever it pleases your damned meneer to settle his debts. And, you: put that bloody chisel down.' He snatched the tool from a hired man's hand. 'My press is going nowhere until it's paid for, you hear?'

The hired men exchanged glances and downed tools, advancing on Wynkyn de Worde, forcing him back against the wall. One of the men stabbed at him with a gnarled finger:

'And what about us, eh? When do we get paid if there ain't no money?'

'Soon. Soon.'

'Not good enough. We don't work for naught. Come, Franklyn, get your tools. We're leaving. Watch out for that damned dog: it looks vicious.'

In truth, anything less vicious-looking than Gawain as he sat, panting, tongue lolling, was hard to imagine, his instinct for confrontation already spent upon Caxton earlier. But, even so, I called him aside as the hired men left in haste. Who could blame them?

'As for you,' Jude snarled at Wynkyn,' You can bugger off, back where you came from. Your sort isn't welcome here. Go on, fuck off to bloody France or Flanders or whatever God-forsaken mud hole you crawled out of. We don't want you in London.'

I saw the Fleming brace himself as though in preparation to fight but then he thought better of it and backed down, shoulders slumping but he would make the final cutting remark:

'I forgive you,' he said, holding his chin high. 'Being a poor cripple, you would know no better.'

Jude's eyes blazed with ire but he could do naught about the words.

Afore trouble could result, or anything more dire than insults could be thrown, I took Wynkyn's arm and directed him out of the door.

'Your master's business with my brother is concluded,' I said. 'But not with me.'

Jude reached for the ale jug and filled a cup for himself alone before easing down upon the bench.

'Now what?' he asked, staring at the dismantled timbers lying on the floor, the metal platen leaning against the fireplace, the great iron screw... all useless now. 'What do I do with the bloody thing now? This is all your fault!'

'My fault? Would you rather have given it away, *gratis*?'

'At least it would be gone instead of strewn all over my house, tripping me up whenever I move. You'll have to get rid of it.'

'Me? How is this my responsibility, Jude?'

'It was your idea to sell it to bloody Caxton in the first place. I knew it would all go wrong but you insisted...'

'And you agreed...'

'Eventually, after you persuaded me and much against my better judgement…'

'You wrote to Caxton of your own volition. I did not force you…'

'It was still your idea in the first place.'

I sighed. This pointless conversation was going nowhere. I could not permit Caxton to drive yet another dagger point betwixt me and my brother. Besmirching my good name was bad enough.

'Mayhap, Stephen will buy the timbers from you. They look to be of the stoutest oak, no worm, few knots. He may give you a fair price for them.'

'How much?'

'I cannot say. I know not the cost of such items.' I helped myself to ale: arguing with my brother was ever-thirsty work. 'What price did you pay for the press?'

'None of your business.'

'A considerable sum, then, plus the cost of shipping it from France…'

'Burgundy,' he corrected.

'And customs, taxes and tariffs, port duties and carriage from Dover…'

'Ipswich and then by boat to Queenhithe.'

'Even farther and the Queen's Geld to pay to unload there and, I assume, you paid a carter to bring it to your door. Altogether, a deal of expense.'

'Bloody thing. I wish I'd never bought it. What about all the ironwork? Stephen won't want that.'

I frowned in thought and drank my ale.

'Sell it to a blacksmith for melting down, though I once saw a great screw not unlike that used to crush the juice from pears to make perry. In Kent that was. Maybe a cider-maker would buy it from you. And the platen, set in a fine frame, would make an excellent shiny mirror… I be certain every part could be put to use somehow.'

'And I'll barely recoup the importation fees. I may as well chop it up for firewood. At least it'll keep me warm come winter. In the meantime, you can shift it out of the way.'

'Nay. My shoulder was dislocated, if you recall. I was told to rest it.'

'You've abandoned the sling you wore before.'

''Twas more of an encumbrance than an aid but I dare not attempt to lift those timbers.'

'Then send that fat, lazy cousin of yours. It'll do him good to work for once, the idle bugger.'

I made no comment, knowing Adam would do naught to assist my brother.

'I must leave you, Jude. My thanks for the ale.' I drained my cup. 'I have urgent matters to attend elsewhere.'

'And you would leave me with all this?' He gestured expansively towards the cluttered floor. 'Bloody typical.'

'I fear so. Ask your drinking companions at the Panyer or the Sunne to oblige you. Farewell and give my regards to Eleanor.'

I went home. The others, including Thaddeus, had dined, somewhat belatedly, but Rose had set my portion aside upon a chafing dish to keep warm. Yet I did not desire food, my humours too curdled with anger at Caxton's behaviour and his ill words towards me.

'I shall eat it for supper,' I said. 'Come, Thaddeus, Bess, we must away to that other matter. I must fetch those items…'

Grace Church Street

Bess directed us to Mistress Anneis Fuller's house by Leadenhall in Grace Church Street. It was a fine building, as were most in this wide thoroughfare, three storeys with pargetted plaster betwixt the heavy oak timbers of its construction. The front had lately been lime-washed and bedazzled the eye in the bright afternoon sunshine. The door was well painted with woad blue and all the downstairs windows were glazed, adding to the dazzle.

Thaddeus stepped around a pat of cow dung to reach the door and rapped upon it with his staff of office, this being an official visit and, as City Bailiff, he would make it plain that he had no intention of suffering any obfuscation, misdirection or lengthy verbal protests from the woman. We knew Mistress Fuller to be well capable of using her sharp tongue as a cutler's blade.

In such a house, I expected a servant to answer the knock but Mistress Fuller herself opened the door. She looked surprised to see us but put on a smile.

'Bailiff Turner, good afternoon to you. How may I assist our ever-vigilant Guardian of the Law?'

'We require you to assist us in our endeavours concerning certain accusations you made of late against Mistress Bess Chambers of Bishopsgate and her niece, Sarra Shardlowe. May we come in? 'Tis better to discuss such matters privily rather than here in the street where we may be overheard by your neighbours.'

'I have naught to hide,' she said haughtily but then realised the good sense in the bailiff's advice. 'But I suppose you must come within. But not her!' She pointed at Bess. 'I'll not have a witch step over my threshold.'

'As you will, mistress, but Master Foxley must join us.'

'If you insist, though I don't see why I should allow him in my home either.'

I gave Bess a coin—I wore an old purse, retrieved from the bottom of my coffer to replace the one stolen from me earlier at St Martin's. 'Twas battered and the strap fraying but it must serve for the present, having but a few pence within. I bade her await us in the nearby George and Dragon tavern before following Thaddeus into the Fuller house.

'Is your husband at home?' he asked, espying a man's boots set beside the door.

'The boots are John's—my son's,' she said, following the bailiff's glance. 'My husband lies in All Hallows churchyard across the way; thank God for His mercies. The man was a hopeless fool. All this...' she waved her arms to encompass the well-appointed entrance hall and the carved staircase to the chambers above before ushering us into an equally handsome parlour. 'This is my doing; the house was my dowry and all the improvements mine. Thank God he died before he could ruin everything.' She took a seat in a velvet-upholstered chair, the queen of her domain. She did not bid us sit; rather we must stand in her regal presence and acknowledge our humble place.

Thaddeus ignored the slight and, without invitation, sat on the cushioned settle, gesturing me to do likewise on a gold-fringed, damask-draped stool. I was unsure whether this was wise, if we desired her co-operation. Mistress Fuller's affront was obvious but, this once, she held her tongue.

'What do you want?' she demanded, all efforts towards courtesy abandoned on both sides—no hospitality was offered.

'Master Foxley, if you would oblige... please explain our purpose to Mistress Fuller.'

I took out the spare wax, rounded and flattened from previous use, in its dish, a candle stub upon a pricket and my tinder box. I struck a spark to the tinder and lit the candle afore holding the dish by its ears to warm the wax.

'What in St Margaret's name are you doing?' Mistress Fuller wanted to know.

'Have a little patience and you shall see,' I replied, enjoying her bewilderment even as she watched the procedure which, I prayed, would shortly prove to be her undoing. Reciting *Pater Nosters* under my breath to reckon the passage of time, with the wax now softened to the degree required, I blew out the candle. I wiped away the soot deposited on the underside of the dish with a linen scrap brought for the purpose and presented the warm dish to Mistress Fuller.

'And what, pray, am I supposed to do with this?'

'If you would take the trouble to push your thumb flat into the wax,' I said, demonstrating how without my thumb actually touching and making a mark.

She obliged, frowning, as I made certain the mark was clear. In order to be certain, I asked her to make a second imprint with her index finger afore I used my finest paint brush to take a little soot from the linen—having found this served as well as charcoal dust—and lightly dusting it over the indentations, making the raised patterns easily determined. Then, peering through my scrying glass, I copied the marks, enlarging them so the design could be seen more clearly. With them completed, I wrote her name and the day upon the paper so that there could be no confusion afore passing it to Thaddeus to initial.

'There you have it, mistress,' I said as Thaddeus passed her my drawings. 'Those are the patterns upon your thumb and finger. You saw me copy them, did you not? They are *your* marks, do you agree?'

'I suppose.' She looked at them closely and then squinted at her thumb. I gave her the scrying glass to observe the patterns more easily. 'What of it? It means naught.'

'On the contrary, it means a great deal.' From my scrip, I produced my earlier drawings of marks made upon the mannequins—labelled accordingly and, likewise, witnessed by Thaddeus. I explained them to her, taking a risk forwhy I had not yet compared them for myself yet I felt certain the two would be as alike as two eggs in a nest. I gave her time to pore over them afore returning the papers to Thaddeus. Thus it was he who announced our findings.

'The thumb marks match, mistress: irrefutable evidence that your hands made those foul images. Mistress Bess Chambers and Sarra Shardlowe did not make the devilish objects. You did. If anyone laid a curse upon Thomas Goulden and caused his death by means unnatural, it was you.' The bailiff stood afore announcing: 'Mistress Anneis Fuller, I'm arresting you upon a charge of murder by witchcraft with other charges to follow.'

She howled in protest as he led her from her fine house, her cries of protest and denial attracting the attention of her neighbours who came into the street to gawp and nudge each other.

'Let me go, you oaf! Unhand me, I say. I'm not guilty of any crime. Those women have done all this: cursed me so I take the blame. Leave me be, you wretch. Take your filthy hands off me.'

Thaddeus was deaf to her ranting, holding her firmly by the arm and hastening towards Cornhill. He had already informed me that, if her fingers had indeed made the mannequins, he would take her to the Compter—the Sheriffs' lock-up—not to Guildhall. He did not intend to risk losing another in his custody but the Compter was not a pleasant place and definitely not for a woman. A pretty lass would ne'er survive a night in there with her reputation intact which had been his reason for keeping Sarra at Guildhall. Mistress Fuller would have to take her chances.

We had found out the widow's crimes but, since her fellows in Grace Church Street did not seem much surprised by the events occurring on their doorstep, I think others had suspected or, mayhap, already knew of her evil activities beforehand. Some among them had been in the mob that destroyed the apothecary shop—I recognised their faces and noted them in my head. If Thaddeus intended further prosecutions for riotous behaviour, destruction of property, trespass, disturbing the King's Peace, assault upon myself and any other charges which might be brought against them, I should be able to point out some at least of the offenders.

Greatly relieved, I took my scrip and hastened to the George and Dragon to tell Bess the glad tidings. She greeted my news with such delight and insisted we should celebrate with a cup of wine, if I had no objection to paying, of course. Which I did not. But then we should hasten back to Paternoster Row to tell Sarra that the real culprit was now taken into the City Bailiff's custody.

'Whilst we be so close, Bess,' I said, 'Would you not wish to see the repairs being done at your house?'

Bess Chambers' shop

We made our way up Bishopsgate Street to Bess's house to see how Stephen was getting on and the progress made towards restoring her home and livelihood. Her door was now hung upon stout new hinges of iron, instead of leather. Most of the window shutters were likewise repaired. Stephen was affixing the last new shutter in position. This one had been so badly damaged beyond mending and its pale wood had yet to be painted to match the others. Otherwise, the outside of her house was now as it should be.

Stephen let us in through the door. The inside was quite another matter though fresh planks and wooden brackets lay ready to build new shelves and a fine, stout board leaned against the wall, awaiting the construction of new trestles to support it upon which Bess could resume serving her customers.

The still room beyond was yet in a sorry condition. Though cleared of debris, shattered glass and broken pots and with the floor swept clean, naught had been done to make it possible for Bess to go about her work of distilling medicaments, making ointments, tisanes and cordials, perfumed waters and scented candles and whatever else an apothecary required to stock. Fortunately, the pentangle was quite obliterated. Everything would need to be begun afresh. Bess had so much to do to start anew but, even so, she now wore a smile.

'Stephen is doing so well, Seb, and my place is secure now. What a relief that is to me and I couldn't afford it without your assistance.'

'You will need Sarra's aid to get all in readiness to reopen your shop.'

'My poor lass. But at least we can now prove she didn't make those wicked things. Oh, Seb, I do believe all will come right in the end.' She smiled again but also wiped away a tear.

'Speaking of those things: I must to Guildhall to lock away the drawings and mannequins as evidence. They must be kept safely from any hand that might ruin them.'

'Or use them for evil purposes over again. We wouldn't want more lives endangered, would we?'

'In truth, Bess, that had not occurred to me but 'tis yet another reason to keep them under lock and key. Thaddeus has the use of the city coffer with four locks, each with a different keeper of the key. He has but one, the Lord Mayor, the City Recorder and the Mayor's Secretary hold the others. That should serve to keep innocent citizens from harm.'

The Foxley Place

I shocked Adam by working at my desk for the entire afternoon though it did not concern our craft. Rather, I transcribed Parker's screed and wrote my report for Thaddeus to make amends for having struck him. In truth, I thought he made over much of very little. My knuckles bore no bruises, having dented soft flesh only, of which, these days, my friend carried somewhat of an excess. Too many cook-shop pies, no doubt.

That done, I looked to Kate's first sewing of gatherings. She, being my apprentice, I needs must oversee her work. But since stitchery be one of most women's natural talents, I should not have been concerned: her work was fine and neat in appearance and secure enough to hold the gatherings as long as the pages should last.

'I commend you, Kate. 'Tis well done, indeed.'

Her face lit up at my words of praise.

'Hugh told me to make the threads tighter than I did to begin with. I feared they might tear the paper but he said loose stitches would be more likely to do that over time if the pages were able to slip about, the threads would wear away at the holes.'

I looked to her betrothed at the neighbouring desk where he was copying out St Mark's Gospel with his left hand. I always wondered that his work could be of such excellence when done cack-handed-wise. Those of a foolish superstitious mind say 'tis thus the Devil's handiwork but I know that for a nonsense.

'Then I commend you also, Hugh, for your goodly instruction. You shall make a fine master one day.'

'Thank you, Master Seb. Kate is an attentive pupil and takes my direction willingly—most times.'

He laughed as she dug him in the ribs with her elbow.

'I always do as you tell me... so long as it's convenient.'

We all laughed together.

'And you shall make a most biddable wife, Kate, of that I be certain, if Hugh may ever tame your spirit,' I said.

'He never will, master, as he knows full well. But he says he'll suffer my short-comings without too much complaint so long as my dinners are as good as Mistress Rose's. So I must practise my cookery skills if I want a happy marriage. Isn't that so, Hugh?'

'Aye, a husband with a good meal under his belt has no cause to berate his wife—or so my Uncle Gardyner says and he should know, having had three wives.'

Later that eve
The Foxley Place

After supper—or dinner in my case—the women folk being fully occupied in the kitchen with washing dishes, tending babes and whatever else, when a knock came at the street door, I opened it myself. We were not expecting visitors and I was much surprised to see William Caxton standing in the twilight upon the doorstep.

'Good even, Master Caxton.' I greeted him in friendly wise—not that he deserved such courtesy after the insults he had flung at me earlier.

'A good even, is it? I think not.' I saw that his eyes were wild-looking; his hands shook. 'Not for you, leastwise. I have found you out, Foxley; you and your wicked schemes...'

'My wicked schemes? I know not of what you speak.' The

fellow must be drunk, I concluded. 'You had best come within,' I said, thinking to avoid a scene in the street.

Rose came from the kitchen as we crossed the entrance hall to the parlour door. Her hands and apron were flour-dusted.

'I heard someone at the door...' she began.

'Aye, this is Master William Caxton, of whom you have heard much of late. Master, this is Rose Glover, Mistress Foxley, my goodwife.' I purposefully introduced them contrary to courtesy which, of course, required a man to be informed of the woman's name foremost. If he did not wish to be courteous then I could do the same.

'Shall I serve ale and wafers in the parlour, husband?' Her enquiry sounded guileless but I could tell she was aware of the tensions betwixt us.

'A cup of ale will suffice, Rose, I thank you. Our visitor will not stay for long.' I escorted him into our fine parlour chamber, decorated recently with a painted hanging depicting the Visitation of the Virgin to her elderly cousin, Elizabeth. Rose chose it forewhy both women were, at the time, with child by a miracle, a condition for which my sweeting had long prayed daily. I could hear the answer to her prayers chuckling in the kitchen—a merry sound much at odds with the sour airs here in the parlour.

I directed Caxton to the settle whilst I remained standing. This was a trick I learned from Thaddeus during interviews with miscreants: have them sit so they feel intimidated as you stand over them.

'Well? What are these wicked schemes you mention? Explain yourself, if you will.'

'Indeed I shall. This afternoon, since you suggested it, I took the trouble of walking to Holbourne, to the Swan-on-the-Hoop Inn, to be precise, there to make enquiries. And what do I discover but that the folk there say the fellow who spent all my money was none other than Jude Foxley. Your no-good, misbegotten brother!'

Dear God! What a fool I had been to tell him of the Swan but I was angry when I spoke of it and ne'er expected him to go there.

'Ah. I can see how this must appear to you.'

'The pair of you destroyed my livelihood and I can see why. As stationers, you fear the competition from my printing press. Setting a felon to investigate his own crime—I dare say you laughed right merrily at that. You knew the whereabouts of my book all the while. Did you keep it here in this house even whilst you enjoyed yourselves at my expense? Did it not bother you that my journeyman died because of what you did? You're murderers, the pair of you... I'll have you both arrested...'

'Hold, hold. Allow me to correct you. I had naught to do with what came to pass. I was not involved in any criminal activity. You asked me to investigate upon the King's and Lord Hastings' recommendations. Do you think they were also party to this scheme, so-called? As for my brother spending your money in Holbourne, did folk there describe the fellow to you?'

'Aye, clear enough.'

'They told me he was young, dark of hair and, I quote, "built like an oak tree". Have you met my brother Jude?'

'Not in person but...'

'Your assistant, Wynkyn de Worde, can describe my brother to you: not so young with fading yellow hair and crippled of leg. Anyone less like an oak these days be hard to imagine.'

'I still mean to have you both arrested... the King will hear of this.'

Rose came then, bearing two cups of ale.

'By the by, husband, I meant to tell you: City Bailiff Turner sent word that he can join us for dinner on the morrow, as usual. Shall I wear the gown I wore when His Grace, the Duke of Gloucester, invited us to sup? Oh, and your cousin will be meeting with Lord Mayor Browne on Thursday next—he asked me to inform you. Will that be all, husband?'

What a clever wife have I? Since Caxton mentioned

King Edward, our family could name our illustrious acquaintances also.

'Certainly, Rose. We shall not detain you. I know you have much to do and I, too, must think upon my business in St Paul's yesterday… with Bishop Kempe.' I sipped my drink and took my ease afore returning my attention to our visitor; 'And Caxton, as I was about to say, the fellow at the Swan did, indeed, call himself Jude Foxley but either my brother has a namesake or, more likely, the fellow was taking my brother's name in vain for his own nefarious purposes. If you were a felon at large, would you be so foolish as to make use of your own name or that of some other? 'Tis simply a most unfortunate coincidence that he chose Jude Foxley. Mayhap, he overheard the name somewhere and liked the sound of it.'

'And maybe all three of you were working together.'

'My brother's injured leg precludes his involvement in any activity which cannot be accomplished whilst seated. Besides, we both of us have firm and unassailable alibis.' I stated this last with as much conviction as I could muster but, truth to tell, I could not recall what I did upon the night in question nor where I was. Most likely, I was here at home, abed with my wife as any worthy, righteous citizen should be.

'So, go ask your assistant concerning my brother's appearance,' I continued, 'And see whether it tallies in the least with the fellow described to you at the Swan. I can assure you that it will not. Now, I bid you goodnight, Master Caxton. Have a care on your walk back to Westminster.'

With which, I relieved him of his ale, half consumed, and escorted him to the street door.

'If you hasten, you may be home afore full dark and avoid being accosted by the Watch as a felon out and about at night without a torch to light your way.' I did not offer him a light nor summon a torch-bearer for him, as good manners required, but I cared not. I owed him naught, whereas he owed me the monies due as per our contract.

311

Chapter 19

Tuesday, the third day of July
Guildhall

IT WAS raining, as if I did not feel misery enough. Caxton's accusations of last eve yet tormented my spirit. Even so, I hastened to deliver the transcription to Thaddeus, that which his man Parker had made illegible, aware that the bailiff must have full cognisance of its contents afore the impending trial on the morrow. He took it from me and perused it briefly.

I shook rain from my hair like a dog, except that a dog as wise as Gawain had chosen to remain dry at home.

'Aye, this I can read. You're re-instated as my secretary with immediate effect.'

'I am not. Find yourself a more capable scribe than Parker straightway. I have not the time to spend nor the inclination to work for you, as you well know. Besides, you expect to have my penmanship *gratis* and I cannot afford that.'

'I buy you ale.'

'Rarely. Concerning which…' I unfastened my well-worn purse. 'Here, 'tis the penny three farthings I owe you for our ale at the Sunne in Splendour.' I put the coins upon the board. 'I would not have you call me debtor.'

'You owed me because you struck me and I deserved compensation. However,' he took a leather bag down from his shelf. 'This is yours; delivered last eve.'

I opened the bag and saw a cluster of gold angel coins. I looked at him questioningly.

'Cobb the Carrier brought it; said you'd know what it was for but demanded a groat out of it, which I paid him.'

'Oh, I had quite forgotten this. 'Tis from the Prioress at Dartford for the Gospel Book we made.'

'Twelve pounds sterling, thirteen shillings and four pence. I counted it. I trust he didn't rob you? Is that the correct amount?'

'Most certainly. Cobb be an honest fellow indeed. My thanks to you for this, Thaddeus. 'Tis an expensive time, what with a new babe and other, er, losses.'

'Well, don't go losing it as you did yesterday. Take better care of it. Now, have you written the report concerning what went on behind St Martin's walls and how we retrieved the escaped miscreant?'

I handed him another neatly written paper from my scrip.

'We?' I repeated. 'Miscreant? Sarra be innocent, as I recall.'

'Escaping custody is an offence in itself. You'd better not have made it seem I was at fault. She was here for her own safety and should have been content to wait for the law to take its proper course.' He began to read, his lips forming each word silently.

'The lass was afraid. She had been named for a witch. In like circumstances, if the chance of escape offered, what would you have done, Thaddeus? Would you have turned away those who came to aid you to freedom?'

'She should have been patient. It was just for one night…'

'Did you explain that to her?'

'I'm not obliged to explain my purpose to those I arrest. They do as I tell them. She disobeyed me. Now, you've caused me to lose my place. Where was I?'

'Have a heart, my friend. She be but a young lass. What knowledge would she have of the law?'

'Ignorance of the law is no excuse, Seb, as you know full well and it applies to all, young or old, man or woman, rich or poor. Justice stands indifferent.'

I sighed.

'Then what would you have me do? Bring her to you with a

313

halter about her neck? Help you lock her head and hands in the pillory or put her feet in the stocks?'

'Oh, I don't know. Just keep the wench out of trouble, can't you?'

'I am not her guardian.'

Thaddeus gave no reply to that except for a meaningful look, which I was unsure how to interpret, afore returning his gaze to the paper.

'I mislike what you've written here…' he said when, at length, he put down the document. 'There is too much made of her ease of escape, as if I left the place unguarded which—as you well know—I did not. And you make little mention of how I persuaded the porter at St Martin's. I need you to rewrite this.'

Without a word, I accepted the paper and replaced it in my scrip forwhy my thoughts were otherwise occupied:

'I wonder if I should tell you…' I began. 'I may have difficulties of my own regarding the law…'

'What now? Another scrape is it?'

'I would not call it so.' I sighed and resigned myself to telling the tale. Something of it, leastwise. 'It concerns a certain Master William Caxton, the printer at Westminster. You may have heard of him?'

Thaddeus nodded.

'What of him?'

'He has reneged upon a contract made betwixt us, refusing to pay my expenses or remuneration, slandering my good name and accusing me of all manner of evil deeds done against him.'

'Then sue the wretch for every penny he possesses.'

'And therein lies the problem: the man has no money. His premises were burned and his livelihood destroyed—these being the very crimes for which he now holds me responsible. Worse yet, he claims King Edward himself, Anthony, Earl Rivers, and Lord Hastings as his patrons… if he should make a case of it. Could he do that, Thaddeus? How does the law stand on such matters?'

'On what grounds does he accuse you?'

'I suppose his best evidence be that I succeeded in recovering his stolen accounting book, therefore, according to his reasoning, I must have known its whereabouts all along. But, since I did not return the money that was taken at the same time, it must be the case that I have either spent it outright or secreted it away to discharge at my own will and pleasure.'

Thaddeus blew out his cheeks.

'Sounds a bit thin, Seb...'

'Thin? The morning mist has more substance to it.'

'But his patrons are powerful men.'

'That worries me the most. As you say: "Justice stands indifferent" but we both know 'tis not always so. If I take him to court, shall I find myself facing their men of law? That would be a battle I could not win. I know not what to do. Advise me, Thaddeus, I pray you.'

The Foxley Place

As I walked home, the rain fell heavier, lightning flashed and thunder rolled across the sky but naught could make my temper any worse. In truth, I did not much like the advice that my friend had given. Thaddeus was most probably wise in telling me to forget the matter but it soured my humours further yet and I chafed at this hindrance to my purpose. Knowing that Justice did not invariably stand indifferent made me angry and bitter.

I had eaten my dinner without tasting a bite and now my apricocks in a velvety cream sauce sat, untouched, in my bowl.

Rose and the others knew of my encounter last eve and how it had upset me. She shook her head in dismay as I shared out my helping betwixt the little ones.

'Tell us a tale, Papa,' Dickon said. 'We can't play in the garden: Mam says it's too wet.'

'Not now. I have not the time.'

Rose raised her eyebrows in question.

'What else do you have to do, Seb? It would amuse us all until the rain abates.'

'I am not of a mind for stories. Go play merrills or fox-and-geese. The boards are in the parlour.'

'Oh, pleeease, Papa. Gawain wants a story. And I don't like the thunder and lightning,' my son added as the storm roared overhead.

'I said nay, Dickon. Now cease your wheedling. 'Tis unbecoming and irritating.'

'Then I shall tell one,' Rose said. 'And listen well. There once was a man: kindly, sweet-natured and honest. Everybody loved him but, one day, an evil-mouthed fellow called the man a thief, saying he had stolen all his money. Of course, the kindly man hadn't stolen anything—he was far too honest to do such a thing—but the evil-mouthed fellow had so upset him that the man became a grouch. He was sullen and ill-tempered and didn't even eat his dinner. He upset everyone who loved him. Well, somebody had to put things right, didn't they?'

The children nodded.

'What did they do?' Dickon wanted to know.

'What would you do?' Rose asked him.

'I'd kick the fellow on the leg—hard,' my son said after due consideration. 'And ride my hobby horse all over him. Gawain could bite him.'

'I'd slice off his ears and pelt him with stones,' Nick decided. 'Then I'd cut off his lying tongue and rip out his guts and make him eat radishes and stab him in the...'

'Aye, I think the fellow is properly dead by now, Nick,' Adam said, grinning. 'You've killed the wretch for certain with those radishes.'

Nick nodded enthusiastically.

'Well, he deserved it. Anyhow, I hate them.'

And the company laughed. I smiled, my humour not utterly amended but much improved by the vision of the children waging war on my behalf. Caxton being forced to eat radishes by young Nick was an image to be long remembered.

'I ask forgiveness of you for my surliness and for being a— what was it, wife?—oh, aye, a grouch. I beg your pardons, one and all.'

With which, the rain eased to a gentle patter and the sun broke through, tearing a great golden hole in the dark clouds.

Bess Chambers' shop

Later, with the storms past—concerning both the weather and my personal tempest—Bess, Sarra and I walked to Bishopsgate, that they might see the progress made in repairing their home. Stephen had been working like a galley slave to have the place made habitable and, outwardly, the building was now in fine fettle as a limner applied paint to the last window shutter. I did not know the fellow. Stephen must have hired him. But I touched my cap in greeting and he did likewise with a pigment-dappled hand.

Bess and Sarra stood, gazing, smiling, admiring the fresh paint, the new door and all else.

Within, Stephen was sweeping up sawdust—a valuable commodity he could sell for kindling or to tavern-keepers, butchers or surgeons to strew on the floor.

'God give you good day, Stephen,' I said, hastening to hold the corners of the hempen sack into which he would shovel the sawdust.

'And likewise to you, Seb.'

Together, we completed the task. He tied the top of the sack and sat upon a stool—new, I noted, to replace what had been broken, waving me to another, not new but with a leg replaced and the splintered seat planed down and scoured with sand to smooth, pale new wood.

'Well? What do you think?' he asked. 'Fit to live in now?'

I looked about at stout shelves along the walls, a fine counter-board on new trestles and a range of small chests for storage.

'Aye. Perfect. Bess can open her shop for business any time,' I said.

As the women came in, the carpenter turned to them:

'I've done upstairs also: the bed, the coffer… all repaired and, as you see, the still room is usable but you'll have to replace all the linens, hangings, pots and glassware. I know little of such things.'

Sarra ran outside and we could hear her feet racing up the stair.

'As for the garden plot…' he continued, 'I mended the paling fence which was broken down but as for the trees and herbs only Nature can put those to rights. I've done my best.'

'We owe you such a debt, Stephen, and not only in coin for your materials, skills and labours,' Bess said, seizing his calloused hands. 'You have remade our livelihood. Our spirits are raised by this and all achieved in so short a time: you have worked a wonder here.' She followed Sarra out the back and I was alone with Stephen for the moment.

'Let me have your reckoning as soon as you may and it shall be paid in full right promptly,' I said.

'A pot of ale now, on account, would be most welcome,' he said, grinning. 'It's thirsty work on a hot day and this sawdust parches a man's throat. I hear the Bull next door serves fine ale in true measures, if you're willing? I'm certain the women can find plenty to do here, putting things straight and to their liking.'

The Foxley Place

Our tardiness in arriving home for supper was readily forgiven since we had such good tidings to impart concerning Bess's place—imbibing ale with a merry companion can also be a lengthy business.

Over a fine mutton and onion pie with fresh peas—our crop being so plentiful we were eating peas for nigh every meal despite giving them away to friends and neighbours by the basket full—the women were discussing what Bess yet required afore returning home: bedding, clothing, cooking pots… stuff for the still room and the shop. The shop was now fit for re-opening but what could Bess sell when all her stock was ruined and her garden spoiled?

'We can spare you lavender and rosemary from our garden to make scented waters,' Rose offered, dandling Ned upon her lap. 'And sage and marigolds for salves and fennel and mint… That will be a start and some things to sell. I can lend you a few pots and pans for now. I'll not need them 'til the time of the fruit harvest. And I know there's meadowsweet aplenty for headaches, nettles for dyes and inflammation remedies and St John's wort for jaundice and melancholy all growing in the hedgerow on the way to Smithfield, so they'll not cost you a farthing. You can borrow the featherbed Pen made use of Sunday night and the pillows…' My wife's generosity caused her to run short of breath.

'I have a spare bag of drawing charcoal,' I said. 'It will serve as well as any other kind to heat the brazier so you can begin distilling. Also, I have more pigment pots than I truly require. You may have a half-dozen of those. I shall see they be washed out first.'

'I'll do that this evening, master,' Kate said.

'Come down to Distaff Lane,' Adam offered. 'The lads' mother had a well-equipped kitchen and I know not what purpose half the stuff serves. There's so much linen napiery we never use. You can take whatever you need. Oh, and…' my cousin paused to steady his voice, 'Her gowns and shifts are yet in a coffer. I couldn't bring myself to sell them to a fripperer. I heard tell your clothes were shredded beyond mending… I'd rather her belongings w-went to a friend…' With which he departed the board in haste, the better to conceal his feelings. The death of Mercy Hutchinson affected him deeply even after so long. Simon followed him to the workshop to share their grief, privily.

'How can I ever repay so much kindness?' Bess used her apron to mop tears.

After supper, when we retired to the coolness of the garden, as was our custom in this warm summer weather, all appeared content. Adam and his lads had gone home and Dickon and Julia played quietly, tying grass stems into some kind of pattern known only to them. Ned slept on Rose's lap. Ralf was out with his Joanie; Kate and Hugh held hands 'neath the apple tree and Bess and Meg were becoming close friends, exchanging knowledge of herbs and remedies. Nessie sulked as usual.

In the peace of the moment, I sat with my drawing board, sketching Rose and the babe. If e'er I should need a likeness for a miniature of the Virgin and Child, the best image was arrayed for me there, beside the henhouse, amidst the pea bines. Never had I seen my dear one more contented than as she gazed upon the downy golden head of the sleeping babe. None would have supposed he was not her own.

'Twas then that I saw from the corner of my eye Sarra slipping away through our side gate, leaving without a word, no doubt hoping to go unnoticed. I could say that I felt concern at the thought of a lass alone on the streets of an evening but, to be honest, 'twas more in the way of curiosity getting the better of me. I wanted to know where she was going and what she intended but one word leapt straightway into my mind: Jack.

To Queenhithe

So intent was she upon her quest, she did not once look back. I followed her through St Paul's Precinct which would shortly be closing its gates for the night. We came out by St Augustine's Gate and turned south towards the river. On Thames Street, she went east, pulling aside into a doorway as a last wagon bearing a load of sawn tree trunks trundled by from Timberhithe.

The smell of salt and fish and pitch was heavy in the still air. Ships' masts pierced the sky as it faded from blue to sunset crimson. The cry of gulls and mariners' shouts came clear. I had little to do with London's riverside—the very sight of waves made my belly churn—but here we were at Queenhithe.

And then I saw it. A shape I could ne'er forget. Of horrid memory yet familiar to me.

The *Eagle* rode low at the quayside, her crew hastening about like ants, doing whatever it is that mariners have to do.

Sarra stood upon the wharf, shielding her eyes, the better to observe the men on board. Whilst most of the stout fellows scurried hither and thither or climbed the ropes to unfurl the sails, a tall man stood by the rail, directing the others. I knew him of old: Gabriel Widdowson—or whatever he called himself nowadays—living, breathing still. The rascal who stole my first wife's heart from me; I should ne'er forgive him yet—foolish as I be—I liked the man. We had been friends. I once saved him from a heretic's fate: a debt he repaid by making a cuckold of me. And there he stood, bold as a pirate's doxy.

Sarra was waving her hand frantically. I wondered how she knew the captain of the *Eagle* but then I saw the object of her piteous farewells. Halfway up the rigging, clinging like a monkey, one-handedly, whilst waving his cap with the other… was Jack.

'Stand-ho,' I heard Gabriel yell. 'Cast off for'ard cable.' On the quayside, fellows unwound a great tarred rope from about the mooring post and threw it into the water. Others swiftly pulled it aboard the ship. As the front end—the bow, if I recalled it aright—swung out, I heard him shout, 'Cast off aft. Make way a-steerboard.' At least, I thought that was his cry as the ship began to pull away from the quay. Ponderously, the vessel moved out into the river until the ebbing tide caught it and it made headway for the perilous arches of London Bridge.

I saw the drawbridge was raised in readiness to allow the passage of five ships sailing on the tide. One departing The Cranes Wharf was huge, flying the colours of Flanders, dwarfing the *Eagle* which nimbly overtook the lumbering vessel to reach the bridge first. Two Hanse ships from the Steelyard followed on and a third came underway from Paul's Wharf, blocking our sight of Gabriel's craft, yet Sarra continued to wave her hand.

Only when a glimpse of its tallest mast beyond the bridge proved that the *Eagle* was safely through this first obstacle on her voyage did Sarra lower her arm. She looked about her, seemingly bewildered to discover where she stood. Quayside workers milled about afore making for the nearest tavern, their labours successfully completed. The lass now stood alone.

Then she espied me. After but an instant of uncertainty, she came to me to be comforted, wiping away tears.

'He's gone now,' she sobbed. 'My Jack's gone.'

Chapter 20

Wednesday, the fourth day of July
Guildhall

A T HOME, matters were returning to normal—or as normal as could be with a new babe. Bess and Sarra had slept at our house for the final time last night.

We were returned from Low Mass at St Michael's and breaking our fast on soused herring when a message came for me from Thaddeus, asking me to attend him at Guildhall straightway. Thinking there must be something amiss, I made haste and found the bailiff in the meagre cell which served as his place of work, munching a breakfast fish pasty, showering crumbs all about. Gawain wasted not a moment in clearing them away, licking his chops then wagging his tail in hope of further largesse. My friend obliged him with the pastry crust, burnt at the edges, though my dog was not put off by a little charring and soot.

'Thaddeus... I came as swiftly as maybe,' I greeted him, breathless from my run through the streets. 'Is there some matter untoward?'

'God give you good day,' he said, seeming in no hurry. 'Help yourself to ale, Seb.'

'Have we time enough to spare?'

'Aye. There's always time for ale but I've got a deal of business to get through and your scribal aid would be appreciated.'

'Oh, is that all?' I wiped dust from the cup with my sleeve afore pouring a small measure of ale from the jug then slumped down upon the rickety stool. 'I abandoned my bread and herring for your sake and all you require is a secretary. I have told you so often…'

'I know, but who else can I ask, Seb? And I apologise about your breakfast but if I'd not made it sound of great importance, you might not have obliged me.'

'And, indeed, I may not. I could return home, finish my herring and be about my own day's work. You forget that I have a business to run, money to earn, mouths to feed.'

'I'll pay you.'

'How often have I heard you say that and not a clipped penny comes my way?'

'This time, I swear…'

'Save your breath. What is it you want written out? I have come here in haste; I may as well put my effort to some use. Besides, you may be able to grant a favour to me and mine in return. Later.'

He frowned at that but then his face cleared as he mentally set the possibility aside.

'I have heard from that useless fellow, Dymmock, Deputy Coroner of London, if you recall? He took the Devil's own time about it, as usual, but tells the outcome of the inquest into the death of one Thomas Goulden. Here, read it yourself.' Thaddeus passed me a parchment with a red wax seal appended. 'And do you have the amended version of what came to pass at St Martin's?'

'Aye.' I fished in my scrip for it and we exchanged documents. 'You now be quite the hero of the piece. I hope that satisfies you.'

The coroner's report was written in a neat, even secretary hand, well spaced for ease in reading. It appeared that Dymmock, as Deputy Coroner, could afford a capable clerk, whereas the City Bailiff could not. The result of the inquest was of considerable interest to me. I read the document through—twice.

'What say you, Seb? You'll see that it was determined by the jury, having been given the learned opinions of a physician and two surgeons, that Thomas Goulden died of "natural causes, namely a seizure brought on by a surfeit of drink consumed over a period of years". That should please you.'

'Aye. I be much relieved… no mention of witchcraft, curses or the black arts. The wretch died of drink and no other cause. Bess and Sarra had naught to do with his demise and their names do not appear anywhere in the document. I praise God that justice has been served—in part, leastwise.'

'One of the surgeons reckoned the drink must have quite rotted his liver and affected his brain…' Thaddeus eyed the ale jug with suspicion but then shrugged and refilled his cup. 'You've got to die of some cause so it may as well be one in which you take pleasure. Tell me why you say justice has only been done in part?'

'Mistress Fuller,' I reminded him.

'Oh, aye, the troublesome and malicious gossipmonger.'

'And maker of false evidence.'

'I hadn't forgotten. Questioning her is another of my tasks for this morning and then I'm at the Lord Mayor's Court this afternoon to make report on that other infernal case for which you rewrote Parker's disgraceful scrawl.'

'May I suggest, Thaddeus, if there be time enough afore we speak with Anneis Fuller, that it may be worth asking her son a few questions. I feel that we may receive but constant denials from his mother. But, as I have heard, this John, being but a lazy fellow, may be more forthcoming with answers, if for no better reason than to be rid of us right swiftly that he may return to his preferred occupation of idleness.'

'You might have a valid point, Seb, but I have business with Lord Mayor Browne in less than an hour but it should be brief. After that, we can go find this John Fuller, if you think it will serve a purpose.'

'In which case, upon quite another matter,' I said to redirect our conversation. 'What do you know of ships which moor at

Queenhithe?'

Thaddeus raised his eyebrows:

'Naught at all unless some crime is involved. Why? What interest do you have in shipping and trade?' He returned to reading my amended report. 'The Bridge Warden would be the fellow to ask. He records the toll paid by every ship for which the bridge is raised, incoming or outgoing.'

'Would he know where each outgoing vessel be bound?'

'Maybe. He could certainly tell you the master's name, who owns it and its cargo. Why? Do you have in mind to stow away and sail to the Indies? Make your fortune in spices?' He put down the paper, smoothing out a folded corner. 'Aye, that reads well enough. You make no mention of my name concerning the escape and you exonerate Constable Hardacre utterly, though I'm not sure he deserves to be let off so lightly. As for what came to pass in St Martin's, it's somewhat vague what you say about the laundresses but, I suppose what you tell of my dealings with that gatekeeper sounds right well. It will serve if anybody enquires further.'

'Why would they? Enquire, I mean.'

'Same reason you want to know about ships at Queenhithe, I should think: sheer bloody nosiness. Or do you have a purpose? I've never known you to take an interest in maritime matters. Are you considering investment in the wool trade? It could be advantageous to you but think of the worries that would come with such a venture: shipwreck, storms, piracy, sea serpents, mermaids…'

'I have no such intentions for the present. Simply that I saw a ship, lately there at Queenhithe, which was once owned by an acquaintance of mine. I wondered whether he owned it still and whither he was bound.' I shrugged. 'A mere passing interest was all.'

As Sarra and I walked home from Queenhithe yestereve, she had spoken of Jack at some length.

'I asked him what he planned to do next. He said he was friendly with a ship's captain who would give him safe passage without question, the ship, the *Eagle,* being in London for a few days, offloading a cargo of timber, pitch, turpentine, furs and amber from the Baltic Lands at Queenhithe, though I never heard of those places. Jack told me the captain, Gabriel, owed him his life; that he'd once been imprisoned and Jack had the idea of painting him with spots to look like the pestilence and giving him a potion to feign death. Then they got him out to bury him—none looking too close at the corpse for fear of contagion. I think he said they put rocks in the coffin instead and buried those whilst the captain escaped, free. In truth, Master Seb, I don't think I can believe such a tall tale, do you?'

'Well, lass, in essence, the story be true, if nigh unbelievable. Those things did indeed occur, more or less as he told you.' I did not mention that it was I who had devised the outrageous scheme.

'Then Jack truly is a hero—unless the captain was guilty, of course.'

'Gabriel's crime was a matter for debate. It depended upon a point of religious conjecture, you might say.'

'So Jack helped *him* to escape. I wasn't the first?'

'Nay, lass, but I suspect you were the first he aided for the sake of love.'

'You think he loves me?' In the gathering dusk, I heard the pleasure in her voice which that possibility held for her.

'He told you of the ship, where it was moored and when it was sailing, did he not?'

'Aye.'

'Why would he do so except in the hope that by then you would be free to come bid him farewell? Why would he wish

327

your lovely face to be the last he saw of England unless he loves you, eh? But tell me true, Sarra, that day of the storm, when you used your scrying skills and a few of Gawain's hairs to learn of Jack's whereabouts... you required no magickal arts, did you?'

'Nay, master, I knew you were searching for my Jack and no other. He told me you would; he was certain of it.'

'I nigh caught him, thanks to you. Why did you reveal his secret?'

'I was in a quandary. I saw, as Jack did not, how concerned you were for his safety and wanted you to know. However, Jack's money was nigh spent and he said he must be leaving the Swan-on-the-Hoop right soon so I took the chance, sure you would take a while to realise how I was directing you and he would be gone by then, on board the *Eagle*.'

'Do you know where the ship be bound?'

'Jack didn't say. I'm not sure he knew... or cared, if it took him far from London.'

'Mayhap, I can find that out, if you wish it?'

London Bridge

I departed Guildhall, leaving my friend to his meeting with the Lord Mayor and did, indeed, visit the Bridge Warden in order to make enquiries concerning the *Eagle*. It maybe that the moment was ill-chosen forwhy the Warden was flapping like a hen pursued by a fox as he attempted to deal with vociferous complaints from the denizens of the bridge.

Apparently, a house of easement, constructed in such fashion that its contents fell directly into the river below, had broken away, tumbling into the waters along with the unfortunates who were making use of it at the time. The like had occurred before but not with the wife of a wealthy grocer in residence along with four others.

The grocer's lawyer was threatening the Warden with a half dozen different legal actions and retributions so vicious they were most certainly of a criminal nature. Others wanted to know who was going to pay for the replacement of the necessary convenience and when could they expect the new one to be in use?

In no way aiding this situation, a liveried esquire was demanding that the bridge's narrow street be cleared for the entrance of his lord's grand entourage. The nobility could not suffer their passage to be littered with obstructions, such as barrows of vegetables, stray geese, dogs on the loose, wandering children and other impediments and why was the Warden not hastening to comply?

I think the harassed fellow was much relieved when word came that an incoming ship from the Low Countries awaited the raising of the drawbridge. He got out his vast ledger, thudding it down upon his stool. Ignoring everyone else, he went off right smartly to collect the appropriate details of the vessel and the tolls thus due, leaving the ledger lying open at the page.

As the man departed and the crowd haranguing him followed on, I seized my chance and read swiftly through the list of ships lately departed. The Warden's script was untidy but legible and there it was, named along with other vessels, including those of the Hanseatic League with unpronounceable names. I read:

This third day of July. The Eagle *out of Bristow, 3 masted carrack, 550 tonnage. Master—Gideon Waterman. Owner— ditto. Crew—48 souls. Cargo—Of fine fleeces, 180 bales. Of mixed fleeces, 337 bales. Of cloth of wool and linen, textiles otherwise various, 305 bolts. Of half-tun casks of salt beef, 161. Of ironware various, 12 hundred weight. Passengers—none. Bound for Calais Staple then Bruges. Tolls incoming and outgoing—paid in full seventeen shillings and nine pence. Pilotage not reqd.*

Gideon Waterman was a name I knew Gabriel used when convenient. 'Twas of interest to me that the ship was noted as carrying no passengers; therefore Jack must be enlisted as crew. And they were Flanders bound. Having escaped London, I could but pray the lad would keep from trouble across the seas but how likely was that, I wondered.

Grace Church Street

Thus, Thaddeus and I met up at the Fuller house soon after nine of the clock on a breezy summer's morn. Thaddeus used his staff to knock upon the bright blue door. We stood back and waited. And waited. A neighbour poked her head out of an upper window across the way.

'If you're looking for Anneis Fuller, she's not there,' the woman called. 'Chucked her in the Compter, so I heard, and serve her right, the old bitch.'

I raised my eyebrows at this from a woman in so respectable a neighbourhood. 'Twas plain that Mistress Fuller was not well-liked by her fellows hereabout.

'It's her son, John Fuller, we've come to see,' Thaddeus told her. 'Is he at home, do you know?'

'Aye, he'll be at home for certain but abed. Without his mother to drag him from it, the wretch'll spend all day there. He sleeps like a corpse and will never hear your knocking. Go down the side alley there and round the back. John won't have troubled himself to bar the other door and you can go in and wake the good-for-nothing rascal yourself. Take a bucket of cold water with you… that's what his mother uses to bring him to his senses.'

'You have our thanks for the advice, good mistress,' Thaddeus said. 'Come along, Seb, let's go rouse the dead.'

We gained entry to the house just as the neighbour had suggested. The back door was not barred—any hedge-breaker could have strolled in as he pleased. What was more, valuables lay around for the taking: a purse beside a chair, gilded candlesticks, silverware upon a carved buffet, even a gold pendant lay openly on a small table.

We climbed the stair. At first, I went quietly on tip-toe but my friend stomped up the treads and, I realised, stealth served

THE COLOUR OF DARKNESS

no purpose if John Fuller slept so soundly.

Our quarry lay fully clothed, including his filthy boots, sprawled atop a bed in such disarray, either he was the most restless of slumberers or the bed had not been remade for days.

'John Fuller! Wake up now,' Thaddeus shouted to no effect whatsoever. 'Wake up, John Fuller. I'm the City Bailiff and I order you...' He grabbed the fellow's arm and shook him. The sleeper snorted, turned over and began snoring loudly. 'I know you're awake, you oaf. Cease this pretence.'

On a stool beside the bed was a jug. It smelled of cheap sour wine. As I gave it to the bailiff, the dregs sloshed in the bottom.

Thaddeus grinned wickedly afore tipping the contents over John Fuller's head. The fellow awoke, spluttering and cursing the Lord God most foully.

'It's not the Almighty come calling,' Thaddeus told him as the fellow contrived to rise from his bed and stand upright. 'Why would He have the least interest in you, you miserable wretch? I'm the City Bailiff and I have questions for you.'

'Fuck off out of my house. I don't care who you are. You have no right...' which statement came with a fist which sent my friend reeling backwards.

I caught Thaddeus to check his fall. Such humiliation was not to be borne. His nose was bleeding and I gave him my kerchief to stem the flow.

'You'll regret this, you bastard whelp,' the bailiff muttered from behind the linen square. 'You've assaulted an Officer of the Law in the rightful execution of his duties. Take him, Seb. You have my full authority to do so.'

Me? I be neither a Constable nor a Ward Beadle.

I looked from Thaddeus—well bloodied—to Fuller who was on his feet, staggering towards the stairs and clearly still the worse for last night's excesses of drink. I grabbed the miscreant by the arm and pulled him around with all my strength. My action was sufficient to upset his precarious sense of balance and he toppled over, face down against the bed. I took a tasselled cord which held back the bed curtain and tied the fellow's wrists behind his back with a stout knot. There! Escape that, if you can, I thought, well pleased with my efforts at performing a constable's work.

'Well done, Seb. That will serve,' Thaddeus said, ensuring that the knot was tight. 'Though this arse-wipe deserves a hempen rope, not a silken cord.'

Downstairs, I fetched a ewer of water from the well in the garden and found a neat pile of finest diaper napkins to aid my friend in cleansing his face, though there was no disguising the rapidly-swelling nose and purpling of bruises.

John Fuller watched us, belligerent of eye, but now tied about with two leather girdles to his mother's fancy chair. His out-pouring of profanities was unceasing.

'Bind his mouth, Seb, for pity's sake. He's giving me a headache.'

I obliged willingly, using another of Mistress Fuller's best table napkins. It muffled her son's words well enough, though his muttering continued behind the obstruction. Trussed up like a Christmas goose, he was helpless but I wondered what we should do with him now.

In answer to my query, Thaddeus said here was as good a place as any to question the wretch. I believe my friend was reluctant to be seen upon the streets with his nose yet seeping blood and snot.

'You begin,' he instructed me. 'Ask what you will but can you make notes also?'

I agreed that I was capable of managing both actions at once. I leaned against a polished board—far too good to soil with everyday meals—but set my paper, ink bottle and pen thereon.

'John Fuller,' I said. 'We would ask concerning your mother…' At which point, I removed the cloth from his mouth.

'That cow,' he spluttered and spat. 'She makes my life unbearable. Nags me from morn 'til night: "John do this; John do that; go here; go there; don't do that…" On and on she goes;

the scolding never ends. How's a man supposed to live with that, eh? No wonder my father went early to his grave just to escape her nagging. I hope you hang the bitch… by the tongue!'

'Indeed,' I said, not committing to any opinion. 'Do you know of the apothecary, Mistress Bess Chambers, and her niece, Sarra Shardlowe?'

'Everybody knows of the tasty-looking wench…'

'Would you know of any reason why your mother might take against those women?'

'O' course. I'm the reason, ain't I?'

'Can you elaborate?'

'Elab what?'

'Tell us more.'

'Aye, well, I took sick with that summer fever a week since or so—lots of it about… the fever, I mean. I asked the ol' bitch to fetch me a remedy. She wouldn't. She said medicaments were too costly to waste on me and, anyway, there was naught amiss with me that a good thrashing wouldn't cure. I know she wanted me t' die of it and be gone out of her way. She hates me: her own son! But I was truly sick and dragged meself t' the apothecary's place. Sarra gave me a remedy… even helped me back home t' bed, she did, and came to tend me every day. It's thanks to her that I'm still alive but the ol' bitch wouldn't forgive either of 'em for savin' me. Wanted me dead, didn't she, the cow?'

With diligence, I wrote down every word bar the expletives which peppered his speech most freely. I would not waste ink upon such filth.

'And then,' he continued, 'She started making these wax things and sticking pins in 'em. I didn't know what they was for but she kept saying that the women was witches, cursing folks… but they helped me when she didn't want 'em to. "Satan's own whore"—that's what the ol' bitch called Sarra. But to me… I think the lass's an angel.'

This last statement somewhat redeemed John Fuller, in my opinion. I looked to Thaddeus: did he have any questions to ask? He shook his head.

'Untie him, Seb.'

I did so, having to use my knife to cut the silken cord. It seemed a crime to damage such finery but I had made the knot so tight I could not undo it otherwise. Fuller unfastened for himself the girdle belts that held him in the chair once his hands were freed. I was yet in some doubt as to whether the bailiff would charge the fellow with assault but he said naught of it.

As we prepared to depart, Thaddeus threw the bloodied napkin aside.

'How do I look?' he asked me. 'Is my nose broke, do you think?'

I gave him a doubtful appraisal.

'If I were you, I should avoid a looking glass for the present,' I advised.

'Mm, as I thought.' Without the least warning, Thaddeus struck Fuller in the face with his fist, sending him staggering back into the chair once more, lips bloodied. 'There. Now, I believe that settles our account.'

I felt shocked at this but my friend grinned as best he was able with his face so painful. Out in the street, he grimaced and nursed his hand. The knuckles were crimson and swelling.

'The wretch has a jaw of iron, damn him. I shouldn't have hit him so hard but it was worth it. He got what he deserved.'

'You should go home, change your clothes afore the court case this afternoon.'

'Not until I've had a drink—wine, for medicinal purposes. I have the Devil's own headache.'

'I shall leave you to your drink, Thaddeus. I must away to my dinner and a full afternoon of labour awaits me.'

Bess Chambers' shop

That afternoon, 'twas a case of all hands to work to furnish Bess's home and shop. Adam and Simon borrowed Stephen's hand cart and went with Bess to collect whatever was needful from Adam's house in Distaff Lane. I trundled a wheel-barrow's worth of stuff from our house to Bishopsgate like a common labourer but it mattered not in so worthy a cause. Hugh and Kate lugged armfuls more of sheets and coverlets and I know not what else whilst Rose and Sarra took the children—along with any sack and basket to hand—to Smithfield beyond Newgate to gather meadowsweet and anything in the way of wild herbs from Nature's bounty. Meg and Nessie did the like from that which grew in our garden plot and might be spared. ('Twas by unspoken agreement that we kept Nessie away from Newgate for fear she would dally at the Shambles with Warin Fattyng along the way. The less she saw of him, the better.)

Ralf was left to keep the shop. His bent back made tasks such as ours difficult for him and someone had to attend to business and serve customers.

Hot and dishevelled, in ones and twos, we arrived at Bess's place. Hugh and Kate were there afore me. The barrow being somewhat spilling over with a featherbed piled high, I had to keep stopping to retrieve contrary pillows determined to make their own way. I should have made a second journey, I suppose.

Hugh and Kate took the featherbed betwixt them, up to the bedchamber and I followed on with pillows. In no time, the bed was made. Hugh propped a ladder Stephen had left for the purpose and began hooking up the tester canopy to the rafters. I stood upon the repaired coffer to thread the hangings along the poles to enclose the bed. I was sweat-drenched in no time and the heat of the day was not the sole cause: balancing precariously to work at a height was not a task I relished but was determined I should not stand there, idle, with so much to be done. I climbed down from my perch and wiped my brow whilst

Kate arranged the faded velvet cloth to best effect. The hangings were old and had once adorned the marriage bed I used to share with Emily. Afore then, Emily's elderly mistress, Dame Ellen, gave them to us so they had had a long life but were well cared for and serviceable still, if a little worn and thin along the folds.

Meg and Nessie came next, bearing the produce of our garden. Nessie was complaining, as usual, about the heat, the distance she had walked and the weight she had to carry.

'I'm not a pack horse, master,' she moaned. 'It's not fair. I carried far more than Meg did. I don't see why I should...'

But lately done with my balancing exploits, I was not of a mind to harken to her and summoned my most withering glare, unwilling to waste words. Besides, 'twas clear that Meg had brought the greater load in a bushel basket, balanced across her shoulders, whilst Nessie had managed two hand baskets only— no more than a morning's marketing. The wench was become idle, truculent and tiresome since that foolishness with the butcheress's son. Mayhap, I should marry her off someday soon to a respectable, mature husband who would not abide such nonsense but, nonetheless, I would have him treat her kindly.

Adam came with Bess, trundling a small cart borrowed from somewhere or other. 'Twas filled at one end with sundry linens of every kind, neatly folded gowns and even a pair of brown shoes of goodly make. At the other end was stacked a motley assortment of pots, dishes, bowls, pans and other kitchen stuff, from spoons and ladles to strainers and graters and—most important for an apothecary—a heavy pestle and mortar of marble stone. Bess's own had disappeared without trace, looted from the premises, most likely, afore Stephen came to make the place secure.

The still room was already looking as it did of old by the time, somewhat belatedly, Rose and Sarra arrived with the flock of little ones and two sack-loads of wild herbs. Sarra put down her weighty burden of a bulging sack under one arm and Julia in the other to gaze about the restored still room. I saw how her malachite eyes sparkled with delight as she swung around, admiring what we had achieved thus far. I could have watched her for an hour but Dickon nudged me.

'Look, Papa,' he said, holding out his hand. 'A nettle bited me. See? And Nick got bited, too.'

I looked but could observe no mark upon his perfect skin as I bent down to be eye-to-eye with my son.

'It *bit* you,' I corrected his grammar without thought. 'But nettles sting. They cannot bite since they have not teeth.'

'Oh, but Sarra mended it and Nick's.'

'Did she rub a dock leaf upon it?'

He shook his head.

'Nah. She spitted on it. Spit's magick, she said.'

'You should say she *spat* upon it, lad. And is it magick? Well, it must be, I suppose, forwhy it appears to have worked. I can see no sign of nettle rash on your hand, Dickon.'

'Is all gone! Sarra magicked it away with her *spat*, Papa. I like Sarra 'cos she's clever. Gawain likes her, too.'

Mm, my instructions in grammar were wasted, it seemed, even as another man—however so young—had fallen under Sarra's spell. As for the dog, that went without question.

Rose carried Ned, sleeping in a sling across her body. She was encumbered with a sack also, pale spires of meadowsweet flowers emerging from the top as she untied it, scenting the room with their honeyed perfume.

'This is marvellous!' Bess declared, beaming as she peered into the sacks. 'Sarra and I can begin distilling waters and making remedies straightway. We'll have the shop open again by week's end, won't we, Sarra?'

Rose pushed a straying lock of hair out of sight 'neath her cap afore delving within the babe's sling. Ever practical, she pulled out a knotted napkin from beside the slumbering babe and set it on the board.

'And don't forget to eat whilst you're working,' she said. 'Since your larder is empty, there are small loaves in there, a piece of cheese, cold mutton left from yesterday and a few pence, enough to buy you ale. Oh, and at the bottom of the sack are yet more fresh peas from our garden, if you're not over-stuffed with them already. Or, mayhap, you can sell them and buy some other worts.' At which moment, the babe stirred, demanding all her attention.

Out of sight, when all were busy elsewhere, I slipped a gold angel into the napkin from the leather coin bag Thaddeus had given me earlier. 'Twas worth six shillings and eight pence to help replenish Bess's empty larder with victuals and to supply any other necessaries she and Sarra might discover they required.

I went into the still room where Sarra was sorting through the piles of herbs: lavender here, sage there, marigolds and those 'biting' nettles.

'Sarra, lass,' I said quietly, yet she jumped as I startled her, so intent was she upon her task. 'Forgive me. I did not mean to…' I steadied her though she did not, in truth, need my aid. She smelled of fresh green plants.

'No matter, Master Seb.' She smiled and a warmth came over me which had naught to do with the heat of summer.

I gave myself an admonitory warning not to act like a foolish youth.

'I made enquiries this morn concerning the *Eagle*. I thought you would wish to know 'tis bound for Calais and thence to Bruges in the Duke of Burgundy's domains.'

'Thank you. I'm glad of it. Do you think he'll ever come home again?'

'With Jack, there be no telling. We should pray for him. That must suffice. 'Tis the best we may do for now.'

'I'll light a candle for him when I can,' she said and forced another smile afore returning to the fragrance of herbs.

Chapter 21

Epilogue

In the weeks following, we had much ado concerning cases at law—some to our great chagrin. Master Caxton brought a suit against Jude, insisting that my brother had reneged upon a verbal contract by refusing to sell his printing press to him. If not for that, I ne'er would have sued Caxton for non-payment of my dues and expenses. At least I had my contract in writing.

As they ever do, the legal matters became entangled and messy. I suspect the lawyers make it so for the sole purpose of further filling their already-fat purses. Suffice to say, Caxton's case against Jude was eventually dismissed and he lost the second, though my would-be remunerations nigh disappeared, defrayed on lawyers' reckonings. I believe, for all the waste of time spent, I was but one shilling and a penny ha'penny richer for it.

Despite his losses, somehow, Caxton found coin enough to have a new press shipped in from the German States and was back in business by Michaelmas. Rumour told that the queen's brother, Anthony, Earl Rivers, advanced the printer a sizable loan, but I know not if that was true.

As for Jude's dismantled press, he sold off the timbers and ironwork, piecemeal, at a considerable loss, as I suspect, but he ne'er told me how much it had cost him to begin with.

Anneis Fuller's trial came to pass as July tipped into August. Adam and I attended court to hear her charged with a multiplicity of indictments, including disturbing the King's Peace, incitement to riot, criminal damage, trespass, defamation of character and assault.

This last, to my surprise, named myself as the victim. I had not realised it was she who pushed me to the ground that day and contrived, somehow, to wrench my arm from its socket. Adam and others bore witness to this, my cousin exaggerating my resulting affliction with such relish that the jury gazed at me with considerable wonder, seeing I could yet stand unaided and with all four limbs correctly assembled.

I was in court, ready to testify and explain my proof that the accused had made those hateful mannequins with her own hands. But I had no need.

John Fuller was more than eager to tell in detail how he had watched his mother fashion them from softened wax and seen her smile and laugh as she pierced them with pins. These last, he said, she'd dipped in the blood of a chicken afore cooking it.

At which, the accused shouted out, naming him for a liar and an ingrate that would speak against his own mother whilst he called her a scolding bitch whose great delight would be to see him buried six feet under.

The proceedings deteriorated into a family outcry, with mother and son each insulting the other until John Fuller was removed from court. However, Anneis Fuller continued her haranguing and the judge had no choice but to order her silenced by means of a gag. Never have I known the like as the crowd cheered and settled down at last.

Found guilty on all accounts, the outcome was announced: Anneis Fuller was to spend three hours each morn of the week-next-coming in the stocks in Poultry to suffer humiliation of whatever kind the good citizens of London chose to administer. She must pay the considerable fine of ten marks to the King's Grace for disturbing his Peace; the same to the City of London authorities for the trouble she had caused; four marks to Mistress Elizabeth Chambers for damage done to her property and another mark for defamation of her reputation. I was awarded half a mark for my pain, suffering and inconvenience whilst my arm was injured.

Finally, and most drastically, Anneis Fuller was commanded to foreswear the City of London and leave within forty days, to remain in exile and not return for five years. A harsh judgement indeed and one I know her son was most eager to celebrate.

The new babe, Ned, has settled into our family and my dearest Rose wears a smile once more. In truth, I had not remarked the lack of it until its joyful return. 'Tis a marvel to see her so content.

And what of Jude? I swear that I did not berate him any further upon the possibility that Surgeon Dagvyle's contraption might aid his knee, yet a while later, he went of his own accord— or, mayhap, Eleanor persuaded him to do it. The tidings are favourable: his leg is become somewhat straighter now but the surgeon says it will take time and numerous applications of his tortuous device afore the knee will be as it once was. Of course, Jude insists that these repeated sessions of excruciating agony do naught but swell the surgeon's coffers but I should rather pay Dagvyle than any lawyer's fees.

The case regarding Adam's citizenship and guardianship of Simon, Nick and little Mundy is yet ongoing. How much longer it may take to resolve, we cannot tell, and it frustrates us all. However we attempt to speed along the men of law, it seems to require yet more money but without making the least difference that we can tell.

At this rate, Adam will have it all to do again when the new Lord Mayor—whosoever he be—takes office at the end of October. 'Tis disheartening for everyone and distressing for the lads in need of a legal guardian though Adam be as good as a father unto them as their own parent ne'er was. I fear we both, Adam and I, now tip coin into the lawyers' bottomless abyss, the colour of darkness whence no light can be seen.

As for Jack? Who can tell? I suppose my conscience should prick me mightily, having made no effort whatsoever to apprehend the young rascal, knowing him for a felon. Yet I sleep sound—when the babe permits. Of his own accord, Jack has departed the city without a judge passing such sentence as befell Anneis Fuller. 'Tis true that a man died as a result of Jack's actions but they were a matter of foolishness and not malice, I be certain. Should I allow youth as a valid excuse for criminal behaviour? Perhaps not but I shall let Almighty God, Our Saviour, be the Ultimate Judge, as is right and proper.

Important Characters
featuring in
'The Colour of Darkness'

The Foxley Household

Sebastian [Seb] Foxley—an artist, illuminator and part-time sleuth

Rose Foxley—Seb's wife, a glover [rescued by Seb in a previous adventure]

Dickon & Julia—Seb's children by his late wife, Emily Appleyard

Margaret [Meg] Russell—an ex-novice nun [acquired by Seb in a previous adventure]

Ralf Reepham—Seb's elderly journeyman scribe [acquired by Seb in a previous adventure]

Kate Verney—Seb's apprentice

Hugh Gardyner—Seb's new journeyman, a previous Lord Mayor's nephew

Nessie—Seb's maid-servant

Gawain—Seb's 'colley' dog

Jude Foxley's Household in Ave Maria Alley

Jude Foxley—Seb's elder brother, attempting to set up a printing business

John 'Eleanor' Rykenor—a cross-dressing live-in friend of Jude [real]

The Armitage Household in Distaff Lane

Adam Armitage—Seb's cousin [actually his nephew] from Foxley, Norfolk, also Seb's assistant at Paternoster Row

Simon Hutchinson—Adam's step-son, now Seb's apprentice

Nicholas & Edmund [Mundy] Hutchinson—Adam's younger step-children

Friends and Neighbours

Stephen Appleyard—Seb's one-time father-in-law [Emily's father], a carpenter,

Jack Tabor—once Seb's apprentice, now Stephen Appleyard's

Bess Chambers—the apothecary & wise woman in Bishopsgate

Sarra Shardlowe—Bess's niece & apprentice

Peronelle [Pen] Wenham-Hepton—a silkwoman, mother of baby Alice

Bennett Hepton—Pen's husband, a well-to-do fishmonger

Joan [Joanie] Alder—a washerwoman and friend of Ralf Reepham

Beatrice [Beattie] Thatcher—a silkwoman, used to be Emily's co-worker

Harry Thatcher—a thatcher, Beattie's husband

The City Authorities

Thaddeus Turner—City Bailiff and Seb's friend

Parker—the bailiff's clerk

Thomas Hardacre—a constable

John Browne—Lord Mayor of London, 1480-81[real]

Andrew Dymmock—Deputy Coroner of London [real]

Others

William Caxton—the first printer in England, based at the Sign of the Red Pale in Westminster [real]

Wynkyn de Worde—Caxton's assistant, a Fleming [real]

Thomas, Jonas and Nathaniel—Caxton's apprentices

Hal Mathers—Caxton's journeyman

Sir Philip Allenby—Seb's customer

Warin Fattyng—a butcher's apprentice [real]

Matilda Fattyng—a butcheress, Warin's mother [real]

The gossipmongers of Bishopsgate:
> Anneis Fuller [widowed with son John, a lazy cutler], Maud, Frances [husband Reynald likes sex] and Philippa [married, husband is friends with Reynald, they fix roofs]

Mary Goulden—a pregnant wife of Bishopsgate [forced to wed wife-beater Thomas Goulden by her father to pay off gambling debt]

Cobb—the Carrier

Folk at St Martin-le-Grand:
> John the farrier & his wife Mary, the 'laundresses' Margery & Dorcas

Francesca Antonia Foxley [Chesca]—Jude's wife and King Edward IV's mistress

Gabriel Widowson—once Seb's journeyman, now captain of the *Eagle* [appears in a number of previous novels]

Thomas Kempe—the Bishop of London [real]

John Dagvyle—a barber-surgeon [real]

Mistress Dagvyle—a barberess

Author's Notes

Writing a historical novel involves combining both fact and fiction. Seb and his family are entirely my invention but readers may be interested as to some of the facts behind this story.

Bess Chambers' secret ingredient is mugwort which, like thyme oil, repels fleas, the carriers of the plague, though this fact wasn't known at the time. Therefore, any insect repellent might be regarded as warding off the pestilence without understanding the connection.

William Caxton was real, famous for setting up the first ever printing press in England in 1476 at the Sign of the Red Pale in the Almonry at Westminster Abbey with Anthony Woodville, the queen's brother, as his first patron. Wynkyn de Worde was real, too, and came from Flanders to work for Caxton. As far as I know, their workshop never suffered a catastrophic fire nor was Caxton robbed. Other members of his printing team are my invention.

John Rykenor, aka Eleanor, was also real, though he/she lived around a century earlier. Arrested whilst dressed as a woman and having sex with a man at the time, Rykenor claimed to have lived with a man as his wife, had sex 'as a man' with several nuns—whom he didn't charge—and, 'as a woman', he did charge a number of Oxford scholars, including one William Foxley, for his services. When 'Eleanor' was arrested in London, the authorities weren't sure what crime she had actually committed [homosexuality was only made a criminal offence in the Tudor era], so they charged her with misleading the customer by pretending to be a female and offering services 'misrepresenting the product'. The punishment wasn't recorded.

In the medieval era, Mystery Plays were a popular form of street theatre performed at Christmas, Easter and Midsummer. Originally, the purpose was to tell the Bible stories to the vast population of illiterate folk and many towns and cities throughout Christendom invented their own traditions. In England, we still have the scripts for those performed in York, Wakefield and Chester, so we know quite a lot about them. Sadly, there is no record of London's cycle of Mystery Plays but there must have been one, surely.

The Duke of Exeter's daughter was an instrument of torture at the Tower of London invented by Edward IV's unpleasant brother-in-law—you've guessed it—the Duke of Exeter. Officially, torture was illegal in England but the monarch could sanction it if treason was suspected. This particular instrument was a form of the rack, designed to dislocate the victim's joints. Whether Surgeon John Dagvyle ever attended an unfortunate victim or saw the device, I've no idea but it made a good story. Incidentally, the king's eldest sister Anne was granted a divorce from Exeter on the grounds of his cruelty—almost unheard of in the Middle Ages—and in 1475, on a return trip from France, the duke's own men threw him overboard to drown. Not a popular guy, then.

The *Ars Notoria* which Seb tried to copy really exists. The Catholic Church didn't ban it outright but it was listed as a 'suspect book'. It was thought to enable quicker study so students could learn Grammar etc. in a few months, rather than years, but it was so complex it took years to get your head around the method. The book also has chapters about foretelling the future and making poisons. One such poison recipe included crushing dried toad, lizard, rats' tails and spiders to a powder and wrapping it in sage leaves and salt. Wax images pricked with pins and dipped in this poison ensure the chosen victim's death. The chapter *Summa sacrae magicae* is about summoning and controlling angels, spirits and demons using Solomon's rings and seals—possibly the plant of that name. An apothecary might have found this book useful but the possible dangers were numerous.

Around this date in 1481, a house on London Bridge called 'the common siege' really did fall into the river, killing five men—not just the grocer's wife, as in the novel. Did you know that the word 'siege' originally meant a seat so this can be translated as 'public seat' or toilets. In the tales of King Arthur, the Siege Perilous was the vacant seat at the Round Table, reserved for whichever knight should succeed in finding the Holy Grail—none ever did. Also, originally, to besiege or lay siege to a town simply meant to 'sit outside' it, presumably in an intimidating manner, and wait for it to surrender.

I hope you enjoyed *The Colour of Darkness* and, if you did, look out for Seb Foxley's next adventure: *The Colour of Malice.*

Acknowledgements

I apologise to all Seb's fans that this novel took such a long time to write. It did not come about without some horrible disheartening errors and a lot of stress so I want to thank members of the Three Daws Writing Group, the Rochester U3A Writing Group and my lovely history students for insisting it was worth all the rewriting to get it finished—eventually. And thank you, Tim, my publisher, for not nagging me for the manuscript.

As ever, I couldn't have done it without my husband Glenn telling me not to give up and supplying plenty of coffee, snacks and technical aid to get me through tricky times when arthritic fingers almost defeated me.

Thank you, everyone.

Toni. 18th February 2025

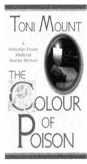

TONI MOUNT

A Sebastian Foxley Medieval Murder Mystery

THE COLOUR OF POISON

TONI MOUNT

A Sebastian Foxley Medieval Short Story

THE COLOUR OF GOLD

TONI MOUNT

The Third Sebastian Foxley Medieval Murder Mystery

THE COLOUR OF COLD BLOOD

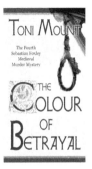

TONI MOUNT

The Fourth Sebastian Foxley Medieval Murder Mystery

THE COLOUR OF BETRAYAL

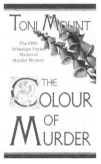

TONI MOUNT

The Fifth Sebastian Foxley Medieval Murder Mystery

THE COLOUR OF MURDER

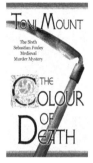

TONI MOUNT

The Sixth Sebastian Foxley Medieval Murder Mystery

THE COLOUR OF DEATH

TONI MOUNT

The Seventh Sebastian Foxley Medieval Murder Mystery

THE COLOUR OF LIES

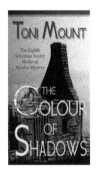

TONI MOUNT

The Eighth Sebastian Foxley Medieval Murder Mystery

THE COLOUR OF SHADOWS

TONI MOUNT

The Ninth Sebastian Foxley Medieval Murder Mystery

THE COLOUR OF EVIL

TONI MOUNT

The Tenth Sebastian Foxley Medieval Murder Mystery

THE COLOUR OF RUBIES

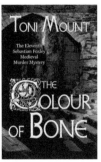

TONI MOUNT

The Eleventh Sebastian Foxley Medieval Murder Mystery

THE COLOUR OF BONE

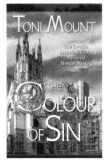

TONI MOUNT

The Twelfth Sebastian Foxley Medieval Murder Mystery

THE COLOUR OF SIN

Meet the Author

Toni Mount earned her Master's Degree as a mature student at the University of Kent by completing original research into a unique 15th-century medical manuscript.

She is the author of several successful non-fiction books including the number one bestsellers, Everyday Life in Medieval London and How to Survive in Medieval England, which reflects her detailed knowledge of the lives of ordinary people in the Middle Ages.

Toni's enthusiastic understanding of the period allows her to create accurate, atmospheric settings and realistic characters for her Sebastian Foxley medieval murder mysteries.

Toni's first career was as a scientist and this brings an extra dimension to her novels. She writes regularly for The Richard III Society's Ricardian Bulletin and a variety of history blogs and is a major contributor to MedievalCourses.com.

As well as writing, Toni teaches history to adults, is an enthusiastic member of two creative writing groups and is a popular speaker to groups and societies.

This is the thirteenth novel in Toni's popular "*Sebastian Foxley*" murder mystery series.

THE COLOUR OF MALICE

Prologue

IT HAD been an afternoon of celebration at the Cardinal's
Hat in Cornhill. Widow Ventham wasn't certain what the
four men were celebrating. Still, they had reserved her back
parlour, in advance, for the cost of eight pence and, so long as
they behaved reasonably in her most respectable house, she was
content to serve them with food, sweetmeats, ale and wine until
they should depart. She prided herself that her inn sold the best
victuals and provided the cleanest accommodation in London.

The four looked to be the middling sort—neither wealthy
merchants nor poor artisans—well-clad but without ostentation.
Sabina Ventham, widowed these three years past, appraised
every male customer with a view to partnership at bed and
board and here at the table was a group of possibilities.

As to their years, judged with a knowledgeable regard, one

was in his late twenties, of an olive complexion, dark of hair and eye but quite comely. She wondered if he was an incomer from warmer lands although, by his speech, he sounded to be as English as King Edward. But he seemed of a nervous disposition, his hands never still. Such as he lacked maturity whereas she required a man of some experience.

Another was in his forties, she would hazard a guess, somewhat stout, broad at the shoulder and still with a full head of brown curls, grey streaked about his ears. Not bad and worth considering. She could picture him hefting ale firkins without too much difficulty.

The other two looked to be in between, in their thirties. Of the pair, the balding, thin-lipped fellow she did not take to, but the other was handsome and smiled at her whenever she caught his eye—which was often indeed. Well, all things considered, she was a fine-looking woman by any account, so she reckoned, and owned this prosperous inn—a fair catch for any man. Thus, even as she wondered upon this fourth fellow's name, she paid him more attention, filling his cup to the very brim and giving him the most generous portions of meat. Blue-eyed and with good white teeth... who could say how things might turn out if she did right by him?

The short winter's day was drawing to a close and the wine yet flowed in the back chamber. The men asked for the fire to be replenished as the night chills crept in under the door and betwixt the window shutters. Candles were called for. The laughter was becoming more raucous; the jests more bawdy but so long as they settled up the reckoning at the end, all would be well.

As she went in with a five-sconce pewter candelabra—no expense spared—the men were examining some strange device, passing it around amongst themselves. It looked to be a hollow pipe about the length of a man's forearm with an ornamented handle. She had never seen such a thing. It seemed heavy in their hands.

'Does it work, though, Jenkyn?' the youngest of the quartet asked.

'Of course it does and cheap at the price, if you want it? Ten marks is a bargain, as I told you,' the stout older man said.

The thin-lipped man whistled:

'My best mare cost less than that.'

'How did you come by it?' the handsome one wanted to know.

'Never you mind. Give it here. I'll show you how it works now we've got candles to see by.'

Widow Ventham put a couple of ash logs on the fire and stoked the flames to a goodly blaze. Sparks rose, dancing up the chimney.

'Can I fetch you gentlemen anything else?' She patted her cap and straightened her apron. 'We have a mutton pie fresh from the oven…'

'Pie would be good,' the thin-lipped fellow said as she reached the door.

'Very well, good masters.'

At that moment, the world seemed to tilt. Lightning flashed, thunder roared and smoke filled the back parlour as Hell erupted in Cornhill. Widow Ventham staggered, clutching the door jamb to keep upright. Shouts and cries came from within the smoke. There was a strange acrid smell. She was coughing, her eyes watering as she turned to see what had come to pass in her most respectable house.

Two men stood; the third was down on his knees beside the fourth who lay prone amidst the floor rushes. Which of them it was she could not tell for the face was naught but a mask of blood. She felt dizzy with the horror of it.

Death, in some new gore-soaked guise, had come to the Cardinal's Hat.

Get your FREE BOOK!

Historical Fiction

The Sebastian Foxley Series—Toni Mount
The Death Collector—**Toni Mount**
The Falcon's Rise—**Natalia Richards**
The Falcon's Flight—**Natalia Richards**
The Savernake Forest Series—**Susanna M Newstead**
The Traitor's Son—**Wendy Johnson**

Historical Colouring Books

The Mary, Queen of Scots Colouring Book—**Roland Hui**
The Life of Anne Boleyn Colouring Book—**Claire Ridgway**
The Wars of the Roses Colouring Book—**Debra Bayani**
The Tudor Colouring Book—**Ainhoa Modenes**

Non Fiction History

The Turbulent Crown—**Roland Hui**
Jasper Tudor—**Debra Bayani**
Tudor Places of Great Britain—**Claire Ridgway**
Illustrated Kings and Queens of England—**Claire Ridgway**
A History of the English Monarchy—**Gareth Russell**
The Fall of Anne Boleyn—**Claire Ridgway**
George Boleyn—**Ridgway & Cherry**
The Anne Boleyn Collection I, II & III—**Claire Ridgway**
Two Gentleman Poets at the Court of Henry VIII—**Edmond Bapst**

PLEASE LEAVE A REVIEW
If you enjoyed this book, *please*
leave a review at the book seller
where you purchased it. There is
no better way to thank the author
and it really does make a huge
difference!
Thank you in advance.